Murder Returns... to a small town

Book 2

Historical Fiction

Alan E. Losure

Yorkshire Publishing
3207 South Norwood Avenue
Tulsa, Oklahoma 74135
www.YorkshirePublishing.com
918.394.2665

BANK BUILDING, GAS CITY, INDIANA

First National Bank corner of Third and Main, Gas City, IN.

The 13th Disciple

Returning Cast of Characters:

Justin Blake	Gas City Marshal
Wilbert Vance	Deputy Marshal
Zeke Miller	Deputy Marshal
Alvin Jensen	Reporter Gas City Journal
Matthew Brooks	Barber/Councilman Second Ward
Davis Huffman	Mayor
Michael Davidson	Councilman Fifth Ward
Doctor Baxter	Medical Doctor
Clarence Stokes	Reverend
Ruth Stokes	Wife
Hugh Williamson	Attorney/'Squire
James Howell	New V.P. First National Bank
Dooriya	Gypsy Girl
Jal	Gypsy Father/Leader

Main Cast of New Characters:

Maggie O'Shea	Widow/Saloon Girl
Virginia Cole	New Arrival in Town
Rachael Marley	Niece of Zeke Miller
George Townsend	Saloon Owner on Main Street
Kyle Holloway	Employee of Saloon
Mort Clancy	Emporium Owner
Constance Wainwright Clancy	Wife
Jane Draper	Sister of Constance
Albert Slocum	Owner of Strawboard Company
Robert Anderson	Strawboard Plant Manager
Harry Roberts	Jonesboro Thug
Adam Lake	Arsonist
Leo Frazier	Lumberyard Owner
Jack Fay	Local Businessman
Tramps	Themselves
The 13th Disciple	?

This book is a sequel to my first book: *Murder... in a small town*. While not a firm requirement, I do recommend that the reader might have a much greater understanding of the storyline if they read that book first (one more sequel will follow). This story picks up one week after the first book ends in September 1894, in a genuine little town called Gas City, Indiana, situated between Fort Wayne and Indianapolis.

With the discovery of an ample supply of available and reachable natural gas in 1887, this little community and those around central Indiana felt that Santa Claus had come to stay and that an endless supply of this fuel would last forever. Main Street was lit by natural gas lighting twenty-four hours a day and the gas was provided free of charge to all factories and businesses that set up shop. Some people have estimated that 90% of the gas supply was simply wasted, and once it started petering out in the early twentieth century, so did the city's once thriving industries.

Alan E Losure

Dedication

I respectfully dedicate this book to the Gas City Police and Fire Department, past and present, whose gallant efforts provide safety to the inhabitants of our local community.

I also want to sincerely thank my good friend, Mrs. Kay Fisher, for her rock-solid support, helpful editing suggestions, and her many, many prayers.

Alan E Losure

Chapter 1
Death Strikes Again

Mort Clancy was a hated man in Gas City, and he couldn't have cared less. He considered himself to be pretty smart, an opportunist actually who saw a chance to strike when the iron was hot in order to improve his position in life. Standing at the bar alone was a nightly ritual as others, men of a lower standard than him, always seemed to give him a wide berth. *No matter*, he thought to himself. *I now have almost everything I want in life, everything I am due.* Clancy had only been a resident in town for eight months and had gone from having nothing to being the owner of Clancy's Emporium on Main Street.

It had been so easy. Having been in the town for only a few days, he learned that the owner of the emporium, a Mr. Chester Wainwright, had suffered a massive heart attack and his poor wife Constance was struggling to run the store alone. That was when the idea hit him. He introduced himself as an experienced clerk, and offered to administer any and all hours necessary until her husband was able to return to work. The offer was graciously accepted by the unwitting woman who then returned to her husband's bedside, until his spirit was finally taken unto Heaven.

Clancy's plan was thus set in motion and, over several months, he set his cap for the wealthy widow who was twelve years his senior. Last month, his persistence had paid off, despite grave warnings from her friends and her sister, Jane Draper. A grieving and apprehensive Constance Wainwright had finally consented to become Mrs. Constance Clancy. That very day, the Wainwright signage was replaced with *Clancy's Emporium*. The modest but elegant two-story home, one block north of Main Street, went from being the Wainwright home to the Clancy home. Even some of the old man's clothing fit his younger replacement. By the time his new wife realized her mistake, it was too late. Clancy now had possession of everything. He immediately returned to his old ways of drinking heavy in the evening and womanizing in several of the local saloons. Mrs. Clancy barred him from her bedroom, which suited him very well since the thought of holding the old hag in his arms made him sick to his stomach. Now, he could freely come and go unseen through the back door. Maybe he could even bring in a late night playmate, too. Quite a few people say that in life one must play the hand that they are dealt, but Clancy did not play by those rules. He believed in simply reshuffling the deck until he got the hand that he wanted to play.

It didn't take long for his new emporium business to dwindle down to near nothing. Once a very popular and profitable store, the local townspeople were showing their displeasure with his obvious scheme by avoiding the store and shopping elsewhere. It was of no matter, as he planned to sell out next month for a quick cash amount and skip town with his windfall anyway. Then providence landed right at his feet. While his wife was traveling in her carriage, her horse was startled by a street car and she was thrown upon the bricked main street, shattering her left hip.

She now spent her days and nights confined to her bed as her health continued to degrade. Only through the constant care and attention of her spinster sister was she cleaned and fed. Clancy hoped that soon the old cow would pass away so he would be free to do everything openly and publicly, without the need to scurry out of town upon a night train to who knows where. Yes, everything was proceeding along according to plan.

Clancy was suddenly reminded of the letter that he had placed inside his rear back pocket. Ordering another beer, he retrieved the envelope and pulled out the letter. Earlier in the day, someone had slid the sealed envelope through the mail slot in the shop's front door. By the time he had noticed it lying on the wooden floor, the carrier was long gone. Thinking it might be important, Clancy opened it but was somewhat baffled by its contents.

You sir are a scoundrel, a liar, a thief, a drunkard, and a womanizer. Your days are now a few hours upon this Earth. Soon you shall meet your master, Satan, and sit at his side for eternity. Isaiah 3:11 "Woe to the wicked! Disaster is upon them!"

Clancy had little doubt that his wife's sister, or her agents, were behind all of this nonsense. *She must realize now that she will be cut out entirely from any of her sister's financial holdings,* he thought. It required a lot more than a stupid threatening letter to scare Mort Clancy. He thrust the letter back into his rear pocket and ordered another beer. The night was still young and, thanks to his wife's dead husband, he had more than enough money to buy whatever he wanted.

Three hours later, an inebriated Mort Clancy staggered toward his home. Even though it was near to eleven p.m., the gas street lights clearly lit up the sidewalks for easy passage. Turning north by the First National Bank, Clancy proceeded up Third Street until he came to North A. This was by far the nicest home he had ever lived in. It, too, would sell for a tidy profit as soon as the old hag got around to passing. Approaching the darkened house, Clancy skirted past the large bushes that lined the front of the house. The rear door was completely in the dark, and Clancy, due to excess drink, fumbled with his keys as he searched for the correct one to open the door.

Suddenly he stopped as a straight razor blade was pressed against his throat. "Drop the keys and move toward the rear barn," a strange voice commanded him. Drunk as he was, Clancy knew enough not to argue with a man holding a straight razor to his throat. As they walked in darkness towards the rear barn, Clancy was aware of other men moving about. One man opened the barn door wide as Clancy felt himself being pushed inside.

"If it's money you're after, I can give you what I have on me," Clancy uttered.

"Shut up and get inside," a voice commanded. He was quickly pushed against his back on the far wall. A pair of additional hands tied each of his wrists with rope by stretching out his arms and tying them fast to exposed studding. A small rag was then shoved into his mouth. Fear overcame him as he wondered what these men had in store for him tonight. Each face was covered with a scarf, and each man wore a hat firmly pulled down to cover his features. Clancy could finally see that there were a total of five men staring at him.

Finally, the leader began to speak, "Mort Clancy, you have been judged by your betters and found guilty of monstrous crimes against your God-fearing gentle wife and this community. You were warned today by letter of the judgment awaiting you for your many transgressions. I am the right hand of God, and have been tasked to dispatch transgressors back into the pits of Hell where they belong."

Clancy's eyes widened as the leader picked up a pitch fork from a nearby pile of hay. The leader took a firm grip upon the handle and slowly approached the throat of Mort Clancy. "I dispatch thee, agent of Satan," the leader shouted as the pitch fork's blades were forcefully thrust into Clancy's throat. The thrust was so firm that the pitchfork remained in the horizontal position buried deeply into the wood, as Clancy's body gave a final twitch.

Heavy streams of bright red blood flowed down the chest of the dead man. The leader took his index finger and dipped it into his victim's blood, before writing a message upon the wooden barn boards and the group departed back into the darkness of the night.

~~~~~~~~~~~~~~~~~~~~~~

The following morning, the sister of Constance, Jane Draper, let herself in through the home's front door with the key that her sister had presented to her. Climbing up the stairs, she reached the bedroom that she knew her sister now occupied twenty-four hours a day. "Please hurry with the bedpan," Constance pleaded. "I fear I shall wet myself soon."

It was a very painful ordeal trying to raise Constance's lower body due to the broken hip. "You are an angel, Jane," Constance told her sister. "I don't know what I would have done without you these past days and evenings."

Making light of her own involvement, Jane replied that Constance would have done the same for her. Taking the half-full bedpan out from under her injured sister, Jane started out of the room. "As soon as I dump this in the privy, I'll start on your breakfast."

Secretly, Jane Draper was about to go out of her mind having to provide this degree of care sixteen hours every day. *That worthless husband never does a thing to help out,* she thought as she opened the back door and walked to the privy. Jane opened the privy door and poured the contents down the hole. Walking back to the rear steps, she noticed a set of large keys lying on the ground. Picking them up, she determined they had to belong to Mort Clancy. Jane looked about and noticed that the door to the barn was standing wide open.

He probably got so drunk last night that he couldn't open the door, she thought. *He's probably lying inside the barn fast asleep. This will give me a chance to really give him a piece of my mind!* Marching at a quick pace, Jane Draper entered the barn only to see the most horrifying image that would haunt her for the rest of the days of her life.

~~~~~~~~~~~~~~~~~~~~~~~

Marshal Justin Blake had to gently push his way through the small crowd of people who had assembled to gawk at the tortured body of Mort Clancy. There was something odd about people wanting to see blood and gore, when logically it would make more sense to avoid it at all costs. The pitchfork was still embedded through the victim's neck and buried deep into the barn siding.

It kept the body of Clancy pinned in an upright, standing position.

To say there was a great deal of dried, deep red blood would be an understatement, as the body's front was completely saturated. A voice from the group said, "It's him alright, Marshal. That's Mort Clancy. Serves him right, too, the way he's done wrong to Constance Wainwright." Several within the group began muttering their approval of what had been said.

Another person then entered the barn. It was Doctor Baxter carrying his medical bag. "Morning, Doc," Justin greeted. "I'm afraid this guy is beyond any medical treatment." Baxter sat his bag down and examined the wound in his neck.

After an examination, he told Justin that he thought the man had been dead since late last evening. "Sometimes I wish we had a photographer on staff to capture horrible images like this," Justin said.

"Is it alright that I have some of the men take him down now?" Baxter asked. "I still need to examine him closer before he's delivered to the undertaker." Justin gave a nod of approval. "You, men, lay the body in the back of my patrol wagon for me. I would greatly appreciate it." The body was then removed.

Justin pointed to the bloody dried writing on the barn's wall. "What do ya' make of that, Doc?" The letters were approximately five inches in length and read:

The 13th Disciple

"Well, I knew of the original twelve but never a thirteenth. It sounds like we may have a lunatic with some sort of God complex," Baxter said. Justin nodded in agreement. "Thanks Doc. Go ahead and take the wagon and I'll see you later. I want to interview the victim's wife and the sister who apparently found the body."

Doc picked up his medical bag, "I'll go with you. I need to check on Constance's condition anyway." Both men entered the home together unannounced. Justin followed the voices which were coming from upstairs. Tapping lightly upon the bedroom door, Justin announced his arrival. "Ladies, it's Marshal Blake and Doctor Baxter. We would like to enter your room." The bedroom door was opened by the sister, Jane Draper.

"Come in, gentlemen," a faint voice could be heard. Doctor Baxter went directly to his patient to check upon her. "Oh, Doc, the pain is simply awful," she spoke in an almost whispering way.

"Are you taking the laudanum I prescribed for you, Constance?"

While Doc was busy with his patient, Justin began to ask Jane some questions. "I understand it was you that found the body?"

Nodding, she told her story. "I was going out back to the... ah... facility, when I noticed the set of keys lying in front of the back door, and then noticed the door to the barn standing wide open. Knowing of my new brother-in-law's drinking habits, I presumed that he was passed out inside and went inside to give him a piece of my mind. What I saw was simply terrible, and I cannot get the image out of my head."

"So I gather you didn't like Mr. Clancy?" Justin asked.

A look of utter contempt swept over the lady's face, "I hated him for all he has done to my poor sister. Marshal, I didn't kill him, in case you are wondering, but I am very happy someone else did. Good riddance to bad rubbish."

At that point, the sickly Constance Clancy raised up slowly in bed and spoke to him, "Marshal, ...may God forgive me for what I am about to say... but if I could have risen from this sickbed... I would have killed him myself for what he has done to me." She then fell back flat onto her bed. There would be no grieving from either lady. It was very plain for all to see.

Turning back to the sister, Justin continued his questioning. "Do you know of anyone who had a personal grudge against the deceased?"

"Actually, I think he was despised by the majority of people here in town. The emporium's business has been going downhill ever since he'd tricked himself into my sister's life. Most people could see the truth for themselves and began shopping elsewhere. And in case you are wondering, marshal, neither of us paid anyone to do such an awful murder. The last thing either of us would have wanted was the constant memory that it happened inside my poor sister's barn."

"One last question. Do the words *The 13th Disciple* mean anything to you?"

A look of complete puzzlement appeared on her face. "No, it means nothing to me." Clearly, she hadn't stayed inside the barn long enough to even notice the writing on the wall.

"Thank you, ladies. We will let ourselves out." As both men began walking down the stairs, Justin asked, "So what do you think Doc?"

Pausing briefly, he replied, "Bed rest with full immobilization is about all we can do for her now. As to the murder, I think you have a madman on your hands, Marshal."

Glancing about, both men noticed the Gas City Journal Reporter, Alvin Jensen, interviewing the large crowd of people about the crime. Tomorrow's newspaper should make for interesting reading.

Chapter 2
A Decision to be Made

Gas City Mayor, Davis Huffman, walked anxiously along the sidewalk as he viewed the evening skyline in the west. Today had been a beautiful and warm September day, but by late afternoon, gray storm clouds were approaching and soon the storm itself would arrive. Pulling out his pocket watch and checking the time, Mayor Huffman knew that he was running early for the monthly city council meeting. He was running early on purpose. Naturally, he wanted to be in place before the rainstorms began, but more importantly, he desired to spend some much needed time alone in order to think.

Do I really want to run for Mayor again? he wondered. Approaching the beautiful three-story masonry Mississinewa Hotel, the Mayor entered and proceeded to the makeshift city room that the hotel seemed pleased to lease out to the city for its official uses. *Some day we need to build us a city hall,* he thought.

Entering the meeting room, Huffman lit the gas lighting fixtures and took up his seat in the center of the long business table that he shared with the five ward councilmen and the secretary. Opening his briefcase, he removed his notes for tonight's meeting and began to review the evening's agenda. Huffman then quickly realized that he could not concentrate on anything other than the question that had dogged him for weeks.

Should I run for re-election as Mayor or step aside and allow another to fill my place?

One way or another, he would have to make an announcement tonight since the November elections were only two months away. He owed it to his party to make a decision. Either he would be their candidate or another must be chosen to run against the already announced Councilman Michael Davidson who represented the other political party.

Leaning back into his wooden chair, Huffman's thoughts began to drift back in time two years ago to 1892. The little town of Harrisburg, Indiana (population of 150) had decided to incorporate and become a city, built on the huge natural gas supply discovered only a few years earlier. A city with a new and exciting name;

Gas City. What else could it be called anyway? Natural gas meant one thing and that was overnight prosperity for everyone. Factory after factory arrived, with the promised unlimited supplies of free natural gas for their every need. With the factories came men and families looking to make their own futures brighter. All of this had not come without some public opposition. Many people deeply resented any changes, especially in the name of the town they had known so well since 1867. Much more was involved than simply changing a name and all of that had to be clearly explained to the voting public.

A town or village is an unincorporated community with no governmental powers or services. To become a city, a modern city, is to become a defined governmental entity. It then provides local governmental services such as a Mayor, councilmen, treasurer, judge or 'squire, and many official positions. In other words, it becomes a self-contained body that is capable of handling most issues without requiring outside assistance. But in the end, the daily growing population's vote tallied yes two-hundred-twenty in favor of becoming a city and forty-five voted no. Gas City then became its new name. Now, only two years later, the city boasted a population of over thirty-three hundred people, and Huffman expected it to reach twenty-five thousand one day when his grand-son would become its elected Mayor.

Looking back, Huffman was proud of his role in all of this but it had come at a great price. The madman who had tried twice to kill him had been a man that he had once considered a close friend who was soon to be hung for his crimes. This was never too far from his thoughts. Many a night he awoke with terrible nightmares, re-living those horrible moments over and over again as the bullets zipped past his head. He could only thank the young Marshal and his deputies for preventing his own murder. Most people had no idea what it's like to be hunted like an animal, and the assassin's bullet had come so very close to killing him... twice. Why would anyone put themselves in a public spotlight that invites the insane to single them out for killing? Still, he was alive and well, thanks to the quick actions of Marshal Justin Blake and his deputies.

They were also able to end the White Cap murders and had driven out a well-orchestrated criminal element operating within the city. *Maybe, working together as a team, the elected officials of Gas City were beginning to make a difference. Maybe another term as mayor wouldn't be so bad? Maybe the worst has now passed, and we can continue to build upon all of our good work?*

This is not the time to cut and run but to remain firm and finish the work ahead. Huffman felt that he had made the final personal decision and would make his awaited announcement at tonight's public meeting.

For the last two weeks, the council had appointed Davis Huffman to fill in as the temporary 'squire or, as others called him, judge or justice of the peace. So far, Huffman had married two couples and sentenced a few drunks and domestic disturbances to a few days in the city jail. It was the thought of handling a serious case that frightened him nearly to death. Having no legal training whatsoever, Huffman had scoffed at the very idea that he should fill in temporarily until a suitable 'squire could be appointed before the November elections.

One local man would be perfect for the job but he had rejected the idea of leaving his law practice to become the city 'squire. Honest as the day was long, Hugh Williamson was the perfect choice and everyone but him knew it. It had taken quite a bit of mild arm twisting, but finally, Williamson had realized the futility of avoiding it any longer and had agreed to appear before the council tonight to throw his hat into the political ring.

He would serve out the prior 'squire's time and then officially run for the position during the November elections. Hearing a door open, Huffman was brought out of his deep concentration as a few people began to filter into the room. The Mayor then returned to studying tonight's busy agenda.

Off duty, Marshal Justin Blake felt it very necessary to appear before the council tonight to make his request to hire two additional deputies. With his friends Wilbert Vance and old Zeke Miller working nights, Justin was left to fend for himself during the daytime. More manpower was clearly needed in order to provide the city with at least one officer on duty at all times. Five officers would allow for this, but getting the city council to agree would take some skilled salesmanship on his part. At the start of the meeting, Mayor Huffman announced his candidacy to run for another term.

Attorney Hugh Williamson was introduced as the new 'squire and was sworn in to take office immediately. Then it was Justin's turn to present his case. He felt he had pretty well covered all of his bases but he saw that Councilman Davidson would be his chief opponent. Davidson stated that the city could not afford two full-time deputies and suggested a full and part-time fill-in position instead. Justin, though unhappy, felt that he could accept this concept... for now... and maybe later he could push for the fill-in position to be upgraded to full-time.

At the conclusion of the public meeting, Justin remained in order to welcome the new 'squire. "Congratulations, Mr. Williamson. I look forward to working with you," he told him as the men shook hands.

"Same goes for me, Marshal. Congratulations on your promotion, too. I think we will make a good team in enforcing law and order," replied the new 'squire. "Any leads on today's terrible murder?"

"I wish that I could say yes. Perhaps it was just a passing tramp who tracked him down to settle the score for an old grievance? We'll keep after it, sir, and I hope to have the man appearing before you soon. Good night."

As Justin walked back to his house, he began running possible names through his head for the newly authorized positions. This was going to be more difficult than he originally thought. *I'll come into the office early in the morning to brief the guys on the killing and see if they have any ideas on hiring these new men*, he thought. Entering the small but well-built home that had been given to him by a dear friend in his will, Justin grabbed an apple out of a bowl of fruit sitting upon his kitchen table. He then proceeded outside to sit on the front porch and relax. He found that he did his best thinking while sitting outside in his favorite rocker. There was much to consider now, and Justin Blake had all the time in the world tonight to think. Justin then noticed a familiar face approaching.

"I hoped I could find you tonight, Marshal," Doctor Baxter said.

"Pull up a chair and sit a spell, Doc. What's on your mind?"

"I found this letter in the rear pocket of the murdered man. I thought you should see it tonight since it might be very important."

Justin motioned for Doc to follow him as they entered and Justin lit an oil lamp. Justin read it several times before commenting. "This fits right in with the killers' bloody message on the wall. Another crazy killer on the loose is just what we need, and this one appears to be God's messenger of death." With a goodbye wave, Doctor Baxter let himself out as Justin returned to his front porch in deep thought. *Here we go again.*

The next morning found Marshal Justin Blake sitting inside a small restaurant having breakfast when he noticed the Gas City Journal Reporter, Alvin Jensen, arriving. Without waiting to be invited, Alvin took a seat at Justin's small table.

"Don't mind if I do," he said jokingly. "Anything new on the Clancy murder case? I saw you at the council meeting yesterday evening. Anything you want to give to a hard working but under-paid newspaperman? What is your opinion on the Mayor's decision to run again?" Alvin asked. A waitress brought Jensen a cup of coffee and he then pointed towards Justin's plate of food.

"I'll have what he's having, but bring it on another plate. I like the Marshal but not that well." The joke fell flat with the waitress having heard all kinds of stupid remarks from other early morning customers.

Justin looked up at the reporter and said, "Sorry, no comment on either topic this morning, Alvin."

Jensen was the type of young man who felt totally comfortable pushing his way into any situation in the hopes of picking up a story that might impress his editor, who also happened to be his uncle.

"Should be an interesting election between the Mayor and Councilman Davidson."

Jensen continued. "No two people could be so different as those two, more like night and day."

Justin hurried to finish up his breakfast, saying, "I can work with either of them. You'll have to excuse me, Alvin. I want to brief my night crew before they go off duty. I'll be seeing ya." Justin fished out a coin, laid it upon the table and left. *A little bit of Alvin Jensen goes a long way,* he thought as he walked over to his office.

Calling his small working space inside the fire barn an actual office was a bit of a stretch of the imagination. Unfortunately, it was what the city had provided and until the funds were appropriated to build an official police station, hopefully along Main Street, it would have to do. Entering the office, Justin couldn't help but notice that there were three men standing inside the small jail cell.

"Looks like you fellows had a busy night," Justin commented to Deputy Wilbert Vance.

Wilbert, who was filling out the paperwork for the evening's report, paused briefly to reply. "Yep, these three felt they could tear apart the Oasis Saloon last night. Maybe we should have let them do it and saved ourselves future problems."

From inside the jail cell, one of the men spoke up. "Let us out, Marshal, and I promise we'll be good."

Over by the stove pouring himself a cup of coffee, an older man spoke up with a chuckle in his voice. It was Deputy Zeke Miller. "Dem two fellers was wild cats last night and all, but now they purr like kittens." Zeke didn't spend much time with book learning during his youth but he was a great friend and a good deputy, despite his advanced age.

"You should have seen old Zeke in action last night, Justin! He has a way of sweet talkin' drunks into giving up without much of a fuss. He must know every man, woman, and animal in town, and folks just take a natural liking to him. Those that don't, get a persuasive tap on the back of their skull by me."

"You two make a very interesting pair," Justin joked. He then filled them in on the Clancy murder. "Does the 13th Disciple mean anything to either of you?" Justin asked. It did not. He then read aloud the strange letter found in the dead man's pocket.

"We sure can use some new help. Do either of you have any ideas who would make a good full-time or fill-in deputy?" Neither could think of anyone in that moment. "Well, if anyone comes to mind, please let me know. You guys can take off, I got this now. I'll march these three over to our new 'squire's office this morning. It's time to get his feet wet anyway."

Newly appointed 'Squire Williamson seemed a little surprised at the early morning showing of lawbreakers for his court. "What are the charges, Marshal?" he asked, with authority in his voice.

"Drunkenness, destruction of property, and disturbance of the peace, Your Honor." Each man was fined five dollars and sent on his way. Luckily each was able

25

to pay his fine or he could expect to find himself as a guest of the city for the next week. After each man had left, 'Squire Williamson turned to the young marshal and asked, "So, how did I do?"

With a smile, Justin replied, "Just fine, Your Honor... just fine."

Northeast of Gas City laid the small quaint town now known as Van Buren. If you stopped any man or woman on the street who lived there and asked them who the town troublemakers were, two names would almost always be given to you. Fred Willis and Tray Johnson. From an early age, those two had taken part in every ruckus, brawl, street fight, juvenile theft, house burglary, masked robbery and, some would say, even worse occurrences. As they grew up, they had become the scourge of the town and were often found hanging out at their favorite uptown drinking establishment, Rood's Bar.

You had to hand it to the two men, they always seemed to have an available alibi that prevented the local lawman from sending them away to prison. Most people would tell you that both would end up dangling by the end of a rope one day. It was only a matter of time. That or perhaps blown away by the working end of a shotgun or, gutted by the blade of a fighting knife.

Only time would tell how they would meet their fate and when they did, there would be no public outcry of great despair.

Willis and Johnson were always seen together, and tonight they stood at the end of the bar discussing their sad financial situation. "We gotta do us a bigger job, somewhere we ain't known, but not too far fer travelin'," Willis said. "Maybe a bank or somethin', so we can get us a stack of greenbacks ta hold us over fer awhile."

Johnson took another deep swig of his cheap beer as he thought about his friend's suggestion. "That might just work," he replied. "But where?" Together the men thought about a few local towns until a decision was finally made.

"Let's drink to our financial future... the First National Bank of Gas City." Tomorrow they would begin their travel plans in order to stake out the bank, but tonight called for drinking, card playing, and maybe an enjoyable bar fight or two. Each man knew the other had his back in any situation and together, they felt like they could take on the whole world and get away with it.

~~~~~~~~~~~~~~~~~~~~~

It hadn't taken very long for the word to spread around town that the First National Bank had hired a beautiful young female bank employee. Newly promoted James Howell, now Vice President of the First National Bank, had personally interviewed Miss Virginia Cole and was very impressed by her resume. After graduating from Tri-State Normal College in Angola, Indiana with a degree in business, Miss Cole had returned home to her city of Auburn with hopes of a career as a bank executive. Instead, she found the position of bank teller and watched through the years as men with far less educational credentials were promoted over her. Finally, in frustration, she confronted her supervisor who brazenly informed her that a woman's place was in the home and that she was lucky to even hold her current position. Clearly it was time to move on if her hopes of proving her own self-worth were ever going to materialize.

Virginia had submitted her written resignation that very day and informed her parents that she was off to seek greener pastures elsewhere. Since Gas City was a major railroad stopping-point, Virginia felt that with all the business and industrial factories in town, she should be able to secure a good position. If not, there was always Indianapolis.

When Virginia arrived in town yesterday, she was informed by the railroad stationmaster that the Mississinewa Hotel was the only place for a lady of her stature to board. Thanking him, but wondering if the old goat was also flirting with her, she proceeded to walk there when a carriage pulled up beside her.

"Hello, Miss, my name is Alvin Jensen and I am a reporter for the Gas City Journal newspaper. May I offer you a lift, Miss...?"

"Cole," she informed him. "Virginia Cole. I'm searching for the Mississinewa Hotel."

Jensen stepped down from his carriage and said, "I would be honored to take you there Miss Cole. Please allow me to assist you. I'll help you with your suitcase."

"Thank you, sir. I appreciate the ride but I find myself fully capable of entering a carriage without any assistance," she stated as she seated herself. "Is it very far from here?"

"No, Miss Cole. I'll have you there very quickly."

Alvin would have liked to have taken the long scenic route to stretch this interesting ride out but knew better than to try that old ploy with this young lady. He realized she was unwilling to converse beyond what she had already said and all too quickly the carriage pulled up in front of the hotel. "Please allow me to carry your suitcase in for you, Miss Cole."

Virginia stepped down without assistance and grabbed her suitcase. "Thank you for the ride, sir. I can handle it from here. Good day."

Tipping his hat, Jensen pulled away and returned to the newspaper office. If this lady was to remain in town, Jensen was determined to see her again.

Finding employment had happened so quickly and strangely for her. After checking into the hotel and freshening up, Virginia Cole had a light lunch in its restaurant then began making her plans. She had already noticed a bank across the street from the hotel and felt that it might be her first stop. *I'll probably have to start at the bottom again*, she thought. *Well, I may as well get started.* She readied her typed resume, walked the short distance across the street and entered the First National Bank.

"May I help you, miss?" a smiling male teller asked.

"Good afternoon, sir. I wish to speak with someone in charge."

With a quick nod, the young man walked over to an open office door and lightly knocked. "A lady to see you, sir," he said softly.

An older gentleman then emerged from the room and with a kindly smile stated, "Please come this way and have a seat, miss. My name is James Howell and I am a Vice President of this banking facility. How may I help you?" He inquired as he motioned her to enter his office and take a seat.

"Good afternoon, Mr. Howell. My name is Virginia Cole and I am seeking employment." She handed him her resume which seemed to slightly startle the man, who acted somewhat uninterested, until he began to read about her education and work experience.

"Tri-State Normal College I see... business degree... three years as a teller at the Auburn State Bank. You certainly have a solid resume, Miss... Cole. May I ask you why you chose to leave your position in Auburn and travel here?"

Virginia was ready for that question, but she had cautioned herself not to sound too abrupt. "Mr. Howell, I graduated with honors at Tri-State and wished to become an important part of my hometown banking institution. Instead I witnessed men, some who did not complete high school, advance over me. When I requested an explanation from my supervisor, I was informed that a woman's place was in the home and that I was indeed fortunate to hold a teller's position. He implied that my position as teller was as far as I could hope to advance at that bank. Mr. Howell, times are changing and I feel that qualified women should receive the same equal chances as men do in their careers. I am not a suffragette, by any means, but I have much to offer, and only ask for a chance to prove it." Virginia watched Mr. Howell's face, wondering if she had expressed herself too harshly and possibly ended her chances of finding employment within his bank.

"My late wife's name was also Virginia, Miss Cole," he spoke with respect. The word *late* couldn't help but be noticed by her. "She often spoke as you do, that women should be offered positions of responsibility that they are qualified for. I think she may have been right, too."

Picking up her resume one last time, he paused as he read it again before laying it on his desk. "Miss Cole, I was recently promoted from the loan officer of this bank to vice president. We have not filled my old vacant position yet so I have been doing both jobs. With your business degree and work experience, you would be qualified for the loan officer position. By the way, our bank has a thirty day trial period for all of our new employees. I will also need to contact your past employer for their recommendation. Would you be interested in applying?"

Virginia Howell was completely shocked by the generosity and trust this man was willing to give to her. "Yes, sir, I know I can handle it and I won't let you down. Thank you for considering me for this great opportunity, sir."

After finding out where she was staying, Howell informed her that he would telegraph the Auburn State Bank for her work history, and requested she stop by tomorrow afternoon for his final answer. Virginia offered her hand and thanked him again for his consideration. Now all she could do was wonder what her old supervisor might say about her. Would he refuse to recommend her out of spite? It would be a long twenty-four hours of waiting for her.

Chapter 3
A New City and People to Meet

Virginia Cole had difficulty sleeping that night as deep concerns swept through her thoughts. What would her stuck-in-the-past ex-supervisor say about her? Would she lose the position of loan officer because of it? It was well after midnight before she finally drifted off to sleep. Tomorrow will be tomorrow, and nothing would change it anyway, so she might as well quit worrying. Awaking early, she enjoyed a light breakfast and then decided to walk the town and visit its small shops. Virginia Cole planned on being at the bank sometime after one p.m. to learn of her fate. Either she would be hired, or it would be time to start visiting other locations in town.

~~~~~~~~~~~~~~~~~~~~~~~

Emerging from a far less glamorous rental over-night establishment, Fred Willis and Tray Johnson had already entered the bank that morning under the pretense of making change for a silver dollar. Each man saw exactly what they expected, no bank guard and two cashier windows for the public. Here was their plan: One man would hold a gun on everyone present while the other circled behind the cashier's windows and empty each cash drawer. The bank vault could not be seen from their vantage point, but if it was found to be open, much of its contents would also be taken. If that was the case, they planned to herd all of the employees and visitors inside the vault and then seal the door shut, thus preventing their exposure too soon. Each man felt this would be easy and openly wondered why they have not pursued this type of easy pickens' before.

As for their get-away, each man owned a horse that was to be hitched outside the bank. After the robbery, they intended to ride east before cutting back north to Van Buren. With bandannas over their face's to hide their features, each man felt that they could return home and lay low for a few days. Should anyone question their whereabouts, there were plenty of friends who were willing to vouch for them anytime. "We were home baking cookies for our sick grandmas," Tray laughed out loud.

The bank job should be a piece of cake, easy enough for their sick grandma's to handle.

While the two men were inside the bank that morning, V.P. James Howell was opening the reply to his telegram that had just been delivered. It was from the manager of the Auburn State Bank. He wished it to be known that their past employee Miss Virginia Cole had been a model employee, and he only wished he had been given an opportunity to speak with her before her resignation, in order to talk her out of leaving. He had also learned of the statement that her supervisor told her that a woman's place was in the home and not in a bank. He replied that the man had not spoken as a representative of the Auburn State Bank, but of his own opinion. He ended by saying he wished Miss Cole the very best in her future career and that she would be welcomed anytime to return there. *Well, I guess that proves my gut feeling was correct concerning Miss Cole,* he proudly thought. *She will make a great addition to our banking team and I am sure a hit with all the men applying for loans!*

Fred Willis and Tray Johnson were on their second quart of beer as they made their final preparations for the bank robbery. Tray owned a .38 Smith & Wesson Double Action Revolver so he was the man to cover everyone while Fred scooped up all of the paper cash that he could. They were planning on leaving the coinage due to its weight and bulk. The boys were not born yesterday. Since the bank closed between noon and one p.m., they would arrive shortly after its doors re-opened for business after lunch.

Returning to her hotel, Virginia made arrangements to remain another day and then laid down to rest as she drifted off to sleep. Awaking before one p.m., she freshened up and waited for the bank to open. Feeling the need for divine help, she prayed that her old supervisor would take pity on her and not prevent her from obtaining the golden opportunity to show what she was capable of. Seeing that it was now time, Virginia Cole left the hotel and walked across the street to the First National Bank. It was now or never, as she crossed her fingers for good luck.

As she approached the glass-fronted set of doors, an unseen hand flipped the closed sign over to read open, while the door was unlocked and held open for her. Virginia paid no attention to the pair of scruffy-looking men who entered behind her. Making eye contact with the male teller from yesterday, she spoke up. "I'm Virginia Cole here to speak with Mr. Howell."

With a smile, the young man replied, "This way Miss Cole, Mr. Howell is expecting you."

That was as far as she got as behind her a loud voice shouted, "This is a hold up! Everyone stay just where you are!" Hearing the shout of *hold up*, Mr. Howell came out of his office only to be met with a masked man with a gun in his hands.

"Grandpa, you and your teller move over by the cashier cage where I can watch you." Apparently Tray did not see Virginia Cole as any type of threat, as he stood directly behind her with his eyes fixed firmly on the men, and the actions of Fred, who was busy pulling out the cash drawers. Neither man had given any thought to how the cash was to be bagged, so Fred had to stop and look around for something to use. He found two empty money bags upon a lower shelf and then began bagging up their loot.

Glancing down upon the counter right in front of where she was standing, Virginia noticed a partial bag of coins that the teller had been in the process of dumping into their cash drawer. Moving very slowly, she laid her hands on the top of the bag and gripped it tightly. She had a plan, but if she gave it any thought then she would certainly talk herself out of it. Knowing the man with the gun was now watching his partner, she calmly said, "Don't forget this bag of bills," as she suddenly swung it with all of her strength around and upwards.

It made a sickening crunch sound as the bag of coins shattered the gunman's nose, who began shouting in agony as a stream of red blood gushed out of his nostrils. The injured man took a small step backwards as his hands went up to his injured face. Virginia grabbed the barrel of the gun, and with all her might, she twisted it downwards and out of the startled man's hand. She now held the gun and it was pointing directly at him.

Fred, who was loading the cash, stopped what he was doing and began to charge directly at her. Calmly, Virginia fired a shot into the floor an inch from the man's shoe. "I suggest you stop right there, as the next shot will be into your manhood. So if you don't want to have to squat to pee for the rest of your life, I suggest you drop to the floor and raise your hands. Do it NOW! Both of you!"

Startled, both men slowly lowered themselves to the floor. Looking over at the young teller, Virginia directed him to go find whatever police officers this town had to offer and tell them what had happened. In a flash, he was out the door. Several men outside in the street heard the shot and entered to see what was going on.

"You men. Come over here and help watch these two," directed Mr. Howell. The townsmen were more than happy to assist.

"Are you alright Miss Cole?" the somewhat shaken V.P. asked. "That was a very brave thing you did. I never saw anyone twist a gun out of another man's hand like that."

"It was something my father taught me many years ago," she told him. At that moment, Marshal Justin Blake entered with his weapon pulled. Seeing a gun in the hand of a beautiful woman seemed to throw him off for a couple of seconds.

"It's alright now, Marshal," Mr. Howell said. "These two attempted to hold up our bank, but our new loan officer, Miss Virginia Cole, stopped them."

At first she didn't quite hear what Mr. Howell had said. Looking down to examine the gun in her hand, she began saying, "Smith and Wesson DA Revolver model two, made between 1882 and 1884, with a rounded side plate on its left side for added strength. Nice weapon, but in the hands of stupid bank robbers," she announced to the startled men.

"May I have the gun now, Miss Cole?" Justin asked as she handed it to him.

"Before you ask, my father is a police detective in Auburn. When most little girls were home playing with dolls, I was being taught the proper use of firearms," she said with a seductive smile. Both men were truly impressed, but tried not to show it.

Searching both of his prisoners, Marshal Blake asked some of the men to help him escort his two prisoners over to the jail. "I'll be back shortly to interview all of the witnesses," he said as the group left.

Tuning to his new loan officer, Mr. Howell jokingly said, "If you are finished with your police work Miss Cole, allow me to show you to your new desk." It was then that the reality hit her. She had gotten the job after all.

The story of the attempted bank robbery, and the beautiful new bank employee who stopped it, spread like wildfire all through the town. Everyone wanted to catch a glimpse of this new lady. Soon she was being referred to as their own version of *Annie Oakley*. Journal Reporter Alvin Jensen remained inside the bank, peppering Miss Cole with question after question as a sketch artist made a rendering of her beautiful face for tomorrow's edition. His uncle had already made plans to print five hundred more copies than usual. Soon the story would be sent out over the wires to other newspapers all over the country. Should the two misfit bandits, as they were now being referred to, ever get out of prison, they would certainly be unable to ever show their faces again in Van Buren.

At the suggestion of 'Squire Williamson, Justin sent a wire to the Grant County sheriff telling him of the bank robbery attempt and the capture of the two holdup men. The sheriff then replied he was sending two deputies by train to pick them up and transport them back to Marion. Justin also heard from the Van Buren Marshal who was thrilled that the two hoodlums had finally been caught in the act.

Justin then returned to the bank to interview his witnesses, but saw that poor Miss Cole was being bombarded by questions from the reporter and other townspeople. "Gentlemen, you'll have to excuse Miss Cole, as I need to speak with her on official police business." Reluctantly, the men began to leave.

"Thank you, sir. They were driving me crazy with all of their questions," a smiling Virginia Cole told him.

"Let us get out of here, get a cup of coffee down at the dinner, and try out these new concrete sidewalks the city recently installed. It's a pleasant walk and it'll give you a chance to unwind," Justin told her as they began walking towards the dinner.

"I appreciate your kindness, sir. What do I call you? Chief of Police or Marshal?" she asked.

"Name's Justin, Miss Cole... Justin Blake and I am the Marshal. Either title is accurate but folks here prefer using Marshal. That was a mighty brave thing you did today in the bank." By now, she was slightly tired of hearing how brave she was. Brave for a woman was what was being implied, but she smiled back anyway.

"Please call me Virginia. It was nothing but a wild impulse on my part. If I had given it much thought I probably wouldn't have done it." As the pair walked along, she suddenly wanted to change the subject. "Are you originally from here... Justin?"

Shaking his head no, he replied that he had moved from Cleveland. "My folks have a farm outside of town and my two brothers are working it. I had no love for farming and worked as a dock worker before moving here in April of last year. Marshal Brewster saw something promising in me and offered me a deputy position that I accepted. Actually, I haven't been the Marshal all that long."

"I'll bet your friend is proud of your accomplishments," she told him. "I would like to meet him sometime."

Justin slowed his pace, realized what he was doing, and picked it back up. "Marshal Brewster is dead. Killed in a shootout recently saving my life." Pointing towards a small home, Justin continued, "That house was his. He willed it to me hoping I might grow to love this little town as much as he did."

Virginia felt Justin's sadness and wished that she hadn't said what she did, but she also had no way of knowing. "I'm guessing you're a family man. Any children?" she replied.

"No, no wife or any serious girlfriend. Working keeps me pretty busy. So tell me about yourself. What do you think of our little community?"

Happy to change the subject, she continued, "It is a much smaller town than Auburn or Angola. That's where I went to college. My parents live in Auburn, and as I mentioned, Dad is a detective. I'm an only child so I know they hated to see me go out on my own, but everyone must leave the nest at some point. By the way, can you recommend a good church for me?"

Justin was quick to nod, "We have several here in town. I go to the Reverend Stokes's church which sets back two blocks from your bank. He and his wife are good friends of mine."

By now they had reached the little dinner, ordered two cups of coffee, and Justin asked his questions while he made his official report. "Thanks again, Justin, for taking me out of that madhouse. I enjoyed our talk.

Now, may I impose upon you to recommend a clean and respectable boarding house for me? I'm afraid the Mississinewa Hotel will prove too expensive as a permanent residence."

Justin broke out in a wide grin, "I sure can, Virginia, and we're close to it now. I recommend Ma Richardson's Boarding House. Clean, quiet, and very respectable. I used to live there myself before I inherited the house. Ma is a sweet elderly lady who won't take any nonsense from anybody. You will come to love her as much as I did. Want to stop by and see if she has any vacancies?" She readily agreed.

Ma met the pair at the door with a wide smile, "Are ya returnin' to me home, Justin me boy?"

After the introductions, Ma was extra surprised that this was the little lady all the folks were making a fuss over. "Ya would be more than welcome here dearie, and feel free ta use me kitchen anytime's ya feels like a cookin', just clean ups after yerself. Here is me open room and if I am a rememberin' right, t'was Justin's old room too." Virginia liked the room and especially liked Ma, and she agreed to move in first thing after work tomorrow.

By the time that Justin had walked Virginia back to the bank, they were laughing together like old friends.

Walking her to the bank door, Justin tipped his hat and thanked her for her time. "I'll be seeing you in church," she told him as she entered the bank.

Mr. Howell seemed happy to see her, but told her to go back to the hotel and rest. She could start officially tomorrow morning. Happily, she agreed. *This was a very good day*, she thought. Justin was still sitting inside his office as his night deputies Zeke Miller and Wilbert Vance entered the office. They were bound to have heard about today's bank robbery attempt. Justin wanted to answer any questions that they might have and also pass on tonight's schedule.

Looking up at Wilbert, Justin burst out laughing. "What the heck do you call that?!" as he pointed towards his new haircut. Wilbert was sporting an odd-looking style, with his hair split down the center and all greased to each side.

"It's the newest thing," Wilbert said as he walked over to look at his reflection in the glass. Zeke was chuckling and shaking his head in wonder.

"Just can't figure out dis younger generation at 'all. Older folks ain't gonna like dat big city look one bit." Wilbert seemed proud of his new look and ignored the gentle ribbing.

"Times are a changing and you old timers need to change with it." Justin got a kick out of being referred to as an old timer, being only a couple years older than Wilbert.

Justin filled the men in on everything that had happened at the bank. "Virginia Cole is an amazing young lady, smart, brave, and also, by the way, quite beautiful. If she were a man, I would have offered her the deputy position," laughing as he said it. "Our advertisement for a deputy will be in tomorrow's newspaper. If we get someone, I will put him in your care for night-time training. I still have nothing new on the Clancy murder. Be safe, and see ya in the morning."

After Justin had left for home, Zeke spoke up, "Ya mentioned changin' with da times, I don't know if dats always a good thing. Takes dat accident with da street car and da bread wagon last week. Horses are naturally afraid of des movin' street cars. Dat team of ponies became frighten' and pulled da peddler's cart right onto da track and breakin' up da wagon fer sure. Not da first time dats happened dis year too. Maybe dem there street cars ain't good ta run up and down da streets a scarin' folks and animals. We did just fine back in da days when W.G. Pittsford ran da stage line, the American Express Company, tween Anderson, Marion, and Jonesboro.

Last one ran back in '67, if I'm a rememberin' right. Too bad dem days are gone fer good."

"Zeke, you can't stop progress. Look at how much we have advanced in the last one hundred years. Maybe in the next century, people will be operating their own private street cars up and down the tracks of every city. There was a story in yesterday's paper about a Professor Wellner's Flying Machine. He said that people will one day soon fly through the air at railroad speeds in his flying contraption powered by cylindrical sails."

Zeke started laughing at the very thought, "Somebody been pullin' your leg, Wilbert." Course, if we had one of dem flyin' machines back in '62, we could have dropped down like a chicken hawk and grabbed old Jeff Davis himself and ended da war. Me... I'll stick with a horse anytime."

Wilbert replied to that, "I think you should, as my Uncle Dan rode with Confederate John Hunt Morgan's Cavalry and Morgan would have shot down your flying machine and fed it to HIS horse." With that bit of humor, both men began their nightly patrols.

Up on Main Street at the Lovett's Opera House, ballroom music could be heard emitting from the third floor. The Flint Glass Workers were hosting a ball that was clearly well attended. "You a dancing man, Zeke?"

Wilbert asked his friend. The silent, stern look he received back firmly answered his question.

"Looks like da work on da new shed fer the firemen is proceedin' along nice," Zeke muttered. The Mississinewa Hotel's property bordered the fire barn, and they agreed to donate a small section in which to house the new hook and ladder truck that the city had purchased for $440. When it was delivered, which should be soon, it would contain the ladders, ropes, chains, and buckets needed at many fire scenes. Many of the firemen had been busy constructing the new shed that would butt up against the old structure.

As the deputies were walking westward on Main Street, they heard a loud shattering of glass outside George Townsend's Saloon. The men were already close enough to see a man standing outside on the sidewalk who appeared intoxicated and who was shouting through the shattered window at the occupants inside. "That'll teach you Gas City trash not ta mess with Harry Roberts!"

Coming up quickly from behind, Wilbert snapped a handcuff over the drunken man's right wrist. The startled man swung his other fist towards Wilbert's face, barely missing him. Zeke grabbed the swinging arm and soon both wrists were cuffed as they then marched the confused man inside to discover what had happened.

"Glad you caught him," Mr. Townsend said. "This man is a pugilist from Jonesboro. He came in here acting big and bad, ready to take on everyone with his fists. My new bouncer threw him out and told him to go home, but he picked up a brick and shattered my window. I want to prefer charges against him for assault and damages, Deputy."

"He'll appear before 'Squire Williamson first thing in the morning," George, Wilbert said as Zeke removed the man for the short walk back to the jail. "I'll be with you in a moment, Zeke," he told his friend.

"I'll need you to come down to the office later and sign the complaint," Wilbert informed the saloon owner.

"We are packed with customers and I don't know if I can get away or not. Would you let my bouncer sign the complaint for me? He was the first one that became involved with this street thug anyway. I would really appreciate it." Wilbert Vance agreed and together with Zeke, they escorted the angry man back to his awaiting jail cell. As he was being pushed inside the open cell, the big man, moving unbelievably fast, swung both of his cuffed hands sideways and straight into the right ribs of Zeke Miller.

A sickening sound was heard as Zeke groaned and bent over in pain. Wilbert, seeing that his prisoner had just attacked his friend, brought his pistol barrel down hard on the top of the man's head, staggering him back into the cell. The cell door was then locked.

"Zeke, how bad are you hurt?" Wilbert shouted. It was clear that Zeke was having trouble breathing and his hands were going instinctively to his ribs.

"I think he broke me ribs. I didn't see da blow a commin' at me," Zeke whispered out in pain. Laying his friend down but away from the cell, Wilbert placed a towel under Zeke's head and ran outside to find men to gently carry his friend over to Doctor Baxter's office.

"Not much anyone can do to fix three broken ribs," Baxter told Wilbert after his examination. "And at his age, it's going to take a long time to heal. His deputy marshal days may very well be over." Hearing all of this, Zeke tried to make light of it.

"Just help me stand up and I'll be ready fer work." As he said this, Zeke tried to sit up but quickly fell back down upon the examination table, wincing in pain.

"I'll keep him here with me tonight," Doc said, "He's going to need someone to help look after him for quite a while. Does he have any family locally to look after him?" Wilbert thought for a moment and remembered Zeke mentioning his married sister up in Fort Wayne.

"I suggest you get her full name and address from him and send her a telegram," Doc replied. With great reluctance, Zeke Miller provided his sister's information.

"Zeke, I'll be back shortly." he told his injured friend. Knowing that Western Union's office was closed, Wilbert headed straight to the Pennsylvania Railroad Depot. They would send out the telegram through their own system. Wilbert was also going straight to Justin's home to advise him of the situation. All of this pain and suffering because some drunk felt like he could take on the world.

Chapter 4
When You Least Expect It

Marshal Justin Blake stood alongside his injured friend, "I feel so bad that this has happened to you Zeke."

Trying not to show his pain, Zeke Miller forced a smile and spoke in short sentences. "Na Justin, it could have happened ta any of us. Just goes with da job. I'll be back on me feet for too long. I just hate I'll be a leavin' ya short-handed and all."

Justin patted his friend's shoulder, "Don't worry about it. I'll find someone to fill in for you until you are ready to return to work. I'd have to hire two men just to replace you. Get well my friend, I'll check on you again tomorrow." Zeke gave him a slight wave and then seemed to start drifting off to sleep.

"I gave him something for the pain" Doctor Baxter said, "He'll sleep through the night. He's a tough old bird, Marshal. He'll be just fine given time to heal properly."

Thanking Doc, Justin felt that it was time to return to the office to make a report on his officer's attack. *I have no doubt this guy will be spending some time courtesy of the Grant County taxpayers*, he thought. Entering the office, he saw that the large man inside his cell was still cuffed.

"Hold out your arms through the bars and I'll remove those. Try anything funny and I'll chain you standing up on your tippy toes all night." The prisoner was happy to cooperate but just enough to get the tight bracelets off his wrists.

"How's grandpa doin'"? He seemed to be enjoying a good laugh, knowing that he had been successful in injuring the deputy. With the handcuffs now removed, the prisoner began rubbing the areas that had cut into his wrists. "I might just have ta sue you Gas City coppers fer cuttin' into my wrists and all," he said with a threat.

Justin was not about to be bullied by the likes of this man. "Assault against a police officer will bring you several years in prison. I hope you relive this evening every night you are incarcerated. In prison, you'll be somebody's baby before too long."

Wilbert entered the office and was not surprised at all that Justin was there. "I'll put on some coffee, it may be a long night," he told him. "So what's going to happen with our friend here?"

Justin wanted to give the thug something else to worry about. "I'll take him before 'Squire Williamson tomorrow morning. He'll pay for damages or do time. Since he attacked Zeke, I'll turn him over to the sheriff and I'm sure the Marion judge will send him away for a long period of time... say twenty years or longer."

That got the prisoner's attention, "Twenty years? Just fer hittin' dat old man?"

Ignoring the prisoner's obvious deep concern, Justin continued. "Yep, I'm guessing he will be about Zeke's age by the time they get around to letting him out."

Wilbert began filling out his portion of the complaint form that saloon owner Townsend would be filing in for his damages. Each man was concentrating on his own paperwork when there was a light knock on their door. Inside came a huge man without an ounce of fat on him that stood around six foot three inches tall.

"Excuse me gentlemen, Mr. Townsend asked me ta come down here and sign da complaint fer him. Name's Kyle Holloway and I works for Mr. Townsend." Both Justin and Wilbert were a little startled at the man's appearance as he stood before them holding his hat in his hands. Mr. Kyle Holloway was a Negro, and a very large one at that.

Justin was the first to speak. "Please come in and pull up a chair. Deputy Vance is working on the paperwork now so we might have some questions to ask you." It was almost comical to see this huge man pulling up such a tiny chair, but due to the smallness of their office, larger more comfortable chairs would not fit.

Seeing Holloway enter the room, the prisoner exploded with anger. "Get that smelly N***** out of here!" he shouted. The harsh words didn't seem to inflict pain on the face of young Mr. Holloway. No doubt he had heard such words all his life.

"Shut up Roberts, and watch your mouth. You don't give orders around here!" Wilbert shouted. With that, the prisoner returned to sitting on his cot but watched closely and listened.

"Mr. Holloway, would you tell us from the beginning what happened?" Wilbert asked.

"Yes sirs, I was in the back room gettin' some cleaning supplies together as one of the customers puked on da floor at the end of the bar. Dat's when I heard a lot of shouting, 'I can whip any you Gas City trash with one arm tied behind me back,' or somethin' like that. Besides cleanin' up the bar and picking up da empties, I serve as bouncer when needen'. Most folks only takes one look at my size and then they back down. Well Sirs, I was a steppin' out of da back room and that fella in dat jail saw me and started yelling bout smellin' N*****. I've heard dat kind of trash talk all my life and just pays no mind ta it when I can, but dat fella, he came up ta me and threatened ta break a beer bottle over my head. Dats when Mr. Townsend ordered him ta leave or be throwed out. Den he yelled, 'There ain't man nor boy here that can do it,' so after see-ins' the approved look in Mr. Townsend's face, I rushed da man, punched him in da gut and throws him out da door. The crowd of men at the bar started yellin' an laugin' and all so's I guess dats what finally got da man's goat as he picked up a brick and throws it through da front glass window. Dat's about da time you men arrived."

"I was one of the two officers who arrived, but I don't remember seeing you inside the bar," Wilbert said.

"Well sirs, as soon as I throwed him outside, I commenced ta cleaning up da mess at the end of da bar. Dat was my job and I figured all you white men will handle da rest."

Justin had set down his pencil and was listening to the story and asked, "Where are you from Mr. Holloway?"

59

"Marion, Sirs. My pappy is a barber downtown. I grows up workin' as a boot black in his and in some white men's barbershops. As soon as I came of age, I was determined ta improve my life, so I came over's here and got a job sweepin' up at Thompson's Bottling Company during da daytime and working fer Mr. Townsend at nights."

Justin was very interested in his story. "Do you live here in town?"

"No Sirs, I gots a little shack outside of da town a little piece. Mr. Townsend is a good man and I appreciates him giving me a job. The cabin also belongs ta him. I know my working there is causin' him some troubles with a few of his customers so I don't figure I'll have da job much longer."

After signing the written complaint for his employer, Holloway stated that he must return to work and left. He was hardly out the doorway when the prisoner opened his big mouth again, yelling, "Open the windows and air this stinkin' place out, will ya!"

Wilbert walked slowly over to the coffee pot, picked up a tin cup, poured some of the hot liquid inside and approached the prisoner. "Would you like a cup of coffee?" he asked. With an outstretched hand, the prisoner was inches from taking the cup when Wilbert threw the contents of the hot liquid into the man's face. The prisoner howled and threatened to kill everyone.

"You saw what he did to me, Marshal!" he yelled.

Justin looked squarely in the man's face. "I didn't see anything." Then he went back to filling out his paperwork.

The following morning at nine a.m. sharp, the prisoner Harry Roberts stood in front of 'Squire Williamson as the complaint was read. Saloon owner George Townsend also appeared so as to answer any questions put to him and, of course, to see that justice was served. The 'squire fined Roberts fifty dollars in damages and five dollars to the school fund which the big man agreed to pay. "Marshal, please return the prisoner to his cell and notify the sheriff that they have a prisoner to pick up." Justice had indeed been served that day.

Walking over to the Western Union office, Justin sent a telegram to the Grant County sheriff explaining that he had a prisoner for their pick up. He also added on a request for any information on a Kyle Holloway, Negro male, about twenty years of age. He chose not to try and use his office wall telephone, which was only satisfactory for local Gas City calls. Perhaps the telephone system would soon be improved and able to reach other cities, so that calls could be heard clearly. Until then, Justin was happy to continue to use Western Union for out-of -town business. Before leaving the office, the operator told Justin that he had another telegram that had just arrived. Opening it, he read the following:

Will arrive your city on afternoon train from Fort Wayne to attend injured Uncle Zeke.

Rachael Marley

Taking the telegram in hand, Marshal Justin Blake used their police patrol wagon to drive over to Zeke's little house to check on his friend. The wagon had been the property of ex-Marshal Brewster, so it seemed only natural that it should be used as a sort of patrol wagon and team for his staff to haul equipment or prisoners to and from jail.

"Knock, knock, it's me." Friends had carried Zeke home from the doctor's office earlier this morning and he was resting comfortably. "I brought you these. I thought it might help you get around for awhile."

Zeke saw what they were. "Marshal Brewster's crutches," Zeke said with a smile. "Dem belonged ta a good man an' I'll be honored ta use dem." Thanks, Justin.

Justin told Zeke he got a telegram from his niece saying that she was arriving today to take care of him, so he brought the wagon to haul her and her luggage to Zeke's home.

"Don't need no fee-male ta take care and boss me around, no sir-ee." Wilbert poked his head inside the bedroom and asked Zeke how he was feeling.

"Like ya would feel if some thug smashed in your own ribs... but thanks fer askin' anyway."

Justin looked over at his deputy and asked him why he wasn't home in bed.

"I got a couple of hours sleep but I was more concerned about how Zeke was doing." Pulling the telegram from his pocket, Justin handed it over for Wilbert to read.

Wilbert then replied, "I see you brought the patrol wagon. Why don't you let me go and see if the Fort Wayne train is on time? I can bring her back here and then return it later.

"Well, I appreciate that Wilbert," Justin told him. "I'm watching out for the sheriff's deputy who should arrive soon for our prisoner. Thanks a lot, that helps me out."

Wilbert only made a face to indicate that it was no big deal then turned to Zeke, "So tell me what your niece looks like and I'll go fetch her here."

Thinking on it for a few seconds, Zeke replied, "She's about fifty-four year old, heavy in the hips like her mother, gray hair and not much ta look at. But don't ya dare tell her I said so!"

"Your secret is safe with me, he said. I'll be back soon." Then he left for the depot. After arriving, Wilbert began checking the time table for arriving trains. He could see that the Fort Wayne train was projected on time and should arrive in about twenty minutes. He then took a seat and waited. As the train arrived, Wilbert walked out on the platform and waited. Several people were also waiting for new passengers to also arrive, with a few standing by to board. It was then that Wilbert noticed a lady of Zeke's general description stepping off the platform.

Approaching her with a smile on his face and his hat in his hand, Wilbert said, "Hello... I'm here for you." Suddenly the woman got a real mean look on her face and commenced to hit Wilbert with her hand bag. "Don't get fresh with me young man or I'll call the constable on you! The very idea! What is this country coming to?"

Wilbert just stood there with a dumb horse-look on his face as laughter erupted behind the older woman. "I have the feeling you're looking for me, officer."

Before Wilbert stood one of the prettiest girls he had ever seen. She stood about five feet five inches tall, had long brown hair, and sparkling blue eyes. Her smile would surely melt butter too.

"I'm Rachael Marley, if that's whom you were sent to locate." Wilbert turned three shades of deep red, knowing that old Zeke had sure set him up to embarrass him in front of his young beautiful niece.

"Yes, hello. Glad to make your acquaintance. My name is... My name is Wilbert Vance and your uncle just made a total fool out of me!" As he helped her and her baggage into the patrol wagon, he felt that he owed her an explanation as to what had occurred, and soon both were laughing at the prank that had been so successfully pulled on the young deputy.

"That's my uncle Zeke," she laughed. Each agreed not to let on to Zeke that his joke had actually worked so well. "Let us not give him the satisfaction."

"Well, here we are. I'm afraid your uncle's house isn't too much to look at." Most young ladies Rachael's age may have hesitated to even step inside such a structure, let alone agree to stay there for a while. Rachael Marley was not like that at all.

"Knowing my uncle the way I do, I wasn't expecting too much away with him being an old confirmed bachelor and all." Wilbert assisted her down then grabbed her baggage.

"Uncle Zeke, it's so good to see you again! Dear Uncle, how bad are you injured?" she asked.

"Just a few broken ribs... I don't need no fee-male taken care of me know how but... it's good ta see ya again Rachael."

Turning to Wilbert, the older man asked, "Any trouble spottin' her?" With a straight face Wilbert replied, "No, sir. She's as you described her." That seemed to disappoint the old man slightly as both of the young people held back from busting out laughing. *Someday I'll tell Zeke about what really happened, but not now*, he thought.

"I'll leave you two to visit. It was truly a pleasure to meet you Miss Marley." Walking up to him she extended her hand, "Please, call me Rachael. Any friend of my uncle is a friend of mine. Goodbye and I hope to see again soon." Driving the patrol wagon back to the jail was a complete blank to Wilbert. Half the town could have been blown away by a tornado and he wouldn't have even noticed. All he could think about was the beautiful face of Miss Rachael Marley.

~~~~~~~~~~~~~~~~~~~~~~~~~~

Two Grant County sheriff deputies arrived shortly after Justin returned to his office. Both men were casually known to Justin, having worked with the sheriff's department in the past. "Here's my report about Robert's attack on my deputy. He broke three of Zeke's ribs. Our civil court is now through with him." One of the sheriff deputies took the report as the other man removed the prisoner from the cell and cuffed his hands, this time behind his back.

"That ought to take some of the fire out from under him. Oh, by the way, you asked about a Negro by the name of Kyle Holloway. Neither our department nor the Marion city police have anything on him. His dad runs a barbershop in Marion. We were surprised he was living over here because we didn't know Negro's lived in Gas City."

Justin said he didn't know it either but that the town was now drawing workers from all over the country. "Just a suggestion on my part," the officer said. "But ya better keep an eye out for White Cap activity now. They're determined to stir up trouble." Thanking the officers, Justin left to go and see the Mayor. He had a favor he wants to ask of him.

~~~~~~~~~~~~~~~~~~~~

"A Negro? You want to hire a Negro as a Deputy Marshal in Gas City? A town that's 99.9% white?" Mayor Huffman said. "I personally would have no trouble with it but many here might. What restaurant will serve him? How will he interact with our female population? I can see White Cap troubles brewing over this. Have any other cities used Negro police officers?"

"Yes, many of the larger cities have used Negro police officers since the 1850's to patrol the Negro section of town. Of course, our city population is almost completely white. I know it's asking a lot of you and the city council to even consider it, and I have no idea if the man would be interested or not. It might just paint a cross hair on his back. He would be under tremendous pressure from some people to resign. My gut tells me it's the right thing to do, not only for him, but for our city and the rest of the local community. It would send a clear message that times are changing. If a man can be called upon to serve his country in a time of war, he should have the same right to hold a job within his community. Maybe this might send a signal to other small towns like ours that every American is entitled to the same rights under our Constitution."

After a brief pause, Huffman said, "Let me poll the other city council members to get their take on the situation and I'll get back with you early next week. I suggest you ponder this idea yourself, Marshal."

~~~~~~~~~~~~~~~~~~~~~

By 11 a.m. Saturday morning, Wilbert was already cleaned up and dressed to revisit with Zeke and, quite naturally, Miss Rachael. She met him at the door with that wonderful smile of hers. Looking around, Wilbert commented, "It sure looks clean and organized in here, Miss Rachael. I bet it hasn't been this clean in many years."

With a chuckle in her voice she responded, "Uncle Zeke fusses every time I dust or clean anything. When he naps I throw out the old trash when I can get away with it. I also strongly suggested that he take a bath but he wanted to know what month it was... so I dropped it. I'm cooking a pot of stew, Wilbert, and you're more than welcome to eat with us. There's plenty." He was happy to stay, and later, even old bachelor Zeke could see that something might start brewing between the two young people.

~~~~~~~~~~~~~~~~~~~~~

Mayor Huffman began polling his city council members on Justin's proposed new deputy. Most were, to say the least, a little surprised, but only a couple openly opposed the idea. Seeing Marshal Blake on the street that afternoon, Huffman gave him the results of his sampling. "Mixed opinions. Two opposed the idea while the others were willing to try it for a thirty day trial period, or use him as your temporary deputy. That's about all I can tell you at this point." Thanking the Mayor, Justin decided it was time to speak with 'Squire Williamson to get his legal perspective on the idea.

"I don't see any reason why we cannot do that Marshal," he told him, "Providing that you are ready to handle everything that will come up. Being the first to hire a Negro in Grant County will be a test case for other departments to review and consider. If you are successful, you will open the door for many worthy men of color, and, at the end, you can improve race relations here. I commend you for even considering this."

Thanking him for his time, Justin sought out saloon owner Townsend. Entering the nearly empty saloon, Justin saw his man sitting at a back table going over his books. "George, do you have a minute or should I come back?" Looking up with a smile, the owner closed his books and told Justin to take a seat.

"Books can wait, what's up?" Looking around to ensure nobody could hear their conversation, Justin lowered the volume of his voice then replied, "First by keeping all of this under your hat." With a quick nodding of Townsend's head, Justin continued. "What can you tell me about Kyle Holloway?" The question seemed to slightly surprise the saloon owner.

"I hope he ain't in any kind of trouble, Marshal?" With a reassuring no, the owner continued. "He's a hard working young man, I'll tell ya that. Jumps right into all the dirty work without waitin' ta be told. Very polite with da customers... even when a few cuss him out. He takes a bit of verbal abuse about his color and all."

"Tell me, would you like to see him improve himself in life even if it means losing him as your worker?"

Pausing to consider his answer, the owner replied, "Yes I would. I ain't had many dealings with colored folks, but this one's a good kid and deserves a chance to improve his life." After Justin left the saloon, Townsend returned to his books but couldn't concentrate. *I wonder what's going on?* he kept wondering.

~~~~~~~~~~~~~~~~~~~

It was just after four a.m. when a persistent barking of his dog awoke farmer Ed Ryan, who lived just north of Gas City. Then he noticed the smell of smoke. Jumping out of bed, Ryan dashed to the upstairs bedroom window to see that his barn was on fire. "Fire!" he shouted. "Mother, help me get the horses out before it's too late!" There was no time for modesty and Ryan ran downstairs and into the back yard in only his night shirt. He was able to open the barn doors to allow one frantic horse the opportunity to escape, before the intense heat from the flames drove Ryan back. Inside, he could hear the terrible cries and groans from six trapped horses as they slowly burned to death. Soon their cries of torment ended, thank God. There was nothing he or his wife could do but drop down on the ground and cry together, as their barn burned completely to the ground.

It was later reported the Ryan's lost fifteen tons of hay, three hundred bushels of corn, six sets of harnesses, a self-binder, mower, a carriage, buggy, cart, and other farm implements. Their loss would be total as he had no insurance. It was later thought that the barn may have been set on fire by passing tramps who were beginning to appear in larger groups within the area.

From a distance, twenty-one year old Jonesboro resident Adam Lake, watched the fire and laughed to himself in genuine excitement. Adam had always known that the sight of a fire aroused him in odd and mysterious ways which one might think of as sexual pleasure. Since he was eleven years old, Adam has occasionally set a small fire here or there just for the fun of it. Burning the large barn was a big step in the right direction for him as fires involving outbuildings or sheds were too small to obtain the necessary pleasure that he was after. Someday he would work up to a house full of people. Also fires at night were far more rewarding for him than daytime blazes, that were often choked in heavy dark smoke. Adam could always be seen around any fire, accidental or deliberately set if people would only have noticed. *More fun to follow soon*, he thought.

Chapter 5
A New Beginning

Sunday morning services were about to start and Justin Blake was running a little late. Arriving just as the doors were being shut, he looked around for an empty seat and made eye contact with Virginia Cole, who managed to save an empty place right beside her on the edge of a bench. "I was wondering if you were coming," she jokingly said.

"Got a little behind this morning, thanks for coming and saving me a seat." Everyone was asked to stand and turn in their songbook to *Rock of Ages*.

After his opening prayer, Reverend Stokes began," I am pleased to announce that a city committee has been formed to collect donations for the construction of a bell tower for our new school. I need not tell you of the Sunday morning confusion that exists with every church ringing their own bell for services at different times. To solve this problem, all church leaders in town have agreed that the newly constructed school bell will be used as a signal for all churches, that services are soon to begin at the same time. I think you will agree this new measure will be a vast improvement over our current system."

Reverend Stokes began, "Today's message will be found in First Thessalonians, Chapter Four starting with Verse Thirteen..." After the church services had ended, Justin introduced his new friend to Mr. and Mrs. Stokes. "So this is the little lady the entire town is talking about. We are very pleased to meet you and I hope you will come to our services again," the Reverend said.

"Thank you sir, I enjoyed it very much," a smiling Virginia said to him. Then Mrs. Stokes spoke, "My dear, why don't you and Justin have lunch with us today? I have a pot of chili already simmering, and we would love to have you." Virginia looked over at Justin and smiled, so he took that as a yes. "We would be delighted." Mrs. Stokes placed her arm around Virginia's shoulder as they started their girl talk while walking out to the awaiting carriage. Reverend Stokes held back to speak with Justin privately.

"My son, I am happy to see you are enjoying life once again. She seems to be a very sweet little lady.... as long as you are not a bank robber!" Both men laughed and after shaking a few more hands with remaining church goers, they left to join the ladies for the ride to their home.

"You men can take a seat as I'll have the food ready in only a few minutes," replied Mrs. Stokes. "What can I do to help you Mrs. Stokes?" Virginia asked as both ladies vanished into the kitchen. Justin was pleased to once again be invited into the Stokes' home. So much has happened in his life since his first visit here early last year. The Reverend's question brought Justin out of his old daydreams, "So are you enjoying your promotion to Marshal?"

"Yes I am, but it's a big change from simply following directions to making all the decisions, and hoping that they are the right ones." At that point, the ladies entered carrying bowls of chili for the men, while returning to the kitchen for their own. Soon a blessing to Almighty God was offered and routine table talk began.

"So, what do you think of our little community, Miss Cole?" the Reverend asked.

"I am very surprised and delighted. In only one week I have gone from being a total stranger, to employed at the bank and meeting nice people like you and Mrs. Stokes."

Everyone at the table noticed that when she said "nice people," she glanced straight into the face of Justin. Mrs. Stokes smiled to herself but said nothing. The intent was obvious to everyone but Justin. "This is very good chili, Mrs. Stokes. Your cooking always reminds me of my own mother's," Justin said.

"I hope you won't mind but I would like to share something with all of you and get your opinions," Justin continued. "I am considering offering a deputy marshal position to a Negro, and I wondered what you think the town's reaction might be?"

Mrs. Stokes was the first to comment, "You know of my family's involvement in the old underground railroad here, as my husband has fussed at me for the old stories I have told you around this very table. So personally I am very pleased."

Looking over at the Reverend, Justin waited for his comment. "Well Justin," he finally began, "We are all God's children, but with that said, I cannot help but wonder if you might be bringing a whole lot of trouble onto yourself. Change comes slowly and some people will not like having a black man in authority over them." Justin thanked each for their comments then he looked over at Virginia. She on the other hand continued to eat in silence and offered no opinion.

At the end of the afternoon, the young people thanked the Stokes for a wonderful time and Justin proceeded to walk Virginia back over to Ma Richardson's boarding house. He couldn't help but notice the change that had came over her as they basically walked in silence. Reaching the house, Justin thanked her for a wonderful afternoon and hoped he could see her again. Without saying a word, Virginia Cole walked into the boarding house and closed the door. A confused Justin Blake then began to make his afternoon plans.

~~~~~~~~~~~~~~~~~~~~

Justin rode his horse *Spunky* slowly out of town towards the home of Kyle Holloway, having obtained the address from the property owner, Townsend, during his earlier visit. Arriving on scene, Justin could see the shack didn't present a very inviting place but was probably good enough for a single man. Knocking on the door, Justin waited for quite a spell before the door slowly opened.

"Kyle, it's Marshal Justin Blake," A weary man stood at the doorway half way behind it, ready to slam it shut at the first sign of trouble.

"I ain't done nothing wrong Marshal," came the quietly spoken words.

Justin realized the man was afraid, "No, I only want to talk with you. Can you come outside and sit on the porch with me?" With suspicious concern on his face, Kyle Holloway did as he was asked as Justin found a wooden box to sit on, so the occupant could use the single straight-back chair.

Justin cleared his throat then began, "Kyle, I have heard good reports about you and your character and I am asking if you would be interested in a night-time deputy marshal position with the city? It pays $35 a month." The man just sat there for a few seconds considering what was just said. He had been afraid that he was being taken off to jail for something he didn't do, and now he was being offered the position of its jailer?

"You're a pullin' my leg ain't ya Marshal?" Shaking his head no with a serious look on his face, Kyle could then see that the white man was serious.

"I have permission from the city council to hire you. As with any new employee, there's a thirty day trial period, but after you pass that, the position becomes permanent. We both know that there will be a few people who won't like a colored man in a position of authority. I'm afraid we'll have folks like that around for a long time, but here is your chance to prove yourself to the other people in town that a man of any color can protect the lives and property of its citizens. Mr. Townsend is 100% behind you and says you can still continue to live here. I know this is a big decision for you to make, so sleep on it tonight and come by tomorrow at the office and let me know your decision. Do you have any questions I can answer now?"

Thinking for a few seconds, he replied. "Would I wear da uniform and have a badge like you white men?" With a smile, Justin told him yes and just to be quite clear on the subject... there would not be white deputies or a black deputy, only deputy marshals working as a team to uphold the law.

"I'll leave you now to think it over. Please let me know what you decide." Justin then offered his hand which was cautiously accepted as the men shook on it. Riding slowly away, Justin reflected upon the problems that he knew would be coming his way. *Nobody ever said this job would be easy*, he thought.

The next morning Justin arrived a little early at work so he would have time to speak with Wilbert about his offer. Stepping inside, he was a little surprised to find Kyle Holloway standing out in the fire barn waiting for him. "Good morning Kyle," Justin offered.

"Morning sir, I gave your offer deep thought and I needs ta turn it down. Me workin' as a real deputy marshal would just cause too much trouble with sum folks. You's too good a man ta live with da memories of finding my body ah hangin' from a tree and all. I ain't too keen on dat thought either. I'll just stick with what I'm ah doin', but I wants ta thank ya fer your kind offer."

Justin was visibly disappointed but certainly could understand Kyle's concerns. Kyle Holloway then left for his daytime job at Thompson's Glass Factory. *What a shame things are the way they are. Maybe someday all this will change,* Justin thought.

"What was that all about?" Wilbert asked Justin as he poured his friend a cup of coffee. "I offered Kyle the deputy position but he turned it down. He felt the town's people were not ready to accept a black deputy marshal. Maybe he is right. So now we are back to square one. The advertisements in the paper didn't produce anyone that I felt was fit for the job. I even placed a help wanted sign outside on the jail you may have noticed, but so far nothing. I know you are stressed to the limit working nights all by yourself."

Wilbert replied, "I'm making it work so far but only covering the basics. If we are going to start your crackdown on enforcing the liquor laws, we will need more help."

Justin took his third swig of coffee. "At least the coffee is better now that you are making it. How's Zeke doing?"

With a slight smile on his face, Wilbert told him about having lunch with him and Rachael. Justin couldn't help but see that his friend was in fact quite smitten with the lovely Miss Rachael Marley. "I guess she'll be returning to Fort Wayne soon now that her uncle is mending," Justin casually stated. A strange look swept over Wilbert's face, one that Justin could easily read. His friend was falling in love and the thought of his darling leaving for home hit him like a ton of street bricks.

Telling his friend to go get breakfast and some well deserved sleep, Justin decided a shave and a haircut might just do the trick. He then headed over to the barbershop of Councilman Matthew Brooks. "Morning Matt," he said, as he entered the shop. There was already one young man in the barber chair so Justin picked up an old copy of the Gas City Journal and leafed through it as the man in the chair continued telling his story.

"Like I was saying, my Uncle Johnny Dexter was an old bachelor when he died. Now this is the strange part, earlier in his life, my uncle was a school teacher over in

Marion and he fell in love with his fifteen year old student, Mary Wiggins. Her parents objected to any thought of her marriage to him, probably due to her young age, so Uncle Dexter moved north of Gas City and built a small cabin and worked the land. He avoided society and slowly added additions onto his property, where he remained for forty years. His only sister, who was my mother, died last year leaving me as his heir."

"Now here is the part where it starts to get even stranger. His old sweetheart is now the mother of six children, one of which is a daughter, age 19 named Gertrude. Uncle's will was read late last week, and it said that if I, as his only relative, married his old sweetheart's daughter within two years of his death, then I can inherent his entire estate. If either of us chooses not to wed the other, I on the other hand only receive a small fraction and the state of Indiana gets the rest. I'm to meet our mysterious Gertrude this afternoon to discuss the possibilities of marriage."

Barber Books thought he had now heard everything, "That's some story young fellow. Maybe you would like a splash of good smelling hair tonic to help you impress the little lady? Only ten cents extra." The young man agreed. "Now you're looking very dapper," he told him. "Good luck with your young lady friend."

Justin settled himself into the old barber chair as the barber cloth was placed around him. "That's a story the reporter Jensen would have loved to print," he joked.

Brooks began to trim his hair as he spoke, "So tell me Marshal, did anything come of your idea of hiring the Negro?" Justin filled him in on his reasons for turning it down. "He may be right as it might have stirred up more White Cap troubles in town," Brooks told him.

Justin continues, "So I'm back to square one and I desperately need additional night time deputies. Maybe I should deputize the city council members?" Justin had said it more of a joke, but the idea did seem to reignite to some degree with Councilman Brooks.

"Actually I wouldn't mind helping out occasionally as long as I don't fall asleep cutting my client's hair. Let me run the idea past the council to get their views on it. I do have experience operating our Horse Thief Protection Association and all." These were a group of men who wore their own badge and whose job it was to capture any horse thief and turn him over to the law. They would then return the stolen horse to the owner. All of this they did for a small annual fee that went into the Association's fund. It was estimated there are well over one thousand members in the county alone and many other similar groups all over the state.

The barber then changed the subject. "I had the owner of the strawboard company in here first thing this morning. Do ya know the man, Albert Slocum? Well, we were discussing all these tramps that are coming and going from town, knights of the road he calls them. He said he is allowing them to sleep on company property out of kindness. Sometimes as many as thirty tramps a night are over there."

Justin then replied," Seems to me he's taking a huge risk with one of them smoking and causing a fire."

Nodding his head in agreement, Brooks replied, "I guess he deprives them of their pipes and matches before admitting them. Still strikes me as a foolish thing to do, though. We were discussing these tramps before the last city council meeting and the mayor thinks fifty to one hundred and fifty tramps pass through Gas City every day looking for a handout. It seems to me that the more we give them, the more will show up." With his haircut and shave completed, Justin returned to work. He had an idea come to him last night that he should approach all of the town's church leaders and ask if they had any members who might fit the profile of the 13th Disciple, someone who had publicly professed those actions or feelings. Taking the letter in hand, Justin allowed each man to read it and offer their own opinion as to the killer's motive. While a good idea, his efforts produced no tangible results.

Consulting his pocket watch, Justin saw that it was nearing noon. *Maybe Virginia will be free to have lunch with me,* Justin thought. Walking into the bank, he found her speaking with an employee at the teller's booth.

"Morning Virginia," Justin said with a sincere smile. "I was wondering if you had made any lunch plans?"

Justin could see a slight hesitation before she answered, "I guess not. I'll meet you outside at noon," she told him.

Justin could still feel a slight chill in her demeanor and wondered what he had said or done to cause it. No matter, he was having lunch with her and that was all that actually mattered. Maybe he was reading too much into all of this and Virginia was not really interested in him after all?

Stepping outside, Virginia pulled a light shawl over her shoulders and tied it in front. "A bit of a fall chill is in the air," she said. Walking together Justin kept the conversation light but as far as conversation goes, it was pretty one-sided. They found a secluded table inside a popular Main Street restaurant and sat down.

"Virginia, may I ask you something? Have I said something that has upset you? You have seemed a bit standoffish since we left the Stokes's home."

Virginia said nothing and reached for a drink of water. Finally she looked up at him and said, "Did you hire that Negro you were talking about?" Justin then filled her in on why it had not worked out.

"Good" she said. "Let me explain something to you, something that happened long ago in my past. When I was ten years old, my best friend Betty Lawrence was kidnapped, molested, and murdered by what they say was an old Negro man. A beast actually. I was sick that day or he would have gotten me also. We had a place in the woods where we played. A private location we would go to and escape the real world, and enter into a make-believe one. He apparently found Betty there and that was where his dirty deed was accomplished. I have never entered a wooded forest area since."

Now Justin could understand Virginia's fear, the mentioning of Kyle had brought up an old, painful memory from her childhood. "Did they catch the killer?" Justin softly asked.

"A group of men formed up and hunted him down about one half mile from the murder. He had a small campsite set up there when they captured him. He was quickly lynched."

Justin reached over cautiously and touched her hands. She didn't pull away from his touch but continued speaking. "I know it's in the past and it's probably not right to condemn an entire race of people for the actions of one old man. Maybe I'll eventually get over my fear."

Justin smiled as he spoke, "Maybe just talking about it will help you to heal. Thanks for sharing it with me. I was concerned I had upset you." The couple now changed the subject and enjoyed the remainder of their time together before Justin walked her back to the bank.

While Justin and Virginia were dining together, Wilbert was having lunch again with Rachael and Zeke. The old deputy was getting around much better using the crutches that Justin gave him, and was sounding more like his old feisty self. "I know dat me bein' off and all is causin' da office ta run short. I hopes ta be back ta work in a few weeks," Zeke said. Wilbert doubted his optimistic timetable but knew Rachael's days remaining in town were probably numbered. The thought of her moving back to Fort Wayne clawed at his soul like a bear claws a tree.

"So, Rachael, I gather you are anxious to return home?" Wilbert asked with a nonchalant attitude.

"Well, yes and no actually. It will be wonderful to see my folks again but I've learned to like this little town and many of its people," she replied.

Zeke jumped in, "Fer a fee-male, Rachael's been a pure joy ta have around. I'm kinda surprised one of dem Gas City fellers ain't asked her out to Lovett's Opera House sum evenin' and all." Wilbert felt his face beginning to blush a deep red, knowing who Zeke was trying to spur on. It was now or never.

"Rachael, I would be proud if you might attend the new comedy show playing there with me. It would have to be this afternoon's matinee showing due to my work schedule."

Turning to her uncle, she then asked, "Will you be alright for two hours?"

Zeke being old Zeke replied, "No... not for two hours, more like four ta be honest with ya. Go have fun, take her to da park, give her a ride on dat steamboat down da river... do whatever young people do des days. Maybe you can talk some sense in ta him about dat dumb haircut he's got!" Turning back to Wilbert, she nodded yes with a smile on her face, then reached over and gave Zeke a big hug.

"Gash, I didn't do nuttin'," he replied as he turned beat-red.

The comedy show at the opera house was rather silly, but the crowd of people present laughed and apparently had a good time, as Rachael and Wilbert laughed along with them anyway. Afterwards, they took a ride on the local steamboat *Eureka* traveling up and down the Mississinewa River. "It's so good to get outside again and be with people," Rachael said.

"It's so good to be with you Rachael. The idea that you will be returning to Fort Wayne soon troubles me terribly. I wish you would stay here." With that said, Rachael reached over and gave him a light peck on his cheek.

"That's so sweet of you to say. Even my uncle suggested I look for work and remain here in town. He even offered to let me stay with him, but I wouldn't want to do that on a permanent basis." As the couple walked back uptown, they passed what used to be Clancy's Emporium.

"Look, they are removing the Clancy sign and putting back up the old Wainwright one," Wilbert said. "I don't blame her one bit for going back to her old name. I bet her old customers will be happy to see it and starting shopping there again."

Standing outside watching the sign men at work was the owner's sister, Jane Draper. "Afternoon Miss Draper. I see the old sign is going back up."

"Hello deputy, and who is this pretty little girl on your arm?" Wilbert made the introductions. "Miss Marley, this is Miss Draper, the owner's sister."

"Hello, how are you! Since Constance is a couple of weeks away from being able to walk on crutches, I convinced her to let me go ahead and change the signage back since 'Squire Williamson is making the necessary paperwork to legally change her name back."

Wilbert replied, "I'm sure everyone will be happy to start shopping here again soon. When do you plan on re-opening the store?"

"As soon as I can hire a proper lady to clerk it. We discussed that point and my sister is very adamant that she will hire no more men." With that, both ladies chuckled. An idea struck Wilbert that he blurted out without giving it much thought.

"There you go Rachael, the perfect job for you so you won't have to return to Fort Wayne." The idea clearly caught Rachael off guard a bit and she noticed that the older sister had begun sizing her up.

"If you're interested, you'll have to come over and speak with my sister. She does the hiring. I'm just her legs until she's up and about. There's a small upstairs apartment above the store that she might let you have if you are hired. Nothing fancy, but useful to live on property. You seem to be a fine young lady and all, just realize that no men are allowed upstairs."

Wilbert was quick to interject, "She certainly is a proper young lady. Rachael's uncle is Zeke Miller, my co-worker. She's taking care of him until he's medically ready to return to work."

With the name of Zeke Miller, Miss Draper started laughing. "I was foolish over your uncle years ago when we were younger, but I just couldn't pin him down. How is the old buzzard doing anyway?"

"He's up and around on his crutches. You certainly described Uncle Zeke... a confirmed bachelor to his dying day."

"I won't hold it against you being related to him if you decide to speak with my sister," Jane Draper said with a smile on her face. "I'll be seeing ya, I gotta get back to bossin' these sign men around or they might hang the thing upside down."

Chapter 6
The Plot Thickens

The Strawboard Manufacturing Company continued to do a good business. Strawboard is a very useful product made of straw and pulp, used in making packing materials and boxes. Sometimes referred to as Jute board or Pasteboard, it has also been used as coverings for books and even roofing material. The owner of the company, Albert Slocum, relocated his factory last year with the promise of free land and natural gas. So far it had proven to be a wise move on his part. His superintendent of daily operations, Robert Anderson, had worked for his employer for several years and held many of the same beliefs as Slocum. Several months ago when the first group of tramps arrived, Anderson was of the opinion that the more you feed and provide them with shelter, the more that will come after. Like feeding a stray cat once, and suddenly it's your cat.

Albert Slocum had a completely different approach to the situation, stating that we are in fact our brother's keeper. Slocum authorized the tramps to sleep on the property at night providing that all matches and pipes were collected beforehand. At first there were six tramps who turned into twelve, until finally some evenings there are well over a hundred men sleeping on site. Slocum had hired a local immigrant woman to occasionally cook stew for them and to provide them with vegetables to enable them to cook off-site for themselves. Slowly Anderson came around to his boss' way of thinking, having been told to seek out the leaders of the tramps. With their help and cooperation, the rest would fall in line.

Slocum now estimated that about twenty percent of the tramps remained day after day while the rest eventually moved on to other locations as a new batch of people arrived. The workers at the Strawboard factory were very much aware of the tramps presence, and wondered what their owner would do when the weather turned to winter. "Work with them and treat them with respect," Slocum reminded superintendent Anderson almost daily. "We are all God's children and it's the duty of those of us blessed with enough, to share it with the poor and the destitute." God's will be done.

~~~~~~~~~~~~~~~~~~~~~

Not far away in a rather poor section of housing built for worker's families, a young woman sat at her dressing table mirror methodically combing her hair. Over and over the hair brush ran through her long black locks as she thought about her recent predicament. Her name was Maggie O'Shea, until recently it had been Mrs. Maggie O'Shea. Her husband Michael O'Shea had been one of the six men killed by the sawmill boiler explosion where he was employed.

Michael O'Shea had been a well-liked and friendly man who had met Maggie in Chicago. Despite the fact that she had been selling her body to men, he had proposed marriage to the young woman. Leaving her past behind them, the young couple arrived in Gas City last fall. Maggie had remained a loyal and helpful wife as the couple had developed genuine deep feelings for each other. All of that had ended that morning. One of the men who hauled logs in by team told the authorities that he had just unloaded and was leaving the property when the steam boiler, which provided power for the saw blade, exploded. The shock of the explosion was so great that he had been thrown from his seat. Timbers had been hurled as far away as five hundred feet. The driver had quickly returned to the terrible scene to find the gang of six men, who he had known so well, all dead.

What he witnessed was pure horror. Bodies were badly mangled from the shrapnel from the boiler. One body was blown up and onto a nearby rooftop. Michael O'Shea's body was scalded by the boiling water. Maggie had often heard her husband remarking that it was an unsafe place to work, and it was only a matter of time before someone was killed. Past workers had complained to the owner, Leo Frazier, about the unsafe working conditions and the age of the old boiler. His response was to fire anybody who complained, thus ending the discussions. Any talk of forming a workers' union resulted in more firings. Michael O'Shea knew that he had no other choice but to report to work, to draw his meager earnings and to hope, yes pray, that his luck would not run out. But it had. Maggie continued to comb her hair in silence, and considered her limited options. Her future no longer looked bright.

The funerals were held the very next afternoon in close proximity to each other. All of the workers killed were newly-arrived immigrants, and the town, shocked in disbelief at the terrible tragedy, chose to remain at home. Several people who were there were shocked to hear the cold-hearted statements coming from the mouth of the sawmill's owner, Leo Frazier. He was speaking to reporter Alvin Jensen when he said, "My company is not responsible or at fault in this accident. You know how these foreigners like to drink... I'm positive the fault lies completely with them. I'll find another old boiler and be up and running again in no time." Even Jensen had been taken aback by the man's lack of compassion.

That evening, Maggie O'Shea sat again at her dressing table mirror combing her hair. Her options for the future were bleak. She still had her good looks but with no education, Maggie would once again be forced back into the only occupation that she had ever known. Perhaps it wouldn't be for too long. Perhaps another man would come along and together they would leave and start again anew. Reviewing her food supplies and meager coinage, Maggie saw that she must renew her prior lifestyle within only a few days. There would be no financial assistance from Leo Frazier. Maggie O'Shea was once again on her own.

The next day, Gas City Journal's editorial expressed concerns about the lack of worker safety in most of the new factories. Quite a number of men, women, and children had been maimed on the job. Couldn't something be done by the owners to improve their safety record and to provide protection to its workers? It was the paper's headlines that caught most of their readers attention: **Liquor Laws Continue to be Broken**.

"The better element of the citizens of Gas City and Jonesboro know that the liquor law is violated every day. Saloon keepers refuse to take out the annual county licenses at one hundred-fifty dollars when they can run a quart shop at their business and sell over the counter the same as any other saloon nearby who is in legal compliance. The law against selling on Sundays, selling to children, and selling after eleven p.m. is also not being enforced. The under-staffed Marshal's office seems helpless in enforcing this particular section of the law. Of course, saloon keepers who continue to violate the law so recklessly have to use a little precaution. Unfortunately, it is not an uncommon sight to witness three or four men entering a saloon on Sunday. This newspaper calls on every law-abiding citizen to assist in enforcing our laws and bringing those in violation to arrest and brought before 'Squire Williamson for swift conviction."

Reading the article, Marshal Blake had to smile knowing that it was bound to stir the pot and possibly move the five councilmen and the Mayor into action. Several had expressed a reluctance to assist in working as acting deputies until the office's current manpower situation was improved. Now due to the public outcry, the politicians must act or risk the wrath of the voters in the upcoming November elections. Willing or not, Justin knew that each man would now come forward and volunteer his services for night duty.

Rachael Marley had given yesterday's afternoon outing with Wilbert Vance a great deal of thought. The possibility of staying longer in Gas City intrigued her. Should she go and speak with the owner of the emporium? There was so much to consider and Rachael felt like it might be time to sit down and speak with her Uncle Zeke. "Uncle, can we talk? I have some things I would like your opinion on," Rachael asked. Zeke poured himself a cup of coffee and sat down at the table.

"I been expectin' we would talk. What be a botherin' ya Rachael?" She then covered the comedy, the boat ride up and down the river, and meeting Miss Draper who was needing a daytime clerk for her sister's store.

"What should I do, Uncle?"

None of this came as any surprise to Zeke Miller who could clearly see the chemistry between the two young people. "You in love with Wilbert?" he softly asked her.

The question required a deep emotional response that Rachael didn't feel she knew the answer to yet. "I don't know. I like Wilbert a lot. I like him probably more than a lot, but love... I just don't know yet. How will I know for sure?"

Zeke didn't feel like he was the right person to advise anybody on the subject of love. He had avoided it personally almost his entire life and planned on being single until the Good Lord called him home.

Reaching out and taking his niece's hands within his, Zeke continued, "I'll tell ya somthin' I never spoke about ta anybody before. I was in love once." The statement rocked Rachael, as knowing her uncle the way that she did, she never even considered that possibility before.

"It was back in '59. Her name was Moo-ne-sha and she was an injun' gal. Prettiest little thing I ever saw too. She and her folks used ta come in at McClure's tradin' post in Marion. Her pappy used ta trade furs for whiskey while she and her momma wanted bright cloth, thread, and needles. I just hung around on Saturdays hopin' I could see her. Her hair was as black as coal and her brown eyes sparkled like de was diamonds. She was fearful of us settlers and never really spoke ta me but I loved dat girl. Smallpox got her later in da year. I never really got over it and I still see her in my mind at nights when I goes ta sleep."

Rachael was truly touched by her uncle's story. "I promise your secret is safe with me," she told him. Zeke smiled deeply but said nothing as Rachael continued. "As for staying here in town, at least for a while anyway, I feel like I'm ready to get out on my own. The emporium job sounds interesting and Miss Draper indicated that there was a small upstairs apartment above the store. Right now finding a job and being out on my own is the highest priority. Wilbert may or may not be in my future, but I'm willing to just let that ride for the time being. I wouldn't want to leave you short-handed here at home."

Zeke smiled, "I appreciate havin' ya and all, but Rachael, I can take care of myself just fine. I plan on returnin' ta work within a couple of weeks anyway. My advice is go see Constance and ask about da job. If ya don't get it, maybe it ain't meant ta be anyway."

That sounded like good advice. "I'll wait until after dinner and do just that," she replied.

By noon, all five city councilmen as well as the Mayor, had stepped into Justin's office and agreed to start working night shifts with Deputy Vance in order to help crack down on the quart shops. Justin made up a schedule where two men would work a shift each with Wilbert, then be off for two days before their shift came up again. He knew that Wilbert would train each to the best of his ability, and Justin felt that the exposure to actual police work may be an eye-opener for many on the city council.

After lunch, Rachael obtained the address from her uncle and soon was at the doorstep of what was the Wainwright/Clancy home. *It was now or never*, she thought as she knocked upon the front door. It took four knocks before she could hear someone descending down the stairway. Opening the door, Jane Draper replied, "Yes, may I help you?"

"Hello," replied Rachael. "I met you yesterday outside the emporium and we discussed the possibility of the clerk's position."

A look of recognition swept across the sister's face, "Yes, Miss Marley, wasn't it? I have already spoken with my sister about you and she would like to meet you. Please come this way."

Together, they started up the staircase. "Constance was involved in a buggy accident and broke her hip. We hope to have her up and walking on a crutch within a few weeks. Here we are." With a slight tapping upon her sister's bedroom door, the ladies entered.

"Constance, this is the young lady I spoke with you about last evening..." Thirty minutes later, an excited

Rachael Marley left the house with a job position and an upstairs apartment of her own. *Now I am going to have to break the news to mother and father*, she thought as she hurried back to Zeke's shack.

Wilbert entered the office to find two councilmen, and learned that they and the other four men would assist not only in coming down on illegal saloons, but anything else that might appear during their night shift. As a precaution, each man was sworn in as a temporary deputy, but would remain unarmed other than being issued a nightstick. Their job was to watch, learn, and provide any assistance that was required. Tonight their fun began. By morning, three men lay inside the jail cell awaiting an early appointment with 'Squire Williamson's court.

~~~~~~~~~~~~~~~~~~~~

An interesting story was being passed all over town by word of mouth. It seemed that a farmer outside of Marion had stumbled upon a hoard of silver half dollars. The farmer had been in the process of clearing a piece of ground previously un-plowed when he stumbled upon fifty-eight silver coins. The coins dated from 1807 to 1834 along with a bone later determined to be the radius bone from a human arm. An old timer remembered that an Indian village once sat upon the farmer's property. He also explained that the Indians drew money from the government and would let the squaws have a portion of it, which they almost always buried. He also said the bucks would take their part and go on a *spree* until their own portion was spent. It was supposed that the Indians may have fled in great haste and that the buried location was forgotten. Either way, a major search was underway for any additional coinage.

~~~~~~~~~~~~~~~~~~~~~

The first day in October had finally arrived, and with it, the bright and colorful turning of the town's foliage. Within the month, they too would begin to fall to the ground and Old Man Winter was just around the corner. Justin had returned to his office, having taken last evening's prisoners over to the 'squire, when a well-known local citizen entered holding a paper in his hands.

"Marshal, I gotta talk with you. I'm being threatened," he said, as he thrust the paper into Justin's hand.

"Have a seat, Mr. Fay," Justin said as he tried to read the letter and hear the words being uttered by the clearly agitated older man. "Let me read this first then we'll talk," Justin said to him. With that, Jack Fay calmed down.

The letter read: *Leviticus 24:15-16 "Say to the Israelite's: If any one curses his God he will be held responsible; anyone who blasphemes the name of the Lord must be put to death."*

"Marshal, that was tacked on my front door and a bundle of switches were laid under it at my threshold." Fay was a reasonably respected man within the community with one major exception; his intense hatred of any organized religion and its churches. Any conversation one had with this man always relegated itself into a lecture on the evils of religion. Town talk said he had completely disowned his only child, a daughter aged twenty-four, because she attended a church.

"I discovered the other evening that my own wife was sneaking around behind my back and attending the stinking religious services too. Clearly someone has cast an evil spell over her to defy my well-known wishes. Some blasted Baptist church is responsible for this outrage! When she returned, I naturally barred her from my home for several days while she apparently stayed with neighbors. Death threats indeed! Clearly these church people are totally insane to threaten a law-abiding citizen with a thrashing, while they practice their black magic and mumbo-jumbo. I'll fight them! Either one at a time or I'll take on the whole bunch at once!"

Patting the bulge in his breast pocket of his jacket, Fay made it known he was ready to fight fire with fire. "Thanks for bringing this letter to my attention," Justin informed him.

"I'll take it back around to the church leaders to see if anyone recognizes the handwriting."

Fay jumped to his feet. "I don't want or need any help from those church devils. Just know that if I die soon, it's at the hands of these religious morons." Then, softening his mood, Fay asked, "What am I to do, Marshal?"

Without hesitation Justin replied, "Stay indoors at night and do not open your door to anyone. I also strongly suggest you ease up on your wife and make peace. Clearly you are being watched."

"Over my dead body, Marshal," Fay finally replied.

"It may come to that Mr. Fay. It may very well come to that."

As a man of faith himself, Justin was shocked by the man's hateful words... words that went against his own personal religious beliefs, but Fay's right to believe in what he wanted was his own business. Justin opened up a desk drawer and removed the first letter found upon the body of the murdered man. The hand writing appeared to be the same. Someone was very serious about warning the often outspoken Jack Fay. *Now how do I stop them before they strike?* he asked himself.

With Wilbert and his new temporary deputies involved in finally getting a handle on the evening problems, it would fall to Justin to stake out Jack Fay's home. Maybe with luck, he could catch this person or persons before they acted out their threat. After briefing Wilbert and the oncoming shift, Justin set off to eat a quick supper and arrived outside the Fay residence after dark. *Now that it's October, it sure starts getting darker earlier*, he thought. Finding a location across the street on a neighbor's darkened front porch, Justin watched and waited. By one a.m, Justin's body was starting to shut down from a lack of sleep when his eyes caught the sight of movement through Fay's front yard. The figure moved past his home and arrived on the front porch of the house next door.

Odd they picked the wrong house, Justin thought, as he began to quietly creep up on the person. The figure tried to open the front door and finding it locked, proceeded to a side window. That window was raised about half way when Justin shouted, "Freeze right where you are and don't move. This is Marshal Blake and you are under arrest."

The man spun around and in a highly intoxicated voice began shouting, "You can't arrest me.... I live here." He then began singing the song *My Wild Irish Rose*. Loudly and out of tune.

"Quiet down," Justin directed. "Show me some identification." The man replied, "Wif-ee locked me out. I gotta go to sleep."

A candlelight appeared in an upstairs window as a female head appeared. Opening the window, she demanded, "What's going on down there?"

"It is Marshal Blake ma'am, I caught a man attempting to crawl through your window who claims to live here." The drunken man began yelling, "'Cause ya locked me out. Open da door, Elsie!" Taking a couple seconds to consider her options, the woman replied, "Marshal, will you please lock him up? I don't want that drunk in my house tonight. A night in jail and a stiff fine might be just what he needs." Justin agreed and cuffed the drunken man's hands.

"Start singing again and my handkerchief goes right into your mouth," he warned. Clearly the Marshal's tone was all it took for him to quiet down.

A voice then called out to Justin. "Marshal, is that the fellow the church people sent to kill me?"

Turning to see who was speaking with him, Justin saw that it was Jack Fay who was dressed in his night shirt with a stocking hat upon his head.

"No, it's your next door neighbor returned home drunk," he told him. "Didn't I warn you to stay indoors Mr. Fay?"

Fay threw his hands up in the air, "Makes no difference now Marshal. My wife has packed up and left me. Ran off to be with her church friends. They can do whatever they want to me now. They have destroyed my life. I am a beaten man."

With those words a depressed and dejected Jack Fay re-entered his home. Justin marched his prisoner into the empty office and locked him inside the cell. The man fell face first into the cot and was snoring before Justin was even out of the building. Justin now had an appointment in his own bed. Later that night, a somewhat startled Wilbert Vance found an unknown sleeping man locked inside the jail cell snoring peacefully away.

Chapter 7
The Ladies Find Success

After some breakfast and a few hours rest, Wilbert Vance proceeded over to Zeke's residence to speak with Rachael, but instead of her meeting him at the doorway, Zeke appeared. "She's gone, Wilbert," he casually spoke. A look of confusion swept over the young deputy's face.

"Gone? You say, she's... gone?" Seeing the sadness in his fiend, Zeke felt he'd probably joked around perhaps a little too strongly.

"Actually Rachael is bein' trained by Jane Draper ta work in da emporium. I was on my way over ta hear what fixins' she may need in dat upstairs apartment. I ain't gonna be able to climb no stairs, so if ya want to come on over with me, you can go see what Rachael needs. This here crutch really helps me walk along just fine, but I plan on givin' it back ta Justin soon and comin' back ta work."

As the men entered the emporium, Wilbert could see Rachael and Jane Draper behind the large wooden counter going over some books. "Come on in gentlemen," the sister said.

Wilbert then replied, "Miss Draper, we only came to see if there was anything Rachael... ah, I mean Miss Marley will require for her apartment." Jane Draper provided an encouraging smile as she stated, "Why don't you show your friend your sleeping room, Rachael."

"But Miss Draper, you told me that men are not allowed inside my apartment?" Rachael pointed out.

"I think we can make an exception this time, go ahead and show him. If she needs anything that's not provided, I may be able to come up with it," as she waved for the young people to ascend the interior stairs.

"How about you Zeke. Gonna try to hobble up them stairs on your crutch?"

Seeing a couple of wooden chairs off to the side, Zeke took it upon himself and sat down. "Ya might as well join me, Jane," He told her. "Me and stairs don't get along too good these days anyhow."

Jane took his crutch from him and set it to the side. "I heard you were injured Zeke. I hope it's nothing serious."

"Nope, just ta couple of busted ribs. I'm doin' just fine."

"Take care of yourself Zeke. We're not getting any younger you know. I do see you occasionally on the street but you never come around. That offer of coffee is always open."

Glancing around the store, Zeke thanked her for the offer. "How's she a doin?" With a reassuring smile, she informed him that his niece was doing quite well actually and catching on quickly. Nodding towards the stairs, she asked, "Are they a pair or just friends?"

Zeke replied, "A might too early ta say fer sure. He's head over heels but Rachael has a good head on her shoulders and ain't da type to just jump in ta somehin'".

Silence followed for almost a minute before Jane Draper said to him, "Where have all the years gone Zeke? It seems like only yesterday that you came back from the war in your fancy blue uniform and marched with the others down that old muddy street."

"I know. Seems like when we was youngens' time went slow, but now it just flies by," he replied. Feeling like she had no other chance to say what was on her mind, Jane finally spoke up.

"How come you and I never got together Zeke? Seems to me we had so much in common." Zeke looked over at her in surprise. "Yes," she continued, "I had quite a crush on you for many years. Does that scare you?" With nervous laughter, Zeke mentioned that he had never been aware of it and changed the subject.

Upstairs, Wilbert scanned the small room that Rachael seemed so proud of. "The cot seems comfortable and the mirrored dresser is more than adequate."

Walking over to the window, Wilbert raised the window up and down. "Works a little hard, but you'll be able to get some fresh air until it turns cold.

"There's no fireplace, but Miss Draper says the heat from the store will keep the room warm. Anyway, with heavy blankets I'll be able to make it through winter alright."

Wilbert looked directly into Rachael's eyes. "I'm glad you decided to stay. Maybe I can see a little more of you now."

Sensing that the time was passing, she replied, "We better go back down. Anyway with me working days and you working nights, I don't expect we will be seeing too much of each other." Her smile had been rueful; one of regret. With that, the couple descended back down into the emporium. For once, Wilbert decided that he hated working the night shift.

~~~~~~~~~~~~~~~~~~~~~~~~~

Over at the Strawboard Manufacturing Plant, Albert Slocum was speaking with the plant manager, Robert Anderson. "Bob, how's the work coming on emptying the smaller warehouse building?" Slocum had earlier directed that it be made available as a cold weather shelter for the tramps now camping outside at night.

"I have a team of workers removing the contents and placing them inside the main warehouse. It'll make it quite cramped this winter for us, but I guess we can make it work," Anderson told him.

"Good, keep me informed. Are you maintaining a level of cooperation from their leaders?"

Nodding the affirmative, Anderson replied, "They seem very appreciative for what you are doing for their men. I also reminded them to maintain a constant surveillance for matches or smoking materials and that any serious miscues might result in you changing your mind in helping them."

With a deep look of satisfaction upon his face Slocum replied, "We are only doing God's work here, Robert."

Working the night shift as a temporary deputy marshal was certainly an eye opener for all of the councilmen. By now, each had taken a turn and they could see that there was so much more involved in the job than they had originally thought. The one councilman that seemed to have really taken to the job was Michael Davidson, the man running against Mayor Huffman for the position of Mayor. Each councilman had also experienced some degree of excitement during their shifts. One of the most unusual was a saloon scrap between plant worker Ed Kirk and a young troublemaker known only as Paint. As these two went at it, Paint had bit half of Kirk's left ear off. The next morning, 'Squire Williamson fined Paint ten dollars for the incident.

The following night, a William Bowen who was employed at the tin plate works had tried to kill his wife and threatened the lives of others. This was the same individual, well known as a bad and dangerous man, who earlier had threatened another man with a shotgun. Apparently Mrs. Bowen, a hard working and well-liked woman by all her neighbors, had been keeping boarders in order to support herself and her family. Mr. Bowen spent his money in saloons and was known as a very jealous man. Last night, he had came home about mid-night with blood in his eyes and began fighting with his wife. Mrs. Bowen, seeking shelter from harm, sought help at a neighbor's home. Bowen had kicked in the neighbors door and came at his wife with a large carving knife. A scuffle then occurred and Bowen had fled the scene only to be later captured by the night deputy marshals. He then appeared before 'Squire Williamson. With court fines and the cost of a new door, the total came to seventy-five dollars. Mrs. Bowen refused to prosecute her husband and so only by her good graces had he avoided further punishment.

~~~~~~~~~~~~~~~~~~~~

Virginia Cole remained after normal banking hours in order to complete the stack of loans that she was processing. It seems that having a female loan officer, and a beautiful one at that, had caused a larger than normal interest in borrowing money. She was enjoying her new job, and the people that she worked with. Her boss, Mr. Howell, was a warm and gentle man who treated all of his employees with respect, a rare thing these days. The bank had closed thirty minutes ago and Virginia finally completed the loan applications and laid them on

Howell's desk. Putting on her shawl and bonnet, Virginia stepped outside and locked the front entry doors. She was hungry and was already considering her dining options, when she noticed a small child sitting alone near the edge of the building with her head braced within her hands. Curious, she walked over to the child.

"Hello," she spoke to the little girl who appeared to be about four years old. "What are you doing here?"

With tears in her eyes, the child began to cry, "I want my mommy." Concerned, Virginia looked up and down the street searching for the child's parents, but saw no one anywhere near.

"What is your name little one?" "Cathy," came the reply. "Well Cathy, I will help you find your mother. What is her name?"

"Mommy," came the reply as the child began to cry again. Taking the poor child by the hand, Virginia began approaching anyone on the street and then shopkeepers as to the identity of the child. Finally, a young couple could be seen running toward them with the woman several paces in the lead.

"Cathy!" The mother cried out. "Oh, Cathy!" as she grabbed the little girl and held her close to her bosom.

Virginia then spoke, "I came out of the bank and she was sitting on the curb crying for you." By now, the young mother was satisfied that her daughter was alright and acknowledged Virginia.

"My husband thought Cathy was with me and I thought he had her. Thank you so much for protecting our daughter." With a gentle smile, the family departed. *I bet she gives him a piece of her mind,* Virginia thought.

Marshal Justin Blake was in the process of briefing Wilbert Vance and the two night time deputies when Virginia poked her head into his office. "Anyone here interested in taking me to dinner tonight?" Justin jumped at the chance and stated that he would be right with her.

"Doctor Baxter has examined Zeke and says he can return to work in a week. He just needs to take it easy and stop being a human punching bag," Justin said. The councilmen deputies then reminded everyone that they had to attend the city council meeting at eight p.m. but that they would catch up with Wilbert afterwards. There was no problem doing this, they were assured.

Justin and Virginia decided upon a restaurant and found a small table and a bit of privacy. "I did my good deed for the day," she told him. "I found a small child unattended outside of the bank a few minutes ago, but now she's back into the loving arms of her parents."

Justin was happy to hear this. The last thing he need-ed was for a small child to be hurt or even worse upon a busy public street. "So how's the job at the bank coming along?"

With a smile upon her face, Virginia described all the loan applications she was processing. "Mr. Howell teases that it is because of me and not really the bank," she chuckled. "One old coot even suggested we run off to South America together!" Justin then asked what she had said to the man

"I pointed to his wedding ring and asked what his wife would say about it, and he kind of got quiet." The food then arrived and they continued speaking between bites.

"Are you going to the City Council meeting to-night?" she asked him.

"I thought I probably should in case anyone has any questions that I need to deal with," he replied. "How are things at Ma Richards?" he asked.

"I'm very satisfied. Maybe some Saturday I could use Ma's kitchen to cook you a meal?" Justin was happy to hear this.

"I'll even wash the dishes afterwards," he told her. It was great to spend time again with Virginia Cole.

The council meeting discussed the following items of importance:

(1) Next month's election voting will be held inside the fire barn.

(2) Merchants are stacking boxes and merchandise outside on the new concrete sidewalks, blocking public traffic from using the sidewalks. Marshal Blake was asked to speak with each offending stores and to remind them that two thirds of the sidewalk must be kept clear.

(3) A representative from the streetcar company complained that mischievous young boys were placing rocks and wooden boards across their tracks causing needless delays. The public was asked to supply the names of any boys seen doing those acts.

(4) The Gas City Land Company has offered a fund of seventy thousand dollars to entice any new factory to relocate. A Porcelain Ware Factory has shown interest in relocating from Crawfordsville, Indiana to Gas City.

~~~~~~~~~~~~~~~~~~~~~~~

Jane Draper informed Rachael that she felt she was now ready to work unsupervised at the emporium. This made Rachael feel good. "Constance and I were discussing the need to have some sort of public contest to help re-introduce the emporium," Jane told her.

An idea formed in Rachael's mind, "Why not have a contest where anyone who spends a dollar or more gets a promotional key. We could have a lock box with, say twenty dollars in silver coinage and on a certain day, maybe two weeks later, people line up to see if their key will open the lock." Jane seemed very surprised by the idea.

"I love it! Let me speak with Constance tonight about it. We'll have no trouble finding a large amount of old keys or even have some cheap ones made up for the size of the lock. Then the customers can reach in and pick their own key. I can imagine a sturdy wooden box with chains and a padlock that everyone will notice in the front window of the store. I bet folks will gladly spend a dollar in order to take a chance at winning twenty silver dollars." Rachael then volunteered to make up the advertising store signage. "We'll need to run an advertisement in the Journal too. This is a great idea, Rachael!" By the next day, the actual key and all of the non-winning keys were made ready and soon the public was buying again at the emporium.

~~~~~~~~~~~~~~~~~~~~~~~~~~~~

Adam Lake felt the emotional need to set another fire, and he felt that he knew the perfect location, the business of the not very popular owner of the sawmill, Leo Frazier. That awful man had been the talk of the town since the accident that killed those poor workers. Even though he had brought in another used boiler, the talk was that the place remained a death trap and nobody wanted to work there. *Maybe a good fire will destroy his equipment and send the old skin flint a message,* he thought. *Maybe a fire is in the public's interest. Maybe people will even praise the man who sets it!* Tonight the fun would begin again.

It was well after two A.M. when the fire bells sounded in town. Men rushed from their beds to the fire barn to harness the fire horses, Roscoe and Prince Phillip. Each horse was raring to pull the town's Christie American Steam Fire Engine to wherever it was needed. Soon the blaze was under control and extinguished. The smell of coal oil was everywhere as the owner, Mr. Frazier, surveyed the carnage.

"This ain't gonna put me out of business, no sir-ee, ain't gonna happen," he expressed to all the firemen and night deputies. Seeing a crowd of onlookers, Wilbert walked over to them.

"Anybody see how this thing was started?" he asked, as people simply shook their heads no. At the rear of the crowd stood Adam Lake who began to walk away slowly into the darkness. It had all been so very easy tonight but more fun was just around the corner

The next day's newspaper headlines read: **Arsonist Destroys the Frazier Sawmill**. Adam Lake cut the story out of the paper and pasted it with all the others upon his small shack's bedroom wall. He enjoyed seeing them and reading them over and over, which made him feel like a very powerful man. *Look at what I can do anytime I want*, he laughed to himself.

Chapter 8
The Gypsies Return

A large band of Gypsies had once again set up camp down by the bridge on the Mississinewa River. Unlike many other locations, Gas City welcomed the people back. During their last visit, a severe storm had destroyed the gypsies' encampment and the good people of Gas City brought canvas and other building materials to help them rebuild. In return, the leader of the gypsies, Jal, had recovered much of the stolen jewelry of the townspeople. Justin waited until the afternoon before riding down to pay his respects. Seeing many familiar faces, Justin kept on searching until he found Jal.

"Deputy Blake, good to see you again," he said as the two men shook hands.

"It is Marshal Blake now. Great to see you too Jal. What's the big event?"

Jal smiled as he said, "It's our annual fall encampment. The King and Queen of all the gypsies' camps are due to arrive in two days and we'll have music and dancing festivities. Please tell your townspeople that our ladies are set up for fortune telling. After the King and Queen visit, we will break camp and move over to Converse. Oh, and in case you are wondering... Beval is here. She is over by the fortune telling tent." Justin thanked Jal and started over in search for her.

Beval was a strikingly beautiful and mysterious gypsy girl that he had met last year. He hoped that she would remember him, as he often saw her face at night before going to sleep. Justin found her, sitting at her place at the fortune telling table while she was fiddling with something underneath the crystal ball table. Walking up as quiet as possible he sat down and said, "I would like my fortune told again, pretty lady." With a startled look, she sat up and instantly recognized him.

"Justin, you startled me! It's great to see you again. How've you been?"

"Do you remember the fortune you read for me, Beval,?" he asked her. Shaking her head as a 'no' answer, he continued. "You told me I was to be promoted, that I would lose a dear friend, and that I would find love in the arms of another. I was promoted to Marshal of

Gas City and my dear friend ex-Marshal Brewster died saving my life." Justin's face reflected the sadness as he paused, "I am still waiting for the third part to come true," he said with a sly grin on his face.

Using her long established poker face, Beval replied, "The crystal ball never lies." Then they both broke out in a hardy laughter. "I do remember taking that wonderful boat ride on the river with you. I have thought of that day often," she mentioned.

"Perhaps we should pick up where we left off?" he suggested. Her sad smile told him what was to come. "I cannot. I have a new boyfriend and Jak is the jealous type and would not understand."

Justin was naturally disappointed, "I was somehow hoping that you might become the answer to the third prediction."

Beval was touched by the suggestion and reached out for his hands while saying, "Dear Justin, you and I come from completely different worlds and neither of us would be happy living in the other."

Justin had his answer. "It was great seeing you again and I wish you all the best." As he was walking away, Beval reminded him that her predictions always come true. "Love will find you Justin Blake. Goodbye, my friend."

Returning to his office, Justin was very pleased to find Zeke waiting for him. "I brought da crutch back to ya. Doc says I can gets back ta work. Can I start tonight?"

Justin had already considered his options. "Zeke, how about working days with me for a short spell? Wilbert's still working with our councilmen at night, and I have my eye on one of them as a possible full time night deputy." Zeke was happy to get back to work.

"I'll be a seein' ya in da morning. I'm gonna go check up on dem fire horses ta see if they's missed me while I was gone."

It will be great having Zeke back and enjoying him on days so Justin could watch out for him for awhile.

Word spread quickly that the Gypsies had returned and many women and yes, a few men, planned to line up before the pretty fortune teller. As a crowd gathered, an older woman in full Gypsy garb asked for the people's attention. "Ladies and gentlemen. No doubt there are a few of you who do not believe in the powers of fortune telling. Tonight we shall disperse those doubts forever, for before you is the beautiful Beval. Her powers are legendary far and wide. Let me tell you a true story that took place here in Indiana just this past summer. A man's mother laid on her death bead. Before she passed, she told him of a large sum of money buried on different parts of her farm, but before she could tell him where, her spirit passed on to the great beyond."

"After her burial, the man dug up various parts of the front yard but found nothing. He then began to have the same reoccurring dream in which his mother instructed him to seek out Beval and have his fortune read. After several nights involving the same dream, he set out to locate the gypsy camp where his mother said she was located at. Beval told the man to dig in a certain point in his mother's orchard and he would find a tin can containing twelve-hundred dollars. He searched just where he was directed and low and behold, found a tin can containing $1,243.50. Such are the powers of Beval. Please line up and see what's in your own fortune." People began shoving as they jostled for their own place in line. Beval's mother had to laugh to herself. That story gets them every time!

Back in town, off duty Deputy Wilbert Vance met Zeke coming toward him on the concrete sidewalk. "Startin' back on day shift tomorrow. Gonna be good ta be back on da job. I was a goin' ta the emporium ta tell Rachael. Wanna come along?" Wilbert thought that was a great idea and together they entered the store. Rachael was finishing up with a customer, "Thank you and please come again," she told the lady with a genuine smile upon her beautiful face.

"Doc's cleared me ta go back ta work tomorrow," Zeke told his niece. "Justin's puttin' me on days for a while, probably so I can look after him."

Rachael was happy, "That's great news. Hello Wilbert, how have you been?"

Busy was his reply. "I like your artwork signs," he told her. "I'll have to come in and buy a dollar's worth so I can win your grand prize."

Rachael glanced around before continuing, "I have a strange story for both of you. We have a male customer that came in earlier today and announced to everyone in the store that he visited a gypsy girl for a fortune reading, and she assured him that he will draw the winning key. He had most of the people in our store laughing at him as he truly believes it. He made his purchase, picked out his key, waved it all around for others to see and left to tell others his story."

Zeke asked, "What's da feller's name?"

Rachael replied, "It's Bob something or other. That's all I know." Wilbert then told Rachael that he would keep his money in his pocket since Bob something or other already had the winning key anyway. Another customer came in and so both men left Rachael to her business and proceeded outside.

Kyle Holloway called out to them. "Deputies, Mr. Townsend asked me ta fetch ya. He's got something ta show ya." Even though both men were off duty, there was no hesitation as they entered Townsend's Saloon. "I fetched um like ya asked me to, Mr. Townsend," Holloway said.

"Thanks Kyle, deputies please pull up a chair and sit down. I have something I need to show you." Townsend went behind the bar and picked up a paper laying near the cash register. "This was slid under the door after we closed last night and I found it when I opened up this morning. The letter read:

Proverbs 11-19: *"As righteousness tendeth to life, so he that pursueth evil pursueth it to his own death." The Lord Commands and I shall obey. The 13th Disciple.*

Townsend continued, "I didn't think much of it until my beer delivery man told me other saloons were talking about receiving the same letter, so I went to three different saloons and saw that they too got the exact thing. Who is this 13th Disciple anyway to threaten me?"

Wilbert looked at his pocket watch and replied, "George, I need to go home and change into my work uniform but can I take this and show the Marshal?"

Shoving it back towards Wilbert, Mr. Townsend said that would be fine. "Any 13th Disciple comin' in here making threats might just meet with the working end of my shotgun," he warned both men. Both deputies had no doubt that he was speaking the truth.

After changing into his uniform, Wilbert reported directly into work. "Justin, we got more threatening letters from the 13th Disciple," as he handed it to his friend.

Justin replied, "I know, another saloon keeper just brought his letter in to me a few minutes ago. We have a real situation on our hands. This crazed zealot has already killed and now threatens more deaths." Wilbert also said he had heard from Zeke and that it would be nice to have the old man back at work.

"Thanks for coming in a little early so we could discuss this privately. Go ahead and brief your two councilmen when they come in on our situation. Meanwhile, I'm gonna do a little more checking before I turn in." Stepping outside the fire barn, Justin's eyes settled on the new shed addition that now housed the recently purchased fire department ladder vehicle that the city had ordered. Something in the back of his mind warned Justin that it was going to be needed soon. He hoped and prayed he was wrong.

Justin already had made plans on visiting Reverend Stokes tonight, to try to get his take on exactly what type of religious personality they were dealing with. Riding over to the Stokes' home, Justin knocked upon the door and was welcomed inside.

"Justin, we were just about to eat. How about staying for supper? We have plenty," Mrs. Stokes insisted. After finishing the meal, Justin passed the letter over for both of his friends to read. "These went out to several saloons here in town. They all read exactly the same and warn of dire consequences unless the saloons comply with their demands. What kind of religious zealot are we dealing with here? Do you have any ideas that may help us catch him before he makes good on his threats?"

Reverend Stokes pushed his dish to the side and brought his cup of coffee closer. "Maybe I should explain the meaning of that word first and give you a little historical background. The term zealot in the biblical sense means one who is zealous on behalf of God. The original zealots were members of an ancient Jewish sect who fought to the death against the Romans, and who killed and persecuted Jews who were seen to be collaborating with the Romans. It would seem to me that this person calling himself the 13th Disciple is conducting a self-appointed reign of terror as a holy crusade against those he perceives as transgressors of God."

"Wouldn't someone like that tend to stand out and be noticed?" Justin asked. With a sad look upon his face, the Reverend replied, "I'm, guessing he or she is capable of hiding their mental illness from others. It has happened before." Justin felt himself turning red with embarrassment, knowing the hidden meaning of Reverend Stokes message.

"I am sorry that this topic has caused you both pain, I shouldn't have bothered you with it," Justin replied as he rose from the table to leave.

"No, my son," Mrs. Stokes said, "You have not reminded us of our pain. We live with that daily, but with God's love and understanding, we find the strength to carry on."

Reverend Stokes walked Justin to the door. "We are happy you came to see us. I don't know if I have helped you or not tonight, but we pray that this madman will be stopped before he hurts or kills again. God bless you, son."

Newspaper reporter Alvin Jensen managed to get a hold of one of the threatening saloon letters and the Journal printed it entirely under the headlines: **Crazed Zealot Threatens Local Saloons With Death Threats**.

The article also stipulated that other religious-sounding threatening letters had been received by others, including one for the late Mort Clancy. How he had discovered this bit of information, Justin didn't know, but suspected one of the minister's that he had spoken with earlier had broken his vow of silence. Anyway, now that everyone who read the newspaper would know the name *The 13th Disciple*. Would this help or hinder their search?

~~~~~~~~~~~~~~~~~~~~~

Labor troubles continued to plague the area factories. The nearby city of Jonesboro was openly referred to now as "scab town" by the union workers of Gas City. Evening saloon brawls were becoming an every evening occurrence for Deputy Vance and his two councilmen. The Sheldon Bottle Company was having problems securing enough boy laborers due to the low wages being offered. The worst bit of news came from the tin plate factory; they have introduced machines into the dusting room. It was rumored that sixty-five young girls and women were to be thrown out of work as a result. Clearly the town was already on edge, and now with the public exposure to the 13th Disciple business, anything could happen.

Albert Slocum has made it his business to return to his strawboard factory after sunday evening services to see to the treatment and condition of the tramps housed in his small warehouse. As he hurried along, a cool evening breeze caused him to button up the top button of his dress coat. *Coats,* he though. *These men will require warmer clothing to get them through our coming winter. I need to contact the area churches and organize a clothing drive for these poor men.* As he arrived outside of the warehouse that he had instructed his superintendent to have ready for their use, Slocum could see the glow of smoking materials from men standing outside the building.

"Gentlemen, I have instructed your leaders a hundred times, that there must be no smoking on this property or you will be asked to vacate my factory grounds immediately." They were new men who had arrived today and did not know the rules, or at least that was what they told Slocum as he confiscated their matches and pipes. "These will be returned when you leave, just see Mr. Anderson, who is my superintendent.

One of the leaders of the tramps came up to Slocum and apologized for the incident. "Mr. Slocum, all I can do is keep hammering it into these men how lucky we are to have a God-fearing man such as yourself to care for us the way you do. God bless you sir." Slocum then mentioned his idea for a clothing drive that he would organize at his and other local churches. Seeing that the tramps were now properly housed, Albert Slocum returned to his home.

~~~~~~~~~~~~~~~~~~~~~

It was slightly after dark when a lone man arrived outside the home of Jack Fay. With a small bundle in his hand, he slowly approached the front door and knocked. He did not have to wait long before the door was opened to him, and just as quickly shut behind him. The visitor remained inside the Fay home for two hours before returning to parts unknown.

~~~~~~~~~~~~~~~~~~~~~

That evening, Deputy Wilbert Vance and his two Councilman helpers were quite busy. Earlier, Vance was forced to shoot and kill a mad dog that had been a great annoyance to local occupants. Women and small children have been in great fear for some time as the dog would frighten them, only to then run away before assistance arrived. As the officers passed through the neighborhood, the dog sprang over a fence and caught

Deputy Vance in the leg. Fortunately, the officer's pant's thickness prevented any injury. Kicking it loose, Vance pulled his revolver and shot the dog through the head.

Later, at about ten p.m., their attention was called to a drunken Indian performing "a scalping dance" on Main Street, threatening to scalp several bystanders. Surrounding the intoxicated Indian, the officers subdued and jailed him to await 'Squire Williamson's court tomorrow morning.

Acting Deputy Marshal Councilman Mike Davidson was the hero of the night as he captured a burglar red-handed coming out of a broken screen door at the Pan Handle Depot Office. The man had forced open the railroad's money drawer and stuffed seventy dollars in cash into his pocket. A scuffle ensued in which Davidson overpowered the bandit, and turned him over to Deputy Vance. The man was not recognized and was thought to be one of the local tramps arriving in town daily. He refused to provide his name and was to be turned over to railroad authorities in the morning once 'Squire Williamson signed the paperwork.

~~~~~~~~~~~~~~~~~~~~~

Adam Lake was feeling the need to start another fire, and an idea struck him that should get everyone's attention. He will set fire to a local farmers' cornfield. With the corn stalks a lovely golden brown, all it would take was a few gallons of coal oil and a windy night. As it so happened, tonight was such a night. Let the fun begin.

Farmer Floyd Benson owned a small farm south of Gas City consisting of soy beans and field corn. He already had the soy beans harvested and was waiting a few more days for the corn to dry out to his liking. This would supply his animals with food, and then he could sell the rest as a cash crop. This was a much needed income for Benson and his wife, who had no children and lived on the edge of poverty. "Honey," he told his wife, "Maybe we'll make enough money so as I can put in dat kitchen pump ya been a wanton' all these years." Unfortunately, all of their hopes and dreams for the following year went up in flames late that night as the darkened sky glowed red from the massive fire completely wiping out their corn crop. From a safe distance, Adam Lake enjoyed every moment of it.

~~~~~~~~~~~~~~~~~~~~~

Zeke Miller reported for duty on day shift and seemed rearing to go. He marched the Indian over to the 'squires court without any hesitation. If he was still in pain, he kept it to himself. Returning to the office, Zeke poured the last of the coffee into a cup and sat down for a break. "How's it feel to be back to work?" Justin asked him.

"Feels just fine. Got pretty darn tired a just sittin' around and doin' nothing while you and Wilbert was short handed and all."

"Zeke, you got any ideas about this 13th Disciple business? It seems you know about everyone in town. We got any strange ones I need to look at?"

Taking a gulp from his cup, he replied, "I knows most of da Gas City and Jonesboro folks but not many of dem new factory folks. Deys comin' and a goin' every darn day." Justin informed him of what the Reverend Stokes said about religious zealots, but together they could not produce any possible leads.

"Think it's da same feller startin' all dem fires? Zeke asked.

Justin couldn't see any connection, "Since there are no warning letters beforehand, I suspect we got two different suspects to consider. The arsonist hasn't hurt anyone... yet, but if we don't stop him then he's bound to sooner or later. We either need more men or a lot more luck to catch him in the act."

Zeke asked if any of the councilmen were show-ing promise. "Funny you should ask, as Mike Davidson has really taken to the job, according to Wilbert. He's the one that captured the burglar we told you about. The elections are just a few weeks away, and if he isn't elected Mayor, I may just have a talk with him as he has vacated his old council seat in order to run. I couldn't care less which political party he belongs to as long as politics are not discussed on the job. We work for who-ever is Mayor."

Zeke chuckled, "Your name is on da ballot I was told." Nodding yes, Justin explained that being an incor-porated city now, his position was also an elected one.

"Why didn't you run against me, Zeke?" Justin said with a wide grin on his face. "Marshal Miller has a nice ring to it!"

Giving Justin his well practiced look of shock, Zeke started laughing, "Ain't gonna happen, no sir-ee, ain't never gonna happen!"

Picking up the Journal newspaper, Justin told Zeke that he wanted to read him a very strange story from Brazil, Indiana. *"The 16 year old wife of Andrew Stapleton, age 65, is lying at her home in a critical*

143

condition, having been in hysterics for the past two days. She asserts that her husband is a witch, and that since she separated from him a few days ago, she has been constantly under his influence. Her attending physician says that unless her condition changes soon, she will die. The affair is creating much excitement."

Zeke scoffed at the story. "Must be one of dem early Halloween storics. What dern fool his age wants a 16-year old wife anyhow?"

Justin felt like teasing the old man a little, so he said, "I don't know, a young wife might just be the thing a man your age needs."

"Bound ta be bad fer da heart," Zeke said, "But I'm a guessin' that's da chance ya take. If she dies... she dies!"

Chapter 9
More Trouble Planned

The MacMhaighstir brothers were immigrants from Scotland who had arrived in Gas City a year ago. Since their last name was of a Scottish pronunciation and spelling, it was changed to be pronounced as MacMaster to comply with its American spelling. Their first names were a bit of a tongue twister also; Ailean (Alan) and Osgar (Oscar). Each brother saw the profit in Americanizing as quickly as possible, so it was one of the first things that they did upon settling in the country.

Each brother, although not twins, looked so much alike that a decision was made by Oscar to shorten his own beard to help them be distinguished from one another. The older brother, Alan, retained his full beard and mustache. Back in the old country, both men had worked as bartenders and they eventually had bought a small tavern that they jointly owned and operated together.

When they arrived in Gas City, both found employment in separate saloons, but desired to once again purchase and operate their own drinking establishment when the opportunity arose. Their time spent separately as bartenders here allowed them the opportunity to see the differences in American saloons from the type of drinking establishment that they had operated previously.

The concept of a "free lunch counter" was new, but interesting. With the purchase of a beer or a shot of whiskey, any man was then entitled to help himself to the salted meats, breads, pickles, and other items which were occasionally changed out. The salted meats made men thirsty so they then purchased more to drink to satisfy that thirst. The brew that the Americans called beer took a bit of getting used to, but if that's what the men wanted to drink, well, that's what they would serve them.

The brothers' opportunity to finally purchase their own saloon came with the death of its previous owner. The last two owners of the White Dog Saloon had met their untimely demise, so Oscar insisted that for the sake of luck, the name must be changed. Looking at his older brother's face, he suggested that they call the saloon Red Beards. Thus the MacMaster Saloon became known as "Red Beards Saloon."

Each brother took a twelve hour shift by himself while the other enjoyed his day off. This schedule worked well as the saloon opened at eleven a.m. and closed at eleven p.m. Gas City ordinances required all saloons to close at that time, but a few continued to take a chance and remain open later. Any owner took a huge risk in doing so, as the hefty fine imposed by 'Squire Williamson was simply not worth it in the long run. The brothers also respected the Sunday closing laws. Let others take their chances, but the brothers wanted to remain free of any trouble with the local authorities and to become good Americans.

One of the early problems noticed by both brothers was the factory workers who lined up to drink away their wages. Each brother knew that the families suffered and marriages were damaged by the need to drink, but the brothers reasoned that if they didn't provide their saloon's drinking services to their customers, others would. Besides, the moral aspects of the business should be left to the clergy to sort out. Since Red Beards had opened, business had been good and so each brother felt that they should obtain their own slice of the American dream. The brothers had rented a small four room house over by the railroad tracks which made traveling back and forth to their nearby saloon very easy. The only time both brothers were at home together was at night and all day on Sunday. So far, this had not been a problem. Though middle-aged, neither brother had any intention of marriage as loose women could be found anyway when the need arose.

Alan MacMaster arose early knowing that his new work day was beginning and besides, it was his turn to make breakfast and start the coffee going. Oscar was fast asleep snoring loud enough to almost shake the windows. Alan was secretly very proud of his younger brother and his dedication to the new family business. Both men dreamed of the day that they became successful enough to hire others to work the bar as they became established local businessmen, who could enjoy the social aspects of that privilege.

Soon the smell of frying bacon permeated the little house, bringing Oscar out of his slumbers. "Rise an' shine little brother," he joked. "Your snoring tis loud enough to wake the dead in Glamis Castle."

Swinging his legs out from under his blanket onto the floor, Oscar looked up with drooping eyes. "Have a hard night, did ya?" Alan asked.

"T'was like the olden days'. Old man Purvis came after a factory worker with a broken bottle, but others jumped him before he killed da poor man," Oscar mumbled as he rubbed the sleep out of his eyes. "That smells good."

Alan then told him to get up and get with it. "I ain't a servin' ya breakfast in bed, ya know." Such was the morning routine of the MacMaster brothers.

As Alan prepared to set the small table, he picked up a scrap of paper laying upon the nearby table. "What is this?" he asked.

"Twas stuck on the door as I entered last night," replied Oscar. "T'was too dark ta see what it says and all. Is dat coffee ready now? I'm a hopin' it's better den the last patch you made. I think ya soak your bloomin' socks in it fer flavorin'."

Alan read the paper aloud: *Romans 13:4 "For he is the minister of God to thee for good. But if thou do that which is evil, be afraid; for he beareth not the sword in vain: for he is the minister of God, a revenger to execute wrath upon him that doeth evil."*

"What does this gibberish mean? Is someone ah sayin' we are evil? Must be mad or somethin', I be ah thinkin'."

With no answer from his still sleepy brother, Alan folded it up and put the paper into his pocket. *Maybe somebody at the bar will be ah understand its meaning and all, tonight*, he thought.

~~~~~~~~~~~~~~~~~~~~~~

The Gypsy encampment was gone. Apparently the King and Queen of the Gypsies had failed to show up as scheduled. Justin knew deep inside he would never see Beval again and it was now time for him to forget her. Some things were just not meant to be. Justin's thought returned to the lovely Virginia Cole. *Maybe I should invite her to attend the Lillian Godfrey comedy show appearing tonight at the opera house?* Feeling that it was the right thing to do, Justin walked over to the First National Bank and stood before Virginia's desk.

"Morning pretty lady," he said with a genuine smile. "I was wondering if you might like to accompany me over to Lovett's opera house tonight to watch a comedy show? It's been recently remodeled with new wall paper and stage equipment. They also installed a new, better sounding piano, I was told. I sure would have hated to be one the men carrying it up three flights of stairs!"

Virginia had a surprised or puzzled look upon her face as she replied, "Well, I'm afraid you're too late. Alvin Jensen, the reporter, has already asked me. Where have you been anyway these past few days?"

Justin was disappointed, especially now being aware that Jensen was attempting to move in on Virginia.

"Works been very hectic, but I'll do my best to make more time in the future. I suggest you get there early, since Marion's opera house burned down, there might be a lot of out of town visitors. Enjoy your evening, Virginia," he told her as he waved and left. Some days it doesn't pay to get out of bed.

Leaving her office, Justin thought that it may be time once again to visit the barbershop of Councilman Matthew Brooks. Entering, Justin saw one man in the chair and three waiting, so he picked up an old newspaper and sat back to wait his turn.

Barber Brooks began speaking to the customer sitting in his chair, "I had a very strange visitor this week. A young woman came into my shop asking about a barber who's been working on and off again in Jonesboro who she has been trying to track down. I didn't have any customers at the time, so the poor girl sat down and between tears, told me her sad life story. I guess she simply needed to talk to someone and I got picked. It seems the lady's parents died while she was quite young and she was taken to the Woman's Reformatory in Indianapolis. There she stayed until turning eighteen. It was then that she met this barber from Jonesboro, who made promises to set her up and find employment if she would only come with him back to Jonesboro."

As he continued to trim his customer's hair, Brooks continued telling the story. "Well, sir, it seems he did find her a place to live but no job came of it, and he soon deserted her, leaving her near penniless. Then with the help of local citizens, she tracked him down as he was working as a barber in Muncie. Unfortunately, before she arrived, word had reached him and he fled to Alexandria. The sequence continued as she was continuously a short distance behind him. Now the word is that he's now back in our area."

The customer he was working on asked, "Why is she so determined to track this man down? He clearly is undependable."

Brooks replied, "Because she is about to become a mother, and the barber is the father."

The customer then jokingly replied, "Guess that proves you just can't trust a barber around women or female dogs!" All eyes settled upon Books to see what his reaction to the insult against his profession would be, but they saw nothing.

Silence followed until he replied, "I have always wondered what it would be like to accidentally let my razor slip and slice off a customer's ear," Brooks said non-chalantly.

The man in the chair instantly froze, "I was just a foolin' Matt, honest I was!"

Things got pretty quiet for the next few customers as the thought of a sharp razor blade made everyone else act like total gentlemen. As Justin took the barber's chair, Brooks asked him, "How long do you figure on using all of us councilmen, Marshal?"

Justin was planning on discussing the topic with him anyway. "If I can, up until the election. I have heard through the grapevine that one of you might be interested in making the job permanent."

Brooks replied, "That would be Michael Davidson. He talks about how exciting being a deputy marshal is all the time. Speaking only for myself, I think he would do you a good job, if you were interested in my opinion." Justin said he was giving it some thought but wanted to see how the election for Mayor came out first.

Changing the subject, Brooks asked Justin what he thought of the new peddler law enacted recently by the state legislature. It allowed all honorably discharged ex-Union soldiers to be able to vend, hawk and peddle goods, wares, fruits, and merchandise by issuing them a free license. No fees could then be charged by any Indiana city official.

Justin said that he had heard about the new law but hadn't given it much thought. Brooks, on the other hand, was against it. "As a councilman I must view it as lost revenue for our city." Justin replied that he wondered if the southern states were doing the same service for their veterans. Brooks said that he didn't know, but it was an interesting question. With his haircut completed, Justin returned to his office.

~~~~~~~~~~~~~~~~~~~~~

Rachael Marley was busy helping customers, when the owner's sister, Jane Draper arrived. "How's business, Rachael?" she asked.

"Busy. Everyone is doing their last minute shopping before our contest ends tomorrow. By the way, how is your sister doing now?"

"Constance is doing much better. We moved her downstairs so she doesn't have to fight those stairs with her crutch. Every day she seems to become stronger and more determined than ever to get well. I'm guessing it won't be too long until we see her back here in the store."

Rachael was happy to hear the news but felt like she needed to ask something that had been on her mind. "Then I'm guessing you won't need me anymore?"

Jane looked at her a little puzzled. "No, not at all. She wants to return so both of you can make the emporium more successful than ever. We're both very pleased with your work performance and how sweet you are to our returning customers." By now, another customer needed help so Jane Draper excused herself to begin inventorying for more supplies.

~~~~~~~~~~~~~~~~~~~~~

Across town at the Jack Fay residence, the lone figure from last evening had returned and gained entry into the house. There he would remain until early evening before departing. Mrs. Fay's current residence remained unknown to her husband.

~~~~~~~~~~~~~~~~~~~~~

Arsonist Adam Lake felt the strong desire to burn another barn tonight. Now all he had to do was locate his prey and wait for total darkness to set in.

~~~~~~~~~~~~~~~~~~~~~

The man known only to law enforcement as *The 13th Disciple* and his four angels made their plans for tonight also. This was to be a Friday night that many in town would not soon forget.

~~~~~~~~~~~~~~~~~~~~

Wilbert and two of the councilmen deputies had a gut feeling that something was going to happen that night. One could sense something in the air that was not right. A strange stillness that no one could explain, but each man felt as ready as possible to handle whatever might occurs. Tonight's plan would be different as each deputy would be posted separately in different locations throughout the city. Unless the saloons became a major issue, each deputy will patrol alone in order to cover more ground.

It was shortly after eleven p.m. when a small barn located on Fourth and South A Street went up in flames. A neighbor who was coming out of his outhouse at the time saw the fire and alerted the town. Fortunately, the fire barn was not all that far away and the responding firemen were quickly on the scene. As they arrived, the firemen realized the barn was beyond saving so they concentrated their efforts on saving the nearby house.

A quick search was made of the home after repeated pounding upon the door failed to bring forth its occupants. It was later learned that the family was out of town in Alexandria visiting with their married daughter and her family.

Naturally all of the deputies responded to the fire scene with Councilman Michael Davidson arriving first. He immediately began questioning witnesses who gathered to watch the fire. The neighbor who first reported the fire informed Davidson that he had seen a man in the darkness running away from the scene and thought that he had thrown something down as he ran. Both he and Davidson searched the area and quickly located a nearly empty coal oil container just as Wilbert and the other councilman arrived. After turning over the suspicious coal oil can, Wilbert took a written statement from the witness. Finally, someone had at least seen the man.

"Do you think you can identify him if you saw him again?" Wilbert asked.

"Sorry deputy, it was just too dark and my attention was naturally on the fire. I couldn't even give you a guess as to his age."

Standing to the rear of the large assembled crowd was Adam Lake, before he causally walked away. *Oh, how fun this is* he thought.

With all eyes watching the nearby barn fire, a freight wagon rolled slowly past unnoticed as it made its way down the bricked street. Its lone driver seemed in no hurry as it traveled westward towards its target. The driver was thrilled about the fire as everyone's attention was being drawn that way. Laying flat in the wagon and hidden away were his four angels. The sound of the hooves of their two horses were not heard by anyone as *The 13th Disciple* continued on toward Red Beards Saloon and their ordained target.

The freight wagon came to a stop in a darkened alley, within easy reach of their destination. All of its occupants were waiting for the proper time to act. Once word of the barn fire reached this section of town, the remaining customers of the Red Beard Saloon, knowing that it was near quitting time already, decided to leave to investigate what was burning. Inside, Alan MacMaster was emptying out the cash drawer that was never left on premises for fear of robbery. He then emptied all of the ash trays into his trash barrel and carried it outside to avoid taking the chance that a smoldering cigar might extinguished their source of livelihood. The trash barrel was always quite heavy with a day and night's accumulation of empty bottles. Tomorrow morning, their hired swamper would clean and mop the place up before opening. It had been another very profitable Friday night and tomorrow's take was expected to be the same or even larger.

As Alan sat the barrel down outback and was preparing to return inside, a sharp razor blade was pressed to his throat. "Whoa there friend," said the quite startled co-owner. "If it's da money ya want, I have's it inside."

Instead of being lead inside to retrieve the cash, Alan was surprised that he was being pushed up against the rear of the building. A rag of some sorts was thrust into his mouth and his hands tied behind his back. With his hands bound tightly, he was spun around to the front, and forcibly marched away, towards the darkened alley. The frightened man could see several men in the darkness. In front of him appeared a freight wagon and Alan was pushed up and over its sides. The four men then climbed aboard and held the frightened man down and out of sight.

Alan could hear the driver as he climbed aboard and started the team moving. Slowly the freight wagon returned to Main Street traveling west and Alan realized that they were crossing the bridge over the Mississinewa River. Other than the normal sounds of nighttime, nothing else stirred. After crossing the bridge, the freight wagon pulled off to the side and Alan felt himself being pulled to the ground near the tree lined edge by the riverbank. He was stood up with his front facing the river, with his arms held tightly by the masked men.

Finally, a voice sounded behind him, "Sinner, you were warned that by doing evil, thou shall be punished by the sword of God. We are your executioners this very night." Suddenly from behind, a sword was thrust downward entering between Alan's shoulder blades and exiting through his stomach. The sword was left in place as his body twitched in the final moments of death before dropping to the ground. Without any hurry, each man re-boarded the freight wagon as it slowly made its way back onto the road and disappeared into the dark night.

Chapter 10
The Aftermath of Terror

Oscar MacMaster awoke early from having a very restful good night's sleep. He was surprised his brother's snoring hadn't awakened him as it usually did. Rolling over, he saw that Alan's bunk had not been slept in. *No wonder*, he thought, *Alan must have gotten lucky last night*. A smile crossed his hungry face. Good for him. Realizing that he must now make his own breakfast, Oscar swung himself out of bed.

~~~~~~~~~~~~~~~~~~~~~~~~~~~~

The old swamper arrived about ten-thirty a.m. for work. He was surprised to find the front door of the Red Beard Saloon unlocked, so he figured one of the owner's must have arrived earlier than normal that morning. Now he'd have to do a better clean up job than he normally does. Entering, he noticed a money bag laying up on the bar top. *It couldn't be*, he thought. With guarded caution, the sweeper reached for the bag and was surprised that it was, in fact, full of money. Looking around he could not find anybody and noticed the back door was also unlocked. Glancing out back, he found nothing out of the ordinary and returned inside. Reaching out, he picked up the bag of money again and bolted through the front door. His days as a bar swamper were over. He was now a thief.

~~~~~~~~~~~~~~~~~~~~

At the same time, Oscar MacMaster was dressing to leave for the saloon. Normally, the off duty brother deposited the night's take at the bank while the other reported to work. Since Alan had still not returned home, Oscar figured that he must have locked up last night's money in their rear safe, so he'd be in later to retrieve it. The brothers always leaft a small amount of coinage separate anyway for the cash register. They'd found that their saloon remained near empty of customers until around lunchtime, when the hungry factory workers arrived for the free lunch counter spread and purchased their drinks. Glancing up at his small mantle clock,

Oscar finished tying up the laces on his boots and began mentally preparing for another twelve hour shift.

A pair of fishermen arrived at the river bank, hoping to catch a few catfish for their lunch today. Instead they discovered a horror that neither man would ever forget.

Marshal Justin Blake and Zeke Miller were completing their uptown patrol when an excited man rode up and said there was the body of a man down by the bridge. Arriving in their patrol wagon, Zeke quickly appointed a couple of bystanders present to keep the crowd back as they awaited the arrival of Doctor Baxter. Clearly, the man was dead but a thorough medical inspection of the body must be made before it could be removed to the undertakers. "A common military type of sword like da officers used in da war," Zeke told Justin. "Why would anyone murder a man dis way? It don't make no sense ta me."

Justin instantly recognized the dead man as Alan MacMaster. "Anybody send word for his brother?"

"I just sent a kid to fetch him," one of the bystanders mentioned.

"What about Doc? Anybody send for him yet?"

One of the men in the group then announced he saw Baxter's buggy approaching. Within moments, a highly disturbed and out of breath Oscar MacMaster arrived. "Alan! Oh my God, Alan. What have they done to you?!" as he broke down in deep sobs.

Doctor Baxter then arrived and began his examination of the body. He has seen just about everything during his long medical career, but never a man executed with a sword this way. At least not since his military days during the war. Wishing to use all of the tact and respect he could muster, after allowing for a few moments to pass, Justin approached the near hysterical brother. "I'm sorry to bother you at a time like this, but we need answers. Who could have done this to your brother? Did he have any enemies or were any threats made by customers in your saloon? Anything you can tell me will be of great importance in my investigation."

As tears continued to roll down his cheeks, Oscar fixed his stare upon the sword. "There was ah letter stuck ta our door, ah sayin' somethin' about ah sword as evil punishment or somethin' like that. I don't remember now."

Justin's ears picked up on hearing that. "A letter? Do you still have it?"

"I don't have it but Alan does. Ask him... I mean... he said he was gonna show it around the saloon last evening. Please catch da man who done this terrible thing ta my brother, den turn him over to me. I'll take care of everythin'." Oscar's friends then led the poor man away from the crowd down by the river's edge.

"It took a lot of strength to ram a sword through this man's back like this, Marshal. I think you can rule out a woman as the killer," Doc told him as he motioned for the body to be taken to his office for further examination.

"Mind if I look through his pockets first, Doc?" A quick nod of approval followed.

Justin searched every pocket and finally found what he was looking for. Though bloody, the writing could easily be read: *"For he is the minister of God to thee for good. But if thou do that which is evil, be afraid; for he beareth not the sword in vain: for he is the minister of God, a revenger to execute wrath upon him that doeth evil."*

From behind, Marshal Blake heard someone say, "I got a pair of good huntin' dogs that might track down whoever did this, Marshal."

Zeke pointed to the wagon wheels in the grass as he replied, "You can see where da wagon brought 'um here and den returned to da main road, otherwise your idea might work out. Thanks anyway."

At that point, a boy ran up to Marshal Blake. "Sir, the bartender at Whiskey Bob's Saloon wanted me ta fetch ya. He says there's a swamper from Red Beards

Saloon inside buying the house drinks with a money bag full of cash."

Approaching the grieving Oscar MacMasters, Justin suggested that he come with him to identify his swamper. "Could you identify your saloon's money bag from others?"

"Yes Marshal," he said, "Our money bag has da initials RD marked upon da bag in blue ink."

Together both officers and the brother walked over to the nearby Whiskey Bob's Saloon as a few men followed out of curiosity. Entering the saloon, MacMaster saw his hired swamper pulling men inside up to the bar with the promise of free drinks. Few working men would turn down this great of an opportunity, even if it was a little early in the morning. "You!" MacMasters shouted to his swamper. "Where did you get dis money?" The swamper attempted to grab the money bag off the counter and beat a hasty retreat out the back door, but Zeke reached out and caught him firmly by the collar. Grabbing the money bag out of the swamper's hands, MacMaster could easily see the initials RB in blue ink. "It's our money bag Marshal," he shouted. "You killed my poor brother ta get it, didn't you! Dirty scum, now I kill you!"

The swamper was terrified at the situation he found himself in. "I didn't kill anybody. I found this bag of money on the bar when I came in to clean up earlier. Honest! The doors were standing wide open but nobody was there."

Justin cuffed the terrified man's hands behind his back. "Look at his small size MacMaster and tell me how this little man overpowered your big brother, drove him in a wagon against his will, and then managed to force a sword completely through his body. Is he a thief? Yes. Is he a killer? No. I suggest you and I go back to your saloon and inventory everything to see what's missing. If the saloon was open all night, your swamper may have worked along with other thieves and cleaned you out. Again, I'm very sorry for your loss. We'll do everything within our abilities to solve this murder."

Zeke gave the cuffed man a little push, "Come along swamper, you've got da appointment with 'Squire Williamson later today," as he marched his prisoner away to the awaiting cell.

As Justin and MacMaster entered the Red Beard Saloon, both were surprised not to see missing bottles from the bar area. "Let's check da supply room," MacMaster suggested. Everything appeared to be there and Justin saw no signs of further burglary.

"Maybe the swamper was a tellin' da truth marshal and he just found da door open. If anybody knew da place was wide open, every bottle would have been stolen. I guess we was lucky on dat point."

Justin found he had to agree, so the swamper would only be charged with theft of the money bag and not with murdering Alan MacMaster.

~~~~~~~~~~~~~~~~~~~~~~

Justin was no closer to solving the murders than when he first started. Also, the barn burner seemed free to burn any structure when the need suited him. He could only imagine what the newspapers would say about the inefficiency of the Marshal's office in ridding the city of the public menaces.

~~~~~~~~~~~~~~~~~~~~~~

The lone figure again returned to the home of Jack Fay and stayed until noon before departing.

~~~~~~~~~~~~~~~~~~~~~~

Saturday morning brought a huge turnout at the emporium. Today was the day that people began lining up so then they could test out their key out on the strong-box containing twenty silver dollars. Rachael opened the doors exactly at eight a.m. as people already had begun to line up. One by one, each customer inserted their key, and one by one each customer left disappointed. By ten a.m., the line was even larger. Still, disappointed customers took their loss in stride, and many bought needed items in the store while they were there. The contest was proving to be quite popular and the store owner was already considering increasing the pot to forty dollars for next year's contest.

~~~~~~~~~~~~~~~~~~~

Since losing out to Alvin Jensen for the comedy show, Justin made it a point to see Virginia as often as time allowed, which was normally at lunch, and occasionally after hours. Today they had made plans to have lunch together at a popular dinner. Arriving early, Justin got a table and waited for Virginia's arrival. Minutes passed by and Justin began to think that she wasn't coming, when a very distraught Virginia Cole entered. She was in tears as she handed him the telegram that she has just received at the bank. *Father attacked by criminal... stop... Not expected to live... stop... Come home. Mother*

"Oh Virginia, I'm so sorry to hear this. How soon are you leaving?" he asked.

"I'm on my way to the depot now. I left my suitcase out front. Will you walk with me?"

"After the telegram arrived, Mr. Howell heard me sobbing at my desk and came to see what was wrong. I showed it to him and he immediately told me to go and take all the time I required, and that he would process any loans for me. That man is an absolute angel."

Justin placed one arm around Virginia's waist as he carried her suitcase, walking the short distance to the depot. Checking the outgoing train schedule, she purchased her ticket to Auburn and together the couple waited on the bench. Justin held her hand as she spoke lovingly of her father and the dangers of police work. Soon the Northbound train arrived and Justin handed the suitcase to the porter along with a tip. "I wish I could be there with you Virginia," he said as she stepped upon the platform. Virginia then reached down and kissed Justin fully on the lips. Nothing needed to be said as she gently waved goodbye to him as the train departed the station.

By early afternoon a long line of customers with key in hand extended outside. Many customers were shopping, and both Jane Draper and Rachel Marley were extremely busy trying to wait on them. There had been no lunch break as it simply wasn't possible to do so. Outside standing in line was the man who they jokingly called Bob something or other. He was telling everyone in line that they were wasting their time and that the gypsy assured him he in fact has the winning key. People smiled at his story, but he was in getting to be an annoying loudmouth. Still, he or anyone of them might have it, as the money was still inside the strongbox waiting for its new owner.

Soon it was Bob something or other's turn, and with a wide grin, and knowing that all eyes were trained on him, he inserted his key and turned the lock. A look of shock appeared upon those present as the lock easily opened. Bob removed the lock, raised the lid and grabbed up a handful of silver dollars for all to see. Everyone present, though naturally disappointed, erupted in a mighty cheer. Bob something or other had won after all. The gypsy's forecast had come true. Bob announced he was going to visit his sister in southern Indiana with the money and quickly departed. The contest at the emporium had proven to be a roaring success. With the crowd of people now dwindling, the ladies took turns going for a late lunch and a little well-earned rest.

~~~~~~~~~~~~~~~~~~~~~~~~~

The clothing drive that Albert Slocum started at his church for the tramps was beginning to pay off. A large pile of clothing was brought into his church by local families, so Slocum directed his superintendent to have it collected and distributed to the tramps in greatest need. Slocum felt pure joy knowing that those in need would be cared for as the nighttime temperatures were definitely dropping. Anderson directed the leaders of the tramps to then distribute the clothing to their own men as they saw fit.

Shortly after lunch, three of their own factory workers came to Anderson's office and quietly knocked upon his door. Deeply involved in a large stack of paperwork, he looked up and told them to come in.

"Mr. Anderson," one of the men stated, "We are sorry to bother you, but the men have appointed us as spokesmen to discuss a developing problem with you."

"Come forward gentlemen," he directed, "What's on your mind?"

"Mr. Anderson, I will come directly to the point. It's these bums. The men are quite upset with Mr. Slocum's policy of housing, clothing, and feeding them while we as hard working men must work twelve hours a day to provide for our own families. Sir, it's just not right that they get to lay around and have everything given to

them. Now we are hearing that one of the glass factories are planning on laying off their own men and hiring
bums at a lower wage. It's a power keg, Mr. Anderson,
ready to go off anytime. All it's gonna take is one fist
fight and there's gonna be a huge riot among the factory
workers against the bums."

Anderson sat back in his chair and thought before
speaking. "Mr. Slocum prefers they be called tramps
and not bums. As for hiring, to my knowledge we have
not let anyone go or hired what's being referred to here
as scab labor."

The worker replied, "Yes sir, that's been the case...
so far, but our own workers are feeling the wrath of
the other factory workers because these bums... I mean
tramps, are housed, fed and taken care of on our own
company property. Should any situation develop, our
men will join with their working brothers against the
tramps. It will get very ugly sir."

"What are your suggestions?" Anderson asked.

"That's easy sir, get rid of these stinkin' lazy tramps
and the problem is solved."

Anderson stood up and walked over to the men, "The
owner of this strawboard factory, Mr. Slocum, is a prac-
ticing Christian. He practices helping others seven days
a week, not just on Sunday as many do. I also believe in

the Christian teachings and as long as Mr. Slocum wants to house, cloth, and feed these poor men, he will do so. Please convey my message to our workers. This is not anyone's responsibility but Mr. Slocum's. Thanks for coming to see me and good day gentlemen." With that, all three men looked at each other with sadness reflecting upon their faces as they left the office to return back to work.

~~~~~~~~~~~~~~~~~~~~~~

Robert Anderson waited for several minutes before walking over to Albert Slocum's office. He didn't want the men to think that he was panicked by what they had told him. "Mr. Slocum, do you have a minute?"

"Sure Bob, what's up?"

Robert Anderson explained the entire conversation to his supervisor. "Bob, I feel it's my Christian duty to help these poor men in every way I can. We haven't replaced any workers with cheaper labor yet, have we?"

"No sir, Anderson replied, "But the men are correct in that other local plants are beginning to consider doing so because I've had casual conversations with other plant supervisors. Should trouble start, I fear that everyone will take out their anger and frustrations out on our facility."

"Then let us pray that trouble won't happen," Slocum warned.

Sunday morning brought a solid attendance to the Gas City Baptist Church as the congregation welcomed all arriving attendees before services started. The Reverend Tyler began by asking its members to stand and sing an old favorite, *Rock of Ages*. As the congregation began the second verse, the rear door to the church slowly began to open. This was nothing new as members occasionally run a little late and all would be welcomed anyway. As the door opened, an unknown man dressed in his Sunday finest began to walk slowly down the aisle towards the front, passing many rear empty seats along the way. Some would say he was walking, but others would later recall that his pace was more as a short stepping stumble, not as a drunken man would do, but more like a man having great difficulty making his legs obey his commands to move forward.

By the time the man was half way down the aisle, he became the center of attention to most of the people present as they continued to sing, but continued to watch as the man moved forward. Reaching the end of the aisle and directly in front of the pulpit of Reverend Tyler, the man fell to his knees, bowed his head and began to cry. Tyler held up his hands for the congregation to stop singing as he slowly stepped down and placed his hand upon the shoulder of the crying man. "My friends, another sinner has come to Christ this day and I ask that you all rise and come forward to welcome our brother, Mr. Jack Fay."

It was Tyler who had met privately with Fay the past few days and evenings, and now a new member in the body of Christ would be added to the fold. Fay felt himself surrounded by well wishers and encouragement, and inside he couldn't help but feel himself to be a different person. Fay then noticed a woman's hand reaching into his and with heavy tears in his eyes, he recognized the joyful face of his wife. Who says that miracles don't happen?

Chapter 11
The Trouble Begins

The Red Beard Saloon remained closed all day Monday as the body of Alan MacMaster was laid to rest. The sword that had so viciously penetrated his body had been removed by Doctor Baxter, cleaned and given to Marshal Blake for examination. It was a common sword and contained no engraved name that might present a clue as to its owner.

As expected, the Gas City Journal newspaper's headlines screamed of the murder of Alan MacMaster, the horrible manner in which he was killed, and the letter of warning signed by The 13th Disciple forecasting his death. It also stipulated that it appeared that the Marshal's office was no closer to catching this fanatic that before. In that respect, Justin could not find fault with what reporter Alvin Jensen said. He was right.

Maybe I should ask the Grant County sheriff's office to take over the investigation? he thought.

The newspaper also warned of the reported labor troubles developing between factory workers and cheaper local labor. The tramps were mentioned, along with the church's donations of clothing organized by strawboard company owner, Albert Slocum. Clearly the town was now in two camps: those wishing to provide food, shelter, clothing and other assistance to those in need of it, and the working wage earners who saw them as a threat to their jobs and livelihood. There were also unconfirmed reports that the management of the strawboard company had been warned that the situation was a "powder keg waiting to go off."

Below all of the important news was a small paragraph telling the story of Bob and his winning of the twenty silver dollars at the emporium's contest. "Well Zeke, I guess a bit of non-threatening news might be good for the town. I expect this Bob something or other is well on his way to his family by now."

Zeke, who had just returned from feeding the fire horses, Roscoe and Prince Phillip said, "Your pretty concerned there's gonna be trouble, ain't ya Justin?"

"Yes I am and we cannot afford to be caught flat footed if there is. I think I would like you to wander through the factory areas today and see if you can learn if there's going to be any trouble tonight."

"Good idea, well I best be a goin'. If I hears anythin' I'll let ya know."

Walking over to the mayor's office, Justin told Mayor Huffman of his concerns that the powder keg mentioned in the paper would actually explode, and that he might require all of the councilmen deputies to drop what they were doing, and come to his assistance. The Mayor agreed and said that he would inform all of the other councilmen to be ready to respond on short notice.

~~~~~~~~~~~~~~~~~~~~~~

It was well after ten a.m. before Maggie O'Shea crawled out of bed. The nightlife was taking some time to get used to again. Sitting before her dresser mirror, Maggie began to comb out her long locks of hair as she contemplated her new life. Maggie had managed to sell her *favors* to four men last evening, so she was able eat today and put back some money for the rent. So far, there had not been any client willing to take her away from the lifestyle. Perhaps tonight she would find one that would.

~~~~~~~~~~~~~~~~~~~~~~

Even a stranger entering town for the first time could probably sense that there was something in the air, something that you couldn't put your finger on, but an uneasiness that indicated something was going to happen. The final piece dropped into place right after lunch when a large group of American Glass Company workers were informed that they were being replaced by cheaper labor and they were not to report to work after today. With this information, the men walked off the job and instead of going home, went directly into the local saloons. The more they talked about it, the angrier they became. All that was now required was a leader to step forward and offer the men a plan of action. By two p.m, that happened. "We're being replaced by those dirty tramps!" one man yelled as everyone within the bar agreed. "We need to contact all of the other factory workers as they get off work tonight, tell them of our plans, and together we'll march onto the strawboard property and crack a few tramps heads!" Everyone was in agreement, knowing that many of the factory workers would join them as they knew their own jobs were now at risk.

Runners were dispatched to all of the local saloons to brief the factory workers present on the plan of action.

"Bring whatever ya can lay your hands on, boys. We're gonna run these worthless tramps out of town forever!" Chosen men were instructed to approach the other factories and somehow to get word to those currently working to meet at seven p.m. for a mass meeting down by the river. Tell one man the game plan and it would spread like wildfire to the others. By tonight, they may well have gained over three hundred armed men, armed and ready for action.

It didn't take long for word to spread all over town that tonight was the night to finally end the problem once and for all. Shopkeepers closed early and those that could boarded up their windows. Mothers kept their children inside and the streets were becoming empty. By six p.m, Marshal Blake, Zeke, Wilbert, and the six councilmen deputies were positioned between the river and the strawboard company. A large crowd of workers were already assembled by the river's edge, and a steady supply of beer and whiskey flowed out of the local saloons to the assembled workers, which only fired up their anger even more.

The tramps were fully aware of the impending situation as many left town early in order to avoid any confrontation. Some had secretly obtained their own weapons such as pipes, pieces of building materials, and a few chains. They wouldn't instigate any trouble, but they also were not going to stand by and allow themselves to be massacred either. Albert Slocum was a nervous wreck, pacing all around and trying to speak inspiration to the leaders of the tramps. His humane plan of providing comfort to those less fortunate was backfiring, and he feared that many might die this very night. Why would God permit this to happen?

The leader of the mob was very happy with the huge turnout of factory workers that have assembled. Many openly carried clubs, chains, and other weapons, and were more than willing to knock a few heads this day. Standing upon a wooden bucket for height, the leader asked for everyone's attention. "Brother workers, your attention please. By now all of you have heard what has happened. Quality workers from the American Glass Company have been fired so management can bring in those scab labor tramps to replace them and put more money into their own greedy pockets!" Many in the crowd booed his words about the American Glass Company.

"Why then has the management of the strawboard company housed, clothed, and fed these vagabonds anyway? I'll tell you why. It is to ensure that the factories have scab labor at their disposal. Why should we work twelve hours a day, six days a week for our well deserved pay, when these tramps have everything handed to them for free as well as our jobs? Friends, are we going to stand for this outrage?" The crowd yelled NO!

"Our families needs must come first over the needs of tramps and corporate profits. Am I right, men?" YES! came the response. "If we don't act to put a stop to this now, hundreds more will come to feed off our jobs. The time for action is NOW! Are you with me, boys?" A huge cheer went up from the men as they began moving towards the property of the strawboard company with blood in their eyes and weapons in their hands.

Standing at the edge of his property between the tramps and the advancing workers was Albert Slocum and Robert Anderson. "Please hear me out men," pleaded the owner. "I have heard what your leader has said and I must tell you that he has made the wrong assumptions. There is no plot to raise an army of tramps to take your jobs. As the owner of the strawboard company, I felt that it was my Christian duty to help the needy as the teaching of my faith requires that of me. My company has not, I repeat, not hired any of the tramps to replace our own workers and I have no plans on doing so. While I cannot speak for the other owners, I can tell you I have heard nothing officially of plans to replace you with these poor men."

Over to the side, Zeke Miller was fast approaching with another man who turned out to be the owner of the American Glass Company. Many men within the crowd started booing upon recognition of him. "Men," he shouted. "Please hear me out!" Slowly the workers became quiet, mostly out of curiosity. "It was I who made the decision to hire what you call scab labor to replace some of our workers, but the men who are housed behind me, the ones you call tramps, were not involved. I had planned on hiring a group of men in Jonesboro, but now that plan is shelved. I will not replace our workers, and those who were told that they lost their jobs may return to work tomorrow as if nothing has happened." A huge cheer went up from the crowd and a general feeling of having won the day. "Go home in peace. No changes will occur at my plant with our present labor force. Violence is not necessary. Go home."

Laughter and happiness could be heard among the crowd as men dropped their clubs and such upon the ground and retreated. Many felt that a drink was in order to celebrate a victory for the average working man, so the saloons did a booming business that evening.

Justin walked over and shook Zeke's hand. "My friend, you just saved the day, great job!"

All the councilmen shook both men's hands and patted Zeke on the back for defusing the situation. No man would be injured or killed this night. The town took a deep sigh of relief. Tragedy and misery had been averted.

"Shucks,... twern't nothin,' Zeke replied with a grin upon his face.

Justin thanked each of the councilmen for their support today and then sent them home. "Saloons might be a little wild tonight boys, so be careful." he laughed as he and Zeke were finally off duty.

~~~~~~~~~~~~~~~~~~~

It was Wednesday afternoon before Virginia returned and found Justin inside his office. "I'm back," she said in a saddened voice. Pulling out a chair for herself, she sat down and began to talk. "Father never regained consciousness. He was at the sight of a break-in questioning two suspects, when one reached for a pipe laying on a shelf, and struck him on the side of his head. The other detective overpowered the assailant and he's now facing a hanging charge. I hope he enjoys the rope around his neck and strangles as he dangles."

Justin could understand her bitterness and said nothing, but reached out to take her hand. "I wish I could wipe away the pain for you, Virginia."

She squeezed his hand, then stood up. "I need to let Mr. Howell know I'm back. How about taking me to lunch tomorrow?" His smile said it all.

The following day, Justin met Virginia outside the bank at noon. "Let's eat at the local diner to give us more time," he suggested. After each ordered the special of the day, Virginia told him that she had something she wanted to discuss. "You were on my mind a lot while I was home. As my father's coworkers lowered father's casket into the ground, I thought about all the fear mother must have experienced daily as she watched him go to work not knowing if today might be his final day on Earth. I suddenly imagined it was you being laid to rest instead of father. Oh Justin, are you positive you want to be a Marshal? There are safer jobs you might enjoy as well."

Reaching out for her hands, he replied, "Yes maybe safer, but probably not as rewarding for me personally. Take the factory jobs for instance. How many times have we heard of someone getting a finger cut off or other serious injury, even being killed? The thought of working a long hot shift in a factory no longer appeals to me. I like being my own boss and I like the men I work with. Nothing in life is one hundred percent safe anyway."

"I know," she said, "But I find myself thinking about you a lot and I'm wondering if we will have any type of permanent future together. At this point I don't know what to say. What are your thoughts?"

Justin smiled at her words, "Let us just take it one day at a time and see where all this leads us. Don't allow yourself to live in fear of tomorrow. Sometimes you just have to put away your fears, trust God, and reach for the brass ring of life."

Looking deeply into his eyes she asked softly, "Are you my brass ring, Justin Blake?"

If they hadn't been in a public place, he would have swept her up in his arms but instead squeezed her hands saying, "Only time will tell for both of us."

The food arrived and the serious discussion of this topic ended. "Say, the Forth Regimental Band will be playing tonight at the bandstand in the park. If you don't have any plans, would you like to accompany me?" She agreed and they had a wonderful time. The evening finally ended with a passionate kiss that both clearly enjoyed.

The days began to pass by quickly as fall days always seen to, with orange leaves falling gracefully to the ground and temperatures hinting that winter's cold will soon be upon them. Tomorrow was Halloween, and the kids would be out soaping shop and home windows. A few of the older boys would be corning houses, either owned by cranky old men or young girls that they secretly admired. It was all in fun, at least to most people.

The day after Halloween, an old farmer came in to complain that the local boys had picked up his outhouse and set it back about five feet. The old farmer said that he went outside after dark to use the facilities before turning in, and following his normal pathway, and actually fell into the open hole. It was all that Justin could do to keep from bursting out laughing at the thought of the old man waist deep in you know what.

A story appeared in the Journal that had the town laughing. It seemed that a "ghostly encounter séance" had occurred at the home of a local family on East Second Street under the supervision of a committee of spiritualists from Indianapolis. A "cabinet" was formed by drawing a curtain across one corner of the room. The homeowners and their friends then inspected the spot, and assured everyone that no white material was available in or around it.

Then the ladies brought the medium into another room and dressed her all in black. The medium then entered the curtained cabinet area as the gaslights were turned down. Soon ghoulish sounds were heard as a figure dressed in a white robe appeared between the parted curtains. No one recognized the "spirit" and it soon departed and a small child spirit then appeared. The reporter who wrote the story said that he was told that the child spirit had a strange resemblance to the medium. The little one carried on a strange conversation until the homeowner became suspicious and grabbed the spirit girl, who was in fact the medium down upon her knees. Boo!

~~~~~~~~~~~~~~~~~~~~~~~~

Election day arrived as most of the townspeople were by now tired of hearing the same old speeches, and were ready to cast their vote. Mayor Huffman easily won re-election. A new councilman assumed the seat left by Michael Davidson's departure to run for Mayor. In a day or so, Justin planned on offering Davidson the vacant deputy position permanently, but that very evening Davidson inquired about it, so the job was offered and he quickly accepted. Davidson would now work the night shift under the training and supervision of Wilbert Vance. As Justin could no longer justify the use of the other councilmen, they were placed on a standby position; only to be called upon if something out of the ordinary occured. Justin thought that some of the men seemed a bit saddened by the news that it was over, but seemed pleased to have helped out.

~~~~~~~~~~~~~~~~~~~~~~

Adam Lake felt the strong desire to burn another structure tonight. Now all he has to do is locate his prey and wait for total darkness to set in. The corn fire had been massive but few were able to witness its destruction. *No*, he thought, *it might be best to remain in town so that fire bells will clang, confusion shall reign, and people will rise up out of their beds to witness his talents at work. How about a school teacher's home?*

Adam Lake had a great dislike for school teachers. His old teacher in Jonesboro had seen very little promise in him, suggesting that there was something wrong with his mind. Due to very poor grades he received, and a feeling of being picked on and singled out, Adam had quit in tenth grade. Unfortunately, the old male teacher died soon afterwards or Adam would have paid him back years ago. Still, there was an old school teacher living in Gas City, and he knew just where the old hag lived. She also lived in a modified carriage house. Not exactly what Adam was looking for, but tonight it would do. The carriage house, or coach house as some refer to them, was originally an outbuilding for horse drawn carriages. To make more housing available at the start of the city's gas boom, the owner who lived inside the house on the property converted it into a small home dwelling. Mrs. Engels, a retired eighty year old school teacher from another city, had settled in Gas City due to family ties here and with her families assistance, rented the affordable carriage house.

Just before early morning light, the owner of the property was awakened by the smell of smoke. He quickly checked his own home but found nothing, then looked out the back window and saw smoke pouring out of the carriage house. Knowing that the old woman was most likely sound asleep and needed assistance to escape the burning dwelling, he managed to kick in the front door, but with the new oxygen provided in doing so, the flames drove him back. By now he could hear the clanging of the steam apparatus as it and the volunteer firemen responded. By the time they were able to start pumping water, the house was totally engulfed in flames.

The fire chief watched as his men surrounded and drowned the wooden structure. That one could not be saved. Deputies Vance and Davidson were on hand standing next to the chief and ready to start questioning witnesses. "Chief, " the home owner replied, "I fear Mrs. Engels may very well be still inside. She's about eighty years old and pretty crippled up."

This was the worst part of being a fireman as every man hoped that his efforts would result in a successful rescue and not a retrieval. "Thanks for the information. We'll check the ruins once we have it cooled down," the chief told him.

The fire chief was casually looking around when he spotted a familiar face standing in the crowd of onlookers. "Deputies," the chief softly spoke. "Do not turn around or move, but I see the young man I told the Marshal about that seems to always be present at these fires. What should we do?"

Wilbert quickly developed a plan, "Chief, I want you to point somewhere towards the fire and act like you are telling me something. I will nod yes and start working my way towards that location and out of sight. Michael, you stay here with your back to the suspect. I'll circle around and come in from behind him. Chief, as soon as you see that I'm in place let Michael know and he'll start towards the suspect. If he turns to run I'll be there to stop him. Any questions?" There were none so the ruse began as planned as the chief pointed, Wilbert nodded and walked away leaving the two men simply talking to each other.

Standing in the crowd of people, Adam Lake was unconcerned. He enjoyed hearing the assembled men speculating as to the cause of the fire. One man even said that he bet the old woman who lived there didn't get out. The news really excited the young man and he had no idea that a deputy marshal was now standing twenty feet behind him. Movement quickly caught his eyes as the remaining deputy in front of him turned and was advancing toward the crowd of people. *Time to make a slow departure*, he thought as he turned to settle back into the darkened shadows. "Hold it, you're not going anywhere" a forceful voice instructed him. Now the other deputy arrived. Adam Lake was now completely surrounded.

Chapter 12
The End of the Line?

Adam Lake sat upon the small cot inside his jail cell contemplating his current situation. Other than his name, he had provided little else that the deputies could use against him. Still, he felt assured that no charges could actually be brought against him as nobody has came forth claiming they witnessed him pouring coal oil onto the structure. The fire chief came into the office to inform the deputies that his men had located the burnt remains of the old woman. "Arson was bad enough, Mr. Lake," Wilbert told him, "But now add murder to the list. You'll swing for this crime. Come on man, come clean, and maybe the judge will give you a life sentence instead of the rope."

"Like I told you a thousand times, I didn't start no fire," he told them.

Michael Davidson then continued, "Then why does the fire chief keep seeing your face at all of these fires?"

"I don't know, I just happen to be there to watch, I reckon," came his smug reply.

"Tell us why your pants had the smell of coal oil on them then?"

"I was filling my oil lamp today and must have spilled some on my pants leg," came his reply.

Wilbert could see they were getting nowhere, so they left him be and continued their patrols. *We'll leave this one for the Marshal to figure out*, he thought.

Justin was aware of the fire and after viewing the scene and the remains of the old woman, and speaking with the Chief, he desperately hoped that his officers had caught the fire bug. Seeing Justin approaching, both deputies wanted to brief him out of earshot of the prisoner. "I feel sure it's him Justin but we cannot prove it," replied Wilbert. "He even smells of coal oil but push come to shove, we have no witnesses that have seen him actually do it."

"I'll speak with 'Squire Williamson in the morning. We can hold him under suspicion for twenty-four hours anyway, but I fear I'll be told we must then release him. If he's our arsonist, I'm guessing he will lay low for awhile before the urge to start another fire overcomes him again. If so, we'll just need to keep our eyes on his whereabouts. Jonesboro police can help us with this one."

It turned out just as Justin surmised. Adam Lake was turned loose due to lack of evidence. Many arrested men would have considered it too close a call to ever contemplate returning to the path of arson again, but not Adam. His close call only emboldened him with the feeling that he was untouchable.

~~~~~~~~~~~~~~~~~~

With her former legal last name now officially restored, Constance Wainwright felt happy to be back at work in her emporium store. The crutch was now only used occasionally when she found herself on her feet for too long. Constance was very pleased that her sister had found the young sales clerk, Rachael Marley, and the two women were fast becoming friends. Sister Jane Draper occasionally liked to drop in to chat but rarely now stood behind the counter.

~~~~~~~~~~~~~~~~~~

Justin and Zeke were near the railroad depot on their daily rounds when they met up with Doctor Baxter. "Goin' some where's Doc,?" Zeke asked.

"Yep, gotta go to Marion. Got a bad toothache and then I need to go to their post office and buy a new pair of reading spectacles."

Zeke couldn't help but to tease his old friend by saying, "I always thought you was blind as a bat anyway, Doc."

Pretending to be hurt, he replied, "A pair of spectacles probably wouldn't hurt you none either Zeke... as well as a bar of soap."

"As long as I can see's my vittles on my plate, I'm happy. As fer your toothache, ya know I can pull it fer ya and save ya a dollar."

"You're not putting those filthy horse pliers in my mouth, so save your breath."

Zeke continued, "Justin, we had a Miami Chief around here by the name of Mesh-ing-go-mesia. He had a brother named Shap-pen-doc-cia who used ta crack walnuts in his teeth with no problems at all. Dem Injuns got good teeth and don't need no dentists. Course, dey got medicine men, not blind doctors ta treat their peoples."

"Next time somebody kicks in your ribs Zeke, go see a medicine man and not this blind doctor!" With a wave goodbye, Doc Baxter went to the depot window for his ticket.

~~~~~~~~~~~~~~~~~~~~~

Around seven p.m. that evening, a man entered George Townsend's Saloon and ordered a beer. Many were surprised as they recognized the lone man who took his beer and sat down by himself at an empty table. The man in question was Harry Roberts, the man who had caused the ruckus months ago and who had thrown a brick through the front window. "I'll serve ya Roberts, but I don't want no more trouble," George Townsend, the bartender, told him.

Roberts said nothing and seemed to only want to be left alone, so Townsend thought nothing more about it and continued serving his customers. Roberts had only returned to town that day having served two months in the Marion jail for his last escapade here in town. *I will have my revenge tonight*, Roberts thought. He consumed two more glasses of beer before bring his empty glass up to the bar and set it down, an odd thing for a customer to do. "I'll be back to deal with you next," he warned

Townsend as he buttoned up his coat and began walking out the front door. Kyle Holloway was at the end of the bar picking up empties and also heard the threat. "He's up ta somethin, Mr. Townsend. Want me's ta follow him?" Thinking that might be a good idea, Townsend nodded yes. Kyle didn't even bother putting on his coat, but trailed behind Roberts along the gas lit street.

Kyle followed behind Roberts wondering where he was going. He originally thought the man might be searching for another brick to smash the new front window, but clearly Roberts had other ideas. After reaching Third Street, Roberts turned south and was walking directly towards the horse barn. Movement caught Kyle's sharp eyes as Roberts reached in a coat pocket and pulled out a large pistol as he entered the fire barn. *Dat man is gonna shoot da deputies!* Kyle Holloway sprinted as fast as he could to try to make up the distance, hoping that he would not be too late.

Inside the marshal's office, Wilbert Vance and Michael Davidson were going over the days log book report when Roberts burst in waving a gun at them. "Remember me boys?" he shouted. "This time it's me holding da gun and I plan on shootin' both of ya, then Townsend and his pet N*****. What ya gonna do ta stop me now?" as he laughed at his own words.

Neither officer could move as clearly they were caught in this man's trap. It was only a question of time before each officer would be shot. Wilbert tried to reason with the man but knew it was pretty hopeless. "Yes please, beg for your lives, I love it," as he fixed his sights upon Wilbert.

The office door exploded with a furry as Kyle Holloway leaped upon the startled figure of Harry Roberts, as Wilbert wrestled the gun out of the crazed man's hands. Davidson stood in wide eyed fear watching the two men overpower the intruder. Kyle threw one solid punch upon the jaw of Roberts who then crumpled to the floor. "My God, man," Wilbert shouted, "Where did you come from and how did you know he was going to shoot us?"

Kyle then explained all that had transpired inside the saloon. "Mr. Holloway, how can we ever thank you enough for what you did tonight," as each man pumped his hand. Wilbert dragged the unconscious man over and into the jail cell having first searched him for any other weapons.

"Bravest thing I have ever seen," replied Michael Davidson.

"Ya can thank Mr. Townsend, sirs, he was da one dat let me follow dis man. I best be a gettin' back ta work now, if you'll excuse me."

"We'll walk with you Kyle as we also want to thank your boss before we start our rounds," Wilbert told him. After telling their story to a packed group of saloon men and its owner, Kyle Holloway became the new town hero and was instructed to put away his mop for the evening, as round after round was served to him by a grateful group of new friends.

Justin Blake was shocked to hear at how close both of his deputies had come to being murdered last evening, and requested that the county sheriff send men to place his prisoner back into their custody. There was simply no way that Roberts could receive a fair trial here, and besides, his longtime incarceration will occur somewhere else anyway. Justin sought out Wilbert for a private discussion. "How did Davidson handle everything last evening?"

Wilbert replied that he had thought him frozen in place but actually there was nothing either of them could have said or done as Roberts had the drop on them.

Justin then asked, "So how's his training coming along?"

"I had him study up on our local ordinances and pepper him with questions when time allows. As for weapon's training, the other evening we went down near the dam and I had him using my pistol for practice. A wild turkey ran out of the shrubs and Mike shot it in the head with one try. He then said that he was taking it home for Sunday's dinner. He owns a .45 already and would like to use it on the job."

"That's fine with me. I need him armed as quickly as possible after this incident. How did Rachael take the news?"

Wilbert replied, "I don't know, as I haven't spoken with her yet. I hope I can catch her before she hears of it by a customer or before it gets printed in the Journal."

Later that morning Grant County sheriff deputies Clark and Patterson arrived to pick up their prisoner. "We're glad to be rid of him," Justin told the men. "Say, let me show you some letters and try to get your take on them." He then handed the threatening letters signed by *The 13th Disciple.* "He's killed a couple of our townspeople," Justin warned.

After both sheriff deputies read the letters, Deputy Clark replied, "It's tough to catch a crazed killer like that with such a small police force. No disrespect intended Marshal, but you'll be lucky if you ever do. Have you tried posting any reward money? Somebody might know something and money has a way of loosening the tongue."

Justin replied that they had not but that it was a good idea and he would approach the city council and the local businessmen for donations. Justin also mentioned he has given serious thought to asking the sheriff's office for assistance on the case. Deputy Patterson said they could search their files to see if anyone like this had ever been identified before and they would let him know. Justin thanked each man and gave the cuffed Harry Roberts a friendly little wave. "See ya in about forty years," he told the sulking prisoner.

The Gas City Journal's headlines read: **Negro Saves Lives of Deputies**. Justin was furious when he read the headlines and immediately marched over to Alvin Jensen's office. "You responsible for printing this headline, Alvin?"

With a deep smile of satisfaction upon the reporters face, he replied, "Yes, why do you ask Marshal?"

"Alvin, why does it read "Negro Saves?" Why point out the man's race? What possible difference does that make anyway?

Alvin looked a bit confused. "Marshal, that's standard practice when it comes to Negros."

"Why? If Kyle Holloway had been a white man, would your headline read "White Man Saves Deputies? Of course not! Why must the man's race even be brought into the article at all? You make it sound like Negros normally cannot be expected to perform acts of bravery. Can't you see what I'm saying? You actually tarnish this good man by implying this unspoken slur about his race."

"Marshal, I'm sorry you see it that way. I was just following our standard policy when it comes to Negros."

Justin than replied as he walked away, "Maybe it's time you review your outdated policy, Alvin." As he left, he passed Alvin's uncle who was the editor of the Journal looked at his nephew, who then just shrugged his shoulders and returned to work.

~~~~~~~~~~~~~~~~~~~~

During her lunch hour, Virginia visited the emporium in order to speak with Rachael. They had been introduced to each other and spoken a few times briefly but never one on one. Looking up with her usual smile, "How can I help you, Virginia?"

"Rachael, I was wondering if you might like to get together tonight after work for a little 'girl talk'? I'm told the diner has delicious pumpkin pie."

Rachael readily agreed, "I would like that very much, let's say seven p.m. First one there can get us a table. I'm looking forward to it. See you then."

Virginia was the first to arrive and chose a small table in the corner of the room. Rachel walked in right after Virginia and sat down and took a seat beside her. Soon the girls were talking about all sorts of things like they have known each other for a long time. "Wilbert tells me you recently lost your father. I am so sorry to hear of it," Rachael said.

"Yes and this is getting into the subject I wanted to discuss with you. My father was a Police Detective in Auburn and was killed by a robbery suspect. I have discussed with Justin that I am deeply concerned about the dangers of his job. You read the paper and probably heard from Wilbert just how close he and the other deputy came to being killed. I was wondering how you were able to live with all the danger."

Rachael became quiet as she considered her answer. "Wilbert and I do not have any kind of understanding yet between us, but I feel there is a solid friendship and perhaps more that may or may not develop in time. His work hours begin when mine ends so it's very difficult for us to actually spend much time together. Virginia, I tend to be a bit independent for a young woman of today's world and I enjoy working and supporting myself. I don't feel I need a man to take care of me, but I do want to marry and have children one day. Just not today."

Virginia nodded, "Yes, I'm the same way. I too enjoy holding an important position and one I might add, that is mostly held by men. Justin seems married to his job, but I can tell he's interested in me. I have gone out a couple of times with other men who I felt were gentlemen. Justin knows it and I think he didn't care for it one bit," she laughed. "Anyway, I'm hoping this develops into something more serious, but it's the dangers of his job that keep holding me back from making a total commitment to him."

"I have also had offers from other men. Maybe I should accept one and see what happens?" Rachael replied.

Virginia had a playful look on her face as she said, "Perhaps a little jealousy might do both of our boys a little good. I'm glad we talked. Now let's enjoy the pumpkin pie."

Chapter 13
A Reward is Offered

While the city council was of little help in providing reward funding for the capture of The 13th Disciple, the local saloon owners and other businessmen were happy to offer their own personal resources in order to hopefully catch and punish the crazed killer. In the end there was enough money committed to include a reward for the arsonist's capture also. The Gas City Journal ran a small paragraph stating: *Reward of two hundred and fifty dollars for information on the killer known as The 13th Disciple. Also a reward of one hundred dollars is offered for information on the barn burning arsonist.* Justin hoped that someone who knows the identity of either man would come forward to claim these rewards so he can make the arrests.

The man known only to a select few as *The 13th Disciple* laughed at the reward offer, but then reminded himself of Judas and the 30 pieces of silver.

Adam Lake wadded up the newspaper in anger that his great work was only worth a hundred dollars to the authorities. *They will pay*, he thought. *Oh how they will pay*!

~~~~~~~~~~~~~~~~~~~~

That afternoon three highly intoxicated men approached Justin and Zeke out on the street. "Marshal," one of the men said while slurring his words. "We know who is behind all dem killin's and fires." Justin, though not convinced at their sincerity still had to ask. "Who?" Pointing at Zeke, they all said, "Him! He's the crime boss mastermind all over the county." Then each man held out their hands to collect their 'reward.' Justin gave them their reward by cuffing the men's wrists together. "Here crime boss," he joked to Zeke, "Take these civic-minded citizens over to the jail and let them sleep this off." Zeke was clearly not amused by their game and frog marched the group to their awaiting cell.

~~~~~~~~~~~~~~~~~~~~

The end of November was fast approaching as the few remaining leaves clung tightly to their branches in what seems a final desperate act of defiance on their part. The winter coat drive for the tramps had a marginal success and Albert Slocum was disappointed at the townspeople's response. Too many tramps lacked even the basics for winter as more and more arrived daily from parts unknown. In an attempt to provide some degree of comfort, Slocum has tasked Anderson with hiring a couple of cooks to provide hot soup and sandwiches for the one hundred-fifty plus now living inside his second warehouse.

Since the labor troubles have ended, there had not been any further threats of violence against the poor men. Slocum would have much preferred serving a turkey dinner for the men at Thanksgiving, but was finally convinced that the cooking resources required did not exist. Still, he had hired a local minister to provide Sunday services for the men. Perhaps by spring, most of the men would travel on to other locations and the terrible odor inside and outside the warehouse could finally be addressed. Many of the strawboard workers found the working conditions becoming almost unbearable to work in.

"Mr. Slocum," Robert Anderson asked, "A word, please. Sir, with your permission, I would like to instruct the tramps to dig four new privy holes. Our current out-buildings are overflowing. They were never intended to handle this amount of extra men. We have enough building materials on hand to construct the required new privies."

"Yes, please put their leaders in charge of all the work and remember, we are doing God's work here." Soon many of the idle men were busy at work. Returning to his office, Slocum began reviewing his always present paperwork when he noticed that something was miss-ing. His gold watch was no longer on his desk where he had left it. Slocum called out to his superintendent who instructed that all plant gates be locked and that nobody was allowed out, as a search of the entire plant was conducted. Workers were asked to empty their pockets which they grudgingly complied with, but the watch was not found. Most men blamed the theft on the tramps. One man was suspected and he was watched like a hawk, but was innocent of the crime.

At last, one of the guards remembered an employee by the name of Wertz who had left early claiming sick-ness. Robert Anderson obtained a search warrant from 'Squire Williamson and together with Zeke Miller, they made a search of Wertz's small room. Wertz's pockets were then checked and the missing gold watch was recovered and returned to Albert Slocum. Wertz would soon stand trial on the charge of theft of personal property. Wertz later admitted in court to passing by Slocum's open office while he was outside with Anderson and, upon seeing the watch, he had grabbed it and left the plant.

~~~~~~~~~~~~~~~~~~~~

Rachael and Virginia's plan on being seen on the arms of other gentlemen was beginning to pay off, as each was being escorted by gentlemen to the American Window Glass Company's sponsored ballroom dance tonight at the opera house. Besides having an enjoyable public evening, word would be passed to Justin and Wilbert that the ladies were not to be taken for granted.

~~~~~~~~~~~~~~~~~~~~

Maggie O'Shea was in total panic, having discovered early that morning that a warning note was laid by her doorway with a rock holding it in place. Though moisture had made some of the words blur, Maggie had no difficulty understanding a threat when she saw it. By now, everyone in town knew of *The 13th Disciple* and that he backed up his threats with murder. The note read:

Leviticus 24:15-16 "Say to the Israelite's: If anyone curses his God he will be held responsible; anyone who blasphemes the name of the Lord must be put to death." The entire assembly must stone him. Ezekiel 16: 35 *"Wherefore, O harlot, hear the word of the Lord."*

Of course, there was also the possibility someone was playing some kind of sick joke on her. Maybe a past client? In the end, Maggie felt that she had no choice but to consider the threat real, but what were her options? *I think tonight I need to make all the money I can make, then skip town after a few hours rest*, she thought. *Why take chances with my life anyway?* What she was doing with strange men in dark locations was dangerous enough, let alone in dealing with the written threat. Maybe she could catch a ride out of town in someone's wagon? At this point, any town seemed safer than this one. Maggie sat the note down on her dressing mirror table and began packing up only what she absolutely needed for tomorrow's move out of town, and hopefully, out of danger.

Deputy Zeke Miller heard his name being call, "Zeke, I need to speak with you." Looking across the street, Zeke recognized Sam Haynes, the owner of

Haynes livery stable, and a personal friend going way back to the early days in town.

"Zeke, I think I need your official involvement in a problem. A couple of glass workers rented out a horse and buggy last evening, got quite boozed up, then proceeded to run my horse half to death. They brought it in early this morning and the poor animal dropped in its stall completely exhausted. I want something done about their treatment of my horse. So far they refuse to compensate me. That poor animal will take days to return to health and I'll lose income."

Zeke was a great lover of horses and the story really upset him. "Where are de at now?" he asked.

"That's them standing outside of my livery. I told them that if they ran I would have them arrested as I know who they are."

Walking over to both men who were still unsteady on their feet, Zeke told them, "Boys, if it were up ta me, I'd horse whip da both of ya fer what you did ta dat poor animal. So ya's got a choice. Ya can pay fer da damages ya owe ta Mr. Haynes or I'll lock ya both up and then have 'Squire Williamson judge ya. Your call, what'll it be?" Reluctantly both men dug into their pockets and paid for the damage.

"Don't ever come back to my livery again," Haynes warned them as the men staggered away. With a quick nod, Haynes thanked Zeke and returned to his place of business to attend to the poor horse.

Shortly after noon, Wilbert was up and dressed as he was unable to sleep. Word had indeed reached him last evening that his Rachael was at the Lovett Opera House dancing with another man. Many thoughts were passing through Wilbert's mind, and none of them any good. *What if she's found someone she likes better than me?* Wilbert was not the type of man who gave up without a fight, so he decided that he must go and see Rachael and discuss the situation. He would enter the emporium under the pretense of needing to buy a bar of Santa Claus Soap and then see where the conversation went from there.

Rachael fully expected to see Wilbert enter the store and was ready for it to happen. As he entered, she became busy with stocking a shelf so that Mrs. Wainwright would have to speak with him first. "Ma'am," he replied softly, "May I have a word with Miss Rachael?"

With a faint smile upon her face, Constance Wainwright approached her clerk. "There's a gentleman to see you Rachael," as she went into the back room to allow the young couple their privacy.

"Yes?" she said, as she addressed Wilbert without any hint of an expression showing.

"Rachael, have I done or said anything to offend you?"

Looking him sternly in the eyes, she replied, "I would have to see you and be around you for that to happen. I'm just tired of sitting around every evening by myself. Since you have never expressed any intentions toward me, I feel I am free to do whatever I want. Maybe someone else might enjoy my company."

Wilbert felt a mass rush of feeling and emotions sweep throughout him upon hearing all of this. Because of his working hours, he might lose Rachael for good and that was totally unacceptable. The very thought of it made him almost sick to his stomach. He realized that he was in fact in love with Miss Rachael Marley. "Now if you'll excuse me, I must return to my work," she told him. With his head down, a deeply saddened Wilbert Vance walked away feeling that he had loved and now lost the girl of his dreams.

Both night time deputy's reported to work to find Justin and Zeke waiting. "I have some news to share with both of you," Justin replied. "I received a very important letter from my home in Cleveland today and I must return there tonight. I'm sorry I cannot tell you more but it's very important to me and I probably will be gone a few weeks. I have already spoken with the Mayor who reluctantly will allow my leave of absence. Wilbert, as senior deputy I want you to trade work schedules with Zeke and assume the daytime duties of acting Marshal. I am very sorry to leave you all short-handed but it's very critical that I must do this. I'll explain more when and if I return. So unless there are questions, I must hurry home and pack, then catch the evening train. Wilbert, make any decision you need to make and I will back you. If needed don't hesitate to activate the councilmen again. Would you do me a small favor though? Tell Virginia tomorrow what has happened. Thanks. Good-bye."

Everyone was quite surprised but felt they could accommodate the new work schedule. "Zeke, go home and get some rest. I'm going to work a double shift tonight and tomorrow to make all this work out. I hope you don't feel any resentment over this?" he asked the old deputy.

"Not a bit Wilbert. Enjoy all da paperwork and all da headaches," as he left for home.

~~~~~~~~~~~~~~~~~~~~~

Maggie O'Shea sat at her dressing table combing out her long hair. As she did so, her mind was on surviving the night and making as much money as possible for tomorrow's departure. Marion was the closest city and if that didn't pan out, she might then try Kokomo. *I need to be aware of my surroundings tonight and stay in the light as much as possible*, she thought, *and then I can make it safely through this night*.

The work night was now over for Maggie O'Shea. She had managed to score with two customers and now that the bars were closing, it was necessary to arrive home safe and sound and sleep off tonight's ordeal. She had thought of asking a man she knew at the bar to walk her safely home, but she knew he would ask for something in return and Maggie was not in the mood for that. So she continued on alone. She did not make it to her door.

Out of the darkness, a hand reached around from behind her and shoved a rag into her mouth. Startled at first, Maggie began to thrash about until a solid punch to her stomach knocked the air, and the fight, out of her. Another set of hands lowered a large burlap bag over her head, shoulders, and arms as another person picked her up and placed her over his shoulder. Panic swept over Maggie as she fought to calm herself in order to breathe. No words were being spoken as she felt herself being tossed into some type of wagon. She could feel hands and a knee weighing her down as the wagon moved slowly down the street to an unknown location. Maggie knew this was no joke being played upon her and realized that it was most likely the people who wrote the threatening letter. Never one to pray before, Maggie now began to do so in earnest.

The wagon seemed to rumble on for quite some distance before eventually turning off into the grass. Maggie was forcefully lifted from the rear of the wagon and taken to a wooded area. The canvas bag was then removed and her arms pulled tightly around the back of a tree and tied in place. Though there was no moonlight, she could make out four... no five men all wearing bandannas over their faces and hats pulled down low. There was a quiet hush as everyone then awaited the leader to finally speak. "Harlot," the leader said, "You have been judged guilty of whoring and leading men to sin. As required by the word of God, sentence shall now be passed." Though unable to scream, Maggie's last image in life was of the men holding large rocks in their hands.

A bloody body was spotted by a farmer coming into town from the east the following morning and promptly reported to the marshal's office. Already having worked eight of his scheduled sixteen hour day, Wilbert had left earlier to get some breakfast before starting the day shift.

Michael Davidson was not yet off duty when the startled farmer entered the office. "Looks like there's a woman tied to a tree on the edge of town east of here," he reported. Deputy Davidson began to write a short note for acting Marshal Vance to follow them to the scene when he returned from breakfast. It was a terrible thing to behold. The woman was tied securely to a medium-sized tree and at its base were five brick size rocks covered in the victim's blood. Michael sent an onlooker back to fetch Doc Baxter although clearly the woman has been dead for quite some time.

Wilbert arrived soon after and together, both men began their investigation. "It looks like they simply beat her to death with these rocks. Very strange. What a horrible way to die," Wilbert replied. "I'm guessing five rocks for five killers. I recognize her too. That's Maggie O'Shea, the wife of one of the men killed in the sawmill boiler explosion. I've seen her a few times around the bars at night and also heard sordid stories about her. Too bad she had to fall from grace this far in life."

Doctor Baxter made an examination and told Wilbert that he figured she'd been dead about six to eight hours. Soon the body was being taken to his office for a final examination before turning it over to the undertaker.

"I sure wish you fellers could stop these killings," Doc replied.

"So do I, Doc. I guess I need to head over and ask around as to where she lived and see if I can find her landlord to let me in. Michael, go home now, I have this covered. You'll be working with Zeke tonight."

Through asking questions, Wilbert was able to locate the landlord who unlocked the rent house of Mrs. O'Shea. Wilbert quickly found what he was expecting to find, a threatening letter signed by *The 13th Disciple*. After reading it, Wilbert now understood why she was killed by the bloody stones. What a time for Justin to leave town.

The Gas City Journal screamed murder in its headlines. They also blamed the Marshal's office for being understaffed as the Marshal was off on vacation somewhere and not doing his job.

~~~~~~~~~~~~~~~~~~~~~

That same morning another group of tramps arrived from who knows where and descended upon the strawboard company. This continued to be a daily occurrence as some sort of tramp telegraph seemed to exist, providing information telling the men that they would be welcomed there. Today's batch looked no different than any other group as they approached the company property. One of the leaders of the tramps stepped outside and welcomed the new arrivals. "Hand over all your matches, smoking materials and any knife or weapons you might be carrying. We will not tolerate any trouble here. If you got a beef with anyone, then take it somewhere else. Mr. Albert Slocum is a Christian man who welcomes us with lodging, clothing, food, and spiritual guidance. His superintendent, Mr. Robert Anderson is my point of contact and also a great man of faith. If you cannot, or will not, follow these rules, please leave now." No-one moved, so after collecting the mentioned items, each man was welcomed inside. "Find a spot to store your bed roll. I've been told today's meal is chicken and dumplings." Those words got the attention of the hungry men who entered and awaited lunch.

Most of the tramps who had been there the longest had already marked out their living/sleeping locations, so each new man knew he had better respect those boundaries and settle into whatever vacant spots were still available. Anderson watched the arrival with some trepidation. "Mr. Slocum, we have about a dozen more that came in this morning."

"Better make sure the cooks have taken that into consideration, Bob. It's probably the only food the starving men will enjoy today."

"Nobody can ever say you don't have a kind heart, Mr. Slocum, but what are we going to do when there's no more room inside the small warehouse for them?"

"I don't know Bob, but I'm sure God will provide an answer in His own due time."

Chapter 14
Let's Try Something New

The idea of going undercover had occurred to Justin Blake one evening while sitting out on his front porch. He knew for it to have any chances of working though, that extra manpower would be needed, and he frankly didn't have it, even using the city council members. Then he mentioned the idea to the Grant County sheriff deputy's, Clark and Patterson, who liked the idea and said they would speak to their supervisor about the chances that they could work alongside Justin and solve both the murders and fires. It worked. Justin came up with the idea of having to leave town, getting off the train in Marion, and changed into tramp clothing with a shoulder bed-roll. "I think I'm not the only one inside this old pair of ragged pants," Deputy Clark joked as he commenced to scratching. All three men were then hauled by wagon late in the night and slept out on the edge of the Mississinewa River to await the morning's arrival of more tramps. They then joined the group and approached the strawboard company.

All three agreed to avoid each other so there would be no indication that they knew one another. This allowed all three men to work independently by watching, and listening. Should anyone need the assistance from the others in a worst case scenario, Patterson had passed out small police whistles easily hidden away inside each man's hat. If any of the tramps knows anything about the arsonist or The 13th Disciple, chances are that the officers may pick up on loose talk. Their plan was to sleep as much as possible during the daylight hours, and then leave the small warehouse after dark and stake out various locations of interest.

Justin knew that some sort of wagon was used in transporting the victims to the murder site and a late night vehicle movement of this type might catch their attention.

Should any man receive important information that he wished the other two "tramps" to know about, their plan was for the man with the information to remove his hat and start fanning himself until noticed by the others. Then one of the officers would approach the sender when the time was safe to do so.

Upon hearing that a woman was murdered last night, Justin was sick that they had not started their undercover work a day earlier. But who would have known that last night was the night the killers would strike anyway? Hopefully they could catch a break soon or Clark and Patterson may well get pulled off the stakeout. Justin felt that within a week, his stubble's and odd clothing may hide his features. Until then, he must stay out of sight from any of the townspeople and his own officers. To assist in this, he had covered parts of his face with soot and appeared to be the well-traveled average tramp. Unless a local citizen got a good look at his face, it was unlikely that he would be discovered. Only Mayor Huffman knew what he and the others were secretly doing. This would be a long and dirty job but if a lead was obtained, it would be well worth it. At least each man had some money tucked away so they wouldn't be going hungry.

~~~~~~~~~~~~~~~~~~~~

"That's all I know Virginia," Wilbert informed her, "Justin seemed to be in a huge rush to get away. I too must go now as we had another murder last night and I need to brief our Mayor and the 'squire on the situation."

"Thank you for letting me know," she replied. Virginia sat there for a short period wondering just what had happened for Justin to have to leave town so suddenly without saying goodbye.

~~~~~~~~~~~~~~~~~~~

"That's about the size of it Mr. Mayor. The warning letter indicates that a public stoning was what killed her. Changing the subject, sir, do you have any idea when Justin will return? I sure wish he was here to lead this investigation instead of me."

Mayor Huffman responded, "No, I have no idea. As for the investigation, I'm sure you will do your very best. That is all any of us can expect you to do, but this crazed killer must be stopped before he kills again. If you require our services, don't be afraid to ask. Good luck Deputy Vance." Wilbert then left to brief the 'Squire.

~~~~~~~~~~~~~~~~~~~

Justin was pleasantly surprised how good his noon-time bowl of chicken and dumplings tasted. Clearly, Slocum was trying to do his very best for the tramps. It was now time for Justin to spread out his bedroll and get some sleep to prepare for their first night. Off to the

side of him was a group of tramps standing around talking as a tramp with today's newspaper was discussing
the news of the murder. "This 13th Disciple must be a
nut job or something," one of the tramps stated. Another
commented on the cruelty of beating a woman to death
with rocks.

Justin suddenly got an inspiration and began playing a hunch. "This 13th Disciple is a Saint doing God's
work as the Bible tells us to do. He should be praised by
everyone of you sinners for his actions," Justin said out
loud. That got the groups attention pretty quick.

"You must be as nutty as this killer is," replied the
tramp with the newspaper. The men all agreed and
turned their backs on Justin. *There,* he thought, *maybe I
just planted a seed.* Glancing over at the direction of the
other deputies, Justin knew they had heard him and were
no doubt aware of the chance he was now taking. Once
word spread around the entire group that the new tramp
supported the actions of *The 13th Disciple,* Justin could
feel himself being shunned. With him siding with the
actions of the killer, maybe it would shake something
loose or get him beat to a pulp by the group. That was
the chance Justin felt he needed to take.

Now it was time to see if there was a freight wagon
anywhere on the property. He found it on the other side

of a small structure. It was an open-sided structure, and there were two horses being kept in the barn section. Pretending to be removing a rock out of his shoe, Justin sat down on the wide wheel as he removed his shoe. *Really no different than any other freight wagon,* he thought. It was, after all, common practice for companies to own such vehicles anyway, so finding one proved nothing.

Anytime that Justin heard any of the tramps discussing the murders, he made it a point of saying that the 13th Disciple was doing the work of the Lord in punishing all transgressors, according to the holy scriptures. "How can it be wrong to follow the sacred words of God?" he pointed out. Still, he was avoided by the other tramps who treated him like he had the plague. Nine days and nights followed with nothing happening and Justin feared that he had wasted his fellow deputies time in a wild goose chase, when at last he was approached. "You really believe all you have been ah sayin' around here?

"I believe in the written word of God. It's all laid out for us... all we must do is follow its teachings. An eye for an eye." Justin told them.

"Walk down to the river and wait. Somebody wants to talk to ya."

At last, maybe all this effort will begin to pay off, he thought.

As Justin began to walk towards the river, a casual glance towards both sheriff deputies indicated they saw that he had been approached, and would remain in the distance but on heightened alert. Justin arrived at the river's bank and sat down to wait. Over a half hour's time elapsed before two different tramps arrived and approached Justin from the rear. "Any idea why we wanted ta talk to ya?" one of the tramps replied.

"I'm guessing you want to kill me and throw my body into the river for my religious beliefs. Go ahead. There can be no greater glory then to die in the service of our Lord."

Neither man spoke so Justin continued on. "Or maybe you think I am this 13th Disciple and you want to turn me in to the stupid flatfoots for the reward money. Go ahead, your charges won't stick anyway."

Both men exchanged looks while the one who had not spoken yet uttered, "I'm satisfied" and walked away, leaving Justin and the other tramp standing alone.

Justin then pretended to act impatient and began to walk away when the tramp spoke up, "We'll be in contact soon."

Justin took his time by walking along the river bank before returning to his bed roll. He suspected that his actions would be closely monitored from now on, and he frankly had no idea how so he could notify the other two deputies of the discussion that had just taken place. Still, nothing would happen until one dark night so time was on his side. Arriving back at his bed roll, Justin removed his hat and began to casually tan himself as both officers watched from a distance.

~~~~~~~~~~~~~~~~~~~~~

Kyle Holloway was a busy man, moving from one daytime job sweeping up at the glass factor floor to picking up and cleaning well after closing time at George Townsend's Saloon. But Kyle had worked hard all of his adult life and wasn't the type of man to start slacking off. No sir, he was very grateful for his working position and occasionally managed to send some cash home to his thankful mother in Marion. Kyle was a good son and would one day become a good father but she, as with all mothers, worried about him and where he was now living. Being the only Negro living outside of Gas City made him a target to men who hated his race. She prayed nightly for his safety. Perhaps one day anyone would be free to live anywhere they wished to without fear of violence upon their person.

Arising early as was his normal daily routine, Kyle ate a bit of breakfast before reporting to his day job. Unbeknownst to him was the sheet of paper stuck through a nail on the exterior door of his small cabin. Kyle reported to work as usual, totally unaware of the trauma ready to overtake his quiet, peaceful life.

~~~~~~~~~~~~~~~~~~~~~~

Thanksgiving was fast approaching as people prepared for their annual family holiday get together. Virginia Cole has processed more personal loans then she had ever thought possible, which kept her quite busy and not dwelling upon the missing Justin Blake. *I was sure I would have received a letter from him by now*, she thought. *I guess he doesn't feel he needs to tell me anything.* At noon, Virginia walked down to the small wooden white post office and, upon seeing Postmaster Harris's bicycle, knew that the mail was now available. *Maybe today*, she thought. Unfortunately no letter arrived. Virginia was about to leave when a familiar pair of voices called out to her.

It was Mr. and Mrs. Stokes. "How have you been my dear? What have you heard from Justin?"

"Nothing," she replied, "Absolutely nothing. It's like he walked off the face of the Earth."

"Well, that's men for you. They just never think. If you don't already have solid Thanksgiving plans, we would love to invite you over to help give thanks for God's many blessings."

Mr. Stokes then entered the conversation, "And if Justin does return soon, please bring him along as well."

"That's very kind of you but I hate to butt into your holiday meal," Virginia told them.

"Nonsense! You can help me prepare the turkey. Please say you will come."

With a sweet smile and a simple nod, Virginia now had holiday plans, but she could only wonder if an un-used empty plate will be set upon their table that day.

~~~~~~~~~~~~~~~~~~~~~~

Rachael made plans on cooking a typical Thanksgiving meal at her Uncle Zeke's home next week and she jokingly asked Zeke if he would like her to invite Jane Draper. The hard look Rachael received told

her NO! "Just Wilbert," he told her, "No she-males."
Poor Uncle Zeke, a confirmed bachelor to the very end.

Even with Justin away and the weight of the office
upon his shoulders, Wilbert was enjoying the day shift
and the opportunity to hold more responsibility. It was
also wonderful to see Miss Rachael more often too. Zeke
enjoyed watching the young couple together and assumed they might even be married this time next year. If
they did, just don't let Wilbert ever call him Uncle Zeke!

~~~~~~~~~~~~~~~~~~~~~

The afternoon rain had finally ended as Kyle
Holloway returned home for a few hours before leaving for the saloon. As he approached his small cabin
on the outskirts of town, he noticed a scrap of paper
fluttering in the wind and took it inside with him. This
was nothing new as his employer and landlord often
left changes to his work schedule this way. Setting the
paper down on his kitchen table, Kyle walked over to
the morning coffee pot still setting on the semi-warm
stove and poured himself a cup. Strong and bitter was
the way Kyle enjoyed it as he took a seat. He hoped the
rain would hold off so he won't get soaked walking to

work tonight. Picking up the paper, he readily saw that it was not from his boss. It read:

> *Oh ye brother of Cain! God in His holy wisdom hath banished ye's descendants to the nation of Nod for eternity, yet ye disobeys the word of God and commiths forth to trespass. Submit to thine fate saith the Lord . The 13th Disciple*

Kyle realized very quickly that this was no idle threat, but a warning from The 13th Disciple that he and his twisted friends were coming for him. Thank God they didn't come last night as he would have been unprepared, but now that he knew about it, he will have a little surprise waiting in store. Kyle Holloway was just not the running type. If they got him, he was going to take a few of them with him. Folding up the threatening paper and placing it into his shirt pocket, Kyle made himself a sandwich and prepared for work. Maybe he'd show it to Mr. Townsend later tonight and get his advice.

It was well into his first hour of work before Kyle decided to show the letter to Mr. Townsend. Without saying a word, he handed the letter to him between serving drinks. Townsend turned quite pail as he read the letter.

"Found it stuck on dat nail you leave me messages on, Mr. Townsend."

"Kyle," Townsend replied, "This guy's a nut job so don't dismiss this threat. Fact is, I want ya to go home now so they can't catch ya out on the road after dark."

"No sir, Mr. Townsend, I ain't a runnin' from no 13th Disciple or any other man whose wantin' ta fight."

Deep admiration filled Townsend's heart. "Then come with me," as he removed his work apron. Turning to one of his regulars he said, "Hey Tony, watch the bar for a few minutes will ya? And keep them Irish fingers out of my change drawer too!" The customer, an old friend, simply nodded as even the boss needs a little time to take care of business once in a while. He and Kyle then left the saloon and walked towards the fire barn.

Zeke and Michael were still inside the office as both men entered. Townsend handed the letter to Zeke, who most people knew couldn't read. Zeke then passed it over, saying his eyes were not so good and asked Michael to read it out loud. The threat got everyone's attention as Zeke said, "Maybe dis is our first good lead. Michael go get Wilbert and fills him in. I'm takin' dis letter to Mayor Huffman fer sum more manpower. Kyle, about when do ya normally start fer home after da bar closes?"

237

"Well sir, dat depends on how much of a mess da customers made," Kyle replied, "But I'd say thirty minutes or so."

Zeke felt this was his time to take charge and lay out a workable plan. "Just leave bout the same time and go home. We'll have people a followin' in the darkness and if dey try ta grab ya, we'll have da manpower ta catch um." At least it was a plan... well, sort of a plan anyway. Zeke took the letter in hand and hurried to the mayor's home.

Davis Huffman was sitting inside his library enjoying an after dinner good book, when he was brought into reality by a loud pounding upon his front door. Mrs. Huffman was passing nearby and answered it. "Sorry ta bother ya Mrs. Huffman, but I gota see da Mayor on official police business."

Seeing that it was Zeke Miller, Huffman motioned for him to enter the library, where the letter was presented to him. "We got us a plan ta catch dem fellers, but I need manpower ta do it. If day don't cum at Kyle tonight, we got ta be ready fer um tomorrow night as well."

"I agree, this seems our best chance. Go get Matthew Brooks, he'll probably go with you. I'm sorry but I have a more pressing engagement for this evening." With that information, Zeke left to get additional help.

"Honey, go out in the shed and bring in my old mud-caked garden clothing and shoes," the Mayor said. "I also need to borrow your hair scissors and then I need you to take me somewhere. Please hurry, time is of the importance." Approaching his old shaving mirror, Huffman eyed his neatly trimmed beard knowing what must be done. After ten minutes, what stubble he had left looked horrible. Exactly what he intended.

Eyeing her husband cautiously, she handed him the filthy garden clothing. "My God, Davis, what have you done to yourself?" Taking her by the arm, they stepped out back as he speedily hooked up the buggy.

"You drive," he told her but realized there was one more important task yet to be performed. Stepping over to his now-unused garden, Huffman reached for hand-fuls of soil and rubbed the dirt all over his face and neck. Entering the carriage, he laid flat upon the floorboards. "I wouldn't want anyone seeing me either if I were you," she scolded her very confusing husband. "You must be mad!"

"Drive slowly through town so as not to attract any attention then drop me off just before you get to the bridge. I may not be home tonight. Say nothing of this to anyone," he told her. At least it was dark. He only hoped and prayed that he had time to make it work.

Chapter 15
It's Now or Never

Mayor Davis Huffman silently rolled out of his wife's carriage just before she entered the darkened bridge. She would then turn around and head for home, but would have many unanswered questions waiting for him tomorrow morning. "All this nonsense... and at your age too!" she had scolded him. Once satisfied he had not been noticed, Huffman then backtracked along the edge of the river until he arrived outside the Strawboard factory. Pulling his hat down as far as he could, Huffman walked among the tramps inside and out, searching for the face of Marshal Justin Blake. Time was of the essence and it was already well after eight pm. After a while, it seemed that all of the tramps began looking the same, and Huffman was beginning to give up hope when he spotted Blake laying on his bed roll.

Using his foot, he kicked Blake on his boot. "Get up, we gotta talk, outside." he said in a deep voice.

Justin was a little startled and wondered if he was again being approached. Slowly he rose to his feet but the tramp seemed a bit agitated. "Move it, I ain't got all day." Glancing over into the corner Justin could see that the tramps actions have caught the attention of the two deputies eyes as he followed the unknown man outside to a quiet location.

"Marshal, I got information you need to know about," the tramp said. There was something vaguely familiar about this tramp's voice, but the thought that he has been spotted worried Justin until he finally realized who was standing before him.

"Mayor Huffman, you are truly a sight for sore eyes. If the voters could only see you now! Your elegant beard has been chopped to bits, so I'm guessing your masquerade tonight is very important."

"Plenty important, Kyle Holloway got a threatening letter from The 13th Disciple and Zeke, Michael, and Matt Brooks will be trailing him as he returns home tonight from the saloon. If nothing happens, we'll be in place tomorrow night also to do it over again and again." At last, a possible break in the case!

"We can't stay outside much longer mayor as I'm being watched. I have two requests I need you to do for me. I have pretended to be sympathetic in the cause of this 13th Disciple and I may have been approached by some of his men, so to remove doubts about this meeting I need you to start yelling at me as loud as you can, then when I tell you to, follow me inside shouting . Then with everyone watching, shove and punch me in the jaw."

"Punch you?"

"Yes, and make it good. It may take suspicion off of you and remove any doubt they have about me. Then wait awhile and approach one of the deputies and brief him so he'll get word to the other one."

"But how can I find them when I don't know what they look like?"

"As soon as you knock me down, take off your hat and fan yourself real good with it. That's our signal. I'll do the same and nod toward you. Better start now and make it good!"

Within moments, someone yelled, "fight" and all of the tramps inside the warehouse became suddenly interested. "You're nothing but a worthless piece of scum and ya better keep your mouth shut around here if ya know what's best or else!" Even Justin was surprised at the strength of the punch to his jaw that caused him to tumble backwards onto the floor. Playing afraid, he crawled like a whimpering dog over to his bed roll as the tramp stood over him shouting and pointing. The room was deathly still until the roar of approval and back slapping began. Caught up in the moment, the mayor finally remembered to remove his hat and kept fanning his face as he was being surrounded by well wishers. Justin sat up and did the same as both deputies watched in total wonderment.

As everyone was congratulating this new tramp, several suggested that they all take a poke at the cowering man, but the new tramp said "Let's leave him alone and maybe he'll learn his lesson." If these had been voters, Huffman could easily become the next Governor of Indiana. Unseen by the majority of the other men, two tramps moved up to Justin's side. "You alright?" one of the men asked. It was the two who had approached him earlier.

"Yes, God protected me from harm," Justin quietly said.

"Good, for tonight you will be called upon by our great spiritual leader to do God's Holy work. Go to sleep my friend, we'll wake you when it's time to go."

As the men walked away Justin made serious eye contact with one of the deputies as he nodded his head while fanning himself with his hat. The message was quickly understood. Tonight was the night.

Huffman was cautiously approached by one of the sheriff deputies who identified himself, as Huffman relayed the entire story to him. He then excused himself saying that he must go but that he will be in the hunt later that evening. "Thanks again for your help Mayor Hobo... I mean Huffman," said the grinning sheriff deputy.

At least Marshal Blake and the sheriff deputies have been made aware of the threat, Huffman thought with satisfaction. Running his hand through his chopped up beard, Huffman felt it was indeed worth the effort. Figuring it must be going on ten p.m., Huffman hurried the distance back to the fire barn, hoping that he could arrive early enough to brief the deputies on everything that had just happened. If not, he would just have to follow behind them and hope for the best.

~~~~~~~~~~~~~~~~~~~~

"Any questions?" Wilbert asked his men. There were none as everything had been gone over time and again, but even the best laid plans go out the window once the trouble starts.

"Alright then, Zeke and I will leave now and position ourselves near the edge of town on each side of the street. At eleven p.m., I want Councilman Brooks to be in position near the bank building. Michael, you'll be in charge from your end. You'll need to be outside this building watching for any type of freight wagon passing by. If it looks suspicious, it may be our men, especially if you see more than just the driver. Zeke and I will be watching from our end, so if we get in trouble one of us will fire a shot for the others to come a running. I wish we could have had more men here tonight, but we gotta do with what we got. We must catch these killers in the act of approaching Kyle's shack. If it doesn't happen tonight, we may very well be repeating this same thing tomorrow night, or even the next. Normally though, it seems the warning letters generate a rapid attack by the killers, so I think this may be it. Gentlemen, I don't have to tell you how dangerous this is so please stay safe and think before you act, and don't fall asleep! I want these men taken alive if possible." Now the waiting began.

~~~~~~~~~~~~~~~~~~~~~

After Townsend's Saloon closed, Kyle Holloway began his normal pick up and removal of trash, sweeping and a clean mopping of the floors. He noticed that Mr. Townsend seemed to not to be in a hurry to leave for home, and Kyle felt that his boss was concerned for his safety, which he greatly appreciated. "Well Mr. Townsend, dat pretty much does it. I'll be a heading home now unless ya gots anything more fer me ta do."

Reaching under the bar, George Townsend pulled out his 10 gauge Remington 1882 double barrel SXS shotgun. "Kyle, I want you to take Old Betsy here home with you for protection. Here are some extra shells too. Keep her as long as you need her. Just cock a single or double hammer depending upon how many barrels you want to fire. Any 13th Disciples come at ya, just let go with both barrels and blast em' back ta Hell." It took a little back and forth before Kyle was convinced to take the shotgun. This was a much better choice than his old muzzle loader at home.

"Thanks again fer all your help, Mr. Townsend. You are a very kind man, sir," he said as he left with the weapon for the long dark walk home.

Kyle felt pretty safe now that he was armed, but he still occasionally glanced around upon hearing noises or seeing branches moving by the wind. Zeke had told him that the deputies would be staying in the shadows behind him to follow him home, so he was not surprised that he didn't see them. There were good people living here in Gas City to be sure.

Deputy Michael Davidson and Councilman Brooks watched intently as Kyle Holloway walked out of the closed saloon. With the natural gas street lighting that burned around the clock along the business section of Main Street, each man had no difficulty in seeing that Kyle was now armed. The deputies allowed him to get about a block ahead before following in the shadows. There was no sign or sounds of any moving wagons upon the bricked street.

By the time that Mayor Huffman arrived at the fire barn, everyone was already gone, and so he continued to trail behind. His only concern now was his appearance as he would be taken for a tramp and possibly one of the killers. Just to be on the safe side, he slowed his pace and would approach the group of deputies with caution.

Wilbert and Zeke could see that Kyle was now in sight and so far has not been bothered by anyone. No wagons had either came by or departed as the edge of town was now quiet for the night. Wilbert waited for Kyle to get ahead before he signaled to Zeke to start moving forward. Once they were within visual range of the shack, both groups would take to the edge of the woods, watch and wait for the action to begin.

Kyle half expected to get jumped as he approached his shack but everything appeared as quiet as it should be. *Maybe deys commin' in da middle of da night?* He thought. *Time ta get ready fer my little surprise.*

~~~~~~~~~~~~~~~~~~~~

Justin had no idea how long he had been asleep when he was shaken awake, "Time to get moving," the voice whispered, so he arose and together walked outside with the man. "Here, tie this around your face," the man said as he handed a bandanna to Justin. The smell of the dirty cloth was nauseating but he did as he was told. They continued walking until out near the road Justin could make out a freight wagon. The driver came to a stop where a group of three waited for the new arrivals. Stepping up into the wagon, Justin felt himself being pushed down as the leader calmly announced, "Let's go," The freight wagon slowly made its way onto the bricked street. Though he couldn't see the two sheriff's deputies, Justin knew they were somewhere close by and watching in the shadows, following the wagon. At least the wagon was traveling along very slowly, so the men won't have trouble keeping up. The only talking that Justin heard was that someone said he was glad to have extra help as the guy was huge. Justin also couldn't help but see the rope with a hangman's noose on the buckboard when the wagon traveled under the gas street lights. It didn't take much imagination to know what the men had in store for Kyle Holloway tonight.

The deputies now watching Holloway's shack naturally assumed that he was inside and by now sound asleep. But that just wasn't the case. Upon returning home, Kyle went inside and put on a heavy coat and hat and had come out the rear door, walking through the trees to the outside privy. While city folks naturally hide their privies behind their homes and out of sight, country folks placed them at the most convenient spot, and the one Kyle had was about fifty feet on the left side of his shack. With double barrels fully loaded, Kyle entered the privy with the gun barrel sticking out the side of the open door. Though it would be a long cold night, he wanted to be able to watch the approach to his property and this location proves to be just right. Any Disciples from Hell arriving tonight would meet up with the working end of Townsend's shotgun. Then Satan can sort out the rest of his flock and piece them back together.

The freight wagon's wheels on the bricked street were easily heard as Justin mapped its location inside his head. At the edge of town, the road turned back into dirt as the wagon continued forward. The intense darkness prevented any of the deputies from seeing it but they could hear its movement in the stillness of the night. Would it continue onward east or turn off in the direction of Holloway's shack? Nobody knew. Mayor Huffman had managed to catch up behind the group but remained hidden just in case it was a false alarm. If a mistake was made and an innocent vehicle was assaulted, word would spread all over town. They just had to be right tonight and Huffman was determined that he would not be the one to make that decision.

As the wagon came into view, it left the dirt street and headed out of town as it made its way to Holloway's shack. "This is it boys, wait for my signal," Wilbert instructed his men. The wagon continued past the deputies and made its approach to the shack. Wilbert saw movement in the back of the wagon but had no idea how many men he would have to deal with in the darkness.

The sound of the approaching wagon had not gone unnoticed by the hiding Kyle Holloway as he cocked both hammers back and made sure that his pocket contained the spare shells. The wagon came to a halt a good seventy-five yards away as the men crawled quietly out of the rear, while the driver remained in position. Wilbert's plan was to wait until the group approached the shack for Kyle, then he and his men would jump them in the confusion. It seemed a reasonable plan but sometimes things just don't work out as planned.

As four masked men advanced towards their target, the driver quietly said, "Drag him out boys." Justin continued to linger towards the rear of the wagon as he searched frantically for his fellow officers. Kyle slowly opened the privy door wider and took aim, "Ya lookin' fer me Devil men?" as he let loose both barrels of the 10 gauge into the lower legs of the group. Kyle exploded from the privy like a wild man shouting as loud as his voice would carry, as he removed the spent shells and inserted two more. With blood in his eyes, Kyle searched for more Disciples to add to his collection.

From behind, Kyle could see several men advancing and shouting orders and prepared to go down fighting. As his men lay bleeding and in agony on the ground, the 13th Disciple shouted and he whipped his horses frantically as the team bolted back the way it came. Justin pulled away the bandanna and dove for the rear of the wagon in a wild attempt to stop the man's get away. Though he was being dragged, Justin simply refused to release his grip. Now the responding deputies dashed to grab the harness of the wild horses and finally brought the wagon to a halt as Justin was able to leap upon the wagon and grab its driver from behind. "Cuffs," Justin shouted, "I need handcuffs." Wilbert and Zeke quickly overpowered the struggling driver and cuffed him. Then Zeke attempted to cuff Justin's wrists too. "You sure you want to cuff me, Zeke?" Justin joked. Zeke showed shock in his face as he recognized his friend.

Seeing that the wagon was stopped and that a group of men had captured its driver, Kyle lowered his weapon and walked cautiously toward the awaiting group. "Wilbert, look who we got here!" Zeke shouted as Justin and the two sheriff deputies made themselves known. The largest laughter came when Mayor Huffman exposed his identity. "Clark and I have some first aid training so we'll take charge of the four injured on the ground," the sheriff deputy offered. The men felt very proud to have worked together with the local Gas City law enforcement to pull it off.

"Bring the driver over to the shack," Justin instructed. "Kyle, bring a lantern outside so we can treat the injured men," he instructed. Soon, the entire front yard was lit up by two lanterns. Wilbert came up to the driver of the vehicle who was laying upon his side and pulled off his mask and hat. "Anybody recognize him?" Justin asked. Finally, it was Mayor Huffman who spoke up. "I do. It is the superintendent of the strawboard company, Robert Anderson."

"God will strike you all down for interfering with my ordained Holy mission tonight!" he began shouting.

Kyle was the first to speak, "So dats da 13th Disciple? He don't look so powerful and all just ah layin' there, does he?" The words struck everyone as humorous with the tension finally broken and a feeling of relief sweeping over the men. Laughter only seemed to drive the prisoner more into a rage as he threatened to bring forth all kinds of plagues and punishments upon these men and the city that they represented. That only caused the men to laugh harder. The 13th Disciple... a self appointed avenger of God... would bother no one else ever again. Still feeling empowered by his temporary position as acting Marshal, Wilbert said, "Now let's load up these prisoners and get them behind bars."

Justin just smiled as he replied, "You heard the man, boys. Our work here is now finished." Zeke went to fetch Doctor Baxter to treat the injured as the others hauled the prisoners inside the fire barn and locked them up.

The often snooty Mississinewa Hotel nighttime desk clerk was struggling to stay awake as he heard the approaching sound of a large and loud group of men. Watching his doorway, he was startled to see a small group of tramps enter the hotel. Not good. Holding up his hands the clerk firmly said, "Stop right there. You're not allowed in here. We're not giving anyway anything. If you don't leave I'll be forced to go get the marshal." That only made the men laugh harder.

Now one tramp approached the front desk, "I'm Mayor Huffman. I want two of your best rooms, bathing facilities made ready, and afterwards, wake up the kitchen staff as these men are hungry. Oh, and by the way, they'll need two bath robes brought to their room. Just send the bill to the city council."

With despicable contempt, the night clerk replied, "If you're Mayor Huffman, I'm Grover Cleveland." This also made the group of tramps start laughing.

The clerk was considering his options when Deputy Wilbert Vance stepped into the room. "Deputy, thank heavens you arrived when you did. Please throw these vagrants out of here." Calmly Wilbert explained who and what they had just accomplished and within minutes, staff members were scrambling to comply with their every wish. "I'm sorry Mr. Mayor, I simply did not recognize you!" the now friendly clerk replied.

Huffman responded jokingly, "Neither will my wife, sir! Now if you gentlemen will excuse me, I'm going home." Justin had already returned to his own home with the thought of a hot soak in his tin bath paramount in his mind. Wilbert informed the two Grant County sheriff deputies that he would instruct Western Union to notify their office of their success and request that their uniforms be forwarded. Both men were too tired now to even care and ascended the stairs to their awaiting baths, food, and beds. More than one complete set of tramp clothing, and the tiny critters infesting them, would soon be burning ashes.

It was good to wake up in a small city alive with excitement. By mid-morning, it seemed that everyone was talking about their brave officers, councilman and Mayor. Huffman decided that there was simply no hope for what was left of his beard and found himself clean shaven and looking ten years younger. Alvin Jensen wrote story after story from the perspective of many of the men involved as his editor uncle cranked out newspaper edition after edition for several days. The story was picked up in local papers and a few as far away as

New York City. Little Gas City will at last have its fifteen minutes of fame.

Justin was too excited to sleep long, so after that much needed hot bath, he returned to work a little early. As soon as everyone was present, Justin personally thanked each man but reminded them that they still had an arsonist on the loose and that they need to concentrate on his capture. "Now go home and get some rest," he told all three, "I can handle it today by myself." As the deputies began to leave, Zeke held back, "Got a second Justin?"

"Sure. What's on your mind?"

Zeke kind of fidgeted for a second or two before answering, "I was a wonder' if ya might put Wilbert back on days? He an my niece are a gettin' thicker than two fleas on ah hound dog, but him ah workin' nights ain't so good. I don't mind workin' nights none if ya wanna change him and me around."

Justin laughed, "That makes you a regular Cupid, doesn't it? I'm sure we can work something out, Zeke."

"I just don't want Wilbert ah thinkin' I was ah sittin' him up for a she-male and all."

"We'll keep this between us. Now, go on home to bed."

Speaking of women, Justin saw it was near time Virginia reported to work and he wanted to be standing at the door, hat in hand. He only hoped she wasn't too mad at him for going off without saying anything to her.

"I'm back," he said in a boyish tone. "How about lunch today and I'll tell you all about it. I got a free dinner for two coming to me over at the Mississinewa Hotel restaurant." The smile on her face told him yes as she shuffled past him so as to be on time to work.

Back inside his office, Justin was very surprised when Grant County Sheriff Wrangler himself arrived with one of his deputies. He knew another man was bringing uniforms for their men, so the sheriff deputies could take their prisoners back for incarceration. Justin felt like it was an extra treat that the man himself cared enough to come along. "Great job you local boys did in rounding up the killers," he said.

"We couldn't have pulled it off without your men, Sheriff. It was an honor to work with them."

Looking up at the jail full of prisoners, the sheriff asked, "Are they medically cleared for travel and have all of the release forms been signed?"

"They are yours. Our local doctor patched up their leg wounds, but they'll require more extensive medical treatment once you get them back to Marion."

Looking around a little confused, he finally asked, "Where are my men, Marshal?"

"I'm guessing they are still sleeping off their long ordeal at the Mississinewa Hotel."

Wrangler directed his deputy to pound on their doors, give them their uniforms, and to tell them to get back ta work. The deputy charged out of the office as instructed. "I gotta sound tough and all just ta keep em in line. I'll give em a couple of days off later ta make up for it. Say, I gotta ask ya about this boy of yours, Kyle Holloway."

"Man," Justin corrected him, "Kyle Holloway is a man and a darn good one at that."

"Ah right, man then. Anyway, I was asked by the Marion Police Chief to evaluate this... man for a possible position as a colored policeman for the colored section of Marion. What is your opinion on him?"

Justin responded with firmness, "I recently obtained approval from the city council to offer Kyle a full time deputy marshal position here, and he turned me down. He was concerned the folks here in town wouldn't accept his authority over them and there might be White Cap troubles. I feel he would be great in that position so I hope he'll get the chance to show what he can do. Want me to send someone to bring him here for you to speak with?"

Shaking his head no he replied, "Won't be necessary. If they want a colored on their police force, well I guess that's their business, not mine. Just tell the boy... I mean man that if he's interested, he is ta see the Chief of Police after Thanksgiving."

Holding himself back, Justin quietly replied that he would personally inform Kyle Holloway and encourage him to accept the position.

Changing the subject, Wrangler asked if they had gotten much information out of the prisoners. "Yes, the four tramps have been singing like birds hoping for lighter sentences. Anderson is definitely the crazy religious zealot who used his position of plant authority to search the groups of tramps for possible followers. It's all here in my report."

"Course you folks are used ta dealing with a few crazy's over here, ain't ya boy?" Justin let the slight pass and said nothing. So much for his impression of Sheriff Wrangler.

Within a half hour, the officers and prisoners had been transported by the Marshal's wagon and were standing by the railroad depot waiting for the train to Marion. Maybe Kyle had been right all along. Some folks, despite their position in life, will continue to look down upon other American citizens. Perhaps if Kyle could be convinced to take up the job, this might be the first step in healing the great divide. Only time would tell. Now it was time to meet Virginia and order a plate of those fantastic pork chops the restaurant was so well known for. Life was good again for Justin Blake.

Chapter 16
Thanksgiving Joy

Reverend and Mrs. Stokes were very pleased that Justin and Virginia had accepted their invitation to join them for Thanksgiving dinner. Though thinner from his long ordeal, Justin appeared fit and quite happy. Both men had been shooed away into the family's library by the ladies who were hard at work in completing the meal's final preparations. "You have made everyone in town very happy this week, my son," Reverend Stokes told him.

"Maybe all but one. I'm told that the strawboard owner, Albert Slocum, has just been coming to work and sitting behind his desk all day, often seen openly weeping. I think he blames himself for all those deaths and the fact that he trusted Anderson. Let me ask you something, sir. Do you think there might be anything you could say to him in person that might help ease his guilt?"

"I don't know Mr. Slocum but I have heard of his deep Christian faith so why don't we give it a try? What if I meet you at your office tomorrow morning, say after nine a.m., and we can take my carriage over to his plant. Maybe he'll refuse to see us, but it won't hurt to try." Just then the ladies called the men to the table and a blessing was offered for the plentiful bounty that they were truly thankful for. Reverend Stokes carved the turkey like a professional and a great time was had by everyone.

~~~~~~~~~~~~~~~~~~~~

Justin arrived the following morning early enough so that he could discuss a manpower change with his deputies. "Wilbert, I want to transfer you back on days and I want Zeke to take your night shift duties. Do either of you have any concern with that?" Neither man spoke up. "Let's make the change starting tomorrow." As the men left, Justin couldn't tell if Zeke or Wilbert had the biggest grin on their face as Justin sat down and started getting caught up in all his paperwork that he was so far behind on.

~~~~~~~~~~~~~~~~~~~~

"Excuse me, Marshal Blake," a voice called out to Justin. It was Kyle Holloway. "Come on in Kyle, glad to see you. I needed a break from all this paperwork anyway."

"Well sir, I just wanted ya ta know I talked to dat Chief of Police in Marion like ya said, and it was all true. He wants me ta start as a beat cop in da colored section of town and I'm ah gonna do it, sir."

Justin arose from his seat and offered his hand in congratulations. "They're getting a fine man for their police force, and I know you'll make everyone proud."

"Well sir, I gots packin' up ta do and folks ta say thanks to. You and Mr. Townsend been mighty nice ta me, and I ain't gonna forgets it none. Goodbye."

Justin was saddened to see the man go. Gas City's loss would now become Marion's gain.

~~~~~~~~~~~~~~~~~~~~

Right on time, Reverend Stokes arrived and together the men set off on their journey to speak with the owner of the strawboard company. Entering the gate was easy, as the guard simply waved them through like he had done for a long time with the tramps. "May I help you gentlemen?" came a voice from behind an office desk.

"Gas City Marshal Justin Blake and Reverend Stokes to see Mr. Slocum."

A look of hesitation appeared on the young man's face before he replied, "Mr. Slocum hasn't been seeing visitors much lately I'm afraid, but... you being the Marshal and all, I guess it's all right. Please wait here while I announce you."

Within a minute, the young man had returned and motioned for the men to follow him as he opened the door to Slocum's office. "Come in gentlemen and please be seated." Momentarily embarrassed by the office's clutter and neglect, Slocum made apologies for its appearance. "It's been a rough several days for me gentlemen, and I fear I may not be my normal self. How may I help you?"

"That is why we're here this morning Mr. Slocum," Stokes told him. "To try to help you understand that continuing to punish yourself for the criminal actions of another person will destroy you. It's bad for you personally and bad for your company."

"Excuse me Reverend, but unless you have stood in my shoes, you have no idea what it's like to have turned a madman loose upon the city. These killings are my responsibility as I refused to see what was apparently before my eyes all the time. Robert Anderson used my tramps, that I cared for, to assist him in his deadly quest of brutality."

"Actually Mr. Slocum, I have stood in your shoes. It was my very own daughter who led the killing spree last year here with the group known as the White Caps. She, like your Mr. Anderson, was mentally ill, but hid her condition very well. I too went through my own period of self doubt and guilt until, with the help of our Lord, I realized that my wife and I were not to blame. Mental illness is a disease, Mr. Slocum, and medical science is only now beginning to realize its early stages. As for the tramps, sir, they are not your tramps, Mr. Slocum, and from where I stand that was your only real mistake."

"But Reverend, helping the poor and the destitute is a commandment of God."

Justin felt he needed to weigh in at this point, "You are an important businessman Mr. Slocum, but you are attempting to mix your business interests with your own religious convictions. That's why it's not working. Even your own employees have said so. Name just one other business you know of that is doing this."

"I feel that Marshal Blake is correct in what he's saying. From his standpoint, a large influx of vagrants can become a potential concern for law enforcement. By all means, make your private donations to any worthy cause you feel is just, but isn't it time to get back to business? I think that once you set the men free, your healing will begin."

"You make it sound like I'm keeping my tramps as prisoners here, sir?"

The Reverend continued, "In a way you are, sir, by robbing them of their self worth by providing for all of their needs. You are encouraging them not to try to break out of their situation and to better themselves, but to remain a victim who needs others to support them."

"That was never my conscious intention, gentlemen. I only wished to do God's work," Slocum replied. "And it appears I have done just the opposite that I set out to do."

Slocum was perhaps finally beginning to come around. "Like feeding a stray cat and after that, it becomes your cat? Even Anderson used that example early on into my housing and feeding program, but I would not listen. I refused to listen to anyone. Even the near labor riot was due to my housing of the tramps on company property. How could I have been so self-centered that I was in the right and the entire town was wrong? It seems now that the first step is to re-focus on my company and send my... ah, the tramps on their way."

Reverend Stokes offered up a healing prayer for forgiveness and strength that was very much appreciated. Saying their goodbyes, each man felt that the healing for Mr. Albert Slocum would now begin. Within a few days, the tramps were told to move on and clean-up crews were hard at work restoring the small warehouse back for company use. Slocum would soon select a new plant superintendent, not based on stern religious convictions but this time based on finding the best qualified man to assume its business duties.

~~~~~~~~~~~~~~~~~~~~~

The December city council meeting only produced one piece of information worth repeating, and that was the vote to increase the monthly pay of the deputies by ten dollars, and the Marshal by twenty. No doubt having learned first-hand of all that was expected of the deputies, the councilmen stood ready to improve the poor pay issue. The successful handling of the 13th Disciple killer didn't hurt either.

~~~~~~~~~~~~~~~~~~~~~

Early on in December, Justin and Virginia made plans to attend the evening's performance of Christmas music at the Lovett Opera House. As they arrived at the entrance, Virginia was somewhat startled to see her widower boss at the bank, Mr. James Howell, escorting another lady to the musical. "Justin, that's Mr. Howell and he has a woman with him! Any idea who she is?"

That was quickly answered by Rachael Marley on the arm of Wilbert Vance. "Oh my, that is Jane Draper, the sister of my employer."

Virginia told her friends that she was very happy to see Mr. Howell trying to pick up his life again, and that he deserved any happiness he could find. With that, the couples entered the stairwell and walked up to the third floor of the opera house. While everyone had been watching Mr. Howell, another set of eyes burned with deep desire for Rachael. They belonged to a man capable of anything, and he was furious to see her on the arm of another. This man was Adam Lake.

Adam had met the lovely Rachael as a customer at the Emporium shortly after she started clerking there. He took his empty three gallon coal oil container there for refilling. Due to the hazards of fire and the dangers of spillage, the emporium kept its barrel of coal oil out back next to the building on a wooden rack. All Adam had to do was tell her what he wanted and they would proceed outside, where either he or Rachael filled his container. She also filled his heart with strange, forbidden desires, and he was determined to get to know her. Unfortunately for Adam, she showed no interest whatsoever in him, other than being polite to a customer. Now she stood ten feet away tonight on the arm of another man. Adam returned home with many new hateful thoughts racing through his twisted mind.

~~~~~~~~~~~~~~~~~~~~

The 1894 issue of the Farmer's Almanac called for a cold, bitter winter throughout Central Indiana and by the look of things, it was going to be right as usual. With the days quickly flowing by, it was hard to imagine that Christmas would soon be there. Work in the emporium had been very busy, but Rachael loved every minute of it. The people here seemed to have Christmas within their hearts as they hurried to and fro with last minute shopping. Children assembled every evening in front of the shops to sing Christmas songs, with an occasional penny being dropped inside their tin cup from a well wisher.

The thought of Christmas at home began to consume Rachael's thoughts as she wrapped a gift for another eager customer. Seeing a break between sales, she felt that it was time to approach her employer, Mrs. Wainwright, about some time off. "Ma'am, do you think I might have a couple of days off after Christmas in order to travel home to Fort Wayne for the holidays to be with my parents?"

The kindly woman was expecting a question along this line and was ready, "Yes my dear. It gets pretty slow in here after Christmas, until after the new year. Go and tell your sweet mother hello for me. I can handle everything here in the store by myself just fine."

Rachael ran over and gave her employer a big hug of thanks. She was planning a small celebration at her Uncle Zeke's on Christmas day, with Wilbert invited. She would buy a train ticket for December 26th and surprise her parents unannounced. It would be wonderful. Rachael then began having thoughts about asking Wilbert if he would like to accompany her to Fort Wayne and meet her family. Would such a bold question from a proper young lady scare Wilbert away? What would her family think? Rachael had felt herself falling in love with the young deputy and wondering if he was as serious about her. Perhaps asking him the question might answer her question, as no young man would want to be presented to a lady's family if he was not seriously interested in her, would he? Then the question that must be considered was, could he even get permission to be away a few days? Rachael would ask for her uncle's advice before she saw Wilbert later tonight. Uncle Zeke would know what to do.

Rachael had decided upon the gift she intended to present to Wilbert on Christmas day; an Ingram man's pocket watch. Mrs. Wainwright had even given her an employee's discount, which helped out a lot. Glancing up from behind the counter, Rachael saw that the pesky customer was back ready to buy some trivial item and would probably start flirting with her again. There was something creepy about him, and while she was always polite, she stood firm in her rejection of his offers for meals or walks. *Why can't this man take the hint*, she often wondered. "Hello beautiful," he told her, "I would like to look at that pocket knife in your display case." She had to point to several before he told her which one, so Rachael suspected he was not really interested in it anyway, but was using it as an excuse to approach her. Setting the knife on the top of the glass display, the man picked it up but never bothered to open its blade. "I think you and I need to walk through the park this evening and get better acquainted," he rudely told her. Rachael picked up the pocket knife, returned it to the case and told him that she was not interested. Anger filled the heart of Adam Lake as he stormed out of the emporium.

"Next time that man comes in, please let me wait on him. You don't deserve that type of treatment," Mrs. Wainwright told her. "Maybe you should tell Wilbert what he's been saying to you."

Rachael only replied that it comes with the job and set about helping another customer. *Brave girl*, Mrs. Wainwright thought to herself.

~~~~~~~~~~~~~~~~~~~~~

"So Uncle, that's it. Should I ask Wilbert to travel home with me or not?"

Zeke leaned back in his chair before replying, "Go ahead and ask him. I'm a bettin' he's gonna say yes, as long as Justin can cut loose with him fer a few days and all."

~~~~~~~~~~~~~~~~~~~~~

"...so if you can spare me for a few days I want to go up to Fort Wayne after Christmas with Rachael and meet her parents," Wilbert told him. Justin just smiled broadly and nodded yes. No sense teasing Wilbert that meeting the parents came before a lifelong marriage commitment. His friend was smart enough to figure that part out by himself anyway.

~~~~~~~~~~~~~~~~~~~~~~~

The one fact that everyone can agree on is that the cold weather brings forth sickness and especially influenza. Doctor Baxter did good business during that time of year, yet lacked the magic pill everyone was counting upon for a quick cure. Rachael Marley awoke that morning feeling achy and a bit light-headed. *No, not now. It's Christmas Eve and I have big plans for the next few days.* Knowing that she had no other choice, Rachael got ready for work as today would be a very busy shopping day. Mrs. Wainwright had said the store would close early, and that information was posted upon the window for the benefit of those who put their shopping off until the last minute. This would be a Christmas Eve neither Rachel nor Mrs. Wainwright would ever forget.

~~~~~~~~~~~~~~~~~~~~~~~

Many townspeople were excited that a traveling team of stage performers were performing their last performance of Charles Dickens' holiday classic, "A Christmas Carol", tonight at the Lovett Opera House. General admission tickets had sold out in advance, but Wilbert made sure that he had obtained two, knowing of Rachael's love for the story, and he wanted it to be a last minute surprise. The play was to start at seven-fifteen p.m. and Wilbert was looking forward to the evening together with his enchanting special lady.

~~~~~~~~~~~~~~~~~~~

Rachael could feel herself getting sicker and sicker as the day rolled on. Twice Mrs. Wainwright suggested that she just go upstairs to her apartment and lay down, but she pressed on anyway. During her lunch period, Rachael did as she was told and laid down while the world seemed to spin before her eyes. Thirty minutes later, she forced herself to return to work. She was beginning to feel like her Christmas plans at Uncle Zeke's, and her trip home to Fort Wayne, might now be in jeopardy. Rachael had waited upon two customers when that awful man appeared again. "Hello beautiful," he said, "I'm here to buy you a Christmas present. Just tell me what you want," Adam Lake told her.

Feeling as though she might pass out, Rachael knew she must go lay down again and ignored the man, walking right past him. He watched her thinking that she was going to pick out her present when he noticed instead that she had begun climbing a set of wooden stairs, holding tightly onto the railing as she made her way to the top. There she opened a door and Adam could see it was a small apartment built over the wooden storage room. *So she lives up there does she, and she wouldn't even respond to my offer. Who does she think she is anyhow? She would be lucky to have a man like me, yet she thinks she's too good to even speak. I'll show her, I'll show them all.* Adam Lake stormed out the front door and began to make plans.

The emporium was a masonry and timber constructed building with a flat roof that had a wooden frame rear storage room added some years later. To gain entry into the rear storage room from the emporium, a doorway had been cut out of the brick and a door added. Keeping it closed also helped to keep the emporium warmer in winter. It was over the storage room that the small apartment had been added along with stairs on the side for easy access. Adam Lake took in all of the factors into consideration as he began to make his plans for tonight's main event. He would fix Miss Beauty for good.

Walking down the outside of the emporium towards the rear of the building, Lake looked up to see a lone small window high above. *That has to be Beauty's window to her apartment,* he thought. Directly under it sat a barrel of coal oil on a wooden platform. The spout was chained shut to prevent anyone from helping themselves to free coal oil. Lake had watched her unlock it several times in the past while filling up his own container of the flammable liquid. If that spout was broken off the barrel, its entire contents would spill. If he used an empty can, he could splash it all over the wooden sidings and Miss Beauty and the storage room will go up in flames so easily. Kicking the barrel with his foot, Lake could feel that it was near full. *Yes, this will do nicely,* he thought. *Now we wait until darkness sets in.*

Having been told earlier that the emporium was closing its doors early for Christmas Eve, Wilbert decided on taking Rachael out for supper, providing anything was still open. He would then present her the tickets for tonight's play as a surprise. Entering the store just before closing, Mrs. Wainwright approached him. "She's sick, Wilbert. I fear she has the influenza bug and has been in bed since early afternoon. Let me go check on her for you." Climbing the stairs, she knocked softly upon the doorway and entered. Within a minute, Mrs. Wainwright had returned. "That poor child is very sick. I'm guessing whatever plans you two have made tonight might just be over. Maybe she'll be better by tomorrow but only time will tell in these situations."

Darn, so much for surprises. "Well Mrs. Wainwright, I appreciate what you are doing for her. Sleep and rest is probably what she needs now." Reaching into his pocket, Wilbert pulled out a ticket to the play and handed it to her. "Here's a general admission ticket for tonight's play at the opera house. You might as well use it and have an enjoyable evening."

A deep smile appeared upon the woman's face, "I tried to get a ticket earlier but was told they were all sold out. Thank you, Wilbert. I will enjoy the play." With that, Wilbert returned to the office.

People began lining up on the concrete sidewalk outside the opera house at seven p.m., so Wilbert stepped to the end of the line and waited. Without Rachael at his side, tonight's performance was more a killer of time than an evening of enjoyment. That girl sure had gotten under his skin and he couldn't think about life without her.

Justin had waited too long to try to obtain tickets but Virginia had the opportunity to attend with another man and decided to do so anyway. She would have much preferred Justin's company had she been given the chance. Looking at the couples standing in line, she again saw her supervisor with Jane Draper. Virginia could only pray for his future happiness. Soon the waiting line began to move as everyone ascended the staircase into the opera house.

Justin was cleaning the inside of his house with expectations of the arrival tomorrow morning of Virginia. She had promised to bake a Christmas ham for their lunch then Justin would present her with the lovely gold necklace and locket he had purchased. He only hoped that she would like it. Virginia Cole was also his good friend and he had sincere hopes she might become his wife in the future. Maybe he was only dreaming on this point but oh, what a dream it would be!

A small sign on the office fire bard door said the office would be closed Christmas day and barring some unforeseen emergency, people were to contact him at home. Justin had instructed his men that he alone would handle anything that came up. "Merry Christmas," he wished each man earlier in the evening. "Enjoy your time off tomorrow as it gets rather busy around here on New Year's Eve and we'll all be working that evening," Justin told them.

Rachael Marley kept a bucket beside her bed, just in case. By now, she knew she would be in no condition to cook for her uncle and Wilbert tomorrow. Sleep was all that she wanted so she softly drifted off again, unknowing of the evil about to overtake her life.

Chapter 17
Fire!

Alone figure moved in the darkness at the rear alley of the emporium. It was near ten p.m. and rather early for the fun he normally had in mind, but with the large crowd of people leaving the theater at the play's ten-fifteen p.m. scheduled completion, Adam Lake would be guaranteed his largest audience yet. So many people would share in his joy and excitement as he watched from the sidelines. Of course there was no guarantee that Miss Beauty would be in her apartment. She may very well be attending the play tonight. Either way, the fire would either kill her or destroy her home and place of business. Adam was satisfied with either. Now all he had to do was time the starting of the fire as the people exited the stairs onto Main Street. He could hardly contain himself with excitement as he reviewed his tools; a hammer, a screw driver, and a large empty tin can. If he was unable to knock the spout off, he will punch several holes through the end of the barrel, then by filling can full with the flammable coal oil, he'd splash it all over the rear wooden wall. It should soak in nicely, so when it was time, his match should readily ignite the wall into a blazing inferno.

Wilbert was enjoying the play, and being familiar with the story, knew that the climax was only moments away. After the actors came back on stage for their final curtain call, there will be a mad dash to exit quickly for home. Many parents planned then make everything ready for Santa Claus's arrival with the hanging of stockings and such.

Adam Lake felt it was time to begin, so he swung his hammer hard, striking the spout. It did not move. He hit it again and again with little effect. By now, he was concerned that the loud noises might attract attention from someone wandering by. Then he spotted a brick that was laying nearby, and after striking the spout several times, a deep split along the seam of the metal developed where the spout was threaded into the barrel. Liquid began pouring out as Lake frantically tried to catch the contents inside the tin can. As it became full, he threw the coal oil on the wooden wall then commenced filling it again. What he hadn't noticed in his excitement was the amount of liquid splashing on his own clothing. His right boot was saturated as he knelt at the base of the barrel. Becoming impatient with the slow process, Lake then manhandled the barrel by turning it so that it began squirting its liquid directly onto the base of the wall. Stepping back, he could see the large puddle of liquid soaking into the wooden structure. Lovely. Now all he had to do was time the fire properly and the fun would begin. His body quivered with excitement.

~~~~~~~~~~~~~~~~~~~~~

At his home, Justin Blake was putting the final touches to his kitchen cleaning efforts. He didn't want Virginia to think he lived like one of the tramps. Being a bachelor, he just hadn't realized how dirty things had become. He expected he would still need two more hours of housekeeping tonight before being satisfied that his home was presentable.

~~~~~~~~~~~~~~~~~~~~~

The sounds of people's laughter caught Adam Lake's ears as he realized the play was now over and the crowd was descending the staircase. Reaching for a small box of matches, Lake flicked his thumbnail over the head of the match as it came to life, then threw it down on the standing liquid. An audible swoosh sound caught his ears as the wall erupted into a dancing mass of flame. But something was wrong, Lake felt intense heat and pain as fire jumped up his leg. His entire body was on fire as he ran about shouting frantically, while trying to beat out the flames with his hands. Lake ran along the side of the building, blindly, unable to comprehend the horror he was experiencing as he fell into the brick street rolling and screaming in agony. Two men who were leaving Townsend's Saloon, saw the horror of a human torch dropping on the edge of the street. One man removed his coat and began beating out the flames as the other ran for the doctor.

"FIRE!" someone shouted as the theater crowd saw the flames shooting up above a structure and began assembling along the street to watch. Jane Draper and Constance Wainwright could see that the Emporium's warehouse was on fire as they frantically watched the flames rise high into the night sky. Wilbert ran down to the scene and began searching the faces for Rachael. He could not find her. Several of the play's attendees tonight were also volunteer firemen. They made a wild dash towards the fire barn to hitch up the fire horses to the Cristie American steam pumper and new ladder truck.

The brave men had learned long ago to always maintain a small flame inside the engine's steam boiler for a quick steam build up that more quickly provided steam power to its pump engine. This was a great improvement over the old hand pump system used for many years. Within only a few minutes, both pieces of fire equipment were on the scene, and the firemen began fighting the fire from the rear alley. Justin Blake and his deputies responded at the first sound of the fire bell and discovered the badly burned man, circled by a crowd of onlookers. Justin asked, "Who are you and did you start this fire?"

A weak answer said "Yes,... my name... is Adam Lake. I... set all... the fires. I like...fires...they... excite me...." Doctor Baxter arrived and made a quick examination of the man's horrendous burns. Shaking his head no to Marshal Blake, Baxter directed a couple of men to very softly place him in a wagon and quickly take the man to doc's office. "I'll do what I can, but he's severely burned." At least Justin now had his arsonist.

Wilbert was in near panic that he could not locate Rachael, so he and Zeke ran to the back of the burning storeroom, grabbed a thirty five foot wooden ladder off the ladder truck and a fireman's ax and then placed the ladder directly under her rear window. As Zeke butted the ladder, Wilbert scrambled to the top and attempted to open the window into Rachael's apartment. It would not budge. Wilbert swung the ax and brought its blade deep between the bottom window rail and the sill. He then pried the window open. Shouting down to Zeke to watch out, he dropped the fire ax and crawled through the black smoke into Rachael's room.

Wilbert could not see a thing, so he decided to use a right hand search pattern by keeping his foot against the wall and sweeping out with his arms to search, calling out her name between heavy coughs and fighting the heat as he crawled along the flooring. Finding nothing, he kept moving and crawling as he swept for Rachael. Finding her bed, he searched it and even under it, but Rachael was not there, so he continued on. Finally, his hand made contact with her leg and he dragged her unconscious body back towards the open window. Wilbert had no idea if she was still alive or not, but getting her into fresh air and out of this heat and smoke was all that mattered at this point. Reaching the window, Wilbert was thrilled to find a fireman on the top of the ladder waiting to enter. He helped Wilbert lift the unconscious woman out the window and over the fireman's shoulder as he descended the ladder with Wilbert close behind him.

The fresh air was starting to revive Rachael as she began to cough out heavy black smoke. Wilbert was at her side along with Zeke. "Lets take her ta my place," Zeke shouted as Wilbert picked her up into his arms. "It's unlocked," he told Wilbert. "Take her there an' put her in her old cot in the extra room. I'll go get help."

The firemen were fortunate that many factors contributed to their quick response tonight as they supplied a stream of water to the burning storeroom. Thick heavy smoke was bellowing from the corner of the roof as two firemen, using the remaining ladder, were successful in ventilating the flat roof. Still, there was no way of preventing the fire and black smoke from entering the main part of the emporium and causing heavy smoke damage. From outside, both Constance Wainwright and Jane Draper stood with tears running down their faces. Seeing Wilbert carry Rachael away, Jane Draper told her sister that she would follow to help Rachael in any way she could. Reaching Zeke's little shack, Jane told Wilbert to lay her down and leave. She would care for and bath Rachael after obtaining sleeping garments from her own closet. Doctor Baxter then arrived and shooed Wilbert away, telling him that the burned man had died. Knowing there was nothing more he could do, Wilbert returned to work.

Christmas morning's sunlight revealed the extent of the fire damage to the emporium. The rear storage room was a complete loss, even though a large burned section of it remained standing. Constance Wainwright and Jane Draper opened up the store's front door and side windows in an attempt to remove the lingering smoke and smell. It would most likely be several days before an agent from the Farmer's Mutual Fire Insurance Association will arrive to inspect the loss. At least the agent would be pleased to learn that the arsonist that had plagued this community had been stopped, dying by his own hand. Few would mourn the passing of Adam Lake of Jonesboro.

Wilbert was asked by Jane Draper not to arrive for a visit until after nine a.m. Rachael was now washed clean and wearing a soft, but warm sleeping gown. Jane even had combed the sleeping girl's hair for her. "She did a lot of coughing last night, but seems more restful now. She occasionally wakes up but drifts back to sleep. Since the poor child lost all of her belongings, I asked a few friends to pass the word about donating clothing for her. So don't be surprised if some of it arrives here today. I'll be sitting in the kitchen with Zeke if you need me," she told him. Wilbert pulled up a small chair next to the cot and began to hold Rachael's hand.

Zeke was tired from being up all night, but was not about to go to bed with the other she-male in his house. Seeing that she had made a pot of coffee, Zeke poured himself a cup, then remembered his manners and offered Jane one too. "Jane, I'm mighty thankful fer your ah helping out with Rachael and all," Zeke told her between sips. She made good coffee, but Zeke wasn't about to tell her so.

"I'm happy to do it. Rachael's such a sweet young lady. Still, I can't see how she can be related to an old codger like you, Zeke."

With a straight face, he told her that Rachael got all her kindness and sweetness from him. Somehow Jane Draper didn't buy that at all. "Well, I'll be heading for home now. If you need help with her, please don't hesitate to call upon me." With a wave, Jane Draper let herself out as Zeke sat there finishing up his coffee. Wilbert had saved his niece's life and Zeke would forever be grateful and in his debt.

As Jane Draper approached her home, she saw an envelope stuck on her door, and for an instant, she thought of the 13th Disciple warnings. Opening it with some trepidation, she was greatly relieved and flattered by its message:

Dear Jane,

> *What you are doing for that poor young wom-*
> *an shows the great character and love that you*
> *possess which are qualities I deeply admire in a*
> *woman. I look forward to becoming better ac-*
> *quainted with you during the new year.*

Sincerely, James Howell.

Perhaps one is never too old to find love and happiness even when you least expect it.

~~~~~~~~~~~~~~~~~~~~~

Another day passed. Arriving for the morning shift, everyone wanted to know how Rachael was doing. Wilbert said that he would like to drop over and see her mid-morning if it wouldn't bother Zeke's sleeping. Assured it wouldn't, the night deputies briefed the day men on the night's quiet shift. Folks just didn't have much money to howl in the saloons right after Christmas, anyway. A few days of quietness was a welcome relief for everyone.

With only Wilbert in the office with him, Justin asked about their plans in seeing her parents in Fort Wayne. "Since we're approaching the New Year, I figured you couldn't spare me, so I assumed Rachael will have to travel alone."

"Nonsense," Justin told him. "Go, we'll manage just fine. If need be, I'll call on the councilmen's assistance again. I'll see you after the first of the year. After all that's happened, you both certainly deserve some time away from here." Wilbert was thrilled with the kindness shown to him by his friend.

Arriving two hours later, Wilbert let himself into Zeke's shack and tapped gently upon Rachael's door. "Come in," a much stronger voice replied. Rachael was sitting up in bed looking happy and content. "Good morning, Wilbert," she said to him.

From the other room, Zeke was snoring so loud it sounded more like the roar of a lion. "How does a pretty girl like yourself ever get any sleep around here?" as he sat back down in a chair and picked up her hand. "How are you feeling, sweetheart?"

Chuckling quietly she told him, "I'm feeling much better now, especially hearing I'm your sweetheart. That was so brave of you rescuing me from that burning inferno the way you did. I remember awakening to the smell of smoke and feeling heat. I crawled out of bed but couldn't breathe and fell to the floor. I remember trying to get to the door but it was hot to the touch, so I crawled towards the window but couldn't open it. You'll remember, it was always very hard to open anyway. I faintly remember thinking that I should break the window, but didn't have anything at hand to do so. By then I was confused and having a hard time breathing. I guess I passed out. That must have been about the time my hero came to my rescue."

Reaching out to touch her shoulder, Wilbert replied he was no hero but only protecting the one he loved. He then reached over and kissed Rachael deeply. "I love you too Wilbert," she softly replied. He then told her about what Justin had said and together they made plans to leave by the noon train to Fort Wayne tomorrow. "Jane has been so wonderful in coming by to care for me. Look at the clothing she and her friends have provided. I'll need clothing for my search for another job. It sounds like the emporium will require extensive repairs before it ever re-opens again. Jane says that Mrs. Wainwright is ready to hire some out of work men to tear down what's standing, clean the walls and shelves in what's still standing, repaint, and begin again, as soon as the insurance company gives her final approval. She's planning to eventually build a larger warehouse made of brick this spring. This time there won't be any apartment in its loft, so you'll have to help me find a new home."

"Rachael, we have much to talk about but let's save it for the train, alright? I better be getting back to work. I'll stop by tonight to make sure you're still planning on leaving tomorrow. Now get some rest. I love you." With that, Rachael soon drifted off to sleep with her heart full of love and joy.

~~~~~~~~~~~~~~~~~~~

Just as they planned, Wilbert and Rachael, along with their luggage, boarded the north bound train the following day bound for Fort Wayne and the meeting of her parents and friends.

~~~~~~~~~~~~~~~~~~~

That afternoon, emporium owner Constance Wainwright walked through the smoke and fire-damaged store with the fire insurance agent. Having learned that the arsonist himself died brought closure in the agent's mind, and he told her that he didn't see any problem in the final payout of her policy. Walking over to the case of pocket knives, Constance pulled one out and said,

"Other than smelling of smoke, these were not affected by the fire. Is there any problem with me cleaning some of my remaining stock and having a fire sale?"

The agent said there was no problem from their end once the claim was paid but cautioned that cloth, food items, and such should be disposed of as the smell could not be washed away. This had been a concern, for Constance was considering her options and now made plans to begin sorting what was still salvageable. There was a small empty store down the street that she thought could be rented for a few weeks to wash and resell what she could. The public always seems to love a fire sale anyway. "How soon can my workers begin tearing down what's left of the storage room?" she asked.

"As soon as I'm completed here, you are free to do anything you wish Mrs. Wainwright." Just the words the spunky lady wanted to hear. Now it was time to apply for a business loan so she could begin making plans for the new brick addition. She would go and see that young female loan officer at the First National Bank. The fact that her sister was seeing the banks' Vice President shouldn't hurt her chances for approval either.

On New Year's Eve, Wilbert and Rachael returned to Gas City from visiting her parents. The young couple had also returned engaged with wedding plans set for

May. Since it was around lunch time, they decided to grab a bite to eat before going to the emporium, having heard in the restaurant that Mrs. Wainwright was there working. "After our walk-through of the store, our first priority must be in finding you lodging, even if it's in the Mississinewa Hotel for a few days," Wilbert told her.

Entering the still-smoky smelling emporium, Mrs. Wainwright gave Rachael a big hug. Then upon hearing of their engagement, she gave Wilbert one too. "Congratulations, I'm sure you two will be very happy together," the smiling owner told them. "As you can see I have these men helping me sort and box up merchandise that I think we can clean and resell in a special fire sale I'm planning later on. Are you coming back to work for me, Rachael?"

"Yes," Rachael replied," As soon as I can find a place to live."

"That's easy," Constance told her, "You can stay at my house. I have plenty of room and I feel responsible that I didn't report that awful man to the Marshal's office and maybe, prevented all of this. Anyway, please move in and take the Rose room. It's the largest and has a good bed. You're welcome to stay there until your wedding."

"Oh, Mrs. Wainwright... you are so wonderful! Thank you so much!"

"Think nothing of it dear. Now take your luggage over to the house." Reaching into her handbag she produced an extra house key. "Jane gave it back to me once my hip healed up so now it's yours. Go now, we'll talk later as I want to get a couple more hours out of these men before they head off to the saloons."

Upon hearing the word *saloon*, both men grinned at each other at the very thought of a few drinks. A Gas City ordnance allowed saloons to remain open on New Year's Eve until after midnight and these men and many others will take advantage of that tonight.

Wilbert arrived at his room at Ma Richardson's boarding house and changed into his uniform. Ma was happy to see him back and genuinely happy with the news he had told her about his upcoming wedding. Wilbert knew that the guys would be happy to have him back at work and tonight should be a very busy night indeed. Walking into the fire barn, Justin said, "Well, well, look who's back. Have a good time with your future in-laws?"

"We're now engaged and Rachael is thinking of a May wedding."

After the expected congratulations from his fellow deputies, Justin got down to business by outlining tonight's plan. All of the deputies were to work in pairs and the police wagon would be parked down by the saloons for quick use when needed in hauling men to the jail. "Don't take any chances tonight with your own safety. I expect 'Squire Williamson will have a full courtroom tomorrow morning."

The night turned out to be even worse than Justin expected with a few fights, loud public singing, and one old timer bent upon shooting up the local saloon. All involved spent a crowded and uncomfortable night in the city jail awaiting their morning fines and punishments.

Chapter 18
January 1, 1895;
Happy New Year!

Ohe thing that can be said about Indiana weather is that when Mother Nature is ready to dump snow and bring forth cold bitter winds, there isn't much you can do about it other than complain. Deputy Zeke Miller had warned everyone that it *was fixin' ta hit* as he told all who would listen, and boy oh boy, was he right! It was the dry type of snow that drifted quite deep wherever it had a mind to drift, and the strong winds were more than happy to assist. Snow began to fall during the early morning hours and hadn't quit by the time Justin and Wilbert waded knee-deep snow to their office. "Wilbert," Justin said to his deputy, "Let's get a couple of our overnight prisoners out with coal shovels and start moving the drifting snow away from the fire barn doors, just in case we have a fire today."

Wilbert walked up to the cell containing seven men from last night's wild celebrations. "I need two volunteers to go out and shovel snow away from the fire barn doors."

No one moved but one man asked, "If we do, will the 'squire go easier on us?"

Wilbert smiled and replied, "Your guess is as good as any, but it can't hurt. Let's go... you and you. Move it. The shovels are in the barn."

Zeke then added, "I'll have some coffee a waitin' fer ya when ya's finished, boys." The promise of a cup of hot coffee sounded just fine and off the men went under Wilbert's supervision to shovel the drifting snow.

"I bet we'll have to take turns repeating this all through the day. I wonder how long this bad weather will last anyway?" Justin asked.

"Snow will quit about ten a.m. but da wind will whip it up till early evenin'," Zeke casually replied. Justin chuckled to himself, knowing of his friend's strange ability to predict the weather, and having learned not to dismiss anything that he said.

"Michael, Zeke, you fellows did a great job last evening. Now go home and get some sleep. Wilbert and I will take it from here."

"I hope the wife's up as I'm craving a large plate of ham and eggs," Michael remarked on his way out the door. Justin lingered a couple of minutes on what Michael had just said. It must be wonderful to have someone waiting at home for your return. Wilbert and Rachael's planned May wedding had been on his mind lately too. It's only natural for a man to wonder what it would be like for him to have a wife. Shaking the thought out of his head, Justin settled back on completing all of the necessary paperwork before they would present the seven prisoners to 'Squire Williamson. Thirty minutes later, Wilbert and the two very cold volunteers were back inside and enjoying a cup of Zeke's bad coffee, as the other prisoners watched silently in envy. That's what you get for not volunteering, boys.

The snow stopped just as Zeke had said it would as Justin and Wilbert marched the seven prisoners over to the room leased by the city inside the Mississinewa Hotel as its court room. "Morning, Your Honor," Justin said as they entered. Soon, each man's case was presented and the fines were issued. After the cases were completed, Justin and Wilbert remained behind briefly to visit with Williamson. There was a good feeling that with the coming of the New Year, the possibility that yesterday's troubles would finally be over and a new day of peace and harmony could encompass the community. Unfortunately, that type of wishful thinking would soon dissipate as a new horror raised its ugly head and returned fear and trepidation into the heart of the little community.

Mayhem Returns... to a small town

The Strangler

Historical Fiction

Alan E Losure

Returning Cast of Main Characters

Justin Blake	Marshal
Wilbert Vance	Deputy
Zeke Miller	Deputy
Michael Davidson	Deputy
Virginia Cole	Loan Officer at First National Bank
Rachael Marley	Emporium Employee
Davis Huffman	Mayor
Constance Wainwright	Owner of Emporium
Jane Draper	Sister of Constance
James Howell	First National Bank V.P.
Doc Baxter	Doctor
Matthew Brooks	Barber/Councilman
Reverend Stokes	Reverend/Friend
Ruth Stokes	Wife/Friend
Spunky	Justin's Horse

Cast of New Main Characters

Agnes Cody	Sister/Woman of the Night
Chet Cody	Brother
Doris Davidson	Wife of Deputy
John Croons	Escaped Killer
Betty Jo	Woman of the Night
Brad Lockridge	Teenager
Glades Rollins	Wife
Pete Rollins	Bartender
Lawrence Wright	New Manager at Strawboard Co.
Ely Lewis	Candy Store Owner
Floyd Acres	Clothing Store Owner
Leland Boggs	Landlord
Amos Bundy	Old Fisherman

Chapter 19
April 11, 1895
Winter Finally Ends

Ask any man or woman on the street if they were happy that Old Man Winter had finally left for good, and smiles of happiness appeared on everyone's face. The weather service officer at Indianapolis reported the month of January to be the coldest for many years. Cold, bitter weather seriously affected the flow of natural gas to many homes and businesses. Even the groundhog predicted six more weeks of winter before returning to his warm hole in the ground. Once the thawing began, the passenger boat, Eureka, was found to be badly damaged by three inch thick floating sheets of ice on the Mississinewa River. At last the weather was improving, and now the townspeople had to deal with the rain. For the first ten days of the month, it had been nothing but solid rain, but today is different. The sun was shining, and warmth has finally returned, indicating that spring was just around the corner.

Most townspeople show little interest in any new arrivals to the city as people come and depart daily, but one brother and sister would have a lasting effect on the community since arriving in Gas City last week. Their names are Agnes and Chet Cody. Here was their sad story: Growing up in Louisville, Kentucky, Agnes knew early in life that her family was different from the other students that she attended school with. Her father was a conductor with the railroad and was constantly gone from home. Her mother was a dark-haired beauty who kept to herself and never entertained friends or guests. It was all because of her young son, Chet.

He was born with mental deficiencies and was kept hidden away from other people. Actually, Chet was a great embarrassment to the family and was kept chained by the leg to his bed in the attic. The child never learned to speak, only grunting and pointing in an attempt to communicate with his family. Two years younger than his sister, Chet was quite often beaten by his mother, either out of frustration, drunkenness, or hatred that she had been saddled with a severely retarded child. Agnes often thought that her mother wished the boy would die and rid herself of the terrible situation.

At an early age, Agnes was told she must never tell anyone, anytime, that Chet existed, let alone that he was chained to a bed in the attic. Neighbors all around never saw the boy as his bed was purposely kept away from the attic window. Occasionally though an odd sort of wild scream would emanate from their home, the neighbors made a point of staying away from the strange, unfriendly family. Agnes grew up without any real school friends as word to avoid her was passed from parents to their children.

Once Agnes turned ten years old, she was tasked with the twice daily chore of taking food to "it" as her mother always called her brother, and emptying the bucket of "its" waste out back in the outhouse. Agnes would never forget the horror that she experienced the first time she had accomplished the terrible tasks alone, as her brother had almost managed to catch her hair and pull her closer to him. She had no doubt that he would have killed her as he seemed to associate her with the almost weekly beatings he received from his mother. What her younger brother lacked in intelligence and in looks, he more than made up for in size. Chet was growing into a huge, overgrown figure. While his facial features resembled more of an ape than a boy, it was his hands that always caught Agnes's attention. They were huge and powerful.

The problem started with the arrival of a telegram informing her mother that her husband had been killed in a railroad derailment accident south of Chicago. At that point her mother, who Agnes was already beginning to despise, began drinking more heavily. Soon she took to the world's oldest profession for income, and was away most nights, returning home intoxicated. At the tender age of fifteen, Agnes Cody took full charge of the household and the total care of her brother. The beatings became more and more frequent these days and her mother seemed to lose all control. One day, young Agnes brought a pan of cold water and a wash cloth up to the attic and began treating what she could of the beating marks. Her brother eventually seemed to realize her kindness, and Agnes began to lose her fear of Chet. She spent more and more time with her brother and in a way not fully understood by her, a bond began to form between the two.

It was shortly after turning seventeen last November, Agnes returned home from school and proceeded to the attic, only to discover the body of her mother. It appeared that another beating with a switch had happened, but this time, her mother had become careless and had gotten too close. This was just what the abused teenager had wanted as he had caught his mother and choked her to death, breaking her neck. Chet still gripped the woman by the throat and was dragging her around like a rag doll. A look of peaceful satisfaction was evident upon her brother's gruesome face.

The fact that her mother was dead had little effect on Agnes, as she had long ago lost any love she had for her. Now a decision must be made as to what needed to be done next. If she contacted the local police, they were bound to have many questions as to why her brother had been chained up like an animal all these years. They would take him away and probably put him in some awful institution. The law may even hang him for what he had done. It was not Chet's fault. He had only reacted to the continuous beatings by stopping the person responsible. Could Agnes turn her poor brother over to the police?

The other solution would be for them to leave town. Looking into her brother's sad face, Agnes knew what course of action she would take. They would run. The first thing she needed to do was to find the key to the padlock chaining her brother to the bed. She had never seen the key, and wasn't aware that he has ever been loose from that terrible chain since he was very small.

Agnes began searching her mother's bedroom, pulling out every drawer and checking the closet. The first discovery she made was finding twenty- three dollars rolled up in a sock. This money would come in handy for their trip. Soon she found three keys inside the wash basin drawer and proceeded back up to the attic to try them all out.

The first key did not fit but the second was a match, and soon the shackle dropped forever from Chet's ankle. At first, he didn't seem to understand that he was at last free, so Agnes took him by the hand and lead him beyond the reach of the chain. Pure excitement filled his face as he realized that he could now move about freely. Bringing him to the small window, Chet realized for the first time that there was a world beyond the confines of his attic prison. He tried to laugh and point as he jumped for joy at seeing new things for the first time. Agnes knew at that point that she had made the right decision.

The next thing she had to do was dispose of her mother's body in a way that nobody would find it. Agnes made a quick supper for herself and Chet as she waited for darkness to set in. Soon it was dark enough to proceed, so she grabbed a shovel from the storeroom and taking her brother by the hand, they started down the stairs. Chet grew very excited in seeing the room below but she tried to calm him as quietness was now required. Lighting an oil lamp, they proceeded outside the back door. Seeing stars for the first time, Chet became very excited, groaning loudly, and reaching out in an attempt to touch them. Agnes understood his excitement and gave him some time to adjust to being outside for the first time in his life. Taking him by the hand, they proceeded back beyond the backyard privy where she sat down the oil lamp and began to dig.

Chet watched his sister trying her best to dig a hole with little success. Several times she handed him the shovel and made digging motions trying to explain how he could do it. Finally Chet understood and began digging. Two hours later, he had produced a deep but narrow hole. It would have to be good enough. Taking his hand in hers, they proceeded back upstairs to get the body. As Agnes reached for it, Chet blocked his sister's effort. This was his play thing. Shaking her head no, Agnes made hand gestures showing them pulling the body downstairs. Finally Chet caught on and together they dragged their mother's body down the stairs, out the back door, behind the privy, and into the deep hole.

Chet wasn't pleased that his play thing had been taken away, but Agnes pointed up at the stars, diverting his attention as she filled in the hole. Straw was then sprinkled over the dirt and with a rake, leaves were pilled upon it. Satisfied, Agnes put away the tools, grabbed the oil lamp, and brought her brother back into the house. That night Chet Cody slept soundly upon his cot without shackles, while Agnes lay in her bed making mental plans for their new life together. Tomorrow their journey would begin.

Chapter 20
Escape

Rising early, Agnes packed two travel bags of needed clothing and a small box of food for their journey. Determined to leave the state of Kentucky once and for all, Agnes located a map of Indiana belonging to her late father, which showed all of the railroad stops. The town of Columbus, Indiana caught her eye and that location would become their future home. They will catch the train north, but how would Chet handle riding a train, she wondered? People were bound to stare at his grotesque features and remember him. Then an idea hit her. She would bandage parts of his face and if anyone should ask, she would say that he was injured and could not speak. Also, many people who have never ridden a train before are quite afraid of their high speeds. Agnes will just have to hold his hand and reassure him everything would be alright. Chet did not fight her as she bandaged below his nose and along his forehead.

Together they left the house for good and proceeded to the railroad depot. Agnes approached the ticket agent with her mother's money asking for passage for two to Columbus. She then mentioned her late father and of him being killed outside of Chicago in the derailment. "I knew your father real well," he said. "He was a good man." The ticket agent then handed her two tickets but refused to accept her money. "Least the railroad can do for you Missy," he told her. Extremely pleased at their good fortune, Agnes took Chet by the hand and walked towards the train. Instead of fear, he was showing joy and great excitement and she had no difficulty at all getting him to board. Once the engine began moving, Chet muttered loud grunts and began waving his arms. People quickly noticed but seeing the bandages, they assumed he was an injured man, perhaps even a wounded soldier and then paid little attention to the pair. Everything was proceeding along just as she hoped.

Arriving in Columbus, Agnes began asking about renting a cheap house and was directed to a man known for that type of housing. She chose one on the edge of town close to the railroad tracks that would enable more privacy for Chet. The house was actually more of a rundown shack, far below the standards she was used to, but at least the rent was cheap. After settling in, Agnes was astonished at how quickly Chet understood the operations of the outhouse. There would be no more waste buckets to be emptied. She cautioned her brother not to go outside during the daylight hours unless he needed to go out back to use the facility. He would be free to go out back after dark to look at the stars. Chet was catching on fast and for the first time in his pitiful life, Agnes thought he was as close to being happy as was possible.

After an unproductive search for a job the next day, Agnes suspected she might have to follow along in her mother's footsteps in search of men. At least it might provide enough to pay the rent and obtain food for her always hungry brother. There was just no way Chet could ever hold down a job. Being only seventeen and still pretty, Agnes decided it offered their only way, so after seeing to her brothers needs, she left after dark in search of the bars and her new life on the streets.

"I ain't seen you before Missy," a past her prime street woman said to Agnes.

"I only arrived in town yesterday. This is my first night. My name is Agnes," she replied.

"Mine's Betty Jo. Then let me give ya some good advice, dearie. Be careful how ya pick-um. Married traveling salesmen are best and ya can blackmail em real easy too," the older woman told her.

"How do I do that?" Agnes ask.

"It's easy as long as ya can read and write. Married traveling salesmen like to brag and boast how important they are. Get em to give his name, what city he's from and his company name. Then first chance ya get, write it down afterwards so ya won't forgets. Then later, send him a letter in care of his town. He'll get it alright. Say ya's gonna send wife-ee a long letter sayin' what he did ta ya, one to his company, and one to da police. Then tell em it's gonna ruin his life unless he sends ya a blank postal money order fer fifty dollars. Tell em ta send it general delivery here and give em a fake name fer da envelope. Tell em it better arrive in under two weeks or da price goes up ta seventy five. If not, a week later wife-ee and da others get contacted. Most of da time, it works since he ain't home ta intercept the mail. Stay safe child."

Thanking Betty Jo for the information, Agnes started searching for wedding bands on men in traveling clothing. This was not the life she expected she would have. As time passed, shortly after Thanksgiving, Agnes, using the tools God had provided for her but never intended in this manner, received her first blackmail money order in care of *Miss Sally Smith, General Delivery, Columbus, Indiana.* She cashed it and put the money back inside an old sock, just like her mother had used for any future rainy days. Soon Agnes was very happy that she had done so. It was late November and a cold, wet night having rained most of the evening. Returning home after her "work" was completed, Agnes saw muddy large footprints all through her rent house and realized that her brother had been out in the world. She only hoped he hadn't gotten into mischief or been seen, as she began cleaning up the mess he had made.

Agnes learned the following evening that Chet's little outing was far more than mischief. He had strangled to death a dark haired street walker by the name of Betty Jo. Someone reported a huge man had attacked the victim from behind and had actually broken her neck. He was then seen running away into the darkness before anyone could obtain a better description. Agnes had no doubt that it was Chet. Something inside his warped brain had snapped again, like a switch was thrown and he had sought out a dark haired woman to strangle. Chet was in his own way re-killing his hateful mother again. At least the police had no suspects, but she sternly told Chet he must stay inside and only venture out back when needed. Poor old Betty Jo.

All remained quiet as Christmas was fast approaching while Agnes continued to ply her trade. Two more money orders arrived the same week as she continued to sock away the money. The holiday festivities were in the air and many young people roamed the streets after dark singing Christmas carols to late evening shoppers. Business was poor in Agnes's trade and finding slim pickings, she returned home early that evening. Snow had been falling all day and over six inches was accumulating on the roads and sidewalks which only contributed to the holiday spirit. Approaching her home, Agnes saw large footprints leading out and returning to the shack and fear gripped her again, knowing that her brother had once again taken a late night stroll.

Earlier that evening, two young ladies were walking home together from attending a dance being held earlier in a friend's home. The owner possessed a new Edison phonograph with several musical cylinder records to which the young people danced to their hearts delight. The evening had been a big success and now it was time to walk the short three blocks to their homes. It was a beautiful night with the air full of falling snow. The near full moon reflected the snow upon the tree branches creating the perfect Christmas images. Suddenly, the blond haired young lady gasped as a huge man appeared almost out of nowhere and began choking her friend and in doing so, raised her about six inches off the ground. Before she could even utter a scream, the blond-haired girl heard her dark-haired friend's neck snap as her lifeless body fell to the ground. She began screaming at the top of her lungs for help as the killer quickly vanished into the night, leaving only fresh footprints in the snow.

Soon neighbors responded to the calls for help and in time, the Columbus police arrived. The poor dark-haired young lady was dead and one officer attempted to interview the near hysterical witness as another policeman began following the footprints the killer left in the snow. Unfortunately, the prints began to mix with other earlier prints and the policeman realized that he had lost the track. The description given, which appeared in the newspaper the following day, was of a huge ugly brute under twenty years of age. Agnes knew full well that "the switch" had once again been flipped on inside her brother's head. It was also time to board a train and get out of Columbus as fast as possible. Pulling out the map that she had used prior, Agnes chose a much larger city in which to hide. In the morning, they would travel to Indianapolis.

Using the old bandage routine again, Agnes wrapped her brother's face once more to hide his features. Thrilled that she had managed to save back her blackmail money, they left once again for the railroad depot. Two city policemen were at the rail yard watching for any large man traveling alone out of the city, but paid little attention as a smiling Agnes and her clearly injured husband walked past them, She then obtained two tickets to Indianapolis. They had successfully evaded the police again.

Using the same procedures she had used before, Agnes found a run-down apartment downtown in Indy in which to live, thinking that the safest place to hide was in a large crowd of people. By now Agnes was having deep concerns about her brother and his once a month killing spree. If he was ever caught during one of his outings, would there be enough evidence to tie him back to her? She was once again becoming afraid of Chet. Although he had never shown any hostility towards her, and feeling what will be will be, Agnes continued on. Soon it was becoming apparent that Indianapolis was a bad choice. There were so many other ladies plying their trade that pickings were slim. Many of the traveling salesmen while in town were staying in the better locations and not venturing down to her location. Many people were speaking about a new gas boom town called Gas City up north of Indianapolis. Agnes felt that if they needed to move, then she would try that new location.

Perhaps a smaller town with growing industry was what she needed.

Agnes could also see a pattern developing in her brother's killings. He could go just about a month without any difficulties, and then suddenly he developed the urge to kill. Knowing that, Agnes felt she had a better understanding of the situation and knew when to start preparing for another fast getaway. By the time March 1895 rolled around, Agnes knew of two prior strangulation's of working women with dark hair that Chet had killed. The police didn't seem too concerned about investigating their deaths as they would a housewife. Agnes was now a full-time working girl herself, so that lack of concern did bother her. Still, nothing had developed to indicate the police were closing in on Chet. All of that changed on the night of March 21st.

The urge to kill had once again overcame Chet, and he set about at night to satisfy it by finding a lone dark-haired working girl. Seeing the large man approaching, the girl managed to get off a loud scream before he was upon her. A lone policeman was walking his beat a short distance away and ran to the scene in time to see the strangler drop the girl's body to the ground. The policeman, pulling his Remington single action revolver, managed to get off four shots at the assailant before the man escaped into the shadows. The officer had no idea if he had hit the man or not but began blowing his police whistle to summon other beat patrolmen. Running up to the body of the woman, the officer saw droplets of blood on the ground. At least he had managed to hit the man before he escaped.

Arriving home that night, Agnes saw drops of blood upon the floor and found her brother crouched down in a corner, afraid, and in pain. Seeing his bloody left shoulder, Agnes inspected the wound to discover a bullet hole. Knowing that something must be done to remove the bullet and knowing that a doctor would report this type of injury, Agnes set about removing it herself. Using a small knife, she began to probe for the bullet. Chet must have sensed she was trying to help him and struggled very little. Eventually the slug was removed, then taking a needle and thread, Agnes sewed up the injury. She marveled at her brother's stamina in tolerating what must have been a horribly painful injury. Afterwards, she put him to bed to rest up. Tomorrow was Sunday and she would be home all day to care for him and also to try and obtain a newspaper to discover what really happened.

After several more days to allow Chet to recoup from his injury, she once again bandaged up her brother's face and they left for the railroad depot. Agnes didn't notice any policemen this time, but they could have been there undercover. Still, there was no difficulty in purchasing two tickets for Gas City and soon they were again on their way to a new life in a new location.

Chapter 21
Wedding Plans for Rachael and Wilbert

Marshal Justin Blake cannot help but laugh every time his deputy changed every subject to his impending wedding. The joyous day was still a month away and Wilbert Vance was as nervous today as if the wedding was tomorrow. Together, he and Rachael had found a cute little house on South C Street and Wilbert had already moved in, under the watchful eye of his landlord. "The lady don't move in until I sees da marriage license," he told the young couple. Both smiled and agreed to his terms without any concern. Rachael was still living at her employer's, Mrs. Wainwright's and would continue working for her at the rebuilt emporium once it was completed.

Rachael wanted to get married in Fort Wayne in the family church that she had grown up in with friends and family members, so the couple planned on traveling up to her parents home two days before the May 12th wedding. Wilbert realized that his co-workers could not attend as the local police force could not just shut down and travel out of town. Justin had offered to allow Rachael's Uncle Zeke Miller to have time off to attend, but he turned him down flat. "Weddins' an funerals... they all da same ta me," he told Justin.

Wilbert wished that he had saved more money so they could have gone into O. Gordon's Furniture Store, on the corner of Second and Main, and bought new furniture instead of the used pieces they were forced to buy elsewhere. Rachael didn't seem to mind it though and Wilbert's only concern now was making her as happy as possible.

~~~~~~~~~~~~~~~~~~~~

The town was abuzz with the news that the Gas City Land Company had signed a deal with the owners of a porcelain ware plant from Crawfordsville to relocate to Gas City. Local contractors were to be hired to construct two brick two-story buildings, two corrugated iron structures, and a warehouse for the plant owners. It was an old established firm with quite a reputation for producing high grade stoneware, fancy wine jugs, and other fine Bristol Glaze novelties. The company now had several thousand dollars worth of orders on their books and expected that many more would quickly follow. Most of their thirty-five workers are highly skilled laborers who would relocate there with their families. The site settled upon for the plant was on the extreme south end of Fourth Street, near the Pan Handle Railroad. The plant owners said they would run a track line up to their facility for the easy loading and unloading of materials by rail. This would place an even greater demand for lodging within the city, and several new construction projects had already begun. Illustrating that fact was that nineteen people were reported to have lived last winter inside one small five room home. However, the local authorities disputed that figure, claiming that there were, in fact, twenty-two living within one dwelling. Additional housing was clearly a must.

~~~~~~~~~~~~~~~~~~~~

The morning started out tragically for Marshal Justin Blake and Deputy Wilbert Vance with the crushing death of a railroad brakeman. The poor worker, a Mr. Charles Gault, was employed by the "Big Four" or the "Pennsy" as it's often called, which actually was the Pennsylvania, Cincinnati, Chicago, & St. Louis Railroad. Witnesses said that the brakeman was attempting to jump between cars during the coupling process and either stumbled on the railing or misjudged his timing. He died instantly. Gas City Journal reporter Alvin Jensen soon arrived and interviewed all of the eager witness for tomorrow's newspaper. Doctor Baxter was summoned, but could do nothing for the deceased who then released the body to the undertaker. Justin obtained all of the information he needed for his report and felt the need for a cup of coffee. "Doc," he replied, "How about joining us for a cup over at the restaurant?" Baxter readily agreed and together the men found a table near the back of the near empty restaurant.

All the men drank their coffee in silence before Baxter began speaking. "Sometimes I wish I had pursued another occupation. There was absolutely nothing I could do for that man other than to pronounce him dead."

Wilbert then asked, "What would you have liked to have been, Doc?"

Baxter thought for a few seconds before responding. "A lawyer. They seem to have it pretty easy. Nobody blames them when their client dies. I guess I shouldn't complain. At least I get to sleep in my own bed most nights. My father was a doctor also who was constantly on horseback for days and nights at a time visiting patients in out-of -the-way locations. The roads were terrible back then, sometimes he even had to tie off his horse and proceed on foot. I've watched him leaving home in pouring rainstorms and bitter cold snowy days. Country folks didn't pay very often, instead paying with eggs or a chicken. What can you do with a chicken when you're on horseback ten miles from home? Back then, malaria was a big killer, spread by mosquitoes with all of the standing water. Once people learned to drain it off, folks started becoming healthier. Pay no attention to me, gentlemen, I'm just being a sentimental old fool this morning."

Justin then replied, "You're a precious gift to our community, my friend, and don't ever forget it."

Wishing to change the subject, Baxter said, "That was a big fire in Jonesboro last night with the Presbyterian church and the parsonage completely destroyed."

"Yes," Wilbert replied. "I hope the late Adam Lake doesn't have any brothers in the arson business." Finishing up their coffee, the men went about their daily work.

A telegram arrived at the Marshal's office that afternoon advising all surrounding cities to be on the lookout for a John Croons. He was to be hung for the crime of murder in Muncie next week but had managed to kill a guard and escape. Description: five foot-five, bright red hair, cold black eyes, and a deep scar upon his right cheek. Apprehend with caution. Justin posted the telegram on the bulletin board for his other officers to review.

That evening, Justin escorted his girlfriend, Virginia Cole, to Lovett's Opera House to enjoy a performance by the Saxon Sisters. He had learned the hard way that if he didn't provide time for the lovely Miss Virginia, some other man surely would. As they stood in line waiting to enter, Virginia once again noticed her supervisor, the widower and Vice President of the First National Bank, James Howell, arm in arm with her boss's sister, Jane Draper. The scene made her very happy as the poor man deserved some happiness these days.

Justin Blake however, was not paying attention to anyone except the man who had walked beside the crowd of people waiting in line for the show to open. He was about five foot-five in height, and had bright red hair with a deep scar on his right cheek. *John Croons,* Justin thought, *And here I am out of uniform with no weapon.* "Virginia, listen carefully. I need you to go find one, or both, of my deputies and tell them that I am following an escaped killer and I need their help. Will you do that for me?" Not waiting for an answer, Justin began trailing his target west down the concrete sidewalk.

Virginia ran across the street the short distance to the fire barn, entered it, but found both deputies gone. Running back to where she had started, her eyes set upon her supervisor, James Howell. The line of people was beginning to move forward as she ran up to him loudly pleading, "Mr. Howell, I need you to come quick. Justin is in trouble and needs assistance."

Howell had a strange look upon his face. "But...I..."

"Please come! He's after some escaped killer and I can't find any of his deputies!"

Nodding affirmative, Howell followed Virginia as she took off running west down the sidewalk. "I don't see Justin anywhere!" she exclaimed in a very stressed voice.

"I see him! There, across the street. He just went in Townsend's Saloon," Howell shouted. "I'll go in, so you need to go see if you can find a deputy," he told her. With great reluctance Virginia continued her search. James

Howell crossed over the street and began approaching the door to the saloon.

Seeing that his target had cross the street and enter Townsend's Saloon, Justin trailed behind and entered. Since he was not dressed in a uniform, Croons should not be alarmed by other people entering behind him. Stepping inside, Justin took a few seconds to allow his eyes to become adjusted to the lighting. There was Croons walking back from the bar with a beer in his hands towards an empty table set against the side wall. Knowing that George Townsend always kept a loaded double barrel shotgun behind the bar, Justin made a slow walk towards the edge of the bar. Mr. Townsend was busy filling orders and so far nobody recognized the marshal out of uniform. Justin squatted down and seeing the weapon leaning against the back wall, picked it up and opened it to make sure it was in fact loaded. His motion caught the eye of George Townsend, "Say...what ya think your a doin'?" Justin looked up directly into his eyes then held a finger up to his lips. Townsend now recognized Justin and began wondering if he was going to shoot up his saloon.

It was now or never. Standing up quickly, Justin leveled his shotgun directly at his target. "Hand up Croons, you're under arrest."

Justin was shocked at the agility of the man as he leaped away knocking over the small table. Croons grabbed a startled drummer salesman who was walking nearby, to use as a shield while he began pulling out a revolver from his belt. "Drop your weapon copper," he shouted "Or I blow this guy's brains all over creation."

Justin realized he couldn't shoot now and wanted to kick himself for getting into this situation. Before he could blink though, a man who had just entered the saloon leaped upon the back of Croons which allowed the frightened hostage the chance to escape. Justin ran up to the struggling men and struck Croons in the back of the head with the butt end of the shotgun. The struggle ended. Helping his benefactor up on his feet, Justin was surprised to see it was James Howell. "Virginia came and got me, saying you were in trouble and needed help. I hope I did the right thing."

Justin was mighty grateful and told him so. Just then, Zeke rushed in to find Justin standing over a man on the floor. "Virginia said you was a needin' help." Zeke cuffed the prisoner's hands while Justin took the man's gun. Together they escorted the prisoner outside. Everyone in the saloon started cheering and back-slapping James Howell for his act of pure bravery. Soon the crowd had pushed Howell up to the bar and someone yelled "Drinks on the house." James Howell missed the performance of the Saxon Sisters that night but celebrated a night that he was not soon to forget.

Outside the saloon, Virginia was overjoyed to see that Justin was safe and, upon hearing that James Howell was a hero, finally allowed her fears to calm down. "I'm sorry you missed out on the performance tonight," he told her as the men walked the prisoner over to his awaiting cell. All Virginia could do was hug his neck and plant a passionate kiss on his lips.

"We make a great team, Justin Blake, and the sooner you realize it, the better off you'll be," she whispered to him. Zeke pretended not to see or hear anything as he never approved of mushy she-males anyway.

The next morning, Zeke Miller and Michael Davidson got off duty and proceeded home. Michael entered his home to smell bacon frying in a pan. "Something sure smells good," as he kissed his wife Doris. "I missed out on the excitement last evening when Justin and Zeke hauled in a wanted criminal."

He and Doris had been married seven years but still had no children. "Where were you then?" she asked.

"Breaking up a fight over at one of the low end saloons."

Doris poured him a cup of coffee as he sat down at the kitchen table. "I still can't believe you like being a deputy marshal. Don't you miss being a councilman?"

"No, not really. Just too political. Huffman's doing a good job as mayor, but I wouldn't want him to know I said that," as he chuckled.

"I'll have your breakfast ready in a jiffy, honey. I bet you are tired, you sure look it. I'll be going shopping after you go to bed. Is there anything you want me to pick up? she asked.

"No, but Wilbert's soon-to-be-bride is working at the old emporium getting ready for their fire sale. Maybe you should drop by and introduce yourself to her."

"I'll do that. How do you want your eggs cooked?"

Soon, breakfast was over and Michael settled in for six hours of sleep while Doris left for the emporium.

~~~~~~~~~~~~~~~~~~~~~

The Journal's headlines boasted: **Bank Vice President Captures Escaped Killer.** Due to "sickness", James Howell did not come to work today because of over-celebration the night before inside Townsend's Saloon.

After receiving an early morning telegram from Marshal Justin Blake that escaped killer John Croons has been captured alive in Gas City, two large Muncie police officers were dispatched to obtain and return their prisoner for his appointed date with the hangman. They were expected to arrive on the afternoon train. Justin had already made plans to have lunch with Virginia so he walked over to the barber shop for a shave and a haircut. Outside sat an object well recognized within the community... a bicycle.

Barber Matthew Brooks only had one customer in the chair, so Justin picked up the newspaper to read as he waited his turn. The customer was Postmaster Harris, who was often seen riding his bicycle to and from the railroad depot picking up or sending out mail. "Yep, the Postmaster general finally had to issue an order tellin' local businessmen that hereafter all mail must be taken to the post office first. Them that worked close to the railroad were a droppin' off their mail right at the mail car which caused a lot of extra work for the mail clerks," he boasted to the barber.

The barber then asked, "Do you think the day will ever come when mail is delivered right to your home?"

Harris replied he didn't think so unless they hired a pack of boys to do the deliverin.' "Hey Marshal, I was down at the Pan Handle Depot this morning and saw three boys smash up their buggy. Claimed the horses got startled. Yea, I didn't believe it either. It sure spilled them onto the ground but they weren't hurt none."

Justin replied, "Boys will always blame a startled horse rather than admitting they were just racing hard down the street."

Matthew Brooks joined in the conversation, "I had a customer come in from Marion this morning chuckling about a story going around their town. Seems that some-body sent the Huntington Democrat Newspaper a tele-gram saying that one half of Marion had been destroyed by fire from a natural gas explosion in a dry goods store. I guess they printed the story without checking it out and now it's a big joke on them."

Postmaster Harris thought it funny, thanked the barber, and was then seen peddling away. "That was good work on capturing that killer yesterday evening," Brooks told him.

Justin replied, "He would have gotten away if it wasn't for the quick actions of the banker. I have a din-ner date today so try to cut my hair evenly this time," he joked. Despite the teasing, Matthew Brooks always gave his customers a good quality haircut.

~~~~~~~~~~~~~~~~~~

Doris Davidson entered the still-damaged emporium and saw a young woman that she took to be Rachael Marley. "Hello, are you Rachael? I'm Doris Davidson, the wife of the other deputy. I'm happy to at last get to meet you."

Rachael was very pleased to make her acquaintance and began telling Doris about their upcoming wedding.

"Once you return and settle in, please drop over sometime for tea and girl talk." Rachael agreed and said that she was looking forward to it. Making her purchase, Doris returned to her shopping.

~~~~~~~~~~~~~~~~~~

As Justin and Virginia sat at the dinner table having their lunch, she asked "What should we get Rachael and Wilbert for a wedding present?" Justin had to smile at the 'What should WE' get part of her statement. Reaching over to caress her hand, Justin told her that he very much liked the sound of her statement. "I hope you will give up all those other men in your life and just concentrate on seeing only me."

Virginia smiled. "In case you haven't noticed, Marshal Blake, I already have."

Feeling that it was finally time to share his true emotions with her, Justin replied, "I love you Virginia Cole."

The sweetest smile appeared on her face as she replied, "I know and I'm very glad. I cannot imagine life without you, darling." Justin now realized that his life may have changed forever.

~~~~~~~~~~~~~~~~~~~~

Across town near the railroad tracks, a groggy Agnes Cody awoke from her night's escapades. She was very happy to have chosen Gas City as it offered so many saloons and traveling salesmen coming and going. She only hoped that her brother Chet would behave himself and stay put. His wound was healing nicely but other than him setting out back at night to watch the stars, he hadn't given any indication of resuming his strangling spree. Maybe being shot had finally made a deeper impact upon his mind and he would no longer feel the desire to kill. Only time would tell if that became a reality or not.

Chapter 22
Honeymoon on Silver Lake

Ο ne evening later in the week, Rachael was playing a game of checkers at the home of Constance Wainwright when Jane Draper came running into the room and dropped down upon the sofa, totally out of breath. "My Heavens," Constance exclaimed to her sister, "What's wrong?"

An excited Jane Draper said, "I almost don't know where to begin. I was having a quiet evening with James tonight when he suddenly asked me to marry him!"

Both ladies jumped to their feet in order to hug the new arrival. "So what did you say?" Constance begged to know.

"I told him maybe."

A look of confusion swept over her sister's face. "Maybe... you told him maybe? Why would you say something like that?"

"I don't know. He just caught me totally by surprise. I'm not a spring chicken anymore and I had all but given up on the idea of ever being asked for my hand in marriage. I wouldn't want James to think of me as a replacement for his deceased wife."

"Jane, that's silly. The man loves you and even as important... he likes you. He wants to spend his remaining years with you. If he was only after a replacement, well, there are many twenty or thirty-year-old's that would latch onto a man of his position and wealth."

Rachael agreed and in brief time, Jane had made up her mind. "I know it's late, but I'm going over there now to his home and tell him YES! I wouldn't want him changing his mind come morning!" Each of the ladies replied that he wouldn't do that and wished her nothing but the best as she departed.

Constance remarked, "I'm so happy for my little sister. Maybe God had a plan for her after all." With all the talk of weddings, it only reminded Rachael that her big day was only a short time away.

James Howell did not change his mind and by weekend, a small group of friends stood by as 'Squire Williamson married the couple inside his office. "It is now my pleasure to introduce to you Mr. and Mrs. James Howell," he announced to all those present. Constance cried, Rachael cried, while the men present wondered why women cry at weddings. The happy couple departed by train for a week's holiday up in Michigan.

~~~~~~~~~~~~~~~~~~~~~

The early days of May passed by quickly and soon it was time for Rachael and Wilbert to board their train for Fort Wayne. "I just know my parents are going to love you sweetheart," she told Wilbert. Almost all of their friends were on hand at the depot to see the young couple off. "Take all the time you need," Justin had told Wilbert. "A fellow only gets married once... or twice," he said with a big grin.

"Once will be enough for me," he replied, with an even bigger grin.

Rachael's parents, Cynthia and Everett Marley, met the train at the depot to welcome their daughter and soon to be son-in-law. They seemed like real nice, down to earth people and Wilbert's fears that he would not be accepted quickly evaporated. Arriving at her home, Wilbert couldn't take his eyes off of Rachael as she seemed to want to do and say everything all at once. The surprise of the evening was given to Wilbert. It was a confirmed registration for a fishing cottage west of Angola where

Mr. and Mrs. Wilbert Vance now had lodging on Silver Lake for five days. It was a small fishing lake, quiet, and peaceful, just the place for a honeymoon. Wilbert and Rachael didn't know what to say other than, "You're too kind." Wilbert felt like he was now a welcomed member of their family.

"Nonsense!" her father said, "You'll also have a flat bottom row boat for fishing. I gather you do fish, Wilbert?"

"Well sir, I used to fish for catfish in the river when I was a kid, but I don't own any fishing tackle now."

"Not a problem, take my Pflueger rod and reel with you and my small tackle box. Just return it when you folks pass back this way once your honeymoon is over. I'm told the lake is known for its Large Mouth Bass and I'm looking forward to hearing a big fish story from you when you return."

Finding a few private moments alone, Rachael casually replied, "You still have time to change your mind buddy, because if you don't, you're mine forever." His kiss told her just what she wanted to hear.

Their wedding day started out with a light morning rain, but by mid-morning, the showers were gone and the sun began to shine through the fading clouds. There was a nice size crowd assembled inside the small

Methodist church as the bride-to-be entered on the arm of her father. Rachael looked so lovely in her simple but elegant white dress and veil. The maid-of-honor was her best friend from school, Carolina. Serving as Wilbert's best man was Carolina's husband, Walter, who presented the couple to the clergyman. Standing behind the couple were Rachael's parents who fought back tears before the ceremony even began. With the final "I do's," Rachel Marley became Mrs. Wilbert Vance. A pleasant dinner was prepared for the happy couple and their guests as congratulations were warmly expressed. Soon, however, it was time for the newlyweds to be taken to the railroad depot for their trip northward. Many tears of joy were shed along the way.

It was a short train ride north to Angola and when they arrived, there was a for-hire carriage waiting to take them to Huggens Eastshore Resort on Silver Lake. "I take people there all the time and pick 'um up too. Just tell me what day and time and I'll be there ta bring you folks back to the depot," the old driver said. Within thirty minutes, they had arrived at their destination. Ruby and Earl Huggens welcomed the newlyweds and gave them the key to cottage number two. "If you folks need anything, we're right here in the larger cottage." Later that night, Rachael and Wilbert walked down to the lake front. "It's beautiful" she told him. "Listen, I can even hear the bullfrogs croaking. Oh Wilbert, I love you so much." He pulled her close as he kissed her passionately under the glow of a full moon reflecting off the calm water.

The next afternoon, Rachael and Wilbert decided to take a boat ride. Walking down to a pier, he found a white flat bottom wooden row boat with a number two on it. Rachael climbed aboard and took the rear seat as Wilbert untied the ropes holding it to the pier and pushed it away, as he hopping in just in time. *Can't fall in the lake and embarrass myself in front of my new wife,* he thought. Placing the oars inside the oarlocks, Wilbert began rowing out into the calm lake. He hadn't rowed a boat since childhood, but it all came back to him pretty quickly. Rowing slowly forward, Rachael was able to look deep into the clear water seeing various fish and submerged lake weeds. Over to their left was a long line of reeds and cattails as Wilbert steered over towards them. "Look, there's some kind of open area within the reeds and lily pads," she mentioned. "Let's go inside, it's probably shallow and maybe we can see a big fish."

"Already married for one day and now you're the captain of the boat," he teased her. As they entered, Wilbert was intrigued with what he saw. "I think I'll try fishing for bass in this cove tomorrow. They're bound to be laying under those thick lily pads." Wilbert reached down to the water's edge and picked a pretty flower lily. It was white with yellow in its center. He handed the flower to his wife who seemed pleased with the offer and placed it in her hair.

"We probably should head back to shore," she told him. "Mrs. Huggens invited me over for a glass of lemonade today and right now that sounds delicious." Wilbert then rowed the boat back to the pier and helped his wife safely onto shore.

"I need to ask about buying some bait," he told her. Walking back towards the cottages, he saw Mr. Huggens inside his garage. "Where can I obtain some bait?"

"Red worms or night crawlers?" Huggens ask.

"Probably night crawlers. I'm going after bass."

"I sell them at ten cents for a box of fifty."

After buying a box of bait, Wilbert set about looking inside his father-in-law's tackle box, and placed a large hook and a round bobber on the line. Tomorrow morning, he was going after the notorious Moby-Bass.

Early the following morning, there was a light foggy haze on the water as Wilbert rowed out towards the cove where the reed and the lily pads were located. He quietly anchored about twenty feet out from where he wanted his bait to drop, just in front of the lily pads. Weaving two night crawlers onto the large fishhook, Wilbert set the bobber's depth at four feet as he wanted the bait to lay neat the mucky bottom. Casting out, he was pleased where the bait landed. Now, all he had to do was sit back and wait for the arrival of Moby-Bass.

~~~~~~~~~~~~~~~~~~~~

It was a quiet morning as Justin Blake sat out on his home's front porch, enjoying the peace and tranquility before going to work. He was wondering how the honeymooners were doing when he noticed a man approaching. It was his friend the Reverend Stokes. "Mind if I join you for a few minutes, Justin?" he asked.

"Please take a seat, glad to see you. Can I get you something to drink?"

"No, I'm fine," Stokes said. "Do you know the widow Mrs. Lockridge from church? She came to see me yesterday about her sixteen year old son, Brad. He has always been a good son, but lately he's taken up with a group of older boys, hanging out in pool halls, and staying out late at night. She's worried that he's going to start getting into bad trouble. I guess some of the boys dared him to steal a coat off the outside sidewalk rack of one of the used clothing stores. He did it but the owner saw the theft and chased him down and retrieved the coat. The store owner knows his mother very well so he didn't press charges. I fear the rate he's going though, you'll soon have him in your jail. I was wondering if you had any ideas on how this boy can be turned around and saved from a life of crime before it is too late?"

Justin sat there for a while thinking before he answered. "I do have an idea, but I need to speak with someone else first. Thanks for bringing this to my attention. I'll see what we can do."

Shaking hands, Reverend Stokes excused himself and left for home while Justin starting making plans to prevent another good boy from going bad.

~~~~~~~~~~~~~~~~~~~

The sunshine finally burned off the lingering haze as Wilbert continued to concentrate on his bobber. So far Moby-Bass hasn't shown any interest in his bait, and he was beginning to think there were no fish here at all. Suddenly, his bobber began moving back towards the rear of the lily pads. Wilbert gave the line plenty of slack knowing that a fish doesn't always automatically swallow the bait. Giving the fish plenty of time,

Wilbert tightened the slack and set the hook. The water exploded within the lily pads and he could tell he had a very large fish on his line, maybe even Moby-Bass! Wilbert pulled and cranked for all it was worth, but this fish, this mighty big fish, kept darting back into the lily pads seeking protection from the unknown force.

Slowly, both fisherman and fish were becoming tired with the fisherman finally winning out as the huge fish was brought up near the boat. *What kind of a fish is that?* Wilbert thought, as it was brought near the surface. Not owning a net, he knew he had to quickly slide a finger into the gill of this mammoth fish and hoist it into the boat or take the chance on losing it. With a steely nerve, Wilbert thrust his finger into the fish's gill and hoisted it into the boat. There the fish thrashed about for a couple of minutes before finally lying still. It was dark brown in color with a greenish-tinted belly. At first glance it reminded Wilbert of drawings he had seen of a prehistoric fish as it had a round tail, large scales, and a top fin that moved snake-like. This fish would win no beauty contests. With great excitement, Wilbert began rowing back to shore.

After docking the boat, Wilbert began making a bee-line straight to Rachael to show off his trophy when he heard a voice call out, "What ya gonna do with that thing?" It was Mr. Huggens.

"Any idea what kind of fish this is?" Wilbert asked with great pride in his voice.

Huggens began chuckling, "Nothing but a worthless dogfish, probably seven to eight pounds. Best let me bury it for you. That's one more trash fish removed from the lake." Wilbert was greatly saddened by this news.

"I want to show it to Rachael first. Man, I hoped I really had something here but it was a lot fun catching it anyway. This thing put up one heck of a fight."

Rachael stayed behind the cottage's screen door as Wilbert held up the large fish. "It's so ugly," she told him. He then explained what it was and soon a hole was dug and the fish buried. Wilbert went out again and again the next few mornings but other than a small bass, had no luck in finding Moby-Bass. Soon the honeymoon was over and it was time to pack up and await the carriage to return them to the depot for an overnight at her parents' home, before proceeding back to Gas City, and the return to work for both of them.

~~~~~~~~~~~~~~~~~~~~

"So that's the situation 'squire. Is this something you feel comfortable in doing for the boy's benefit?" Justin asked squire Williamson.

"Yes, I think it is well worth the effort if we can prevent him from going bad. I'll await your signal that you're ready. Will the reverend inform the boy's mother of our plans?"

"Yes, once I brief him. Tonight I'll send one of my deputies out to set things in motion," Justin told him. "Thanks for your help, sir."

That evening, a young Brad Lockridge was shooting a game of pool with his new found friends when Deputy Michael Davidson walked into the poolroom and began scanning the occupants. The pool hall manager became nervous knowing there were underage boys inside his facility, and he was facing a possible fine. Walking over to the manager, Davidson said in a low tone, "Which boy is Brad Lockridge?" The manager, relieved somewhat, was more than happy to point the boy out. Lockridge, with pool stick in hand, was taking aim when Donaldson walked over and snapped a cuff on the boys' right wrist. "Hey, what's the big idea?" Lockridge shouted. Both of his friends saw what had happened and began moving towards the deputy.

"Stay back unless you both want trouble," Davidson cautioned them. Not sure what to do next, both of his friends cautiously stepped back. "Brad Lockridge, you are under arrest," as he placed the other cuff on the boys other wrist. "Let's go," as they left the pool hall.

"What's this all about?" the boy began shouting. "I ain't done nuttin' wrong."

"Attempted theft of a dress coat and shooting a game of pool while under age. Now move it." Davidson remained very firm with the youth and quickly had him behind bars. All additional demands for information were simply ignored as he was forced to settle in for the night. The youth didn't seem so big and bad now that he found himself in jail.

Justin arrived the following morning and totally ignored the questions and demands from young Lockridge. Turning to Davidson Justin asked, "What do we have on him?"

"Theft of a coat, playing pool under age, and we suspect he and his gang might be behind a few house break-ins recently." The youth flatly denied he was involved in the break-ins but in doing so, gave the indication he might know who was.

"I'll have him over at 'Squire Williamson's court at eight a.m. sharp," Justin casually remarked. "Good job, see you tonight." Soon, it was time to march his new prisoner over to the courtroom and Justin handed the 'squire the prisoner's written charges, which he reviewed silently before speaking.

The 'squire addressed the prisoner. "I have a written statement before me from the clothing store owner stating that the prisoner attempted to steal a dress coat from his outside clothing rack. Also, Officer Davidson arrested the underage Lockridge inside a poolroom, another violation of the law. How does the prisoner plead, guilty or not guilty?"

"I didn't intend to steal the coat, Your Honor. My friends just dared me to do it for a lark."

"So young man, are you saying if your friends encouraged you to kill someone, you would do it as a lark?"

"No sir, we just thought it would be fun to take it, but I'm sorry I did."

"So I take that as a guilty plea? I sentence the prisoner to thirty days in jail and a fine of thirty dollars. Is the prisoner prepared to pay his fine today?"

A visibly shaken young man stood before the 'squire, "No sir, neither I nor my widowed mother have that kind of money." He dropped his head and began to sob quietly.

Now it was time for the 'squire to offer his olive branch. "Young man, I would be willing to wave the jail time and the fine if you would agree to and abide by another proposition. I see that you are a high school student and you have another two weeks of school left. If you'll agree to return to school, report afterwards with your schoolbooks to the Marshal's office for a period of thirty days, and work unpaid under his supervision, I will allow you to return to class this morning. What do you say?"

A greatly relieved Brad Lockridge readily agreed and gave his word that he would comply with the 'squire's ruling. He was then released and ran straight to the high school. After a few minutes, 'Squire Williamson left his chair and came around to discuss the matter with Justin Blake. "Well, how did that go?"

"Perfect Your Honor, and thanks again for your assistance. You missed your true calling, sir." You could have been a famous stage actor like Edwin Booth.

Chuckling at the complement, Williamson replied, "With my luck, more like John Wilkes Booth!"

"We'll take it from here and let you know how things are progressing."

Chapter 23
Situations are Developing

Agnes Cody was very happy to receive another money order blackmail payment in care of general delivery to a Miss Amy Jones, her new phony name that she was now using. The fifty dollar money order had come from that fat traveling salesman from Kokomo. He was sure full of himself, she remembered. This was the third money order she'd received since moving to Gas City in early April. Her scheme was certainly paying off handsomely, as none of the men were willing to take a chance on her threats to expose them. *Men are such fools,* she thought.

This time Agnes planned on spending some of the money on herself for some new clothing and make-up. She might even go to Guthrie's second hand store and buy newer clothing for Chet. If so, the clothing needed to be dark in color, just in case he ever resumed his night time outings. It had been the longest period Chet had gone between strangling women, and Agnes hoped that he had finally got it out of his system. His wound had now healed cleanly and her brother no longer favored his injured shoulder. Only time would tell how he'd behave from now on. With cash in her pocket, Agnes then entered the local meat market to purchase tonight's food. Normally they've been living off occasional lower cuts of meat when the money was there to buy them, but today she felt like splurging, so she purchased two large steaks to fry up before going to work. Agnes has long given up on trying to teach Chet how to use a fork and spoon as he insisted on picking up all of his food with his fingers anyway. Tonight, they would eat very well.

~~~~~~~~~~~~~~~~~~~~~~~~~

Pete and Gladys Rollins had been married a little over three years. Pete was the bartender over at the Oasis Bar, a lower-end establishment located near the river and conveniently close to several factories. He works the five to eleven p.m. shift six days a week serving beer and whiskey to thirsty working men. His wife, Gladys was a large woman, plain in her features who did not work outside of their home, which was a small four room dwelling they rent very close to where Pete works.

Neighbors would later say that the couple appeared to get along just fine, as nobody remembered hearing any fighting going on between them. But there was a great secret that Gladys possessed. Gladys frequently went to visit another man for a few hours while her husband was at work. The man was a small-framed German immigrant by the name of Hans Gruber. Hans worked as a day laborer at one of the glass factories and had known Gladys before she had married Pete Rollins. Hans likes his women on the hefty side and never criticized her weight, unlike Pete who complained that his wife was simply eating too much. Weight gain ran in her family and Gladys ate no more than the average woman, but Pete was never convinced of it. She found comfort in the non-complaining arms of Hans and wished things had turned out differently in her life.

Gladys was always careful to return home no later than ten-thirty p.m. so her husband would find her in bed, pretending to be asleep. She knew her husband loved her and that she was running a big risk in doing this to him, but her emotions were dictating her actions and not her head. While Gladys thought that she was hiding everything quite well, she was mistaken as a couple of the neighborhood busy-bodies had already noticed her comings and goings at night. It didn't take long for the women to put two and two together. It was now only a matter of time before her husband would find out the truth they surmised. People who play with fire will eventually get burned by it.

~~~~~~~~~~~~~~~~~~~~~~~~~~

Sixteen year old Brad Lockridge arrived after school outside the Marshal's office not having any idea what the next thirty days will have in store for him. Was he still some kind of prisoner? Stepping inside, he decided to play it calmly and see what happens. "I'm here Marshal, now what?"

"Mr. Lockridge," He was trying to sound formal for the benefit of the situation, "Until school is out, I want you to report here daily and work doing what I and the other deputies direct you to do. We'll send you home before the nine p.m. town curfew. Starting tomorrow, right after school, you are to go home first, eat something, kiss your mother goodbye and then report directly here for assignment. Once school is out, you will report here daily at seven a.m. daily and work until released. Are these instructions clear to you?"

"Yes Marshal Blake, quite clear," he replied.

"Good. Now let's go on patrol. If I or any of my officers enter a saloon or pool hall, you are to remain outside. If you meet any of your friends, you are to avoid all communications with them as you are on my time now, and not your own." Together, Justin and the youth left the fire barn as Brad fell in slightly behind the marshal's pace.

"How are you going to explain to people why I'm with you?" Brad asked.

"I'm not. To do so would only add to your embarrassment and that's not what we in the law enforcement field are all about. We serve to protect the public, not to frighten or bully it. We would lay down our lives to protect the innocent." The youth had never considered it from that angle. His friends have always told him cops were just there to make life miserable for people like them. He would watch and see if the marshal's actions backed up his fancy words.

~~~~~~~~~~~~~~~~~~~~

The afternoon train returned the new Mr. and Mrs. Wilbert Vance to the city. Wilbert hired a man to transport them and their wedding gifts over to their new home. After unloading everything near to the front door, Rachael and Wilbert, with marriage license in hand, proceeded over to their landlord's next-door home and presented it to him. The old man stood there reading over the document carefully before handing it back to Rachael. The moment struck the newlyweds as funny, and they began laughing which prompted the old man, missing his two front teeth, to laugh with them. The old bird wasn't as tough as he let on after all.

As Wilbert unlocked the front door, he ceremonially picked up Rachael and carried her across the threshold as was customary for newlyweds. "Put me down," she teased, as she placed a light peck upon his cheek. The couple were now home. "Please carry the gifts and suit-cases into the bedroom and I'll start unpacking," she told him. After completing his assigned tasks, Wilbert informed her that he was going to the office to let Justin know they were back in town.

A short time later, Rachael heard a light knocking on the front door. It was Constance Wainwright and Jane Howell. "We saw your husband and he said it would be alright if we visited you for a few moments," Jane told her.

"Please, come in ladies," A happy Rachael Vance informed her friends. "I'm happy you stopped by. This isn't as grand as your home, Constance, but we'll be happy here."

Constance replied, "It's a warm and inviting little house. So how was your honeymoon?"

"Wonderful! After the wedding, we had five days in a cottage on a lake near Angola."

Jane replied, "James and I passed through Angola on our wedding trip up into Michigan. I'm glad to see you're back in town."

"Thank you. We are happy to be home," Rachael replied. Turning to Constance, she asked about how the emporium construction was coming along.

"The building is now completed and my new merchandise are beginning to arrive. Jane and I began stocking shelves yesterday. I'm pushing for a grand re-opening on June 1st. When are you coming back to work?"

"I'll be there in the morning," Rachael informed her.

"Well then, we better be on our way and let you get back to work. Goodbye Rachael. Glad to have you back." After her friends had left, Rachael looked about wondering, *Where do I begin?*

~~~~~~~~~~~~~~~~~~~~

Wilbert entered the fire barn and into the office. He saw Justin and a young boy going over some paperwork. "We're back."

Justin grinned then responded, "Well, if it's not our old married man. Deputy Vance, this is Mr. Lockridge. He will be assisting us for a few weeks."

Sensing the formality of Justin's introduction, Wilbert offered his hand, "Happy to meet you Mr. Lockridge. Well Justin, I wanted to let you know I was back and will be at work in the morning. Much happen while I was away?"

Shaking his head 'no', Justin replied, "Another dog was poisoned, a few more drunks wanting to fight and... oh yes, down at the baseball fielded yesterday the Hat Store Team beat the Gas City Nine Team by a score of 13-4."

"Sorry I missed that. Well, see ya in the morning. Nice meeting you, Mr. Lockridge."

After Vance was gone, the youth turned to Justin and said, "Mr. Lockridge makes me sound old. Can't you fellows just call me Brad?"

Justin had been waiting for this question to come up. "Well Mr. Lockridge, first names are generally reserved between friends. Are you implying you wish to become friends?"

Thinking on the question a few seconds, the youth replied, "Sure. Why not... I'm game."

Justin smiled for the first time, hoping that a little progress had just been made. "Then Brad it is. Let's start our afternoon patrol now, shall we?"

~~~~~~~~~~~~~~~~~~~

Across town, Mayor Davis Huffman was getting his ears pinned back by about twenty deeply agitated women. He had been walking towards his office when he found himself surrounded by the ladies demanding that he hear their pleas. Before he knew it, he had basically been *kidnapped* and thrust into one of the ladies' homes, while the group gave him a piece of their mind. They kept reminding him over and over that many stores were selling cigarettes and tobacco products to children as young as nine years old, and that a bell needed to sound for the nine p.m. curfew, which also needs to be enforced. They also informed him that young girls are being enticed in to wicked ways, and that drug stores continue to sell beer on Sundays. One lady went on to say that long lines can be seen forming out the back door of drug stores where beer was being sold by the pint. "I'm told men and boys go behind the prescription counter, buy beer and often drink it there, which we know is against the Nicholson law."

They kept hammering away at Huffman, often shaking their fingers directly in his face until he pledged to look into the matter with Marshal Blake. Finally, the ladies became convinced that they had made their point and Mayor Huffman was allowed to continue on his journey. He was then told that they expected to see positive results, or he would hear from them again. *Now I know why women were not given the vote,* he thought.

The ladies were not through yet as they then contacted Alvin Jensen and bent his ear for over an hour. A newspaper story was then published outlining their complaints and demanding that the Nicholson Law be strictly enforced. Pint shop owners and tobacco stores suddenly felt pressure to enforce the law, and did so for a period of time until things began to quiet down. Then their old selling habits returned to normal.

~~~~~~~~~~~~~~~~~~~~

The warm days continued to drift away and soon school was finally over. Young Brad Lockridge switched over to the evening shift with Zeke Miller and Michael Davidson. Everyone was beginning to notice that Brad was starting to become more of a team player, rather than a lone individual. He often used the word *we* when discussing patrols or office procedures. Over half of his thirty day sentence was now over, and secretly Brad was having the time of his life. Walking with the deputies made him feel a part of something important, and time after time, he witnessed the officers performing their duties for the public good. His opinion of law enforcement officers had now turned one hundred and eighty degrees and he was beginning to see the good that they provide to the local community.

So far the two older boys who had got Brad into the situation had remained at a distance. That changed dramatically when Brad and Zeke were out on an evening patrol. Zeke instructed Brad to remain outside while he entered a saloon on South H and Third to speak with the bartender. Brad's two older friends were on their way over to the pool hall and, seeing Brad all alone, they dashed up to speak with him. "Gettin' your fill of the coppers yet?" the tallest one asked. "Ditch him and come along with us. We're gonna shoot a few games of pool and discuss a break-in we got planned."

Brad told them no. "I don't want any more trouble with the law, so please go without me from now on."

The other one began laughing, "Sounds like the kid has changed sides. What's ya afraid of anyway, that old man?" Flipping out a knife, he then said, "Watch me as I gut the old fool." Just then Zeke came outside and saw the two troublemakers between him and Brad.

"Here now...what ya fellers a doin'?" Zeke said as he approached the group. The one with the knife started to make a lunge at an unsuspecting Zeke Miller. In a split second, Brad knew what to do. He grabbed the moving arm and forced it upwards as he shouted, "knife!" Thanks to Brad's quick actions, the blade missed Zeke altogether and hung up in the air as Brad struggled to keep the blade away. Zeke pulled out his truncheon, commonly known as a Billy Club, and hit the attempted killer on the head who then dropped like a rock onto the ground. The other youth stood there wide eyed as Zeke quickly cuffed his wrist. "Thanks Brad, ya saved me life," Zeke said. Together they stood up the shaken assailant and cuffed him to his friend. "All right tough guy, get a movin'," as Zeke pushed both thugs towards the awaiting jail cell.

Soon Deputy Davidson was located and he interviewed Brad as he began assembling the official report. The thug who had the knife sat upon the cot rubbing the back of his head, but said nothing as the older and taller one began, of all things, to cry out in fear. It brought home the fact to Brad that just acting tough doesn't make a man tough. He also began to picture himself inside that cell with them. *If the 'squire hadn't given me the sentence he did, I would have followed in their path straight to jail,* he thought. He had been given a second chance in life, and any final doubts that Brad Lockridge had finally disappeared that night. He would become a model citizen from now on. Upon hearing of Brad Lockridge's actions, 'Squire Williamson instantly commuted the rest of his sentence. Brad then asked the 'squire if he could just continue out the rest of his sentence anyway, as he had discovered that he really enjoyed police work after all.

~~~~~~~~~~~~~~~~~~~~~~~

During the lull times at the Oasis Saloon, bartender Pete Rollins continued to think about his wife's odd behavior. He searched his mind over and over trying to figure out exactly what he had done that caused her to pull away from him. Maybe it was time for him to surprise her with flowers or maybe even a box of candy. Expensive for sure, but maybe it might warm her heart. It was worth a try. With the eleven p.m. law requiring the closing of Gas City saloons, Rollins always gave a "last call" about five minutes before the saloon shuts down. Then it was a struggle to get some of the men to leave. But once the beer tap was turned off, they finally gave up and go home. Then Rollins emptied the cash register of today's take, recorded the amount in a ledger book and then locks the money in the owner's safe. While this was going on, the swamper cleaned and mopped the floor, emptied the trash and smoking materials, and finally locked up once Rollins was gone. That generally had Pete Rollins home before midnight.

Rollins had begun to suspect his wife was pretending to be asleep as he crawled into bed with her. He often reached out to touch her shoulder, hoping to at least cuddle with her, but the icy reply of being ignored continued. *Maybe tonight will be different, he thought. If not, tomorrow we must talk this out even if she is unwilling to do so.*

After closing up, Rollins walked the short distance home in total darkness and entered his home. All was quiet, as normal as he removed his heavy work boots and clothing and approached his bed. This time, he sensed something was different. The bed was still made. *What's going on?* Reaching out for the oil lamp setting on the kitchen table, Rollins lit it and walked through his small house. Gladys Rollins was not there. *Where could she have gone at this late of hour?* Then worry overcame him, maybe she had packed up her clothing and left him for good? Rollins reached under the bed and his fingers toughed the small travel bag they owned. He then looked in her drawers and saw that her clothing remained. *She must be visiting with a sick friend,* he thought. *I wonder why she didn't leave me a note?* Rollins sat down in a kitchen chair and awaited the return of his wife. In time fatigue finally overtook him, as he laid his head upon the table and went to sleep.

It was the loud pounding on his front door that awakened Pete Rollins from his deep slumber. Standing there was a man that he did not know telling him to come quick as his wife had been found down by the river. Rollins quickly redressed into last night's work clothing and ran as fast as he could down towards the crowd of people he saw beginning to form. A farmer on horseback coming into town early to visit a friend had crossed over the wooden bridge over the Mississinewa River. As was his normal custom, he glanced back down at the river to judge its depth, when his eyes noticed something peculiar. There was a body laying along the river's edge. The body of a woman. The farmer then raced his horse down the brick streets to the fire barn to notify the marshal's office. Zeke had volunteered to fetch Justin and the Doc while Michael went directly to the scene.

As Pete Rollins approached, he hoped that his wife was only slightly injured. Perhaps she slipped on the wet dew grass last evening as she was returning from her quest. It was the looks on the faces in the crowd that told Pete that it was much more serious. Laying down the slope near the water's edge, was the body of his wife. "Gladys!" he cried out as his emotions took over and he sunk to his knees in trembling anguish. Deputy Davidson struggled to keep the crowd of people back as Marshal Blake and Doc Baxter finally arrived. It was very apparent the woman was dead, as her head was bent at a very odd angle.

"Think she fell and hit her hear on a rock or something, Doc?" Justin inquired of his friend. Looking back along the pathway where the body now lay, Justin saw that no large rocks were present.

"I need to get the body back to my office to make a full examination. I'll get back with you later today," Doc replied. "You men, who among you has a wagon we can haul the body back in?"

A local man stepped forward, "Might as well put her in mine, I guess, Doc." Soon four men gently picked the woman's body up for transport. "I'll ride back with you," Doc told the man with the wagon.

Justin approached the stricken man, "I'm sorry to bother you with questions, sir, but I need some answers. What is your full name and your connection with the deceased?"

Trying his best to regain his self control, he replied, "My name is Pete Rollins. She is my wife, Gladys. I work as a bartender at the Oasis Saloon during the evening shift. When I got home last night, Gladys wasn't there and the bed was not slept in. I figured she was visiting with a sick friend or something so I waited up for her return."

Justin then asked, "Mr. Rollins, what time did you return home last evening, and was it customary that your wife was not at home when you arrived?"

"No Marshal, she's always home in bed when I get there just before midnight. I have to count the money and lock it up before I can quit work. Who did this to her marshal, and why?" He then began to break down in tears. Justin realized that he needed to give the man a little time before resuming his line of questioning, so he went up on the hill to question the crowd of people. "Anyone here know anything that might help in our investigation?"

Several men and a few women began looking at each other, and Justin picked up on their behavior pretty quickly. "So, what is it?" he asked them directly.

Finally one of the women spoke up, "I don't want you to think I'm telling tales or anything Marshal, but there's more to this than you know. Several of us live very close to the Rollins home and it's pretty common knowledge that Mrs. Rollins goes to visit a man after her husband leaves for work."

This got Justin's attention pretty quickly. "So how do you know that and what's the man's name?"

Feeling slightly empowered by now, the lady continued, "She passes by our homes going there in the early evening and returns about ten-thirty p.m. I don't know the man's name as we just call him 'the German'."

"Anyone here know the name of this German?" Justin asked.

Someone in the back of the crowd shouted out, "Gruber. He works at the Sheldon-Foster Glass Factory. I don't know where he lives though." Justin completed taking his notes, but hated that the poor grieving husband was hearing all of this.

Suddenly Rollins charged up the hill and into the crowd. "What you just said can't be true! My wife wouldn't do such a thing," he shouted. Nobody in the crowd said anything, and with their heads down, they began to leave. Pete Rollins just stood there in shock with the realization that their silence answered many questions that had haunted his mind for quite some time. Justin approached Rollins now that the crowd was gone and asked the big question: "Did you kill your wife. Mr. Rollins?"

Rollins's face reflected shock at this question. "No sir, I did not. I never knew she was seeing a German behind my back. I swear this to you on my own mother's grave." Justin told him not to leave town as he may have more questions later on. It was now time to interview the German by the name of Gruber at the Sheldon-Foster Plant.

Chapter 24
The Interview

Justin caught a ride back to the fire barn in order to get a cup of coffee and plan out his interview with the German, Hans Gruber. "There you are," Wilbert said as Justin entered the office. "Where was everybody this morning?"

Justin filled him in on the murder of Gladys Rollins and the reports that the married woman also had a German boyfriend. "Doc says it will be a while before he has any results so let's go over what questions we need to put to this Hans Gruber when we visit the Sheldon-Foster Glass Factory," Justin said.

"If he killed her, he may very well have skipped town. Why hang around only to be arrested and then hang?" This was not meant to be funny, but the jest of it reminded both men of the seriousness of their upcoming investigation.

"You're right. We had better get over there and find out. Let's take the patrol wagon in case we feel we have enough grounds to arrest him."

The Sheldon-Foster Glass Factory was a relatively new facility in town. It was built close to the river and had access to a rail spur for the easier shipping of its products. A lone guard shack stood outside its fence with an old-timer sitting on a wooden stool. The old man, who had to be pushing seventy-five, just waved them through without bothering to see who they were. "Excuse me," Justin said to him. "I'm Marshal Blake and this is Deputy Vance. We understand that you have an employee working here by the name of Hans Gruber. We need to speak with him urgently on official police business."

The old-timer seemed a bit excited that something was changing his dull, normal routine. "Marshal, ya say? Well... I guess I can go ask about 'em and bring 'em out here. That is unless ya want ta go find 'em fer yourselves?" Justin requested the man be brought out here so the entire factory would not be aware of the interview. With that, the old-timer disappeared inside. About ten minutes had passed before the old-timer and another man approached the guard shack. Wiping his dirty hands onto a cloth he carried in his back pocket, Gruber spoke in a heavy German accent, "Ja, I am Hans Gruber. Why are da police askin' bout me. I am no thief," he said in a defiant manner.

Justin went right to the point, "Do you know a Mrs. Gladys Rollins?" The question clearly stunned the German and he delayed in answering until pressed again.

"Ja, I know Gladys. Why does da police ask? Did she make da complaint against me?"

It was decided ahead of time that both men would take turns questioning the German if he was still here, thinking that it might help break him down quicker and bring forth a confession. Wilbert then asked, "Were you with her last night?" This clearly upset the German now that the police knew about their affair. Hans began to worry deep inside. This was not sounding good.

"Ja, we was together at my house. Does her husband find out?"

Justin was pleased he was not attempting to lie and continued to ask, "What time did she leave your house?"

No longer acting cocky, the German continued, "'Bout same time as always, ten-fifteen ta ten-thirty p.m. She gots ta get home before her husband gets off work. Why are da police askin' des questions of Hans?"

Wilbert now had the opportunity to bring the main question home by saying, "Her body was discovered early this morning by the river. Why did you kill her?"

Hans Gruber's face turned pure white as the realization of the question hit him like a stone wall. "My Gladys... dead? I didn't kill her. I never killed nobody. Who says I killed my Gladys? Show him ta me. He lies!"

The old-timer inside the guard shack was straining to hear every word of this and couldn't wait to tell everyone inside the factory once the lawmen were gone. This certainly was not a normal boring day, no sir-ee!

Justin then followed up, "Adultery is against the law, Gruber, and we can run you in if we want, but I want to hear your confession. Did you have a fight with her? So is that why you followed her and killed her on her way home last night?"

"Nicht, nicht, we had no fight! I killed nobody! Nicht!" Gruber was angry but scared at the same time.

"We'll be back tomorrow morning to speak with you again. Don't attempt to run, Gruber, you can't escape the law. Think about what we have asked you. It may go easier on you if you just confess to the crime and be done with it," Justin added.

"I no run. I killed nobody. I work and go home, that all I do," Gruber pleaded.

"We'll be seeing you soon Gruber," Wilbert informed him as the pair left the glass factory property. By noon, the old-timer's story about the lawman's interview with Gruber was spread all over the factory.

As they began returning to their office, Wilbert asked Justin why they didn't arrest him on the charge of adultery. Justin chuckled, "His married lover is dead so I don't know if we can hold him on that charge now or not. So what do you think? Did he kill her?"

Based on what you have told me, Wilbert said, "I'm thinking her husband found out she was seeing another man, followed her after leaving her lover's house, and killed her in a fit of jealousy and rage." Justin said that he was thinking along the same line but wanted to get Doc's medical report before proceeding further.

~~~~~~~~~~~~~~~~~~~~~~~~

It was after lunch before Doctor Baxter arrived in the fire barn's office. "Nasty business," Doc replied. "The victim's neck was broken and her throat was covered in huge bruises that extended all around her neck clear to the back. She was strangled to death and the killer had to have powerful large hands in order to break the neck of a woman her size."

Justin looked over at Wilbert before replying, "That just ruled out her boyfriend. He's just a little fellow. While he may have been able to strangle the woman, I seriously doubt he could have broken her neck. His hands were not all that large either but her husband is a large enough man to do it, and he certainly had the motive. We're going to pay Pete a little visit tomorrow morning. Thanks for the report, Doc. I want to go see 'Squire Williamson about the adultery charge now." After conferring with the 'squire, it was determined that it was not worth perusing charges now that the other party was dead. 'Hearsay evidence,' the 'squire had told him. Hans Gruber would get off lucky as far as the law is concerned.

~~~~~~~~~~~~~~~~~~~~~~

After making arrangements for his wife's burial the following day, Pete Rollins went home and just sat at his kitchen table staring at the wall until it was time to go to work. His mind was clearly elsewhere and he wondered if he could concentrate well enough to still attend bar tonight. There was an extra large crowd of drinking men inside the Oasis Bar that evening, whether out of loyalty to Pete or for their own morbid curiosity. That would be left for others to decide. Pete never said a word to anyone as many offered their condolences for the loss of his wife. He simply filled their glasses and took the customers' money.

With the story about the German's interview by the police now all over town, Pete couldn't help but hear some of his drunken customers talking about it in too-loud-of- voices. It was later stated that during the entire time Pete Rollins worked at the Oasis Saloon, that not one person ever saw him take a drink while on duty. That changed about nine p.m. that evening when cus-tomers noticed Pete reaching for a bottle of whiskey and a glass. He then left from behind the bar and sat himself down at a small table in the back of the room. Pete sat facing the wall so as not to see anyone, and began to drink very heavily. His customers, not wanting to bother the poor man as he drank away his sorrows, began to use the honor system, helping themselves to their own drinks and laying coins on the bar counter top. This went on until about ten forty-five p.m. when all of a sudden, Pete Rollins stood up and walked out of the Oasis Bar. Without anyone to announce the eleven p.m. curfew, drinking continued unabated until it was forcibly shut down later that night by the deputies.

Rollins staggered towards his home at a fast pace, entered it and reached for his Colt 45 pistol he kept inside a small drawer. He checked it to ensure it was fully loaded, then tucked it into his belt and walked out, leaving the door to the home standing wide open. Rollins had learned the full identity of the German and where he lived due to the loud boasting of his inebriated customers. He walked at a fast pace to that location and paused briefly outside the doorway. The small house was much like his own, built small and cheap for the benefit of the working man. He could see that no light was protruding from the windows and Rollins assumed the German was in bed sound asleep. Raising up his large right leg, Rollins kicked in the door. It literally exploded, almost coming off its hinges as the big man entered and moved straight into the bedroom.

Enough moonlight was coming through the bedroom window where Rollins could see a startled figure setting up in bed. "Who is dat? What does you want?" the German shouted. "Damn you rascal," Rollins shouted as he pulled his weapon and pointed it at the man in bed. "You dishonored and killed my Gladys and I'm gonna kill you." The first shot struck Gruber in the forehead and killed him instantly, as he lifeless body fell back downwards. Rollins advanced closer and pumped three more bullets into the man's chest. He then paused to savor the moment. It was done. The German would destroy no more marriages. Rollins could hear several dogs in the neighborhood starting to bark and knew many people would soon arrive to investigate the shots. It was time. Rollins put the barrel to his temple and pulled the trigger.

Chapter 25
The Deed is Done

It didn't take very long for the two nighttime depu-ties to arrive and push the gawkers away from the murder scene. A very tired Doctor Baxter determined that they were, in fact, both quite dead. Zeke wondered if Justin should be awakened, but after discussing it, he and Michael felt it best to let the poor man sleep. This was clearly a murder-suicide, and it involved two men already interviewed by Justin only yesterday. Zeke re-trieved the Colt 45, thankful that a souvenir hunter had not picked it up prior to his arrival. "I wish these peo-ple would choose a more appropriate time to kill them-selves," a slightly grumpy Doctor Baxter told the offic-ers. "I'll dig the bullets out tonight and have a report for Marshal Blake sometime in the morning." Retrieving the patrol wagon, the bloody bodies were transported to Doc's office for further examination.

"I hope we did right by not waking up Justin," Michael Davidson told Zeke.

The following morning, a well-rested Justin Blake was briefed by his deputies. "You boys did very well last night. I'll leave it up to your judgment if you feel I need to become involved. It's your shift and I have total confidence in both of you." That made each man very happy to hear that they made the right call. Justin then continued, "Do either of you feel anyone else was involved in the woman's death other than one of these two?"

Both men said they felt the husband was the killer and his action in killing her lover was for reasons well understood. Justin agreed and the case was officially closed. Soon everyone in town felt the same way. That is, all but one. Agnes Cody knew the truth. The death of the dark-haired woman was the work of her brother, Chet. His need to occasionally strangle dark-haired women had finally returned after a long period of inactivity. At least someone who was dead is being blamed for the crime... this time.

~~~~~~~~~~~~~~~~~~~~

It was Doris Davidson's turn to host an evening tea at her home. Since she and Rachael had met, they found they had much in common as well as their husbands working together. Virginia Cole enjoyed being asked but felt a little uncomfortable as she was only a special friend to Justin Blake, and not a married woman. "I hope you ladies like brownies," Doris asked as she passed out the treats. "My friends tell me I make the best brownies in town." After a few bites, everyone agreed she was right. "More tea, Virginia?" she then asked.

"No, thank you. I've had quite enough." Looking over at Rachael, she then asked, "So are you folks all ready for the grand re-opening of the emporium tomorrow morning?"

Rachael smiled with excitement, "Yes, I think so. We've had so many people drop by saying they can't wait to start shopping there again. I know that Constance and Jane are nervous. I told them everything will turn out all right. There will also be a full page advertisement in the Journal tomorrow." All agreed that that would bring in a steady flow of customers. Rachael then asked Virginia, "So how is Mr. Howell?"

Virginia startled smiling with a gleam in her eye, "He's acting just like a newlywed. He has photos of Jane on his desk and you never see the man without a smile on his face. I'm so happy for him and glad he was able to discover love again." Soon it was time to depart as the ladies heard the chiming of the wall clock signaling eight p.m. Time sure flies by when friends share their evening together.

The grand re-opening of the emporium was a huge success as all three ladies worked without a break as they waited on customers. Constance's fears were quickly put to rest as old friends, and a few new faces, made their way into the crowded store. The emporium was back... bigger and better than ever before.

~~~~~~~~~~~~~~~~~~~

Virginia Cole was deep in concentration on a loan request when an unfamiliar voice standing by her desk said, "And who is this lovely creature?" Startled at first, Virginia looked up at the handsomest man she had ever seen. He had brown, wavy hair neatly trimmed, and the brightest light blue eyes that seemed to capture her full attention. It was his smile that captivated her, feeling herself almost drawn into it. Standing beside this gentleman was her supervisor Mr. Howell. "Mr. Lawrence Wright, I would like to introduce to you our loan officer, Miss Virginia Cole. Mr. Wright is the new plant superintendent at the strawboard company." Virginia heard little of her supervisor's introductions as both parties seemed totally captivated with each other. "I am happy to make your acquaintance, Mr. Wright." Virginia felt herself blushing, which only produced a larger smile upon this man's face. She also noticed that he quickly scanned her finger searching for a ring. Finding none, Lawrence Wright replied, "Miss Cole, it's an honor and a privilege to meet such a talented, respected, and beautiful member of this institution. I look forward to seeing you again very soon." After both men had left, Virginia attempted to regain her concentration with the paperwork, but found it almost impossible to do so.

That evening Justin Blake had arranged to take Virginia to a comedy show at the opera house. The audience found the skit most humorous, as did Justin, but Virginia seemed most reserved. He even asked her once if she felt alright, but received a somewhat unemotional shrug in response. As they left down the stairs, Virginia asked if they could find a place to sit in the park and talk. Finding a park bench, the couple sat down and Justin waited to hear what was troubling her.

"Where is all of this leading to, Justin? I mean, do we have a future together as a couple or will we only attend an occasional comedy show?" Justin was thrown back a little by the heavy questions, and he didn't know if he could express himself the way that he wanted.

"Virginia, you know that I love you, and I think I understand where you are going with your question," he told her. "Allow me to say a couple things. I had a dream a few weeks back that still continues to haunt me. In the dream, Wilbert was killed on duty and I had to approach Rachael with the terrible news that her husband would not be coming home to her. It woke me up with a fright and I was unable to go back to sleep. I thought of the dangers each of us face almost daily and I then pictured myself being killed, and that Wilbert would have to approach you. That thought frightened me, Virginia. Not that I was dead, but that you would have to be told that news and somehow have to live with it."

Virginia then replied, "I know of the dangers to your job and have accepted them. But look at the attempted bank robbery I faced. I too could have been killed. I desire to one day have a husband, a nice home and children, but I just don't know if that's what you really want. Maybe just a couple of evenings doing something together is all you really feel is necessary. It's not enough for me though and I want you to know I think the time has come that we should start seeing other people."

Justin felt like a hot knife was just stuck into his breast.

Virginia stood up, "I'm walking home now and I wish to do so alone in case I begin to cry. Goodbye Justin." Watching Virginia walk away brought deep emotions to the surface within him. Maybe he had been too cautious in all of this. Justin Blake arose from the bench and walked home, a very sad and depressed young man.

~~~~~~~~~~~~~~~~~~~~

The following day, a young man entered the fire barn and told Wilbert Vance he wanted to give himself up to the law. Curious as to who the man was and what he had done, Wilbert requested his name and the crime committed. "My name is Jim Geiger, formerly a telegraph operator for the Wabash Railroad out of Springfield, Missouri. I'm being haunted by the ghosts of the train wreck which my neglect caused."

Wilbert had the feeling he was in for an interesting story, so he motioned for the young man to take a seat. "When I saw the awful mistake I had made," he said, "I ran away and succeeded in my escape. Since then I have wandered all over the country, but the scene of the wreck, mixed with the cries of the injured and the dying, haunted me, and even to the present time I see it all. My conscience accused me of being the cause of the loss of so many lives, and it has almost driven me insane. Lately, however, they have found me out and have been following me wherever I go, and for that reason I have come to give myself up."

Holding in his smile, Wilbert ask, "Who has found you out?"

"Oh, it's the dead ones, their friends, and others, and they are all around me. See, here they come now," and with a shriek, the man suddenly jumped from his chair and pointed to the wall. "See, they are coming, two by two, and are going to avenge their brothers, sisters, and friends. Save me, save me! I made the mistake of giving the wrong orders to the engineer and caused the train to wreck. I hear the injured screaming now, I must go."

As the young man finished his story, he almost sank to the floor with exhaustion. Wilbert was now convinced that the man was insane, so he locked him inside the cell and called for Doctor Baxter. Soon the young man was in the care of Grant County medical authorities. Out of curiosity, Wilbert telegraphed the Wabash Railroad authorities and discovered the young man had been their Springfield telegraph operator five years ago when the train accident occurred. Self-imposed guilt had clearly driven the poor young man insane.

~~~~~~~~~~~~~~~~~~~~~~~

Later that afternoon at the First National Bank, Loan Officer Virginia Cole received a small package from a young delivery boy. It was wrapped in white paper with a string binding all corners. Using a pair of scissors, Virginia snipped the string and unwrapped the paper to reveal a book. Its title was *The Time Machine* by H.G. Wells. Opening the cover, she found a scribbled note.

My Dear Miss Cole,

> *I pray that you may accept this small token of my esteem, and that you will enjoy reading this very unusual story as much as I have. May I also ask if you have ever enjoyed the thrill of riding a bicycle? I am very much involved in wheels, as I belonged to a wheel club in Toledo and plan on starting one here soon. May I be so bold as to offer you a ride on my wheels today after you finish work? I shall await your company outside in the hopes that we may become better acquainted.*

Respectively Yours,
Lawrence Wright.

Virginia was both excited and a bit afraid at the thought of becoming better acquainted with the new gentleman from Ohio. She had cried most of the night after she broke up with Justin and had secretly hoped he would follow her and take her into his arms. Unfortunately, that had not happened. With the passing of each new day brought the possibilities that her intuitions about his non-committal feelings were correct.

Wheels, as people are now referring to bicycles, had indeed become most popular. It will be difficult to peddle the machine with her long dress, but she had seen other women accomplish it. *Why not try it?* she thought.

Stepping outside at the closing of the bank, Virginia saw Lawrence Wright standing next to his wheels. "Thank you for the gift of the book, Mr. Wright," she told him. "I look forward to reading it."

"It was my pleasure, Miss Cole. As you can see I brought my wheels along hoping you might take a spin. Have you ever ridden wheels before?" he asked.

"No, I have not, but I think I may like to try sometime," she told him.

Smiling, he replied, "There's no time like the present to learn. It's really quite simple. Sit yourself down upon the seat and gather up your dress so it will not catch inside the moving chain. Each hand should grip the handle bars like so, and then begin peddling. When you are ready to try, let's move the wheels over here to the dirt road." The bicycle was repositioned pointing north and Virginia ascended the seat. "Are you ready Miss Cole?" With a quick nod of her head, Wright gave the bicycle a gentle push and off she went.

Wobbly at first, Virginia soon got the hang of it and peddled down a couple of blocks before turning around as she returned to his location. This was a thrill she had never before experienced. Movement and independence without the help of a man, the freedom to go when and where she wanted to travel. Approaching him, Virginia yelled, "Oh, catch me please," as he grabbed the handlebars so she would not fall. The smile on her face and the excitement in her voice said she totally enjoyed the experience.

"That was so much fun, Mr. Wright! Thank you for allowing me to try this," as she removed herself. "My, you have a nice set of wheels, sir."

"Yes and a very modern one at that. I purchased it in Ohio and used it in our wheels club. It is a Cleveland number 18 and cost me one hundred dollars."

Shocked at the high price, Virginia said that if she had known that she would not have ridden it. "Are all wheels that expensive?"

"For you, I would suggest a second-hand ladies' wheels. Affordable and still enjoyable."

Virginia's smile still hadn't left her face as she said, "I don't know how to thank you, sir for this very enjoyable experience."

"You can thank me by calling me Larry. That's what my friends call me and I do hope we shall become friends."

"Alright ... Larry, you may also call me Virginia."

"May I and my wheels walk you home, Miss Virginia?"

With a smile and a nod, the two began walking away together. Across the street, Justin Blake had witnessed the entire thing and felt almost sick to his stomach as he completed his rounds of the town. Was Mr. Wright now her Mr. Right?

In just a few days, Lawrence Wright had organized the few wheel owners in Gas City and Jonesboro into forming *The Gas City Wheels Club*, with Wright elected as president.

The group met at Guthrie's Clothing Store but quickly outgrown that location. It seemed almost every evening the group of riders were buzzing up and down the streets at breakneck speeds. The wheelers were quickly recognized by the public and almost daily new members were added to the club. Many of the older citizens complained about the wheelers on the streets. They were frightening horses and sometimes interfering with the street cars, they complained. Soon the Gas City Journal ran a small story in the paper entitled *City Seems Bicycle Mad*. In it they told a brief history of the safety wheels, their costs, their tread pneumatic tires, and that over one thousand companies were now making bicycles. Soon the wheels club grew to two hundred members, with the favorite wheels being the Ben-Hur Safety, made in Indianapolis. Advertisements for the purchase of bicycles became common in all area newspapers. The Gas City Exchange began renting bicycles out and did a quite fair rate of business. One day a man gave a fake name and didn't return the bicycle. Virginia purchased a used ladies set of wheels and continued to ride occasionally with Larry, as women were not allowed admittance to the wheels club.

Almost daily, the paper ran an editorial penned by a local complaining about the wheelmen being allowed upon the streets and that they were a public menace with their fast riding. City council members had already ruled that riders of wheels had as much right upon the public streets as anyone else, but that didn't squash the feeling of many. Times were certainly changing.

The month of June passed by without any major incidents. A local man died who had claimed for all of his life that the world was flat. A husband and wife team of burglars were apprehended, but what made it more interesting was the fact that the husband stayed home with their eighteen month old baby while the wife entered homes in broad daylight searching for rings and watches. After stealing over two hundred dollars worth of jewelry, she was apprehended by Marshal Blake as she was exiting a nearby home. They are both now sitting inside the Grant County jail having been tried and convicted by 'Squire Williamson.

Miss Virginia Cole was seen frequently on the arm of Lawrence Wright, strolling through town most evenings and occasionally attending shows at the opera house. Justin had never mentioned anything personally to his deputies, and although they were fully aware that Virginia was now seeing another man, they were careful never to mention it in the office. For that Justin was mighty grateful as he decided to completely throw himself into his work and had put in many additional hours. Working also helped to reduce the pain he felt inside that he would never admit to anyone. Justin continued to attend the Reverend Stokes' church almost every

Sunday and could be seen sitting alone on the pew, sad and lonely.

Since her break up with Justin, Virginia also pulled away from the weekly get together hosted by Doris and Rachael. She missed their company and always went out of her way to speak to each as she met them in various places around town, but she felt it best not to attend further get togethers. The ladies sensed this and eventually quit inviting her. Besides serving tea, checker games became the evening's entertainment, often lasting until near nine p.m. Both Rachael and Doris were quite good at playing checkers so they enjoyed the challenge of competition. Occasionally, Constance dropped by for the social aspect of the evening and was always welcomed. With the new admittance of Utah into the Union, a new forty-five star flag was to be unveiled at the Gas City 4th of July Celebrations. Bands as far away as Muncie would lead the parade down Main Street followed by the Jonesboro Grand Army of the Republic Post #409 members, as well as their offspring's, the Vicksburg Camp, Sons of Veterans. Zeke Miller, a member of the G.A.R. would again march with his companions along the parade route. A large speaker stand had been assembled in the park where out of town speakers were to later address the public with rousing patriotic speeches.

Weather permitting, a grand display of fireworks was to commence after dark.

Virginia and Lawrence watched and waved as the parade went by carrying the nation's newest flag. The day was rather warm, and energetic youngsters hustled beer to the thirsty for the marked up price of ten cents. Many thirsty men scoffed, then reached deep into their pockets for the dime. Other vendors sold lemonade and sandwiches to the crowd. Lawrence purchased two lemonades then asked Virginia if they could find a quiet spot in the park to talk as he had something important to discuss with her. Finding a park bench, the couple sat down. "There's something I have been meaning to discuss with you Virginia....."

Chapter 26
Things Are Not as They Seem

Several more days passed by before Virginia felt she knew what she needed to do. After work, she did a little shopping then ate a light supper before going home and changing out of her work clothing. Donning a plain casual dress, she mounted her set of wheels and peddled over to the home of Doris Davidson. Michael had already left for work and Doris was in the kitchen washing up the dishes when she heard a light knock on the door. Opening it, Doris saw Virginia Cole with a very troubled look upon her face. "I need a friend," she said as Doris welcomed her inside.

"You look troubled Virginia. Let's go sit on the couch and talk. Can I get you anything?"

Shaking her head no, Virginia sat on the couch in a very rigid manner. "I really don't know where to begin," as she began to cry. Doris reached over and comforted her friend until she was able to compose herself. "There, there, honey," Doris said, "Take your time, I'm here for you."

In time Virginia began, "I've made a really bad mess of things and I don't know how to resolve them. Justin and I had a bit of a falling out last month and I began seeing a new man in town, Lawrence Wright. He was so refreshing and alive, active in his wheels club and most importantly, he made time for me in the evenings. Because of him I even own a set of wheels myself. Anyway, I could sense he was starting to get ideas about me, as he tried twice to kiss me, but I rebuffed him each time. That only seemed to encourage him even more. Well, we attended the 4th of July celebration the other day and after the parade had passed, he said he wanted to speak to me concerning an important subject."

"Doris, I became quite concerned that he may be planning on proposing to me, or at least that was what began swirling around in my mind. We found an unoccupied bench and he slowly began to speak. He told me he was already married and that he and his wife had separated three years ago while she returned home to her parents in Pennsylvania."

Doris gasped loudly as she brought her hand up over her mouth. "The cad! The nerve of him doing this to you! Well I never..."

Virginia continued. "He then asked me to wait while he filed for divorce so he could then marry me! As you can imagine, I leaped to my feet and shouted that I never wanted to see or speak to him again! He tried to take hold of my arm to prevent my leaving, but I shouted for help as two gentlemen were close by and both came to my aid. I'm so upset at myself for allowing all this to happen in the first place."

Doris patted her friend's hand, saying, "This is not your fault! You had no way of knowing he was not what he pretended to be. The man should be horse whipped. He certainly is no gentleman."

"Actually," Virginia continued, "That isn't the worst part. While I liked Larry as a person and enjoyed his company, I was never in love with him and certainly would not have married him. I still love Justin Blake but because of my foolishness I drove him away for good."

"Why do you say that dear?" Doris asked.

"With Jane and Rachael getting married this spring, I began wanting to be proposed to by Justin and settle down with him for the rest of my life. Instead, I handled it all wrong and pressured him to make a decision. When

I didn't get the answer I wanted, I broke it off with him. I had hoped that he might see Larry as a threat and decide he wanted me. But instead, he gave me space and we haven't spoken since." Virginia began to cry again, wiping away her tears with her handkerchief.

"My dear, you are hardly the first woman who has tried to lead her man to the altar and failed. Men are sometimes more like little boys in that they can't see what's been laid before their eyes. It has to be their idea, and when they are ready, we as women must act surprised. Not to pry, but what did Justin give as an excuse for not moving toward marriage anyway?"

"He told me of a dream he had about Wilbert and... well, you know firsthand the dangers our men face in police work. He said he didn't want someone to have to tell me he wouldn't be coming home. I know he's still very bothered by the loss of Marshal Brewster. I should have seen that he was actually thinking about me, but I took it as a rejection and over reacted."

"Michael says that Justin is a very unhappy man these days, working extra long hours and just not himself. The other deputies are aware of the problem, but don't want to butt in." She then continued, "Being married to a deputy marshal is difficult. When Michael leaves for work in the evenings, a little piece of me dies until

I know he's safe at home with me again. I don't know if a woman ever gets over the fear of losing her man."

"I know," Virginia mentioned, "My father was a detective and was killed in the line of duty. Mother will never get over her loss."

Doris continued, "So my advice is to ask yourself if you are willing to live with that type of fear hanging over your head or not. Even factory workers are maimed or killed on the job these days. But getting back to Justin, if I were you, I would go speak with him and lay your cards out on the table. That way you'll know for sure if it's over or not." Just speaking about all of this was a great relief to Virginia who thanked Doris for her help and promised to think over the advice she was given.

~~~~~~~~~~~~~~~~~~~~

Across town, Agnes Cody was unaware that her brother Chet had ventured out two nights that last week looking for another victim, but returning late at night without finding satisfaction. Agnes had received another blackmail check that week and was very happy with her situation. That plus her nightly work was keeping the wolves at bay and food on the table. She often wondered if Chet was aware of her occupation, but finally determined that he wasn't able to grasp any understanding of it. Chet had never displayed any type of sexual interest in women. With his looks and mental condition, it would be near impossible anyway. Agnes's thoughts drifted back to David.

He was a regular customer who seems to have fallen in love with her, which struck Agnes as rather peculiar. David has asked several times about coming over to Agnes's home, but she flatly forbid it, not knowing what her brother would do. Still she had to agree that the man was persistent. This week he went so far as to suggest that they leave town together and become a couple. If it were not for her brother, Agnes may very well have taken him up on the offer as it was probably the best offer she could ever expect from a client anyway. She hoped that David would not present a problem when dealing with her other clients. He was a nice enough fellow and was employed at one of the local factories, the name of which she couldn't remember. So many men tended to blend together when mixed with shots of whiskey. It was time anyway for Agnes to start supper then get ready for her evening work.

Zeke and Michael were still in the office that evening enjoying a cup of coffee before beginning their rounds. Things had been quiet lately and it gave the officers a much needed rest. Michael, knowing that Zeke couldn't read, liked to inform him of news stories that were printed in the newspaper. "Here's one that might interest you Zeke, they had an accident over at the Marion Old Soldier Home that killed a man. Seems they were firing off a twenty-one gun salute with their cannon for a National Salute on July 4th with all the old soldiers lined up, as a large crowd of visitors stood by. The firing squad sergeant gave orders to begin firing the salute. The first discharge went off as normal but the man who was swabbing out the canon apparently used a dry swab, for as the powder was rammed a second time, a hidden spark ignited causing it to discharge. It blew the poor old soldier's arms off and mangled him pretty good. He was picked up lifeless and was laid to rest with full military honors. Says here they may quit using the cannon now."

Zeke replied, "I never did care fer cannons anyway. Da Rebs were too good at aimin' em at us. Well, I guess we best be a goin'," as both men left to begin their evening patrols.

~~~~~~~~~~~~~~~~~~

It was well after one a.m. when Agnes Cody staggered back to her little rental home. It had proved to be a profitable evening and she looked forward to sleeping it off in her cot. As she opened the front door, she heard a familiar voice behind her say, "So this is where you live. I want to come in for awhile." It was her persistent client, David.

"No, no, you cannot come in," she scolded, but David was already pushing his way inside.

"I won't leave until we have a little fun. You got a husband locked up inside here or something?"

"David, I beg of you, please leave now!"

He stood there in the kitchen laughing, "Not yet I won't. Come here and give me a little kiss."

Suddenly Chet was upon him as quickly as a mountain lion would be on an unsuspecting deer. David never knew what hit him as Chet's huge hands were around his neck in an instant, squeezing with all of his strength, as his neck gave way with a faint snapping sound. Chet just stood there holding the dead man like a rag doll. This was exactly what Agnes feared most. "Chet, take that body out somewhere deserted and get rid of it. Don't let anyone see you." Her brother seemed to understand and with one arm carried the body away into the darkness. *How much longer can this killing go on* she thought?

~~~~~~~~~~~~~~~~~~~

A group of early morning factory workers noticed a man laying up against a tree down by the river. Thinking the guy must be sleeping off an all-night-drunk, one of the workers produced a pack of firecrackers from his pocket. "Let's have a little fun, shall we?" Approaching the tree from the rear, the worker lit the fuse and tossed the pack directly beside the sleeping man. As the firecrackers went off, the men howled with laughter as they expected the sleeping man to jump out of his skin. Instead, the man never moved. "He must really be hung over," another man said. The men approached the sleeping man, but quickly realized why he didn't jump. The fact that his head now lay flat on top of his shoulders said it all. "He's dead, best someone go get the law." One worker said he would while the others circled around to have a better look. "Anyone know who he is?"

The worker didn't have to go too far as he found Zeke Miller and Michael Vance completing their final round of the shift. Zeke said that he would fetch the marshal and Doc. Vance asked the assembling crowd of onlookers if anyone knew who the dead man was. From near the rear, someone shouted, "David. I don't know his last name. He works at the Chicago Edged Tool Co. I've

played cards with him a time or two. Pretty nice fellow."
*Now it shouldn't be too difficult to obtain a last name
and maybe track down who last saw him last night and
where*, Michael thought.

Doctor Baxter arrived and saw that medical attention
was not required. Zeke pulled up in the patrol wagon
and after being told Doc was finished with his initial
examination, the body was hauled to his office. Justin ar
rived just as the wagon was leaving the scene. "Another
broken neck with strangle marks, Marshal. I'd say we
got us a very large killer on the loose." Just what Justin
didn't wanted to hear first thing in the morning. "I'll see
you later with my report."

Wilbert arrived about this time and Michael shared
with him and Justin the first name of David and where
he supposedly worked. Wilbert said he would go to the
factory to see what he could discover. With the wagon
gone, Wilbert began walking and soon arrived outside
the factory. There was no fence or gate shack so he
walked inside, saw an office and entered. "Yes," a young
man said, "May I help you sir?"

"I'm Deputy Vance. We're investigating the death
of a man by the name of David that's said to work here.
I'm trying to obtain a last name and maybe speak with
any of his co-workers or friends."

The young man went out on the factory floor and spoke with another gentleman who, after making a search, returned and said something to him. The young man then returned to the office. "Deputy, we have a David Eubanks employed here that failed to come to work this morning. Could that be your man?"

"If I may speak with a couple of his co-workers I can determine it one way or another." The young man went out and after a short period of time, two middle aged men in dirty work clothing entered the office.

Confused and a bit worried, each man approached Deputy Vance. "Men, can you give me a description of David Eubanks." After they provided one, it appeared he had his man. One of the men asked if David was in trouble with the law. "Not now I'm afraid, he's dead. Do either of you know where he was last evening? When was the last time you saw him?"

A look of shock swept over both men. "How? What happened?" one man asked to know. "David is a good man who likes to play cards, drink a little Rye, and chase the women." Both said they had no idea where he was last night as they hadn't seen him since work yesterday.

Vance continued a line of questioning. "Ever hear him say anything about being in trouble or fearing for his life?"

The other man spoke up, "No, actually he was quite happy. Said he was in love with a whore and they might run away together soon." The other man nodded knowing of the story also.

"Did he ever mention the girl's name? I would like to talk to her as she might know more about this."

One of the men looked at the other saying, "I know he mentioned her name but ... I can't recall it. How about you?"

A look of recognition came to the face of the other worker. "Agnes! Her real name is Agnes, but she goes by another name for some reason." Thanking both men, Wilbert reported back to the office to brief Justin for the report. Once the lower-end bars open at eleven a.m., he planned on going to each and speaking to the bartenders, but knowing that it may require the night crew interviewing the evening bartenders to actually find someone who knew her. Slowly the pieces to the puzzle would come together.

~~~~~~~~~~~~~~~~~~~~

Wilbert and Justin were inside their office when Doc Baxter arrived. "Want a cup of coffee Doc? It's fresh," Wilbert asked him.

"As long as Zeke didn't make it, sure, thanks." Wilbert poured a cup as Doc sat down. "Marshal," Doc said, taking the offered cup. "That man was strangled so violently that his neck was broken. Same as with that woman down by the river. Deep bruising clear around to the back of his neck. Only large powerful hands could do that kind of damage."

Justin shook his head, "I was afraid that might be the situation from what you said earlier. We got the victim's last name. It's Eubanks and he did work at the Chicago Edge Tools Company. We have a lead we'll be checking up on tonight, but meanwhile, what size of man do you think we are dealing with?"

"I would say huge with long powerful arms and hands. Not the typical man you see on the street corner. It's his mental condition that worries me though. He must be capable of blinding rage, and with his physical abilities, he's capable of almost anything. The sooner he is stopped, the better for all of us." With that, Doc gave them a wave and departed.

Wilbert then said, "I wonder if we should run an ad in the paper asking the public if they know of such a man?"

"I don't know, it might have every large man in town singled out by the curious. Let's see where our investigation goes from here first. I want Zeke and Michael to scour the bars tonight. Somebody must know of this Agnes woman. In the meantime, we'll all keep our eyes out for this man. He shouldn't be hard to miss."

~~~~~~~~~~~~~~~~~~~~~

It was going on six p.m. and Justin was alone in the office. He was reading a police report warning of an escaped killer from Richmond Asylum when someone entered the room. It was Virginia Cole. "Hello, Justin," she spoke softly. "It's good to see you."

Standing up, Justin replied, "Virginia. It's great to see you again. Please have a seat," as he pulled out a chair for her, which she declined.

"I know it's not very lady-like, but I came by to see if you would have supper with me tonight? The diner has the beef stew you like so well." With a deep smile, Justin took her by the arm and proceeded to the nearby diner.

After placing their order Virginia replied, "This is like old times. I have missed you and I have so much I want to say, but not here in this crowded dinner. After you brief your evening deputies, do you think we could take a walk in the park together?"

"I can think of nothing I would like better than to be with you again, Virginia."

Later the couple walked the park arm-in-arm. "I didn't know if you would be willing to speak with me again after the horrible way I treated you," she said. Virginia then told him everything concerning Larry up to her conversation with Doris. "There you have it. I guess I was trying to push you into a lifelong commitment you were just not ready for, and I used another man as a weapon to hurt you. For that I am terribly sorry and I pray that one day you will forgive me." Justin pulled her into his arms and kissed her with deep passion.

"There is nothing to forgive sweetheart, so let's not speak of it again," he assured her.

Chapter 27
Wheelmen vs. Dogs

An incident took place one evening in town that set tongues wagging and citizens taking both sides of the issue. It was bound to happen eventually and finally, it did. Mr. and Mrs. Ely Lewis each had acquired a set of wheels recently and enjoyed an evening ride together after supper before darkness sets in. Last evening, both bicycles passed in front of the home of Mr. Floyd Acres, a local clothing store owner. Mr. Lewis, who operates a candy store on Main Street, was riding his bicycle approximately two lengths ahead of his wife when out of nowhere came two small terrier dogs running towards each bicycle barking and snapping. Startled, Mr. Lewis kicked outward to keep the dog away when he heard his wife scream and the sound of her bicycle wrecking upon the dirt road.

Quickly, Lewis stopped his bicycle to come to the aid of his terrified wife. Mrs. Lewis lay upon the dirt road crying out in fear as one of the small dogs kept barking and snapping at her. With the instinct only to protect his wife from further harm, Lewis pulled out his 1890 Smith and Wesson Model 32, Double Action Revolver, and began firing at the threatening dog. He managed to hit the creature on his second attempt which caused the dog to yelp in great pain. The other dog that had lunged at his legs then ran away.

Lewis then put away his gun and went to examine her injuries. Mrs. Lewis's leg was moderately scraped from the fall but she remained terrified from the incident that had just occurred. The other dog continued to bark at them from a distance. Hearing the two gun shots and the loud yelping of his injured dog, homeowner Floyd Acres had ran up to Lewis and the altercation began. Fists were flying as loud, vulgar cursing was shouted, clearly heard by the neighbors who came outside to see what was going on. Hearing the two gunshots, Deputies Miller and Davidson arrived at the scene and pulled the fighting men apart.

"He shot my dog! I'm pressing charges against him," shouted Acres to the deputies.

"His dogs came out on the public street and attacked our wheels. His dog lunged at my wife and caused her to wreck. It kept trying to bite her," replied Lewis.

The deputies had no choice but to put both men under arrest and let the 'squire sort it out tomorrow. Both wives posted bond for their husbands and both men agreed to appear at the 'squire's court the following morning at ten a.m. After hearing both sides of the continuing argument from the men, 'Squire Williamson issued a ten dollar fine to each man; to Lewis for firing a concealed weapon within city limits and Acres for allowing his dogs to run wild and threatening public's safety. Both men began yelling that his own fine was unfair. The 'squire then threatened each with ten days in jail if another word was said on the matter. Both left in a huff after paying their fines, but the matter wasn't over quite yet.

Two days later, a letter was published in the Saturday edition of the Gas City Journal entitled: **The Rights Of Wheelmen.** *"We would be pleased to have the following questions answered by the reading public. Must a man, when riding upon the public streets on a bicycle, put up with molestation of dogs and do nothing to protect himself?"*

"Yesterday evening while my wife and I were riding along the south side of our fair town, we were accosted by two dogs who apparently were intent upon biting us. I was riding a little ahead of my wife, and on looking around, saw that my wife had fallen from her wheel and one of the dogs had ran upon her barking and snapping. Fearing for my wife's safety, I shot the dog. It was then that the dog's owner, a local owner with a cheap and unscrupulous reputation, assaulted me physically, causing both of us to be arrested and brought before 'Squire Williamson."

"I understand that the discharging of a weapon within city limits may rate a fine, but what I would like to know is this: Does a man, riding upon a public highway, not have the God given right to protect himself and his loved ones from bodily injury? Or in so doing, does the law now protect only the dog and all persons who keep them? Our idea has always been that the public highways are for people and not for the benefit of dogs. Must a man that is caught in this situation submit to allowing the dog to chew on him until tiring, while offering no resistance? What would you do? (We think our correspondent acted exactly right.- Editor, Gas City Journal)

Floyd Acres was absolutely furious after reading the editorial and of being referred to as "cheap and unscrupulous" within the article. While his name was not printed, many people would easily be able to acquaint him to the story. Still fuming over the loss of his dog and the public humiliation that this man had caused him, Floyd Acres began developing a plan of action. Taking pen to paper, he composed the following reply that was soon published in the Journal:

A Reply to The Wheelmen *"As the injured party named within the coarse and inaccurate letter printed by this newspaper recently, I feel it my duty to set the record straight. Do wheelmen have the right to plug away at anything and everyone they feel hampers their 'right' to recklessly speed though our public streets, frightening horses and ladies? If a small child approached a wheelman, does the said rider feel he has the right to shoot the child?"*

"The reader will be asked to evaluate their own personal experiences while riding within a horse drawn wagon or upon horseback. At some time in the past you most likely encountered a barking dog. Did you then produce a weapon and fire upon the poor creature? No you did not, as a dog will quickly lose interest and retreat to

the safety of its home. Dogs have a built-in mode of protecting their owners from harm, which was exactly what my poor dog was doing from fear of these wheel contraptions that should be banned from our public streets."

"As to replying to the crude and vulgar comments made of me by a man, well known within the community for selling overpriced candies that are known to make small children and ladies quite ill, I would simply say that his reputation as a skinflint and a scoundrel speaks for itself."

~~~~~~~~~~~~~~~~~~~~~~~

Justin Blake entered Matthew Brook's barbershop for a haircut the following Tuesday morning and found that the conversation was all about the reply that appeared in yesterday's newspaper. The topic was causing a divide among the populace as each side had its strengths and weaknesses. Most of the older townspeople had no use at all for wheels and wanted them banned from the streets altogether. "Them wheels are a public nuisance and all they do is frighten the horses," one of the older men said. Another said they were only a fad and would quickly die out or eventually be banned all together.

Another replied, "Wheels are givin' women funny ideas about independence and equality too. Soon they will be a wantin' to wear britches and smoke cigarettes in public. I hear tell them saddles on the wheels are stimulating them, if you know what I mean, so women should be banned from riding them, period. I tell you them wheels are the downfall of our civilization."

The oldest man then spoke up, "You fellers' ain't got nuttin' ta gets all worked up about. Folks will still be ridden horses fifty years from now and them wheels contraptions ain't gonna be around much longer."

Justin just smiled to himself and looked at the newspaper until something that Barber Matthew Brooks said caught his interest. "Yep, I saw old Floyd Acres packing a gun this morning. I fear there's gonna be some bad trouble between him and Ely Lewis before all of this gets sorted out." Justin made a mental note to have Wilbert approach both men and warn them off.

The following morning, Ely Lewis was eating his breakfast as he prepared for work. "I'm not afraid of Acres," he boasted, "And if he pushes me, I'll drop him dead in the street." Despite trying to reason with her husband, Barbara Lewis worried that he may very well shoot him or end up being shot. After he left for work, she got down on her knees and asked God to watch over her husband and to keep him safe.

Across town a similar discussion was going on over breakfast. "He shoots my dog then trashes me in the paper. I hope he likes his little surprise this morning." When pressed as to what he had done now, Floyd Acres only smiled.

As Ely Lewis walked towards his candy store, he scanned the streets for any sign of Floyd Acres. *Best to be careful*, he thought as he prepared to enter, but something odd caught his attention. It was a large home-made painted sign of a skull and crossbones with the lettering, **"Beware- Poisonous Candy Sold Here"** Lewis became furious that it had been outside his store for who knows how long. People in town would now be laughing at him behind his back or wondering if the sign could be true. It was bound to hurt his business. He took hold of the sign and brought it inside in case he needed to present it as evidence one day in court... after he had killed Floyd Acres. *Two can play at this little game*, he thought.

The next morning a sign appeared outside of Floyd Acres Clothing Store that read "**Clothing Manufactured Here by Chinese Slave Labor**." Both men were now prepared to kill the other on sight.

As if it couldn't get any worse, both men acted that night in continuing their feud. A bucket of yellow paint was splattered on the front doorway of Floyd Acres home, while a brick was thrown through the window of the candy store. Each man returned home for lunch swearing to their wives that they were going to kill the other that day. After her husband had returned to the candy store, Mrs. Lewis went to seek out an old friend for help. She went to the home of Reverend and Mrs. Ruth Stokes.

Opening the door, Ruth Stokes was pleased to see Barbara Lewis. "Do you have time to talk?" Welcoming her friend inside, they proceeded to the library where they would be more comfortable.

"It's been a while Barbara, and I've been hearing things about Ely that has Clarence and I very concerned."

"That's exactly why I am here and I have a favor to ask of you. This silly feud between Ely and Mr. Acres must end or someone's going to kill the other. I prayed upon this problem this morning and I feel you may be able to help resolve it."

"How can I help?" Ruth Stokes asked.

"Go and approach Mrs. Acres for me. We both need to work together to save the lives of our husbands and stop this silliness before it's too late. Will you do this for me?"

Without any hesitation, Ruth Stokes replied, "Yes and you're coming with me." Both ladies then prayed and asked God to help them in their quest. Together they proceeded across town to the Acres home. With HIS help, they'll put an end to all of the foolishness... before it was too late.

As the women approached the Acres home, they could see the yellow paint splattered on the front door. "Did your husband do that," Ruth asked? Barbara only shook her head in total disgust as they knocked on the damaged door. As Mrs. Acres opened it, Ruth Stokes spoke first, "Mrs. Acres, my name is Mrs. Ruth Stokes and this lady is Mrs. Barbara Lewis. We are seeking your help in stopping your husband's from killing each other. Will you speak with us?" From inside the doorway a much relieved Tina Acres replied, "Oh thank God! Come in ladies, do come in!"

What started out a little awkwardly, they quickly became very friendly as all agreed they must act together before it was too late. Tina Acres even served tea and soon the ladies were laughing together as if they had always been friends. They quickly decided the three of them would pay each husband a visit at his store and the wife would lead the conversation while inside. Unless each husband agreed to let the matter drop completely now and forever, each wife was prepared to stop speaking to them, cooking, cleaning, doing laundry and being agreeable to any involvement of a physical nature. With two other ladies as witnesses, the men would either fully comply or suffer the consequences of their wives' wrath.

Barbara offered the suggestion that they visit the candy store first, as she was anxious to give her husband a firm piece of her mind. The three ladies marched inside and poor old Ely Lewis never stood a chance. Realizing that he was boxed in a corner, he agreed to his wife's terms, but only if Floyd Acres agreed also. With the knowledge that Ely Lewis has already agreed to drop matters, Floyd Acres was reluctant but finally agreed to end the feud. It was now finished and common sense has finally prevailed. Who says women are the weaker sex?

~~~~~~~~~~~~~~~~~~~~~

Across town down by the river, a poker game was underway inside the Last Chance Saloon. Three men had been playing for near an hour and lady luck seemed to have blessed each man until moving on to the next guy, who then began winning. In the pot in front of Jesse

Harper was almost all of his money. This last hand would decide if he rode out of town with enough money to last the rest of the month or left as poor as a church mouse. Harper figured the other two men to be locals, but had been cautious not to divulge too much about himself. He was a wanted man in Kokomo for pistol whipping and robbing a drummer, and it was that man's money that now lay before him on the poker table.

After the last cards have been dealt, each man studied the hand before him and considered his betting options. "I'm out," one of the locals replied while pitching his unseen cards down on the table. "If you gentlemen will excuse me, I have things to attend to," as he stood and left the saloon. Now it all came down to one hand. Harper searched the face of his opponent, searching for any indications of a bluff. His eyes rested on the man's stick pin on his tie. Harper deeply admired it and wondered how he could get it away from this local hick as he glanced back down upon his own cards. He held three tens, a very solid hand, and was considering raising the bet.

Across the table, the other man also searched the face of this young man, thinking he saw a bit of a smile when his opponent last viewed his cards. The gentlemen held three queens. "I'll raise you five dollars," Harper said. The man looked down on his remaining cash of three silver dollars. "Throw in that stick pin to cover it," Harper replied.

"I'm calling," the other man said. Harper laid down his hand with a huge grin upon his face. The other man smiled even broader as his hand clearly won the game, as he stuffed the bills and coins into his pocket. Harper was disgusted with his bad luck.

"Nice playing with you young man," the winner replied as he stood to leave. Seeing that his opponent was clearly broke, the winner slid four bits across the table to him. "Here, go get yourself a pack of tobacco. They got a real good looker down at the emporium," as he walked away.

Harper picked up the coins and spun them between his fingertips as he considered his options. *If they got a good looking woman working at the emporium, they may also have a cash register full of good looking easy money*, he thought. Leaving the saloon, Jesse Harper mounted his horse and slowly rode east straight into town.

The emporium was quite easy to locate right on Main Street as he tied his horse on the hitching rail. Entering the store, a small bell above his head signaled the arrival of a new customer. Store owner Constance

Wainwright was in the back room going over stock inventory and paid no attention to the bell, knowing that Rachael Vance would tend to the customer's needs. "Good afternoon, sir, may I be of assistance?" a smiling Rachael Vance asked the young man.

"I need a pack of Mail Pouch," he told her.

Rachael walked over to the rear shelf and picked up a pack of the tobacco. "That will be...." Rachael stopped in mid sentence as a pistol was now leveled at her head.

"Give me all your money now! Put it in a sack... do it quick, pretty lady or else."

Rachael, maintaining her composure as she looked around for a bag to use.

"What are you doing? Don't even think about pulling a gun on me or I'll shoot you dead," came his threat.

"I'm looking for a bag to put the money in," she told him. Just then another customer walked in, a middle-aged woman who, upon seeing a gun being pointed at Rachael, began shouting and screaming as she quickly ran out of the store. "Murder, he has a gun, help, police!"

This caught the attention of Constance, who did a quick peek out the store room door and evaluated the situation. She then stepped out the back door of the storeroom and moving as fast as she could with her still mending hip, made it to the Marshal's office to inform

them of the robbery in progress. Wilbert was alone behind the desk and upon hearing that a man had a gun on
his wife, he jumped to his feet and ran towards the front
of the emporium.

Rachael found a cloth bag that Constance used in
taking money to the bank, and began filling it with money. Trying to stall for as along as possible, she grabbed
each coin drawer slot and began filling it by hand, pen-
nies first. The man with the gun was looking rather nervous by now and began shouting "hurry up, hurry up!"
Looking upon Rachel's face he then replied, "My you
are a pretty one. Why don't you come with me and let's
split this one horse town together?" Rachael's stern face
gave him her answer.

From out front of the emporium a voice shouted,
"You in there! This is Deputy Vance. Come out with
your hands up. We have you surrounded." Wilbert actually was the only lawman present as Justin was oversee-
ing the 'squire on business. *Maybe a local will come to
my aid?* Wilbert thought. *Lord, don't let anything happen to Rachael.*

Hearing the challenge from the deputy, Harper
reached around the counter and grabbed Rachael as a
human shield. "I have a woman here with a gun to her

pretty head. Any trouble from anyone and I put a bullet in her brain. Do you hear me, deputy?"

Stalling for time, Wilbert's eyes became fixed on the single horse tied to the hitching post. An idea came to him but he had to accomplish it quickly before the gunman came outside. Coming up to the horse, Wilbert loosed both cinch straps on the saddle buckles then stepped up on the sidewalk in front of the store window "Here I am, tell me what you want?"

Using Rachael as a shield, Harper opened the emporium's door, "Toss your weapon inside here deputy and raise your hands where I can see them! Any funny business and she gets it, understand?" Wilbert tossed his service revolver inside and stepped back out in the street with his hands up. Slowly, the robber emerged with Rachael. He looked about and saw people only watching with no signs of any other weapons. Satisfied, he instructed her to unhitch his horse as he kept his eyes fixed on the deputy. With the horse now freed and pointing eastward, Harper gave Rachael a huge push towards the arms of the deputy as he grabbed for his saddle horn, inserted his boot into the stirrup and fell flat upon the ground as the loosed saddle slid sideways. Confused, he struggled to rise up but found Deputy Vance already on top of him, twisting the gun from his fingertips. With a few hard placed fists to his head, Harper's day was through and cuffs placed on his wrists.

"Rachael darling, are you alright? Did he harm you?"

"I'm fine Wilbert, thanks to you." She then gave him a kiss as the crowd of people began hooting and clapping. By the time that Justin had returned from the 'squire's office, the jail cell had a new prisoner soon to be hauled off by a Grant County sheriff deputy. Harper soon learned that it doesn't pay to hold hostage the wife of a Gas City Deputy.

Chapter 28
Carnage

Justin Blake held an early morning meeting with his deputies. Smiling at Wilbert he said, "Now that Wilbert has ended our recent crime spree, I think it's time we refocus on our attempts to discover who this Agnes is. I'm guessing the bartenders probably know but won't tell us out of some form of misguided loyalty. If we're going to crack this strangler case, I feel we must find this woman and question her. She could be hiding in fear or has already left town. I have a plan I want to discuss with you to get your take on it. What if we activate Mayor Huffman and Barber Brooks as temporary deputies with the four of us and we hit the lower end bars and arrest every woman of the night we can find? Maybe we'll get lucky and Agnes will be one on the women we arrest. The strangler attacks late at night and these women may end up being his next target. It's in their own interest to help us."

"I like the idea," Wilbert said, "But I would suggest we concentrate on the hours of eleven p.m. to one a.m. That's the prime time for these women and if we work longer into the night, word will only get out to allow them to hide from us."

"Good point, Zeke what do you think?"

"With six of us visitin' da bars down by da river we can cover more ground lots faster, especially if we use da patrol wagon ta haul em here quick, but shouldn't someone be here in da jail watchin' over dem we catch?"

Wilbert smiled as an idea came to him. "Justin, what if you asked young Brad Lockridge to serve as a special deputy that night? I bet the boy would jump at the chance, and all he would have to do was remain behind in case anyone else came in to report another problem."

Justin liked the idea and said he would approach him today. Everyone agreed that this special operation would begin the following night in order to give the mayor and the barber more time to prepare. Each person was to be in the Marshal's office at ten forty-five p.m. so they could go over the night's plan of action. "I'll also brief 'Squire Williamson on what we're going to be doing. At the very least it will show that we are attempting to remove vice from our city, and maybe we'll get lucky and actually get a solid lead out of it," Justin said. By early afternoon, everything was in place for tomorrow night's raid.

~~~~~~~~~~~~~~~~~~~~~

It was just a typical day for Agnes Cody as she made breakfast for herself and her brother. Chet had been on edge a lot lately, being disagreeable and moody. He seemed unhappy as he grunted and fluttered his arms as if he was trying to tell her something. While she had love for her brother, many a day passed by when she wished that life had turned out differently for her. She had been told by a bartender that the local lawmen were asking about an Agnes who worked the bar scene. Apparently her dead client had spoken of her to friends at the plant. She made a mental note to never give out her real name to another client again.

~~~~~~~~~~~~~~~~~~~~~

Justin and Virginia attended the evening perfor-mance of the Hamilton and Phillips Opera Troop show-ing of "A Southern Rose" at the Lovett Opera House. While not a fan of opera, Justin enjoyed his evening with Virginia very much. Since they had gotten back together, there seemed to be a closeness that didn't quite exist before. A bond, if you will, that the two were now solidly a couple. Virginia pointed out Lawrence Wright on the arm of another young woman. Some people just never learn.

~~~~~~~~~~~~~~~~~~~~~~~~

Michael and Zeke were out doing their evening patrols when Michael asked him a question. "What would you think if I asked Justin about getting us a pair of wheels to patrol with? We could certainly get to places much quicker than walking."

Zeke began to laugh, "Not fer me, no sir-ee. I ain't never gonna gets on one of dem wheel contraptions."

Michael continued to press his case, "But times are a changing, Zeke. In just five years it'll be a new century, the twentieth century. Why, just the other day there was a story in the paper that businessmen in Cleveland were buying horseless carriages as a public transportation system. Their motors come from Germany."

Zeke just shook his head as he chuckled, "Them things don't work and they ain't gonna be around no longer than them wheels are. Mark my word, you'll never see em in your lifetime."

"You may be right, as I ain't never seen one either." Scanning the westerly skyline, Michael said, "Looks like rain is headed our way."

Zeke replied, "Nope, gonna pass right over us." It did not rain that night just as Zeke said it would.

The following late evening, all of the deputies and a very eager Brad Lockridge had assembled in the fire barn for their final briefing. Justin passed out extra sets of handcuffs in case there were several ladies of the night present when each bar was entered. Justin assigned two bars to each man, and he and Wilbert would do three apiece. "If you can, cuff the women together then put them in the patrol wagon and bring them back here to the cell. Don't get into any type of verbal confrontation with any of the men, but if needed, arrest them too. We'll take those straight over to 'Squire Williamson as he'll be ready to try the bunch after our raid is over. Since we're not equipped to handle a large group of women prisoners for any duration, Zeke has volunteered to haul the entire bunch to the Grant County jail as soon as the 'squire passes sentence. I've already notified them and they will be standing by to take our prisoners. Any woman who points out this Agnes woman or helps in our strangler investigation will receive a lighter sentence by the 'squire. Any questions?"

Young Brad Lockridge held up his hand, like he was in school. "Marshal, what do I do if somebody comes in looking for a deputy?"

"Just take down his name and what the trouble is. We'll get back with them later." With that the men loaded up ın the patrol wagon and Zeke drove down towards the river where the low end saloons were. It would be an interesting couple of hours.

By one-thirty a.m. the jail cell held eight women of the night, all mad and yelling to be let out. Justin asked the extra deputies to remain on duty until the group could be taken straight over to 'Squire Williamson's special night court. Each woman was cuffed to another and escorted over to the awaiting courtroom inside the Mississinewa Hotel. The 'squire then interviewed each woman separately, asking for details about Agnes and any information they might have about the strangler. None had any information to provide and didn't know any Agnes. One woman said, "Your Honor, if we knew anything about that killer we would sure in blazes tell ya." Learning nothing of any importance, the 'squire sentenced each woman to thirty days in the Grant County jail and then returned home to bed.

Thanking the 'squire for his help this night, Justin and his deputies escorted the prisoners outside to the awaiting patrol wagon. Still cuffed to one another, a rope was passed between their shackles and then tied off securely to each end of the exterior of the wagon so Zeke needn't worry about escape attempts. With a wave goodbye, the wagon left on its journey to Marion. Thanking each man personally, the extra deputies and Wilbert left for home. Justin entered the office then and thanked young Lockridge for his assistance tonight. "I can't wait until I come of age Marshal," he told Justin. "I want to be a lawman." Seeing that he had a few hours before his shift started, Marshal Blake went home and crawled into bed. He was asleep within just a few minutes.

Unbeknownst to everyone was that Agnes Cody, their wanted woman, was arrested tonight using her fake name, and was now on her way to jail for an entire month. *What's to become of Chet?* she thought as the patrol wagon continued its journey out of town.

~~~~~~~~~~~~~~~~~~~

A hungry Chet Cody awoke to a quiet house. Despite his diminished mental abilities, he was aware that something was different as he went room to room searching

449

for his sister. The more he searched, the more confused he became, finally sitting down at the table as he waited for food. Hours passed and no food arrived. By noon, Chet began to search out whatever was in the house that he could eat. He munched all day on the small amounts he could find, even eating raw eggs. He had no grasp on how to cook anything and by nightfall had consumed everything that he could find. The following day brought even greater anxiety as Agnes still had not returned, and he was very hungry. Chet continued to search every room over and over again for his missing sister but to no avail.

Leland Boggs had not received the weekly rent due for the home of the strange woman. Boggs disliked having to beg his renters to pay their rent, but sometimes his rough appearance at their doorway was enough to get them to hand over their rent money. It looks like he'll have to pay a visit to the woman's rental today and demand she pay up or get out. Approaching the small house, Boggs banged hard on the door and waited. There were no sounds coming from inside and he wondered if she was still in bed. Every couple of hours Boggs returned and banged hard on the door, but got the same results. At the end of the day, he determined he would use his own door key if she didn't open up. Maybe she had fled. Sometimes they do that without giving any notice. Boggs pounded even harder on the door, but received only silence in return. Pulling out his key, Boggs let himself in and was appalled at the condition of the home. It looked like the place had been ransacked by several men. *What a mess to clean-up before I can rent this pigsty out again* he thought.

Boggs found himself walking through the deep clutter as he made his way to the bedroom. "Anybody here, it's the landlord," he said in a loud voice. Suddenly a force of unmeasured power snatched him up by the throat and lifted him straight up in the air. Boggs's eyes protruded in absolute horror as he caught a fleeting glimpse of something huge and monstrous as his wind pipe was crushed. Chet Cody has killed again. After shaking the body like a dog would a rag, he dropped it and continued his unending search for food within the wasteland that was a house.

Four days have now passed since Chet had last eaten and he was now more like a wild animal than ever before. He looked at the body lying on the floor, and with his damaged brain, he began to think of it as food. Inside a drawer in the kitchen was a knife that he had watched his sister cut up meat with many times. Chet had never held a knife before, but at this point, his instincts took over. Taking it by the metal end, he cut himself on the hand, and in fear, threw it down on the floor. He then stood there staring at it and finally took hold of the handle as he looked upon it in wonderment. Chet drove the blade into the left arm of the dead man and with only a little effort, sliced off a piece of flesh, which he savagely shoved into his mouth. Food. Chet Cody hurriedly began cutting more and more flesh from the dead man and devoured it. Chet Cody, the strangler, was now also a cannibal.

Days passed as he gnawed the last bits of flesh from the bones. Lacking any traits of personal hygiene, the beast of a man was covered in blood and gore with an odor completely indescribable except that of a rotting corpse. Something deep within his brain told him he should collect the bones and remaining gore and bundle it up in a blanket. He then waited until the wee hours of the morning to take the bundle out of the house and disposal of it down by the river then return home. In a few days he must go in search of more food once the remaining flesh was gone.

~~~~~~~~~~~~~~~~~~~~~~~~

Amos Bundy always looked forward to Saturday mornings as he and his young grandson Billy, have a long-standing agreement to go fishing in the river together. Whether they caught any fish or not was not what was important to Amos. He was building memories for his grandson to fondly look back upon one day when Amos has gone to meet his Maker. He and Billy have a system when it comes to fishing. Billy would cross over the bridge and begin fishing that bank while Amos tried the other. If one or the other started catching them, the other would soon join on that side. This way they could cover more ground as they slowly made their way down river.

It was the terrible smell that first caught Amos' attention, long before he noticed the bundle lying near the edge. He wondered if an animal had died on the river's bank as he slowly made his way fishing in that direction. Seeing a blanket bundled up, and knowing that the terrible odor was originating from it, Amos located a long stick and flipped the edge of the blanket over. What he saw brought memories of pure horror to his old eyes as he could see the teeth of a human skull showing. The last thing Amos wanted was for Billy to see this, but the Marshal needed to be notified quickly. "Hey Billy," he shouted across the river. "I need you to do something for me that's real important. I want you to cross the bridge back onto this side then go fetch the Marshal for me. Tell him your grandpa needs to see him at the river bank and that it's very important. Once you do that, go on home and we'll fish another day." Billy, visibly disappointed, did as he was asked and took off running for town. Amos was determined that nobody needs to see this awful thing as it's sure to cause panic in the hearts of the townspeople.

Justin was getting briefed by Michael and Zeke when young Billy arrived and told him what his grandpa said. "Tell Wilbert to meet me down by the river as soon as he comes in. I'll ride Spunky down to see what this fuss is all about. Go get some sleep." Justin had little difficulty finding Amos as he was waving frantically with both arms. Arriving, the smell caught Justin's attention as he approached the old man.

"It's just awful marshal," Bundy said. "There's the remains of a dead man in that blanket. I saw his skull."

Justin used the same long stick to take a quick peak then flipped the blanket back over it. "Has anyone else seen this?" he asked the old fisherman.

"Not to my knowledge, sir, and it's best they don't if ya ask me."

Justin replied, "I completely agree so I need your assistance. I want you to take my horse Spunky and see if you can locate my deputy. Tell him to fill the patrol wagon with straw and bring it here. Then ride over and tell Doc to get here pronto. Just tie Spunky up along Main Street somewhere. I'll find him later. Will you do that for me, sir?"

Without any hesitation, both man and horse were off as directed. Justin hoped that the straw might absorb some of the mess when the bundle was later taken to Doctor Baxter's office for examination.

Soon Wilbert arrived with straw in the back of the patrol freight wagon and upon smelling and seeing what was bundled up, the poor man went over to the river and vomited. Justin fully understood and came close to vomiting himself a few times. Doctor Baxter's carriage arrived which seemed to catch the attention of a few people who tried to get in closer for a look, but the smell drove them back. "Doc, I didn't know if you should see this before we brought it over or not. Looks like somebody skinned him. Makes me sick just looking at it."

"Oh my God!" Doc said. "Who or what would do such a terrible thing?" as he began to look closer at the remains.

"We put straw in our wagon to haul it over to you place. Maybe then it won't permeate into the boards of our wagon."

"Yes, let's get it loaded up but I don't want that awful mess inside my office. I'll examine it outback and then it can be taken straight over to the undertaker," Doc told him. "I'll be over later with my report. I should have trained to be a lawyer instead of a doctor. They have a pretty easy life and they only skin their clients for money." With the reluctant help of a couple of bystanders, the bundle was loaded on top of the wagon's straw and taken behind Doc's office under a shade tree. Neither Justin Blake nor Wilbert Vance ate any breakfast that morning. Clearly they had a mad-man loose in town.

Before lunch, Doctor Baxter arrived with his report. "Marshal, in all my thirty-two years in the medical profession, I have never experienced anything like this. We have a cannibal on the loose."

Justin about fell out of his office chair, "What? A cannibal!"

"There are visible teeth marks on many of the larger bones from gnawing, as well as deeper cuts from a knife. His meat was picked clean. It's a sight I'll never forget."

"So what do we have, any identifications on the body?"

"Yes. There was a small coin purse with thirteen dollars with the initials L.B. written inside it. It's here inside this paper sack. Stinks to high heaven. He was probably around five feet six inches and rather heavy set. I hauled the remains over to the undertaker and brought your wagon back. You'll probably want Zeke to clean out the straw and scrub it down pretty good. Well, that's all I have. Good luck, Marshal."

"Thanks Doc, I owe you one," Justin replied. Justin grabbed his hat and went over to brief the mayor and the 'squire on the results of Doc's report. *There's probably no way of keeping this bit of news out of the paper,* he thought. He was so right.

Chapter 29
A Town Gripped in Fear

The headlines in the morning Gas City Journal said it all: **Man Eaten By Cannibal**. Alvin Jensen had done a first rate investigating job in piecing together the gruesome story, even describing the gnawing of the victim's bones. The initials L.B. were said to be inside a coin purse containing an unknown amount of money. Justin knew that the story would send fear into the hearts of the local community. Yesterday after speaking with Doc, he had asked Wilbert to go over to the city clerk's office inside the Mississinewa Hotel to obtain a list of all local men who had the initials of L.B. Three names were discovered and each contacted. They were safe at home and knew nothing about the murder.

They then expanded their search into Jonesboro and obtained four names, three of which were alive. The fourth was a man who owned rental properties in

Jonesboro and Gas City. With the Jonesboro marshal, they went to his home but found it empty. Neighbors spoke of seeing the man, Leland Boggs, several days before. A list of his owned properties were obtained and both police agencies began searching those within their jurisdiction. Arriving outside the small rental property of the Cody's, Wilbert was met by a terribly bad odor emanating from within the structure. Forcing the front door, a bloody mess was discovered inside. Wilbert quickly backed outside and sent word for Marshal Blake. They had discovered the crime scene. What Wilbert didn't know was that the strangler had vacated the property the night before and was now living like an animal out in the woods.

Tying bandannas around their faces to try to keep from breathing in the horrible odor, Justin and Wilbert began searching the home. Even with all of the windows opened, the smell was simply awful. Justin found women's clothing inside the bedroom with letters and paperwork, indicating they have found the home of Agnes Cody, along with different aliases she had used. Wilbert pointed to the other cot and some very large man's clothing. "Somebody quite large has been living here with her and I bet a week's pay it's our strangler."

"I agree," Justin replied, "but why would he eat his victims? He's probably eaten the woman too and we haven't found her remains yet. Look here, inside her drawer is quite a bit of money rolled up inside a sock. So we know robbery wasn't a motive. We are dealing with a maniac, Wilbert. It looks to me like the victim, Mr. Leland Boggs, came here to collect the rent, was murdered and then eaten here. I'm going to inform the Grant County sheriff of our discovery. They may have information we don't have yet."

~~~~~~~~~~~~~~~~~~~~

This story spread far beyond Grant County, as far away as the West coast. Cannibals did not strike very often, but when they did, the reading public became fascinated in a morbid sort of way. The next day at the Grant County jail, Agnes Cody sat in her cell hearing two jailers discussing the cannibal of Gas City. The newspaper covered the discovery of a small rental full of blood and gore where the cannibal apparently had lived. It also mentioned the name of Agnes Cody who had lived there and was missing, presumed dead and eaten. Agnes knew then that her brother had degraded into a terrible beast and she could no longer help or control him. Once her remaining three weeks in jail were up, she would leave the state forever using her new assumed name. Chet would have to make it on his own, but she didn't know for how long and fully expected he would soon face his demise. *It cannot be helped*, she thought, *I've done the best I could*. At least nobody had associated her with the killing as she gave the phony name of Alice McDonald to the police when they had arrested her in the bar. Soon Alice McDonald would leave this place and start a new and better life somewhere else. For the first time in her life, even behind cell bars, Agnes Cody felt free.

~~~~~~~~~~~~~~~~~~~~

It was a very warm September evening as an elderly woman worked alone in her small kitchen. Mrs. Rice was widowed at a young age and never chose to consider another man as her late husband had been the love of her life. She expected to join him one day soon in the kingdom of Heaven. Active in her church, Mrs. Rice could always be counted upon to attend any and all events, so tomorrow's church picnic was no exception. She had worked all evening preparing two pies for the picnic, an apple and a cherry, using fruit she canned herself in June from her own trees. Removing the pies from her oven, Mrs. Rice was most happy with the results as she laid them inside her pie safe. It was built for her by her husband and was a prize possession that she treasured. Due to the heat of the oven, she had her kitchen window and door opened as the screen door was enough to keep any interested insects outside. The aroma was wonderful and a tempting thought came to her to sneak just a little bite before taking them to church tomorrow. Of course she wouldn't do that, she knew, as she smiled at her finished handy work.

Now it was time to wash up all of her dishes, so she began the clean up process. Earlier she had set her kettle of water to boil on the stove and it appeared to be ready. *Someone needs to invent a device that washes dishes for you*, she thought. As she started collecting her dishes, the kitchen door was loudly jerked open, ripping it off of the hinges as a man-beast suddenly entered. It looked more ape-like than man. It was bare-chested and completely covered in hair. The odor was beyond description. With a loud grunting noise sound, it tore through her kitchen as it sniffed for food. Locating the pie safe, the beast ripped off the doors and stabbed its fingers into a pie as it wolfed down the desert.

Backing away near her stove, Mrs. Rice let out a loud piercing scream that made the man-creature turn towards her. It raised its hands upward as it began to approach as if it meant to strangle her. Glancing down at the stove, Mrs. Rice picked up the kettle of hot water and threw it at the creature. The hot water splattered the creature's chest as it let out a howl of pure agony. It then darted back the way it had come. Frightened and trembling, Mrs. Rice staggered through her home emerging outside her front door and ran to a nearby neighbors' home for help.

Later, Wilbert and Zeke looked in wonderment at the carnage left behind by the creature. From her description, they couldn't determine if it was a large bear, a man, or some form of ape-like creature, but they quickly recognized the odor that it had left. Same smell as in the cannibal's house. Mrs. Rice was one lucky lady to have survived its attack and probably the first to do so. Using a lantern, Zeke found a huge man-shaped footprint outside in the dirt before losing the prints in gravel. *Whatever dat thing is, it's after food so maybe we can set a trap fer it?* he thought. He'd discuss the idea with Justin in the morning.

Mrs. Rice was much too afraid to sleep at home that night, choosing instead to stay with her young niece's family.

The following day, the Gas City Journal ran a short story about Mrs. Rice and her ape-like creature encounter. Many folks thought it more of a prank pulled by kids, as hunters were quick to tell that there are no apes or ape-like creatures in the forests around Gas City. Still, something had entered her home and so many people just took on a 'wait and see' attitude. A few men inside Matthew Brooks' Barbershop thought that the whole thing was a hoax to sell newspapers. Talk of forming a hunting party with hunting dogs was discussed, but never materialized. One man said that he would be happy to shoot it so he could mount its head over his fireplace mantel. So much loose, brave talk was common inside the barbershop.

~~~~~~~~~~~~~~~~~~~~~

Now that Virginia Cole and Justin were back together again, she began accepting invitations to evening tea and checker tournaments held every couple of weeks, split between the homes of Doris Davidson and Rachael Vance. Virginia felt bad that she was not in a position to offer a meeting place, but the ladies assured her that it was just fine and not to be concerned. One may be surprised that checkers had become a popular part of their get-together, but it allowed for a healthy competitiveness while still allowing the ladies the opportunity for standard girl talk.

When it came to checkers, Rachael was proving hard to beat. "Wilbert says they think the man-beast is the same one who ate that poor man. I find it very disturbing something that horrendous could happen here of all places," Rachael said as she moved her checker piece on the board. "He really doesn't want me out at all at night until they catch the thing, but I don't want to become a night-time prisoner trapped within my own home."

Doris then replied, "I hear the same from Michael but... here I am! Whose move is it anyway?"

Virginia then said, "Your move, silly. After this game is over, I probably need to return home or Ma Richardson will worry that I ran off arm-in-arm with the ape-man." Three moves later, Rachael won the game and the ladies all decided to call it a night. Saying their goodbyes, Rachael and Virginia walked a short distance together before Rachael arrived home. "Please be careful and don't pick up any ape-man on your way home," she jokingly told Virginia. Ever vigilant, Virginia Cole arrived home safe and sound.

~~~~~~~~~~~~~~~~~~

"I like your plan Zeke," Justin replied after hearing Michael and Zeke out. "How would you go about it?"

Zeke then said, "We thoughts we would camp down by da river one night and cook up a bunch of scrap meat we can gets at the butcher shop, den wait fer da critter ta show up. We'll keep a puttin' on more and more scrap meats all night so as ta give em a real good smell ta enjoy. Michael and me will be armed with shotguns so as ta graze but not kill em."

"What night are you planning on doing this?" Justin then asked.

"Can't do it till two more nights 'cause we'll have fog and rain scattered about till then."

Justin had learned long ago that if Zeke said fog or rain, there would be fog or rain. "I'll arrange to obtain a large box of scraps from the butcher as bait. I'll use straw again in the wagon so you can haul it down to the campsite. I'll probably mosey on down myself that evening to check on you fellows. Just promise me you won't take any chances. This man-thing is a killer." Both men nodded and Justin knew they would use extreme caution. Maybe this will work, he hoped. Two men camping out in the dark with the smell of meat cooking over an open fire. Mighty tempting bait indeed.

The light evening rain and fog happened just as Zeke predicted, but the following evening of what's being called *the bait trap night* was very pleasant for a September evening. The campfire would feel good to both men once it became dark. Both planned to remain awake until midnight, and then each would take turns sleeping for an hour while the other attended to adding more and more firewood and meat as needed. A three quarter moon was a big help as it certainly increased visibility. If the creature came, the deputies felt they could see it and had great confidence in their plan. Justin wandered down to the campsite shortly after ten p.m. to check on the men. "How's it going? You sure can smell that meat cooking from over a block away."

"Only had a couple of curious townspeople a commin' by ta see what's we was a doin' and all," Zeke replied. Justin remained for about an hour making smalltalk before wishing his men success. "Wake me up when you get the thing," Justin said with confidence. Unfortunately, the plan did not work as at that very moment, Chet Cody, the strangler and the cannibal, was on the opposite outskirts of town where he began approaching an elderly farmer's chicken coup.

~~~~~~~~~~~~~~~~~~~~

"Tom, wake up." the farm wife said as she shook her sleeping husband. "There must be a fox in the chicken coup. Spike is barking up a storm." Tom Leffler slipped on his boots and grabbed his shotgun. He was sick and tired of foxes trying to kill his chickens, and tonight he hopes to send the blasted critter to fox heaven. Their dog, Spike, was having a barking fit until a loud yelp was heard... and then silence. With shotgun in hand and a determined look on his face, the old farmer advanced into the darkness towards the unknown.

After about five minutes of not hearing anything, the wife quickly dressed, lit an oil lamp, and proceeded outside to find her husband. As she approached the chicken coup, she saw a huge figure exiting the coup with handfuls of chickens clutched tightly in its fingers, as it ran into the darkness. There upon the ground lay the body of her husband.

~~~~~~~~~~~~~~~~~~~~

"Neck's broken and signs of deep strangulation, Marshal," Doctor Baxter quietly whispered to Justin and Wilbert. This was awful. The bait trap was set the night before on the west edge of town, but the strangler attacked his victim on the rural east edge of town. It also appeared that the family's dog was killed the same way.

"Zeke mentioned he has a friend with a good blood hound tracking dog, and this may be our best bet to track this beast down and capture it before the scent goes cold," Justin said. "I know the man vaguely so let's go over to his farm and see if he's receptive."

Chapter 30
Tracking the Killer

"My husband is out in the barn doing choirs, marshal," Mrs. Walker replied. Thanking her, Justin and Wilbert began walking over towards the opened barn door. "Mr. Walker, it is Marshal Justin Blake and Deputy Wilbert Vance. We need to speak with you, sir."

Fred Walker was a stout, no nonsense type of farmer who handled most difficulties that developed by himself. A self-trained blacksmith, Fred managed to make or repair just about everything needed for his farm. He is the type of man who would never consider going in debt for anything, saving up and paying cash or simply doing without. He was locally known mostly for his dog Duke, the best tracker in the county. Fred was the type of neighbor who never bothered anyone but could be counted upon in an emergency, and today certainly qualified for that in Justin's mind.

"Morning gents. Am I in trouble with the law these days?" he jokingly replied.

"Fred, we'll come right to the point. We require Duke's services in tracking down a killer living somewhere on the outskirts of town, maybe in the woods. He has killed men and women and killed your neighbor Tom Leffler last night."

The news of his neighbor's murder shook the man physically. "Tom was a good, Christian man, and a helpful neighbor. I'll send the missus over today to help comfort his poor wife. Marshal, my dog Duke will track 'em down. When do ya wanna start?"

Justin pulled out his pocket watch, "It is about nine-thirty a.m. now. What if we all meet up at the Lefflers at eleven so I can have a little time to obtain more armed men." That sounded like a mighty good plan. "Wilbert, I hate to have you wake up Zeke and Michael, but see if they'll meet us there and tell them to be armed with our office's twelve gauge shotguns. Same for you, and grab one for me. Bring that full box of shells along too. I'm going to see the Mayor and our councilmen and as many volunteers as I can find in town."

Justin was successful in rounding up Mayor Huffman and Barber Brooks, along with a few of the Horse Thief Protection Services men and local businessmen. The office patrol wagon was then loaded with the armed men and together they proceeded east of town to the meeting location. Soon everyone was assembled and Justin was thrilled to see fifteen armed men ready to do their part in ending the nightmare, once and for all. Justin thanked everyone for their services and then had them raise their right hand to be sworn in as special deputies. He reminded everyone that their goal was to capture this man-beast alive if at all possible.

"Here's my plan, I want Zeke to pick four or five men, then to take the wagon back west through town and assemble on this side of the Mississinewa River. We in this group will follow Mr. Walker here and his dog Duke. Mr. Walker assures me that Duke will follow the scent even if it's a few days old, which it isn't, as the killer was here before daylight. If Duke picks up the scent, we'll form a wide curve and spread out so we can maintain eye contact with one another. We'll attempt to drive the killer towards you men along the river. Watch out for the bridge and don't let him pass over it into Jonesboro. Zeke, we have no idea where exactly where the dog may lead us. He may even take us straight into town, which I pray won't happen. You men along the river will just have to judge our location by the baying of Duke, and move accordingly. I need not remind you not to approach the man-beast if we trap him between us, as he is cunning and kills quickly. If our prey is not located, then I'll have to come up with another plan. Either way, thank you for your assistance today. Be careful and good luck."

Zeke picked five good men and told them to get inside the patrol wagon while he spoke with Justin. "Zeke, any questions?"

"Nope, plain as can be. You drive 'em and we'll capture 'em."

"Be careful my friend and happy hunting," Justin said with a wave of his hand towards the men on the wagon. Soon they were out of sight. It was time to begin the hunt.

Fred Walker appeared to be enjoying the important role that he and Duke were playing in today's manhunt. Walking over to where Walker was speaking, Justin picked up on the ongoing conversation... "And many others use a short tracking harness leash but I prefer a twenty foot leash, as it gives Duke more room to move around."

"How old a scent can Duke follow?" was a question someone in the group asked.

"Bloodhounds can follow scents many days old. He'll pick up the scent and then stay with it until he's located our man. Even if he should lose it, Duke is stubborn and will stay with it until he picks it right back up. If the man crosses the river on us, we'll try to pick him up on the other side."

With that statement, Justin felt compelled to interject, "Actually my authority ends on the Jonesboro side. If our man crosses the river, I'm afraid we're done today. I should have gotten their police involved in our hunt today but I didn't think about it. Darn it."

"I have a question," another man asked,"If Duke corners the man, will he attack him physically?"

"No, once he locates his prey, Duke shows little further interest. Marshal, I think we're ready whenever you say." Justin gave a quick nod, so Walker brought Duke over to the doors of the chicken coup and quickly the dog picked up the scent as he, with nose to the ground, began to lead the way. Justin reminded everyone to fan out and follow the lead of the dog. Duke led them through a corn field then into a wooded area as he occasionally bayed loudly, excited to be on a hunt once again.

~~~~~~~~~~~~~~~~~~~~~

Chet Cody has been living within the woods southeast of town since leaving his blood-soaked home. Making himself a sort of lair with soft leaves and branches, he slept during daylight hours and roamed about at night. He was confused with his new surroundings and was always hungry, forced to eat field corn, tree bark, roots and any dead animal he was able to locate. The weather in late September was turning cool at night and being bare-chested and now barefoot, Chet was beginning to suffer. Instinct, not intelligence, kept him alive day to day. From behind him, he began hearing a dog baying loudly and the sounds of men approaching far in the distance. Instinct warned him to rise up and hurry along further away from the approaching noise.

"Duke has a strong scent," Walker told his fellow hunters as they proceeded along. Thirty minutes passed before the dog led the group up to his sleeping lair underneath a maple tree. "Looks like something or somebody has built itself a place to lay," one of the men spoke. After the dog had sniffed the lair and after circling the area, Duke then lead the group on the newly laid trail of the fast-moving figure.

From down by the Mississinewa River, Zeke could tell by the baying of the bloodhound that the hunting party was moving south-westerly, still further from town. "Let's move further down fellers," he told his men. "Just follow me and keep spread out."

The sound of approaching men and dog made Chet Cody move even faster along. He had no idea what it was that approached, but survival dictated that he keep moving away from the sound. A couple of times he saw movement behind him in the distance as he kept moving away. Being out and exposed in broad daylight terrified Chet as much as the unknown noise as he now ran at full speed.

One of the men yelled out, "I think see something large moving up ahead." That got everyone's attention as each man strained to look for himself. Was it a man or a deer? "Yes," another shouted. "I see it too and it is approaching the river bank."

Zeke and his group also saw the figure way up ahead and were running toward it, trying to make up lost ground. It was huge and appeared as hairy as described by the witnesses. From a distance, they could make out the figure approach the river bank and stop, as it looked back towards the hunting party. It apparently had not seen Zeke and his men approaching from a distance along the river's edge, but was fixated upon the baying of the dog behind it. Suddenly it darted into the river, wading in cold water waist deep and emerged on the other side of the river bank, disappearing into the tall grass. It was gone and the hunting team only succeeded in driving their prey into Jonesboro. Great disappointment was experienced as both groups finally met up at the crossing point of the river. They were five minutes too late. The Jonesboro authorities would need to be warned that the killer is now in their jurisdiction.

Late that night, a solitary large figure forced open the rear door of a small used clothing shop in Jonesboro. The prowler then tried on most of the clothing that had been folded up neatly on shelves and tables, discarding unwanted clothing on the floor, until settling on some that fit. The worst part was the horrendous present the burglar left; a pair of blood-soaked, stench infested pants. Chet Cody would now be warmly clothed for the change to cooler weather. Somehow the old couple who lived above the shop didn't hear the noise, or they too would have been killed had either of them came downstairs to investigate. Now fully clothed, Chet Cody retraced the way that he had came earlier, crossed back through the cold river, and by dawn's early light, he had returned to familiar territory. His lair lay exactly as he had left it as

Chet curled up and was asleep within minutes. Tonight when it was safe to do so, he would once again begin his quest for food.

~~~~~~~~~~~~~~~~~~~

The annual meeting of the Gas City Land Company was held that evening inside the Mississinewa Hotel. The stockholders present seemed very pleased with the information the board of directors offered, as the future of the city seemed bright. The land company had three factories ready to relocate there with two expected before winter set in.

~~~~~~~~~~~~~~~~~~~

The city council also met again after a four week absence. Items discussed were:

(1) Expanding the concrete sidewalks to new locations as seen fit by the street department.
(2) Ask the city attorney to commence legal action against the street car company to make sure they comply to the thirty minute accommodation schedule for the city.

(3) Complaints about the smell and sanitary condition of the meat at the butcher shop on First and South F Street were addressed. This complaint was referred to the city health officer.

~~~~~~~~~~~~~~~~~~~~~~~~~~~~

Over in nearby Marion, a Barber's Union Boycott was being considered. One hundred local businessmen who were seen to be using non-union shops were to be notified by letter to immediately stop patronizing the shops or a boycott of their business would be initiated. Local Gas City Barber, Matthew Brooks, was watching this development with keen interest.

Other newsworthy events in Marion were reported in their city newspaper:

(1) White Caps were burning Negro homes owned by Jews. Marion police were investigating.
(2) Mrs. Allen, a recent young widow, received a White Cap notice warning her to move out of town within ten days.
(3) The notorious Mitchell Webb, colored, was recently released from prison for cattle theft,

returned home but then eloped with his sixteen-year old sister, Clair. Their three older brothers quickly followed the pair, but Webb pulled a revolver thereby forcing their retreat. This has naturally caused a great indignation to this deeply religious family by their wayward son's terrible and near unspeakable actions.

(4) A local man, while playing baseball, was struck severely in his temple by a baseball bat and later died.

(5) Two local brothers employed to dig a nearby well were suffocated when the sides of the wall collapsed, burying them both ten feet under the loose dirt.

Chapter 31
School Begins Again

The city health officer found the public's complaints regarding the terrible smell of the neighborhood butcher shop to be legitimate. The store's owner was mopping up the blood and stench and then dumping it outside the rear door on the ground where the heat of the day made the odor unbearable. Under the threat of city-imposed health fines and possible closure, the store owner promised to stop this unhealthy practice. At night, the smell attracted a confused Chet Cody like a bee to honey, but search as he did, he was unable to locate the food and so was forced to look elsewhere.

~~~~~~~~~~~~~~~~~~~~~~~~~

The first day of school was always a challenge for the faculty and students alike, and today seemed to be no exception to that rule. Superintendent of Gas City

Schools, T.A. Cummings, was a stern and harsh man whose motto, ***Spare the Rod- Spoil the Child***, was well known and feared by students of all ages. Even some of the teachers felt that Superintendent Cummings too harsh in his treatment of students, but feared agitating the old man whose authority was never to be questioned. Hanging inside his office was a wooden sign with his motto neatly hand-painted upon it. Directly underneath it hung what the students had come to grudgingly call "Old Thunder." It was a large twenty-four inch Hickory wood paddle, custom built to Cummings' specifications. With a four inch width and a thickness of three quarters of an inch, Old Thunder could put a real hurting on the backside of any pupil foolish enough, or careless enough, to feel its wrath. Eight, one inch holes were drilled through its center and the handle was custom made to fit comfortably in the hand of its user.

It was established school policy that any faculty member, male or female, who experienced difficulty with a student within their classroom must send that student to the superintendent's office where proper punishment was to be administered. Many a farm boy's rear pants became dust clouds when punishment was administered. The spanking rule could also apply to female students as well, although this was quite rarely enforced. To be sent to the superintendent's office was a sure sign that Old Thunder was to be meeting with someone's backside very soon. Nobody knew exactly how long Superintendent Cummings had been in the Gas City school system, either as a teacher or as an official. Younger grandfathers and fathers alike were all able to relate stories about their own dealings with Old Thunder and it could clearly be said that little love for the old man existed within the community. It was felt that he enjoyed punishing children a little too much.

Willey Scott hated freshman English class and barely managed to get through each day. His friend Tony sat beside him and the two were constantly picking on one another or tossing a wad of paper at the other. Finally, the elderly female teacher had enough of their nonsense and sent both boys to the superintendent's office. Willey and Tony fully understood what was in store for them both. Leaving the classroom, there were many smirks and fingers pointing their way as each remaining student knew what was in store. Quite often, the entire high school could hear each swat of Old Thunder and the resulting screams of its receiver. Students tended to become quite pleasant to their teachers in class after such a punishment is administered.

On the outside of the superintendent's office was a small sign saying K*nock Before Entering.* Neither boy was in a hurry to do so, but knew that they had no choice. Knocking lightly, a voice from within the small room announced, "Enter." Seeing the two teenagers enter his office, Cummings stood up and reached for Old Thunder. Nobody visited the old man unless a punishment must be rendered. Cummings was not feeling well today and was thrilled to have a little entertaining distraction from his tiresome job. "What did you boys do this time?" the old man asked as he held the paddle within his hands.

"We were acting up in our Freshman English class, sir," came the reply from Willey.

"Well, we cannot have any of that nonsense going on in class, can we? You boys are here to learn, not to cause mischief. It sounds like a little punishment is in order today. Who wants to go first?" came the reply from Superintendent Cummings. It was observed that the man had a disturbing, sick sort of smile upon his old face. The sound of the impact of Old Thunder and the boys' screams of anguish filled the hallways of the high school. Students sitting quietly at their wooden desks couldn't help but wonder who would be his next victim.

It took the combined effort of both boys to physically return to class. Neither could sit, so they had to stand in the back of the room as quietly as they could. Since English was their final class of the day, and with the aid of fellow students, both tried to walk home. They found that they could not make it. One boy, who no longer attended classes due to his own beatings at school, happened to pass by in a wagon and offered to haul each boy home. Both Willey and Tony had to lay upon their stomaches for the trip home. Their pain was terrible, but both were worried what pain they'd further experience by the hands of their fathers when they heard that their sons were spanked in school.

As Willey slowly shuffled inside his family home, his mother was cutting up a chicken in the kitchen for the families evening meal. "What happened to you?" she asked.

"Old man Cummings beat Tony and I with his wooden paddle," came a weak reply as he went into his room and laid face first upon his bed. His mother followed him in and scolded him, "Whatever you did today, I'm sure you deserved it, Willey. You can expect another when your father returns home tonight." The boy laid there trying to wish away the pain and dreading what was to come.

Willey Scott Sr. was a factory worker who always arrived home tired and hungry. Tonight was no exception. "Fried chicken," he exclaimed as he kissed his wife's cheek. "My favorite. Special occasion?" he asked.

She then informed him that HIS son was spanked at school today and was laying on his bed. Walking into his son's room, he asked, "So do you want to tell me about what happened?" Young Willey then informed his father what he and Tony had done in class and what had happened with Mr. Cummings.

"Well I hope this serves as a lesson to you son, that you must obey your teachers at school. Mom is cooking fried chicken for supper, so let's go get cleaned up and forget about this, alright?"

"I can't stand up, Dad," the boy told his father.

Out of curiosity, the father pulled up his son's shirt to look and was shocked at the site. "Mother, get in here quick!" The boy's back was a deep, dark crimson angry shade of red that indicated it extended even further down. "Son, how far down were you spanked?" the mother asked.

"He hit me twelve times from the center of my back to half way down my legs." The father then asked his wife to step out of the room and close the door.

"Son, I need you to drop your drawers so I can see this." With embarrassment and great reluctance, he did so. Both butt cheeks were a flaming deep red with severe bruises and what appeared to be scattered welts. "Did Cummings do this to your friend Tony as well?" The answer was yes.

Great anger seethed inside Willey Scott as he grabbed his hat. "I'll be back shortly," he told his wife. "I'm going over to speak with the other boy's father." Soon it became apparent that the other boy had been beaten just as bad as his own son had. Both boys were taken that evening to Doctor Baxter's office for a medical examination and treatment. Each father requested a written medical evaluation of their son, along with a three day medical excuse to remain out of school for healing. After taking the boys home, both fathers went directly to the Marshal's office to register legal complaints against Superintendent Cummings for assault and battery with cruelty to children.

Justin was finishing up his briefing to the night deputies before leaving for home when both angry fathers entered and explained the situation to them. After reading Doc's medical evaluation and seeing their three day home recuperation slips, Justin then sent both deputies to the home of Superintendent Cummings to place the man under arrest. Justin asked each father to go home, and told them that he was on his way over to brief Mayor Huffman and 'Squire Williamson on the situation. Cummings was speechless as handcuffs were placed on each wrist. "Spanking children is sometimes necessary to ensure proper learning," he pleaded as he was lead into the fire barn's jail.

Later that evening, Superintendent Cummings appeared before 'Squire Williamson to answer the charges brought against him. Pleading not guilty, bail was set and a future court trial was to take place soon. Cummings left the 'squires office as mad as a wet hen. "I'm going to turn this one over to the Grant County sheriff," the 'squire told Justin. With his day's work now completed, Justin headed for home.

Many might have thought that Superintendent Cummings would have stayed away from school for a few days, but no, he was right back in his office the very next day. Both of the boys were given an excused medical three day pass by the principal once the doctor's report was provided. By noon, every student and teacher within the high school knew of Cummings' arrest the night before. Most wished that he was still behind bars. No corporal punishment was given out to any student for the remainder of the week.

What Cummings did not know was that a grand jury had convened in Marion, and at that very moment, an order for his immediate arrest was being drawn up under the charge of assault and battery with cruelty to children. By Friday afternoon, a Grant County sheriff's deputy arrived at the high school to place Superintendent Cummings under arrest. Also removed from his office was his little motto sign as well as Old Thunder, both to be entered as evidence at his court trial. Within days, the Gas City school board drew up new written guidelines concerning the topic of spanking. Both Willey and Tony were considered local heros, having finally slain the wicked Cummings dragon.

~~~~~~~~~~~~~~~~~~~~~~~~

"That's right marshal, it happened about ten-thirty p.m. last night," the man explained. "He was a big fellow with long arms and ape-like features. He was down on his knees ah diggin' in the dirt round back of the butcher shop. Soon as he saw me, he bolted quick as a flash into the darkness. I swear I hadn't had a drop of drink that night." Looking into the face of the Marshal and his deputy, he continued on, "I guess you boys don't believe me either. My wife says I must have been dreaming."

Looking over at Wilbert, Justin replied, "Actually sir, we do believe you and we'll investigate your story. Thank you for letting us know." With that, the man left the office. "Well Wilbert, it would seem our strangler has returned to our side of the river. Got any ideas?"

Wilbert then replied, "What if we set up some metal animal traps, you know the kind that snap with sharp metal teeth. We could place meat all around it and catch him in the leg?"

Justin just shook his head. "We're dealing with a human being here, and not an animal, even though he seems to act more like an animal. But the idea of baiting a trap might work. I wonder if he's returned to his sleeping lair?"

Wilbert then said, "It won't pay to use the dog anymore as he's smart enough to just cross over the river or go elsewhere once we approach. It probably would take fifty men to try that trick again anyway. Nobody has reported seeing him during the daytime, so I'm guessing he sleeps during the day and forages for food at night when he's less apt to be seen."

"Maybe we need to ask Zeke to bring in his field glasses he brought back from the war. From a distance, we could look to see if anything is lying down during the day. I might even volunteer to climb up a tree for a better view myself," Justin replied.

~~~~~~~~~~~~~~~~~~~~~~

"How about lunch?" Justin asked Virginia as she sat behind her desk filling out paperwork.

Looking at the wall clock out in the public area, Virginia quickly nodded yes then got back to work. Meeting her outside at noon, the couple walked arm in arm down to the dinner. "You seem troubled, Justin. Is anything wrong," she asked?

"It's that strangler case. This has been one of the hardest cases I have ever been on. He just seems to come and go at will. Even with setting up the tracking dog and all of those men, he still alluded us. I should have had more men across the river just in case he got past us. Last night, a man thinks he saw him behind the butcher shop digging in the blood soaked dirt for food. I'm going to speak to the men about watching that area pretty close tonight, maybe even staking it out myself so the men can patrol the city."

Reaching across the table, Virginia caressed his hand. "You're already exhausted with all of the long hours you put in and I'm worried about your safety.

Nobody blames you for not catching his ape-man. You really need more office manpower."

"I blame myself. Too many people have already died at his hands. Enough of all this. Let's change the subject. How have you been, sweetheart?"

"Just fine. We are meeting over at Doris Davidson's tonight for more tea and checkers."

With a big smile, Justin expressed surprise that anyone would still want to play checkers with Rachael being as good as she was at the game. "It gives us an opportunity to share girl talk with one another. Checkers is actually just the excuse," she added.

"Be careful, and tell the ladies to get home early tonight as we'll be staked out pretty close to the Davidson's home." Then the couple's food arrived and they continued speaking of other less serious topics. At one point, Virginia caught Justin staring intently at her and stopped talking to ask, "Why are you staring at me? Do I have something showing in my teeth?"

With a broad grin, he replied, "No, nothing like that. It is just that you seem to get prettier and prettier every time I see you."

~~~~~~~~~~~~~~~~~~~~~~~~

That evening, Justin briefed his night crew about the man's claim to have seen someone fitting the description of the suspect behind the butcher shop. He asked that they watch that location multiple times during the night, but if they did see him, they were not to approach the figure alone. "Check your weapons to ensure that they're fully loaded. Feel free to carry a shotgun tonight for added safety," he suggested.

Michael injected that darkness was the big enemy as even if they caught sight of him, there was not enough light to track him down and arrest him.

Zeke then added, "Maybe we could borrow a couple of dem red railroad lights from the Pan Handle? Maybe even put em by somebody's rear porch so we can grab em quick if we need em. Sure beats a carrin' dem around all evenin,'" he added. "Oh, as fer da field glasses, I'll bring em in and just donate em to the office. I don't use em anyway."

"Why not use my place to store the lights? I live just three houses down from the butcher shop," Michael suggested. Justin liked the idea and asked him to go and see the railroad agent about borrowing two full red lanterns and some matches. "If you spot the suspect, and if he won't surrender, shoot him in the legs if it's your only chance to capture him. We need him alive if possible. Be careful my friends," Justin added. At least some sort of an evening plan was now in place. If the strangler didn't return tonight, Justin and Wilbert would check out his old lair tomorrow morning, and if they got lucky, they would obtain as many men as they were able to find to attempt to corner and capture him out in the open.

Chapter 32
Stake Out

C het Cody had awakened very hungry that afternoon and reasoned that grass and tree bark was not satisfying enough to fill his aching stomach. Meat was what he craved, and lots of it. He searched for the remains of any dead animals and even back-tracked to the river's edge looking for any fish floating on its waters. Nothing was found as he returned to his lair and waited for darkness to descend upon the land once more.

~~~~~~~~~~~~~~~~~~~~~~~~

It was Doris Davidson's turn to host the ladies evening get-together, and for the occasion, she baked her famous triple-layer chocolate cake. As Rachael and Virginia arrived, the aroma of the special treat filled the air. "You're going to make me fat," Virginia laughed as a thick slice was placed upon a small desert plate and handed to her. Tea was then served and the ladies began filling their evening with news and normal conversations. Rachael sat smiling most of the evening and everyone suspected she had something to tell them, as they patiently waited. Finally, she couldn't silence her news any longer, "I went to see Doctor Baxter today and he tells me that Wilbert and I will be having a baby next summer. We promised each other not to tell anyone yet, since I'm at the early stages of my pregnancy but... you ladies are my friends and all." Doris and Virginia were so happy for her and the topic then changed to babies and the raising of children, which neither really knew much about.

Doris wanted to know how Wilbert took the news. "He's still recovering from it. He thought I should immediately take to bed, but I told him that was silly and old timey. I want to continue working at the emporium for a while longer until I start becoming uncomfortable. Constance will ensure that I stay off ladders and not carry heavy boxes, so I'm not concerned."

After more cake was offered and declined, it was time to begin their checkers tournament. Rachael was clearly the better player, so the ladies had devised a plan. Doris and Virginia would play first and the winner was to take on Rachael for the best out of three games. With

Rachael's mind on babies, she didn't play as well as usual and was defeated by Doris, who celebrated her victory with another piece of chocolate cake. Looking up at the small mantel clock, Virginia announced it was time that she headed back to the boarding house, and again wished Rachael and Wilbert the very best of luck and happiness.

~~~~~~~~~~~~~~~~~~~~~

Justin arrived home after work but chose not to change out of his uniform. Something odd, a strange feeling perhaps, told him that he needed to go help out in tonight's stake out. It was going on nine p.m. when he left his house and proceeded over to the Donaldson home. He planned on picking up both lanterns with matches and taking them with him over to the butcher shop. As Justin arrived, he saw Virginia stepping outside the Davidson's home and called to her. "Virginia, it's me."

A little startled by having her name called out in the darkness, Virginia replied, "Who is me?" she jokingly said, knowing full well that the voice was Justin's. "So this is what you do at night, calling out to women from the darkness?"

A bit annoyed he replied, "I thought I warned you to get off the street before dark? We're expecting the strangler to pass close by here tonight, and now I really cannot take the time to walk you safely home, so you'll have to go straight there on your own." She told him that she was a big girl now and could safely find her way home. Together they walked towards the front corner of the butcher shop where he kissed her and sent her on her way. Justin looked around and saw a large tree across the street. *"That's where I'll hide out tonight*, he thought. Arriving at that location, Justin sat one of the lanterns down behind its large trunk with the box of matches, then grabbed the other lantern with a handful of matches, and went looking for his deputies.

It only took a few minutes to locate his men, knowing their patrol pattern as well as he did. "I see you couldn't stay away," Michael teased his boss. Justin briefed them that he was going to stake out the front corner of the butcher shop until daylight, in hopes of seeing the strangler approaching. He said he would light his lantern as a signal that the suspect had arrived. He then asked for a volunteer to take the other lantern and position himself on the back corner of the butcher shop to do the same. Zeke quickly volunteered, so Michael would continue the night patrols alone tonight. "This may very well be a waste of time, but I feel we need to try it just in case he returns," Justin said. Both men settled in place watching over their assigned areas looking for any red light from the other man. Now the long wait began.

~~~~~~~~~~~~~~~~~~~~~~~

Instinct seems to have directed Chet Cody to return to the rear of the butcher shop. The smell of blood emanating from the ground greatly excited the big man, but being spotted had driven him away the night before. Now that it was dark, Cody feels more comfortable in trying again. Meat must be found tonight, even if his instincts warned him of the dangers as he cautiously darted between darkened houses, moving towards his target.

~~~~~~~~~~~~~~~~~~~~~~~

There was a cool crispness in tonight's air, as Zeke buttoned up his coat collar button. He wondered if the railroad lantern might give off a little heat, but realized he could not take that chance. Rubbing his hands together occasionally before putting them in his coat pocket, Zeke almost wished the strangler might show up so he could move around and generate more body heat.

A movement suddenly caught his eye as a large figure approached the rear of the building. The large unknown man dropped down to his knees on darkened ground and made some odd moaning noises as if he was smelling the dirt. Slowly, Zeke picked up the lantern and matches. *If I lights this lantern like Justin says, it's gonna scare da feller off,* he thought. Not sure just what to do, Zeke pulled out his pistol and waited. *Maybe I can squeeze to da side of the trees in the darkness and go fetch Justin?* Just then there was a very loud noise as the huge man jerked the rear door of the butcher shop open and went inside. Zeke quickly lit the lantern and prayed Justin would see its red glow.

Justin heard the loud noise first as the red glow filled the night's sky. Pulling out his own pistol, Justin ran across the street and peaked around the edge of the building to see what was happening. He didn't see the strangler but saw Zeke running with the lit lantern toward the rear doorway. He joined him there as both men prepared to enter the butcher shop. Inside, the strangler was stuffing himself with whatever meat products he could find, but became aware of a strange red glow behind him. Turning, he was terrified to see a red fire ball moving toward him as voices shouted, "Hands up, you're under arrest!" Not understanding the workings of a lantern and being afraid of fire all his life, Chet panicked and ran towards the front plate glass window, thinking it was a way out. Glass shattered as the big man's body smashed through the glass as he rolled to a stop outside. Cut and bleeding, the big man limped into the darkness. "After him, we can't let him get away," Justin yelled, as both men stepped through the broken window frame. Blood droplets covered the ground from cuts the big man had received. Holding the single lantern out in front of them, both officers tracked the droplets of blood until they disappeared into the grass. "Now I wish we had that tracking dog with us," Justin said, with anger in his voice. It was at about that time that they heard a woman's loud terrified scream. "Over there, let's go!"

Approaching the house from the side, Justin told Zeke to take the front door as he would enter from the rear. "Don't hesitate to shoot him if you have to," he told him. Zeke entered the already opened front door and stood in the parlor with his weapon ready. In the corner of the room stood a terrified middle aged woman screaming as a huge figure of a man with reaching arms, was quickly descending upon her. Zeke took aim and fired, striking the strangler in his left arm. Yelping in pain and knowing who had caused it, the wounded man then turned on Zeke, moving so quickly that Zeke hesitated briefly before firing again. A huge right hand found its mark around Zeke's throat as the strangler lifted the struggling deputy off the ground and shook him before pitching him towards the doorway. Justin heard the shot but was having difficulty forcing open the bolted kitchen door. He arrived inside the parlor just as Zeke was being thrown through the air.

Justin fired two shots, striking the strangler who then began advanced towards him. The woman now saw an opportunity to fight back. She picked up her lit glass oil lamp, and threw it at the large intruder who had invaded her home. The glass lamp burst at his feet as the flammable liquid and fire met, splattering burning liquid upon his legs. The strangler shouted in fear and pain as he made a wild dash upwards toward the staircase. Perhaps memories of safely while living all of those years upstairs in an attic flashed before his eyes. They'd never know his reasoning for sure as he was now engulfed in flames as he ascended the stairs screaming out in absolute terror.

Justin knew that he had to get the woman out of the burning house quickly, as the fire was beginning to rage. "Take my hand," he shouted as they moved towards the open doorway and out of the smoke. Justin saw that Zeke was lying on the outside steps so he picked up the deputy and moved him out near the street. "Bring the red lantern over here," he shouted to the woman. Michael who saw the smoke and flames quickly responded to the site. "Go get Doc, Zeke's been hurt!" In a flash, Michael was gone. Glancing up, Justin could see that the house was now starting to become fully engulfed. The horrible screams that everyone could hear coming from deep within the burning house suddenly stopped, and Justin knew that the strangler has finally met his end. Try as he might, Justin could not get Zeke to open his eyes or speak as he began to fear the worse for his old friend.

~~~~~~~~~~~~~~~~~~

"I'm sorry Marshal, there was nothing I could do," Doctor Baxter said. A neighbor had brought a blanket to the scene to comfort the injured deputy. It was now used to cover over his body. Marshal Justin Blake and Deputy Michael Davidson stood by their dear friend, unable to move or to think straight. Shock now swept over both men as they grieved for the death of Zeke Miller. Mayor Huffman, hearing the responding fire engine, arrived on scene to realize that neither officer could perform his immediate duties at the moment. He then took charge and obtained a written report from the distraught woman and kept the onlookers away from the body. Justin would always be eternally grateful for the Mayor's quick actions and fortitude this night.

The firemen were successful in preventing the house fire from spreading to its neighboring homes, but the structure proved to be a total loss. The charred remains of the strangler were later removed and destined for a pauper's grave with no way of identifying his name. In the days ahead, no one came forward to claim the body, so Chet Cody's cross was only marked with the name *unknown*.

Great sadness and gloom swept through the town upon hearing of the killing of Deputy Zeke Miller. Nobody had an unkind word to say about the old timer, and many an old story about him was shared with friends. Rachael took the death of her Uncle very hard, but at least she had Wilbert to console her through the days ahead. It was felt some sort of memorial service should be held in Zeke's honor. Rachael chose the Reverend Stokes's church as it was available that day and large enough to hold the expected crowd. Nobody could quite remember old Zeke ever sitting foot inside a church before, but knew him to be a God-fearing man anyway, so it was thought he would approve.

Justin Blake blamed himself completely for the death of Zeke Miller. "If only I had taken the front door instead of Zeke, I may have stood a better chance of capturing the strangler and Zeke would be alive today," he told everyone who would listen. "I feel responsible for his death." It was Virginia who sought out Reverend Stokes and asked him to speak with Justin privately before the services in order to console the guilt that he was feeling right now.

Reverend Stoke came up to Justin and placed his arm upon his shoulder. "My son, it's not for us to question the will of God. This was not your fault. That responsibility lies with the killer who now sits at the feet of his master, Satan. Every day we make decisions that impact the lives of others, as well as our own. When we arrive at a crossroads, we are faced with the question. Do we turn right or left? Your important position of town marshal requires you to make decisions that help protect the community every day. Don't start second guessing yourself because of this tragedy. Have faith in God and trust HIS decision in this matter. Our friend Zeke was called home for a reason neither of us have any control over."

The reverend continued, "I remember speaking with Zeke shortly after the death of Marshal Brewster. He told me he didn't feel bad over the death of the Marshal, as he figured that was the way the crippled man wanted to go out by saving your life, and once again, being a productive member of the department. Don't you see Justin? That's how Zeke wanted to go out too. A deputy doing his job right to the very end. Zeke clearly saved that woman's life when he brought the killer's wrath onto himself. He should be remembered today as a hero. Let's go out there now and celebrate the life of this fine man who gave his all for his community." A healing prayer was then offered, asking God to help Justin and his friends during this time of great sadness. Leaving the office, Justin felt like a great weight had been lifted from his shoulders. Today he would help the community celebrate the life of his wonderful friend.

Even Reverend Stokes was pleasantly surprised at the large turnout for Zeke's memorial. Every seat was filled, with people lining two to three deep along the aisles. Several late arrivals stood outside hoping to hear what would be said inside. It had been discussed that this memorial needed to be more of a celebration of life than a religious service, and Justin wanted to be one of the first speakers.

"Let me tell you about my friend, Zeke Miller," he told the audience. "When I arrived in Gas City two and one half years ago, Zeke was the first man I met. Actually we met on the train that brought me here. The next person I met was my dear friend Reverend Stokes, who was also on that train. Both men made me feel right at home that day and helped me get settled. I found out later that Zeke had even spoken to Marshal Brewster about hiring me as a deputy. That was just the type of guy Zeke Miller was, and I know I'm not telling you folks anything that you don't already know."

"One of the first things that surprised me about him was his ability to forecast the weather. I remember the day he announced a tornado would be heading our way, and I watched as everyone took him seriously, and started to batten down the hatches. And yes, a tornado, or a cyclone as he called it, came that evening. I quickly learned never to disregard any of his weather predictions." Many heads in the assembly began nodding.

"The day Marshal Brewster made him a secret deputy was another special moment in my life. Zeke was as proud as he could be, and I knew that only his lack of education held him back. Still, he more than made up for it with his good old horse sense and life experiences. Let me share one incident with you folks today, where he taught me a vital lesson in dealing with people. We were walking along on patrol one afternoon and there was a couple walking about twenty feet ahead of us. Somehow, the lady's coin purse became dislodged and fell to the ground. Before we could call out to warn her, a young boy of about eight years grabbed the purse and shoved it into his pocket. I was ready to move on the boy when I felt Zeke touch my arm and say, "Follow my lead." He marched up to the boy and informed him that we saw him snatch the lady's purse and that he was under arrest. Of course the boy began to cry, but Zeke would have none of that, and soon Zeke escorted him into the office. There, he took the coin purse from the boy and commenced to place the boy inside the jail cell. Fascinated, I went along with Zeke's lead. After saying the boy's father will have to be locked up also, the boy began to cry, said that he was sorry and would not ever take something that wasn't his ever again. That was when Zeke told the boy a true story about this area's local history."

"It seems a stranger to the area hired a Mr. Martin Boots and his young son to show him around. The stranger was on horseback as Boots and the boy walked along side. As the group went over a small hill, something fell out of the stranger's saddlebag. The young boy picked it up and then handed it back to the stranger. It was the man's land speculation purse, containing over eight thousand dollars. Delighted at the young boy's honesty, the man offered the boy one hundred dollars reward, which was the boy rejected out of moral purposes. "You don't reward someone for doing the right thing," a young Boots told the man. That land speculator went on to purchase land here that eventually became Grant County. Zeke then explained that by being honest, the boy had helped folks to settle here and that without his honesty, life would have turned out different for all of us."

"Zeke's story touched the young boy's heart and he agreed to return the purse to the woman and accept no reward for doing the right thing. I learned so much that day and many other days just being around him and following his example. I'll also never forget the evening I brought Zeke over to Lovett's Opera House to see the hypnotist." As he said this, people in the audience started chuckling as they remembered the story as well.

"It sounds like many of you were there that night also. For those who were not, the professor hypnotized Zeke, turning him into a human chicken." The people sitting out in the church began to laugh, with a few shouting *chicken-man*! Even Justin began to laugh at the memory. "Poor Zeke, he was so embarrassed that he laid pretty low for several weeks afterwards."

"So in conclusion, I guess I would just like to say that Zeke played an important role in the lives of many of us here today, and I for one will sure miss him." Justin then took a seat as a few more spoke before the service ended in prayer. Zeke Miller was laid to rest that day, wearing his best clothing, in the presence of friends and neighbors who would never forget him

Chapter 33
Life Begins to Returns to Normal

Justin sat with Virginia inside the kitchen at Ma Richardson's boarding house as they enjoyed a cup of coffee together. "I just can't believe he's gone," Justin said as he paused to look into her beautiful face. "I really want to thank you for all of your support these last two days. You've been right at my side and I fear I may have leaned a little too heavily upon you."

Virginia reached out for his hand, "Not at all. That's what couples do for each other. Just know that I love you, and I'm here for you always."

Justin smiled up into her eyes, "Sure you want to hang around me? The job's kind of dangerous as you can see?"

Looking at him sternly, Virginia reminded him that they had already covered this topic before, and she was sticking by him through thick and thin. *How did I ever luck out in finding a girl as wonderful as Virginia Cole,* Justin thought? *I guess it's time I do this.*

Suddenly nervous, Justin replied, "I hear tell October makes a good month for weddings."

Virginia wasn't about to let her man off the hook that easy. She casually replied, "That's what I've heard also," then stared at him without expression. Justin realized that she was going to make him say all the right words.

"Virginia Cole.... will you..."

Acting like she was puzzled, Virginia replied, "Will I what?"

Summoning up all of his nerve, Justin completed the sentence Virginia longed to hear from him. "Virginia Cole, will you marry me?"

"Yes!" she shouted as she flung herself into his awaiting arms.

~~~~~~~~~~~~~~~~~~~~

The following weeks brought a letter from 'Squire Williamson to the rental home of Mr. and Mrs. Wilbert Vance. Both parties were requested to appear in the 'squires office at ten a.m. that Friday morning. "What did we do?" was the question each one asked the other. Arriving at the appointed hour, Rachael then discovered she had been named as Zeke's beneficiary to his property and savings. Williamson informed them that Zeke had approached him the day after their wedding and asked that a paper be drawn up for him to put his X on, making her his heir. Zeke's small house wasn't much to look at, but after a thorough, solid cleaning and some general repairs, it will make a nice family home for them and the new baby due to arrive next year.

"It'll seem very strange living in Zeke's house," Wilbert told his wife.

"Uncle Zeke did this out of love for both of us and to honor his wishes we'll do it. I only wish he had lived long enough to learn about the baby," she told him.

"It's my guess he's up in Heaven right now shaking hands with our child and filling it's head with all sorts of wild, colorful tales." With that, both laughed at the very thought of it.

~~~~~~~~~~~~~~~~~~~~~~~~~~~~

When Agnes Cody was released from the county jail this past summer, she purchased a railroad ticket west to St. Louis and never looked back. She was determined to end her days as a prostitute forever, and start a new life for herself. After arriving in town, she answered an advertisement as a live-in housekeeper for a widower gentleman. Her employer was a watchmaker, fourteen years her senior and seemed a pleasant sort of fellow. Agnes left her past behind her and soon determined she would become his new wife, hopefully by Christmas. The watchmaker didn't know that she had set her cap for him, but he would soon enough as Agnes knew how to make a man take notice of her. *The old boy won't know what hit him when I get through,* Agnes thought.

~~~~~~~~~~~~~~~~~~

On Saturday, October 14th, Miss Virginia Cole officially became Mrs. Justin Blake in a public ceremony held at the Reverend Stroke's church. Wilbert Vance stood up as best man and Rachel as her Maid of Honor. A small reception was hosted at the Donaldson family home and was well attended by friends and well wishers. While welcoming everyone who came to greet the newly married couple, Justin began to reminisce on his life. It was only two years ago when the gypsy fortune teller Dooriya had read him his fortune in her crystal ball. The first two of her predictions, the loss of a dear friend and a promotion came true. *The third and final prediction of my life has finally came to pass,* he thought. *Tonight I will finally find love in the arms of the woman I love.*

End